BRUCE BOONE DISMEMBERED

POEMS, STORIES, AND ESSAYS

BRUCE BOONE DISMEMBERED

POEMS, STORIES, AND ESSAYS

BRUCE BOONE

EDITED BY ROB HALPERN

Nightboat Books
New York

ISBN: 978-1-937658-58-8

Cover Design by HR Hegnauer
Design and typesetting by HR Hegnauer
Cover art by James Holley, *untitled*, 2008, found-items on cardboard backing.
    Copyright © Bruce Boone. From the Bruce Boone Papers, The Poetry
    Collection of the University Libraries, University at Buffalo, The State
    University of New York.
Text set in Garamond Premier Pro and Helvetica Neue

Cataloging-in-publication data is available from the Library of Congress

Nightboat Books
New York
www.nightboat.org

TABLE OF CONTENTS

Introduction by Rob Halpern I

Early Poems

    Karate Flower 1

    Writing Poems—Is Something Else 7

    He's the Lover/of My Soul 9

    A Natural Form of Love.................................... 11

    from Sleep.. 12

    Dodo the Cat Gives Himself to the Universe and

        Later Writes Poems...................................... 17

Remarks on Narrative: The Example of Robert Glück's Poetry 18

Gay Language as Political Praxis: The Poetry of Frank O'Hara 22

Toward a Gay Theory for the '80s 78

Writing Power Activity... 92

Writing's Current Impasse and the Possibilities for Renewal 97

Language Writing: The Pluses and Minuses of the New Formalism ... 106

La Fontaine (with Robert Glück) 123

"Stoned out of my gourd": A Review of Dennis Cooper's

    The Tenderness of the Wolves 137

Kathy Acker's *Great Expectations* 145

George Bataille: A Fave "New" Writer and His Vile Books 152

Perception of a Body Among Writing's Parts 158

Bruce Boone Interviewed by Charles Bernstein 171

Dark Queer Suite 208

    Stephen King Poem 208

    Buddies In Space 210

    John Wieners, American Poet 211

    Pulp Terror 212

    Lovecraft 213

Letter to Stephen King, The Horror Writer 214

The Last *Soup*: New Critical Perspectives 225

The Truth About Ted 230

An Excerpt from *Carmen* (A Visit with Roy) 242

Three Letters from *Carmen* 246

David's Charm 255

A Narrative Like A Punk Picture: Shocking Pinks, Lavenders,

    Magentas, Sickly Greens 264

Hollywood Celluloid Nuke Madness 269

Mirage—or Where's the Party? 277

For Jack Spicer—A Truth Element 282

Spicer's Writing in Context 291

Robin Blaser's New *Syntax*: Pointing Up Ahead, Behind, Wherever .. 296

Robert Duncan and the Gay Community—A Reflection 309

Review of Robert Duncan's *Ground Work: Before the War* 331

Beat Poetry's Populism 334

The Queen Beats 341

H.D.'s Writing: Herself A Ghost 352

Beverly Dahlen 355

Steve 360

from *He Sleeps with the Angels (Pink Sperm)* 367

The Sense of Utopia: Bruce Boone in Conversation

    with Eric Sneathen 375

A Stele for Jamie.. 387

INTRODUCTION

Bruce Boone Dismembered began one afternoon almost seven years ago over tea with Bruce in his Castro flat where he's lived for thirty-five years, much of that time with his loving partner, Jamie Holley, whose artwork graces the cover of this book, and whose passing in 2009 the concluding piece in this collection devotedly mourns. Bruce and I had just returned from a long walk around the base of Twin Peaks as the thick fog cascaded into the neighborhood like it would everyday like clockwork beneath an otherwise crystalline October sky. I was then working on my preface for the reissue of Bruce's 1980 New Narrative classic, *Century of Clouds*, and was still in the process of grasping the full range of his writing, so I asked him between sips of sweet jasmine and threads of conversation if he might help me compile a list of all his published works. Well, you know, I really didn't keep a very good record of that sort of thing, Bruce responded, and besides, he went on, who would ever be interested?, to which I replied, How about *me* for starters! And just then, as I've often had the occasion to rehearse, Bruce reached beneath the sofa where we were sitting and he pulled out a clutch of manually typed drafts of several texts that looked as though they'd been collecting dust for decades and I immediately noticed one title typed in fading Courier caps that read GEORGES BATAILLE: A FAVE 'NEW' WRITER AND HIS VILE BOOKS. What's that?, I asked while trying to contain a pang of crazy excitement and anticipation, and where was it published? Hmmm. . . well, let's see, Bruce replied, without certainty as to it ever having been published at all. It would take me another five years to learn that this essay on Bataille had indeed seen the light of day, though I only finally verified this when I discovered Bruce's *curriculum vitae* among Robert Duncan's papers at the University at Buffalo Library, which accompanied a letter Bruce had sent to Duncan back in '70s requesting a recommendation for a residency. Would that I had only discovered this CV years sooner and spared myself the uncertainty and speculation! As it turns out, the text of Bruce's essay on Bataille, whose "vile books" were just then crashing against the walls of the American academy in a number of new translations, among which Bruce's own translations of *Guilty* and *On Nietzsche* would soon be counted, an essay I had relegated, together with other drafts Bruce showed me that day, to the fugitive, the aborted, or the lost, had been published after all, although not where one might have expected, say, in a bona fide literary magazine of some sort—but rather in *The Advocate*, a glossy gay weekly whose articles featured more pedestrian entertainments, fashion, health, and sex. This sign of heady times didn't astonish me, it simply confirmed Bruce's commitment, often associated with New Narrative, to bridge "high" and "low," art and commodity, gold and glitter, academy and gutter, Parnassus and Sodom. The title of the essay alone succeeds in doing just that as does the whole of Bruce's writing life, so much of which he generously gathered and packaged for me that afternoon—loose pages and drafts, pamphlets and zines, journals and books—and I carried it all home in a brown paper Safeway bag, like concealed treasure. As I traversed Dolores Park back to the Mission, it was hard for me not to stop in my tracks to begin reading on the steep bank of the park's hill where so many half-naked men availed themselves of the late afternoon sun. It was then that the idea of helping Bruce to edit a volume like the one you now hold in your hands, dear reader, came upon me like a little *coup de foudre*.

• • •

Bruce Boone Dismembered collects poems and talks, reviews and interviews, as well as stories and essays spanning nearly four decades of Bruce Boone's writing life. The aim of the book is to introduce that life to a new readership while expanding the availability of Bruce's out-of-print work. While some of you may come to this volume already engaged by Bruce's writing, others among you may have only heard rumors of his involvement in the San Francisco writing scene in the late 1970s where, together with Robert Glück and Steve Abbott, he helped to inaugurate a literary movement called New Narrative, which connects avant-garde and identity-based writing communities while incorporating both high-cultural rigor and pop-cultural trash. Still others might come to this book already familiar with Bruce's writing by way of his innovative scholarship on Frank O'Hara. Maybe you've already read Bruce's *Century of Clouds* and *My Walk with Bob* (both of which are still in print, and so not included here). And then again, perhaps you've never read a single word of Bruce's writing. In any case, this book is intended for all of you!

The earliest pieces presented here date from the 1970s, and the most recent from 2011, save a 2018 interview. While he continues to write and publish—a five-hundred page poem entitled *Wallpaper* has just appeared!—most of the works in Bruce's published corpus live in the half-light of out-of-print editions, unfamiliar literary journals, underground zines, gay periodicals, "fag rags," self-published pamphlets, and blog posts, making *Bruce Boone Dismembered* long overdue. Although we initially intended to include only work that has seen the light of day in one form of print or other, some unpublished texts emerged during the process of gathering this material whose virtues argued persuasively for inclusion. Two examples of the latter bear mentioning: "The Queen Beats," originally presented as a talk for a 1997 conference on The Queer Beats, at the San Francisco Art Institute, which we recovered in draft and lovingly edited for this volume; and second, the selections from Bruce's aborted novel, *Carmen.* For anyone familiar with Bruce's work, the history of *Carmen* can be confusing, as three other pieces in *Dismembered* were originally published under the sign of this mercurial project: "The Truth About Ted," "David's Charm," and "An Excerpt from *Carmen* (A Visit with Roy)." The work that ultimately became *Carmen,* however, is an unfinished epistolary project and a cosmic fantasy wherein Bruce adopts the avatar of Virginia Woolf's Orlando to perform the fluidity of an ever-changing sex/gender identity, the complete text of which exists only in one unperforated accordion file from a dot-matrix printer. The selections from *Carmen* that we chose to include in *Dismembered* appear here in print for the first time.

· · ·

Bruce's writing of the late 70s and early 80s negotiates seemingly incompatible aesthetic strategies and their corresponding social values. On the one hand, there are the strategies and values associated with the modernist avant-garde (estrangement, materiality, and construction); and, on the other, those associated with identity-based social movements (transparency, communication, expression). Situated between various liberation struggles and the AIDS crisis when the politics of representation became a battlefield, this tension between avant-garde innovation and politicized identification was concretely lived by writers and artists, like Bruce, whose work was poised to run headlong into the social and cultural repressions of the Reagan era. At the time, the terms of this antagonism were being theorized in the academy under the signs of "cultural studies" and "postmodernism," and while the latter in particular might seem moribund today, it was quite relevant to the terrain of Bruce's work. Fredric Jameson himself—among the most notable theorists of "postmodernity"—was a friend and mentor whose influence can be felt in Bruce's writing. "Gay Language as Political Praxis: The Poetry of Frank O'Hara" and *Century of Clouds* bear the mark of Jameson's influence most directly, even as they explore tensions between Marxism and identity politics, specifically gay liberation and feminism, in ways Jameson might not endorse. In one of its culminating passages, *Century of Clouds* narrates the occasion of Brucc's presentation on O'Hara at the Marxist Literary Group's summer institute, presided over by "Fred" himself, a presentation that the narrator refers to as an "intervention" in the institute's failure to address the struggles of gays and women. That presentation would eventually become "Gay Language as Political Praxis," which aimed, "modestly enough," Bruce tells us in *Century*, "at articulating gay language usages in a poet whose reputation till now had not included any official recognition of this important aspect of his writing."

During this period, Bruce was committed to a marxian analysis of culture, which for him was inseparable from community politics. One approach to the relevance of Bruce's work today might privilege the model it offers—one of many possible—for bringing literary innovation, social identity, and political struggle together in one body of work. The opening lines of *Karate Flower* (1973), for example, offer an exquisite illustration of the way these preoccupations manifest in Bruce's early writing:

Oil, that's what I admire, to run the machines.
And gasoline with a cleanliness like war.
But there is another part of me, the grandfather
who made chocolates.

As Bruce explained to me one afternoon while discussing the poem over coffee and figs in his sunny living room, "Karate Flower" aims to catch every possible "enemy" in its grasp by way of its capacious "you"—a commodious direct address capable of embracing "everything and everybody"—so that were the poem to succeed in its rebarbative attack, it would succeed in destroying every adversary standing in the way of social justice! Already, in these opening lines, we can hear the tensions between socio-economic and personal concerns, politics and identity, as Bruce's earliest work overlays cultural and political questions with psycho-social dilemmas while foregrounding contradictions involving language, desire, and history. The poetic labor here is utopian, and its aim is that of preparing ourselves to live in a livable world. "We are moving toward a future," the speaker of "Karate Flower" announces, "Quickly, come hold my hand. / Everywhere I see red, and the time of dispatch." While clearly informed by Bruce's Marxist sensibilities—he was reading Lenin at the time and attending meetings of the Progressive Labor Party—the poem nevertheless intimates that a revolutionary future might be too simplistically imagined by his radical peers to be adequate or acceptable. The poem culminates with a crescendo of phrases, a cascade of effects, and a cymbal crash of intensity as it declares belief in a Communist horizon, and yet the narrator remains self-consciously bourgeois and ambivalent—familiar contradictions, no doubt, but inimitably rendered.[1]

The stresses aroused by Bruce's early poems are the same stresses that inform his scholarly writing on Frank O'Hara, which realizes a desire to demonstrate to himself and others that he could play the academic game and write serious scholarship, while then gaining the credibility to abandon the protocols of respected criticism in order to pursue a more innovative and idiosyncratic approach to the critical essay as a form. Bruce's dissertation, *Frank O'Hara's Poems*, for example, pursues close literary readings of

---

1 *Karate Flower* first appeared as an 8½ x 11 stapled pamphlet with Hoddypoll Press, whose editor James Mitchell published a range of literary books and zines affiliated with Gay Lib, work recently collected in a volume entitled *Gay Sunrise: Writing Gay Liberation in San Francisco 1968-1972*, edited by Mitchell himself (Ithuriel's Spear, 2019).

various poems—often quite brilliant readings—focusing on things like the construction of a first-person singular "I" as both the contrived prosthetic of an historical person and the site of a sincere life-writing, at once artificial and consequential, a tenet that would become a staple of New Narrative.[2] Drawing heavily on Saussure, Barthes, and Lacan, Bruce's doctoral work defaults to a literary post-structuralism that was still just emerging in the academy in the mid-1970s when Bruce was writing his thesis. Just as the critical preoccupations associated with post-structuralism realize a wholesale shift in post-1968 intellectual culture toward theory and away from revolution, Bruce's dissertation bears the mark of a tacit prohibition on explicitly positioned politics which, like a return of the repressed, surges forth in "Gay Language as Political Praxis" (1979), as if Bruce were avenging himself on a dissertation committee that had dissuaded him from pursuing a more radical scholarship.

"Gay Language as Political Praxis" is a *tour de force* and remains a high-water mark of early O'Hara criticism. At once a fully realized convergence of Cultural Studies and *avant la lettre* Queer Theory, Bruce's major contribution to the scholarship on O'Hara appeared in the first issue of *Social Text* beside Jameson's now canonical essay, "Reification and Utopia in Mass Culture." In turning away from the theorists associated with post-structuralism mentioned above, Bruce turns toward more revolutionary figures like Volosinov, Fanon, and Benjamin to critique the major readings responsible for O'Hara's reception within the academy, including those of Helen Vendler and Marjorie Perloff. Bruce aggressively and persuasively characterizes this reception by its conspicuous refusal to engage seriously with O'Hara's queerness before moving on to advance his own reading of O'Hara as the cultivator of a specifically gay language whose subtlety and nuance are keenly attuned to the social struggles of an oppressed group.

This essay is complemented by Bruce's astonishing activist manifesto, "Toward a Gay Theory for the '80s," his most overtly engaged political work, which critiques the making of gay male subjectivity under

---

2 An excerpt from the first chapter of Bruce's dissertation was published in *Homage to Frank O'Hara*, edited by Joe LeSueur and Bill Berkson, 1978.

conditions of late capitalism. Responding to the emergence of a post-Gay Lib era when public displays of homophobia were underwritten by the likes of the Anita Bryant campaign and the Briggs Initiative in California to banish gay teachers from the public school system, Bruce's political pamphlet analyzes the ties that bind gay culture to commodity culture, while proposing a set of practical steps for organizing the gay "ghetto," using labor unions, health clinics, and community centers to resist homophobic intimidation. While seemingly unrelated to literary concerns, Bruce's manifesto builds on one of New Narrative's points of departure by arguing that everything in consumer society assumes an aesthetic dimension, including the gay community itself, defined by a logic whereby not only commodities, but feelings, affects, desires, and pleasures appear divorced from their own material conditions. But rather than debunk gay identity as just another delusion of our commodified lifeworld, "Toward a Gay Theory for the '80s" pushes beyond a critique of the commodity as false consciousness in order to affirm the commodity's significance in the making of gay subjectivity itself.

These politically charged works from the late 1970s and early 1980s achieved their full realization off-the-page in the Left/Write Conference of 1981, which Bruce helped to organize, an event whose aims were faithful to the values of the Gay Liberation Front, which integrated sexual, gender, and class politics, while also including the goal to create a Left Writers' Union. From our contemporary vantage point on the other side of the culture wars that defined the artworld of the 1980s, the Left/Write Conference remains compelling in its effort to reconcile tendencies sadly siloed by the New Left. And in the modest shadow cast by Left/Write across the '80s, it's refreshing to read Bruce writing about the "vanguard" quality of then emergent minority writing, dispatching the divisiveness that often pits "identity-based" writers against those writers associated with the avant-garde. In an interview with Jocelyn Saidenberg for the online accompaniment to *From Our Hearts to Yours: New Narrative as Contemporary Practice*, Bruce brings all of these things together:

> My take on New Narrative probably came from fierce identity politics. (Earlier though, there was already a strong sense of

social justice that my commitment to Catholicism in Vatican II years gave me). At first this was largely inchoate—or else just gay politics. Then during the St. Cloud Marxist Summer Institute when I started mixing with activists of other identities, I realized there couldn't be a robustly radical gay movement without solidarity with other gender and ethnic movements, and this, knitted with a strong left orientation, lead me to writing a short pamphlet to this effect. A little later this led Steve Abbott and myself (then joined by Robert Glück and others) to concoct the idea of a Left/Write Conference—to be able to be a platform for solidarity among the various local groups of ethnic/ gender/ sexual writers—and this coming at a time when many of these groups were not just independent of each other but even at odds with some or all of the others. What eventuated in my opinion was a writing, New Narrative, that would reflect some of these inter-political trends, at least in our own writerly generation, if not in others.

. . .

Whether composing narrative or essay, story or poem, Bruce's writing finds pleasure in the space between theory and gossip, refinement and sloppiness, high-minded idea and pop-cultural schlock. And pleasure, like emotion, has everything to do with politics, as he writes retrospectively in his "Afterword" to the reissue of *Century of Clouds* (Nightboat Books 2009):

> In my book, a politics once polemical wants to be emotional, perhaps a vehicle to joy, elation, even ecstasy. In my own experience politics emerged first as a purpose: I, we (Marxists), wanted something to happen, we wanted to change something. But in writing, emotion takes charge of the politics, so everything gets turned around: the political becomes the means to the production of affect in the reader, just as affect and emotion likewise lead to politics.

In the letter of recommendation on behalf of Bruce's application for the residency that I mentioned earlier, Robert Duncan referred to a quality of Bruce's writing related to this emphasis on emotion: "He starts from a confidence in the authenticity of his existence that is of an order outside literary manner." This notion of "authenticity" may seem old-fashioned, if not retrograde, but it takes on another quality when seen as inseparable from the art of representing emotion. As Bruce's work arouses and attunes our damaged subjectivities at a moment when social forces threaten most to alienate us from one another and ourselves, as well as from our writing, authenticity and artifice are crucial to the making of emotion as a literary effect, and this idea touches all of Bruce's major concerns as they migrate across *Dismembered*, flickering like a strobe between community affirmation and a self-professed negativity, from gay sunshine to queer darkness, two poles that refute the mutual exclusions of dualist thinking as they interpenetrate in as many ways as there are pieces in this book.

Building on these ideas, it's worth proposing that the "high risk" of Bruce's writing is ultimately emotional, concerned not with "transgression"—and here Bruce amicably parts company with Georges Bataille and Dennis Cooper—but with the unfolding of genuine feeling. As he writes in the same "Afterword":

> The book centers on emotions. At the same time it's a record of analyzed ecstasies. The vehicle is words, and nothing but words, words I tried to employ in such a way so as to lead readers to the possibility of their own ecstasy. There is ecstasy, but there are also the devices that trigger it, and neither ecstasy nor those devices can function without each other [...]

• • •

After "Gay Language as Political Praxis," Bruce conscientiously assumed a rather relaxed stance toward all academic matters. How many centuries did it take scholars finally to discover all of Montaigne's faulty quotations of Cicero?, Bruce asked me one afternoon while walking down 19th Street toward Castro in defense of his own unscholarly tendency to misquote.

These are dangerous times! The earth is burning!, he continued. Why should consistency of measure mean anything now?, he said, referring obscurely to the standardization of metrics under Louis XVI in response to my concern with the stylistic inconsistencies you might notice across these pages, in defense of which Bruce concluded his argument with an emphatic *Who cares?!!!*

As you make your way through *Dismembered*, dear reader, you will see how Bruce's writing from the mid-1980s abjures normative rules and their effect of "smoothness" in order to achieve a more roughly hewn texture faithful to patterns of casual talk without ever disavowing its own writerliness. Put yet another way, he nourishes a writerly shorthand that includes the reader in a knowingness that allows for compression, distillation, exclamation, interrogation, and ellipsis in the unfolding of something more faithful to emotional thought. In works like "The Perception of a Body among Writing's Parts," for example, Bruce's writing begins to incline deliberately toward "unprofessional" form: sentence syntax strains, ideas appear telegraphically, texts abut other texts with minimal connective tissue, and tonal gesture is privileged above the representation of ideas. I asked Bruce about these tendencies as we were editing "A Stele for Jamie," an excerpt from his yearlong mourning blog that concludes this book, and Bruce asked me in turn to think of the Vergilius Romanus, one of the earliest extant codices of Vergil's *Aeneid*, where one finds no separation between otherwise discrete words. That's where all this is heading!, he said.

This drift toward entropy, this breakdown in normative orders of experience and communication, carries the afterglow of Bruce's interest in Bataille, whose negativity resonates throughout *Dismembered*. "Writers, let your language be grounded in a more material degree of negativity," Bruce writes in the draft of a talk called "Negativity" that he delivered at New Langton in 1985, and which he and I had begun to reconstruct for inclusion here, a task that proved in the end to be too arduous an endeavor. "The slightest resistance to accepting negativity," Bruce continues, "annihilation, extinction, etc., halts the intensity or flow of aggression that is required to condemn and even extirpate our inclination to maintain normal, received social pretenses instead of subverting them." Bruce theorizes and activates "the negative" idiosyncratically in many of the works included here, often under the sign of "the dark"—from the poems in "Dark Queer Suite" to his review of Robert Duncan's *Groundwork*, and from "The Queen Beats" to the essays on Jack Spicer—lending popular expression to an elevated concept. "I think the time has come to openly express the loss of the *dark* in the blinding, calculating *light* of writing today," Bruce writes in "*Mirage*, or Where's the Party?" And in "The Perception of a Body Among Writing's Parts," he embraces this negativity, together with all his writerly values— anti-academicism, emotion, artifice—while illustrating them by way of writers he admires and loves, writers as different from one another as Kathy Acker, H.P. Lovecraft, Charles Bernstein, Ntozake Shange, and of course Stephen King.

While never departing from the concerns motivating his early poems and essays, Bruce's later writing carries within itself an ongoing interest in the Zen proposition "all form is emptiness, all emptiness is form," and it's useful to recall this while reading *Dismembered*, not only as a spiritual mantra, but as both an ethical rule and an aesthetic value informing the whole of Bruce's lifework. This idea even animates Bruce's revaluation of pop culture whose fugitive energy and transitive evanescence endlessly yield illustrations of that emptiness, like Amiri Baraka's "changing same," or "the new." And like *zazen*, with its emphasis on the ephemeral nature of all things as they move along currents of eternal transformation, Bruce's writing illuminates that emptiness without ever believing to master it. But emptiness doesn't amount to nothingness!, I hear Bruce disabusing me. Things are just always changing, becoming other things!, he goes on, before illustrating. Think of O'Hara, Bruce says, and how he runs the extra mile in poems like "The Day Lady Died" to unite the cosmos and the daily, the eternal and the transitory! And then, with a sudden flash, it all clicks into place and I understand the presence of Kurt Cobain and Bjork who appear like apparitions across *He Sleeps with Angels*, at once singular avatars and arbitrary ornaments, exploding in a firmament under the intense pressure of imminent heat death, the effect of which is both emptiness and form at the same time.

• • •

There remains one dimension of Bruce's writing life that can't go without mention. I'm referring to his work as a translator of Georges Bataille and Pascal Quingard. Given the importance of his translation practice, and its relevance to all of his writing, I'm sad that we were not able to include in *Dismembered* the text of a talk Bruce gave in 2007 as part of a series on "Translation as Social and Aesthetic Practice," organized by the Nonsite Collective. Bruce's talk was largely extemporized in performance, and does not exist as a publishable text. In summary, his theory of translation is rooted in the Gnostic mysteries and wedded to his understanding of translation as a spiritual practice. One of Bruce's key propositions derives from the idea of *disjecta membra*, which refers to a collection of surviving fragments, texts and manuscripts, like the book you are holding. The concept extends metaphorically to refer to scattered parts of the body, organs and limbs, and it's this metaphoric relation between writing and the body that Bruce literalizes when he asserts quite seriously that the price a translator must pay for a real translation is dismemberment: "The cost of the translation is the translator him or herself." This is one of Bruce's theses. "It refers to a constitutive loss on the one hand (for the translation coming into being) and destructive on the other hand. It occurs in the dismemberment of the translator. His dismemberment is the opening of the hole or conduit that passes to the other world." (These quotations are drawn from a draft of Bruce's talk.) In short, "dismemberment" connotes the toll that writing takes on the body as both writing and body become portals to the Outside. Alluding to this idea, Bruce shared the following with me by email: "Like the physical erosion of the body that occurs in vatic sessions of His Holiness the Dalai Lama with the Tibetan State Oracle, the body of the translator—usually a femme and skittish young monk— suffers the consequences of delivering true oracles." When pressed further, Bruce extends the comparison to the Delphic Sybil translating the Oracle, or the Voudon Priestess translating the Divinity, for whom the practice of translation has everything to do with possession and dispossession, with becoming the conduit between irrational demiurge and rational script. "Go tell my horse!," sings the divinity, according to Zora Neale Hurston, one of Bruce's favorite points of reference here. But when one is "ridden by Apollo," as Hurston describes the priestess like a horse straddled by the godhead, one all but loses one's rational sense, only to lose it for real to a scribe who goes and turns all those divine grunts and moans into perfectly legible sentences. How else is one to turn the mumbled phonemes of an unintelligible god into Greek hexameters?, Bruce asks. It only requires a small leap to consider this theory of translation as a theory of writing more generally, a theory whose practice has resulted in *Dismembered*, and this seems like an appropriate place to conclude this introduction.

. . .

A note on the construction of this book: As Robert Glück writes in his "Long Note on New Narrative" referring to the Left/Write conference, "We accomplished on a civic stage what we were attempting in our writing, editing and curating: to mix groups and modes of discourse." This goal of mixing groups and modes of discourse also characterizes our approach to *Dismembered*'s organization as we've conscientiously chosen to mix genres and styles, audiences and periods, in order to better reflect Bruce's refusal to countenance generic expectations and protocols. In our effort to make this volume as inclusive as possible, we had to make some difficult decisions, and so there remain many unpublished works by Bruce that I wish this book could have sampled if only to alert those among you who might be interested to know of their existence. For example, there are two-hundred pages of an essay called "Robin Blaser and Ufology: Interface Deployed" that places Bruce's convergent interests in Gnosticism, Buddhism, UFOs and the Mother Ship, beside Blaser's notion of "the Outside," all of which offer a set of interchangeable metaphors for the cosmic unknown and our part in it. There is also the whole of *He Sleeps with the Angels (Pink Sperm)*, another unpublished manuscript exceeding two-hundred pages, one of two previously published excerpts of which appears here. Among other works, there exists a seventy-page unpublished poem in manuscript called "The Agencies' Aggression (for Phil Whalen)," as well as various versions of "Negativity," mentioned above. There are also many additional poems, both published and unpublished, all of which I mention here to leave a negative trace of work that exceeds this book's frame.

· · ·

Bruce Boone Dismembered has been years in the making and would not have been possible without the help of many who aided in the process of recovering lost works, transcribing analog texts, and guiding the effort in innumerable ways. Gratitude to Chris Daniels, Robin-Tremblay McGaw, Kevin Killian, Kaplan Harris, Evan Kennedy, Brian Teare, Charles Bernstein, Stephen Motika, Lindsey Boldt, James Maynard, Eric Sneathen, Robert Dewhurst, Lee Azus, and Robert Glück. Special thanks to the Poetry Collection of the University Libraries, University at Buffalo, The State University of New York, where the Bruce Boone Collection lives.

—Rob Halpern
August 2019

BRUCE BOONE DISMEMBERED

POEMS, STORIES, AND ESSAYS

EARLY POEMS

KARATE FLOWER

Oil, that's what I admire, to run the machines.
And gasoline with a cleanliness like war.
But there is another part of me, the grandfather
who made chocolates. When I was young I plucked
bonbons like roses or anything ridiculous
you choose to admire. And I admired the beautiful.
Then a shot rang out. It was the archduke
or it was a president I hated. There were wars
and I kept quiet and waited a very long time.
Sincerity does not necessarily go unnoticed.
Now I wear a gun.

I'll tell you my past. First Hawaii.
My teacher told me, Study the stars,
for beauty is cold as money. And wasn't
I as innocent as you, then? I went
to school and I learned. Why bother?
Let the judges decide between us.
As I weakened I fell in love with orchids,
And children like sand-dabs on the beach.
Women taught me piano lessons. My father
gave me a rifle, I will always treasure
his coldness. From him I learned to hate.
But you must think it is better to give
than receive, or why did you come to this
goddamned place anyway? Where do you
think I was in Pearl Harbor? Please
don't think I'm innocent. We were
only unsuccessful.

And now we have the operatic
divers, the sleek-skinned ones. And
Andre Gide. I hate him for what he
did to Saigon. There we have the
french colonial style, and the jungles
are american craters—do you complain about
the palm trees I wear? It is just one american
indian after another I keep sleeping with because
another exoticism is always more interesting than
the one you have now. We are not the same.
You are rich and I am not, and that is the
difference between us. I don't believe in
your fucking. It's passionless and without
pain like your fathers, the bilious
waves that bring in the shrieking tourists,
they just keep fucking and fucking,
red-faced bloated men with their silver-haired
ladies of California.

And don't you know
where the loot goes? Oh god, don't I
want to go home too? I hate you for
your generosity. I could even forget
about the money and I could put up
with the heart-attacks and old folks homes,
I could even get to like Harry Truman,
but I'm not even talking about the past!
A metaphor is just another dumb shirt to
wear. But how are you supposed to talk
to people, go join a nudist camp? Let's
see how many different places we can put
our cocks. It makes a big difference,
doesn't it? No, it doesn't matter in the
slightest. I want a handsome surfer
on my shirt, but so what? Just because

I live in Hawaii doesn't mean I'm
in paradise. Rimbaud and Frank O'Hara
called it Africa, but I call it Sherman's
March through Georgia because it tightens
round my waist, because it's the only possible
way to live. With a tug. What do you know
about etymology, and how about Saint-Just?
Do you think Bastille Day is just another
holiday? It's the rolling Trans-Siberian
Railway carrying the petite Jeanne de France
and Blaise Cendrars across the tundra. I'm wearing,
I'm wearing and I'm worn. Do we have any
idea what the Guillotine is? the black-
and-blue marks without benefit of clergy.
And see how many bishops and queens there are!
Innocent children! something important is
happening! Let us hope for the compassion
of those who will follow us. For it will
come. Ça ira. Rhetoric makes me your double.
We look upon our jailors with dogs' eyes.
We think, he is on the wrong side of the bars.
Let's be silent, and beautiful Havana will
fall. Our rhetoric is upside down.

Why am I telling you all this? "Cry Me
a River," says Big Tits. I am telling you about
my personal history as a headache that
makes excessive demands on my time. I am
giving you a textbook lesson in guerrilla
warfare. Imagine Lenin, caught in his past,
a Swiss sanatorium. He writes with too much freedom.
Someday his train will arrive.
When the day comes, there is nothing left but
dreams. And then the time of sleep comes,
we wander to the gardens of our stolen wealth.
It's the scene from METROPOLIS, and we find

our families, our country, our lovers. But
that is just one of those Lenins. And we are
still above ground.

So am I free then to go
to the games room and play with those puzzles?
Years ago my grandmother gave me the best set,
the interlocking flowers that were to be my
trousseau or bassinet. I could have learned
her impetuosity, but that smile has never ceased
to be a silver urn to fascinate me. I have
your history as well.

It was grandfather,
we were told, who made the chocolate. A
misconstruction—for a German-Swiss arrived
in Milwaukee that day. It was simple enough.
The people made the money, and the people made the
chocolate. It was the German-Swiss who kept
the money, it was the German-Swiss who ate
the chocolate. But we mountains remained
mountains. There. I am a German, I wear
a rope. And I will not permit you to be
sentimental about this. What is the point,
if you do not understand that we have no parents
and we have no country, we have only Russia
to go back to. The money was in vain.
And the guilt had no purpose. I have known
this personally as I have known that the factory
in Milwaukee was an unsuccessful theft and
love it still for its caresses, like a
can of yellow plums on a dusty shelf.

Then grandfather died and the thinking stopped,
but everything went on as before. The profits were
salmon slapping their tails to go home,
to spawn their mess of roe on the front steps.

We stepped around it. I forget which war it
was, but I had the true friendship of a true Nazi.
Don't laugh, for I envy you each of the guns
I pick up. I aim them at the faces in the
newspapers, yours, but I will lose my nerve if you
keep on weeping like this. I think I have the
right to expect laughter when I dissimulate. But
you are the cause, you took away the money.
You took away the past. So I keep wishing for the train
to come rolling in, so I can go to Petersburg. I
want all the faces in the newspapers to be yours,
each president, each leader, each poet, for faces
are the light of the world. Grandfather, hurry!
Hurry my train. Or the fuse of my laughter
will ignite the stars. I am waiting to put the
match to my fragile line, I stand in your place.

Now I want to execute our privileges, grandfather,
disabuse our common purpose and move only in fright
so that our words will be the delicate nerve endings
of a better race. I'll be womanly, you'll put on
flowered shirts. I'll be Madame La Veuve, but you
will remain what you are, my death, the hurricane
I constantly dream of. Hurry grandfather!
Our embrace will take revenge on the world.
Mother, my mother, why did you take away the
past, and now my only mistress must be the blade!
Do you see how it shines? In my slow glazing eyes
the flowers are fading. Why did you put them
there? In the spring you won't pick them.
The men with no faces, the executioners, have already
picked them, plucked and trampled them. Oh,
inanity of nature! inanity of this
world of desperation! Rock your cradle of
yellowing newspapers, sorrowing mother.

I have left to join the armies of each side,
and the dark Kremlins of compassion will come
cascading from my side till all my red trains
go rocking and sliding into the sun for crazy happiness.
The chocolate factories will make only tanks.
Grandfather, I have not left you.
We're only going to Petersburg.
But when the rest of you hear this, remember my voice.
It is yours. I ask your forgiveness. I was unable
to be myself, and I became you. In the extremity
of my solitude I have tried my best to live,
but my lies are only too evident: they are yours.
Let us be like Russia, then, as vast and impersonal.
Let us be the world.
Dear friends, I can no longer vilify you.
We are moving toward a future.
Quickly, come hold my hand.
Everywhere I see red, and the time of dispatch.
Seize it: take my hand, take his hand,
take hers. And the fathers and mothers
will lie still and peaceable at last.
I am walking above ground
and can see only birches, kilometer on kilometer,
the birches of Russia, and the white of the plains.
We are not our own, we are for
the sons and daughters who will follow.
Give them your hand.

Karate Flower was published as a stapled mimeograph chapbook by Hoddypoll Press, edited by James Mitchell (San Francisco, 1973).

WRITING POEMS—IS SOMETHING ELSE

I don't know what
you write poems for
because everything is off someplace else
except for the bad things
of course. That's
what I have faith in.
And who could really expect
any change—maybe
a little more money sometime
is all I can think of—
and what about my
hemorrhoids and constipation
& spindly ankles—the most
I could say is maybe
it's like Dylan—he was skinny too—do
you think anything will change?
I know I'll never finish
graduate school. A few reds
or yellows would make me
feel pretty good. The only
line I memorized from Brecht,
he was watching to see
his cigar didn't go out,
the earthquakes were coming.
Grandmother plays canasta
3 times a week
she never messed her panties
once in 103 yrs, you can
count on it.
I used to want to write poems
like Frank O'Hara—I'll
never have the money though.
& I don't know about Art.

Once when I was
in graduate school
I chased after a hairdresser
to L. A.

"Writing Poems—Is Something Else" was published in *Veins of the Earth: Poetry by Michael Ratcliff, Bruce Boone, Stephen Mark, and James Mitchell* (San Francisco: Hoddypoll Press, 1970).

HE'S THE LOVER/OF MY SOUL

Suddenly I am thinking of Francis,
which is a sissy name and the name
                              of the one
I remember (why?) in the sixth grade
he wet his pants
                    we were in love and catholics
we were always looking back fondly and sadly
because catholics always do
                              we were looking back
as sissies do
                 yet we were in love

all the world loves a lover
                         but does it
when their names are Bruce and Francis?
we showed it by chasing girls
                              and tearing their clothes
but we carved our names on the sacred heart
we knew the language of flowers
                              and aside from us
they only talked to girls
                      filling the glorious
churches of our hearts
                      making us gasp for breath
for the blueness of the sky
                              where love shot out
the flame, the choir, and all that heaven ever gave
it gave us to think
                    we were in the second grade again
as proud as kings
                    and I remember running down the hall
                    and all the girls would run
for the grief and joy

"He's the Lover/of My Soul" was published in *Angels of the Lyre: A Gay Poetry Anthology*, edited by Winston Leyland (San Francisco: Panjandrum Press/Gay Sunshine Press, 1975).

A NATURAL FORM OF LOVE

When I see heterosexuals holding hands
                    and kissing in public
something in me is a little disgusted
though I would not dispute
                    anyone's right
to the satisfactions they choose.
People's sex life is their own business.
                                        Besides,
many famous men in history
                    have been heterosexuals, equally
famous women, too.
                    Where
would Western Culture be
                    without
Eloise and Abelard, in philosophy,
        George Sand and Chopin, in music (and literature),
or Olivia de Haviland and Clark Gable,
                            (in *Gone With the Wind*)
in our contemporary times?
                    If you think of the Brownings
you can easily see
                    how this form of love
can enhance the lives of those
who feel it
                    and lead to great and lasting achievements.

"A Natural Form of Love" was first published in *Sebastian Quill*, no. 3, edited by
James Mitchell (San Francisco 1972).

from SLEEP

You get the eagle on your ass in this country, and you are in big trouble. The bastards ruined Dick Haymes, it wasn't Rita Hayworth, it was the eagle. All the eagle wants to do is put you in the slammer.

JOHN GREGORY DUNNE

Toward the end of a time of fitfulness and a
flattering spirit, my lucidity swept down on me like
a Welfare Office of the mind that burned me, and scorched
and coated the finny bones of my spine and sent me
spinning out like a damp rag on a field.
May I express my clinical awakening as a fragment?
A psychiatrist, if you prefer, which was my eye, the
needle through the back of my mouth. Syringes which
were dirty, leering promises, the pair of pliers
which they held. What was it then but the chill
of death, the absolute of cold, which never, I knew
could be me? A fragment, a motionless rag, and the
whirring sound in the forebrain like a drill. And
then there were splinters and fragments and chips of
teeth that once were my own, and they sank and filled
me up with bone. A smiling like saws was around me,
and on the other side, rods like slats, or like
numbers, made a fence to change the names I knew,
and looking forward and beyond I saw an unfamiliar
face in a frozen grin on a scream.

Then, I said, laughing uncles sold real estate
and prospectuses for shiny new cars or empty desert
land. When was it, then? And they grabbed my shoulder
and squeezed out pain and asked me which did I like,
dollars or cock? When I said cock they said, ha-ha, boy,
you sure got a lot to learn, don't you, son?

They pointed out the elevator, and the little man
in the Philip Morris cap shouted out, 'Ground Floor
here, Get in now for the express to the top!' Then
everybody left and the steel doors slammed shut,
and I was alone for ten whole years.

There was nostalgia, there were colleagues
with tight smiles and watery chicken broth. The future
snarling like a Hoover vacuum-cleaner that won't
catch, and men in suits hand me business cards that
say IDEAS LIGHT THE WORLD, HAVE YOU HAD AN IDEA
LATELY? And I am nervous with fake emotion. A letter
arrives or a summons. It says: Study now with MASTER
CHARGE, first 30 days free. A future free from
financial worry can be yours. Sign here. Should I?
I mean, did I? The Board of Regents appoints the
Angel Moroni from Salt Lake as Chairman of Graduate
Studies, who turns out to be a huffing puffing little
man with beady eyes and a voice that says shoe stores in
Omaha. So I flunk my exams, and the beady-eyed fat man
grits his teeth and says, 'Where I come from we got
places for troublemakers like you. Wanna try again,
Mr. Wise Guy?' And he snickers to his colleague Professor
Hide-in-the-Closet-with-a-Luger, the man who holds
his cards close to his chest and never takes chances.
Anxious to please, Tall-and-Funereal saunters up to me,
he whispers in my ear, 'you got a great career ahead of
you, kiddo, why don't you just commit suicide and save
us both some time?' A distance closes, and I
hear church music promising me the fabled knowledge
of good and evil, but delivering nothing. So the professor
demonstrates his life to me. With a wink he hands me
two quietly strong scholarly works on the theme Poetry
the Tragic Muse, a series of magazine articles on
gracious living arrangements and an informative little

brochure on property management entitled 'Light for
Uncertain Eyes.' Church music again. A boy soprano
is singing 'Shall We Gather?' The congregation looks
to him for cues. Then the knowledge of good and evil
comes to me, and I am filled with sorrow. The professor
tells me he admires Jack Spicer for his poetry but
how terrible he was a homosexual. I know the
worst is to come. Quickly writing out a will that
leaves his wife the entire estate, he puts a finger
to his temple and threatens to blow his brains out, and
I say I think I'm interfering with something so I guess
I better go. Fat boy sneers, considers the performance an
unqualified success. On the spot he pays Bones the
agreed-on Six Big Ones in cost overrun, promises him
a renegotiated contract with travel expenses to Colma,
City of Cemeteries, so the professor can study the
Radio Theory of poetry. The game is up, so Fatso takes
a quick powder, to get out while the getting is good. Which
it is, for Fat Stuff. But Tall-and-Skinny's finger is
on a real trigger, and I am feeling very sick, as he
asks himself sincerely, 'Is it so bad to be a little
dishonest now and then?' and blows himself to Kingdom
Come. And my thoughts on the value of university life
reach new lows on the despondency scale. The sign on
the back of a toilet door on Telegraph Avenue says, 'Dracula
is Lord, Dracula is $.'

Out of here and on, then. If a person were to tumble
like a laundry load in an empty laundromat against the
plastic window, who would there be to see the empty
faces churning by again and again but himself? A
philosophy can hear the sound of a tree falling, it
falls and it falls and falls again and becomes itself.
The philosophy notes this by writing it down. In the
parable of the empty laundromat and the parable of

the falling tree there are persons of integrity, one of
them has integrity and does not change, and the other also
has integrity and does not change. So they go on
disputing and no one has benefited a jot or a tittle.
And does it make a difference? Cramped horizons and
cheap blue-serge overcoats. Heavy foods, Moralism.
I start to ferret for my bad days, like a drinker
for his alcoholic bad breath, and life's grabbers
and takers see me as their own, the thin men of the world's
ill-repute who pick up pennies. And on the horizon
an in-law's Yom Kippur threatens to take away my
lover. It is time to stop, it is definitely time.

So I pull the handle on the slot machine once,
and an ugly piece of shit comes out. Muscular and
large and cheerful, it makes porn movies for a
living, eats vegetarian food, makes healthful love
three times a day and dies without compunction in a
sack on the back porch of a dilapidated flat on Divisadero St.

So I pull the handle on the machine and out of the
chute slides a woman who looks like a man looking like
a woman, and I long to be that woman. Then a man comes
through the door. And when he puts on his gangster's
mask he says, 'Let's make lust and murder.' And then the
man and the woman make lust and murder till they
become a dusty heap of bones and die on the back
porch of the man's dilapidated flat on Divisadero St.
And so I pull again on the handle of the slot machine
and fall into a deep trance: a fish the size of a bloated
carp floats by, some apples and oranges and a large
grapefruit. I am my needs, a single-minded voice
saying, I want, I want, I want! A murderous balloon that
I am ready to launch, a dirigible carrying foreign
nationals to a dark destination somewhere in central

Europe and outside is the cold dark air and the cabin
with the glittering rich. What am I? Am I these
lives? The cold closes in. In the gulags some carry
bayonets and place rubble walls of barbed wire. Some
others live in compounds in Florida and California, they
eat briny finger shrimp or go swimming every day. And on
a compost heap outside Havana a DuPont sits with his
orchids, and everywhere there are orchids, nothing
but orchids. In the jungle Fidel Castro waits patiently.
So I seek out death like a fancier, but he hides from
me and there isn't any finding him.

[...]

(For Jonathan 11/18/76)

This excerpt from the long poem "Sleep" is published here for the first time.

DODO THE CAT GIVES HIMSELF TO
THE UNIVERSE AND LATER WRITES POEMS

Dodo the cat enjoyed the winters
In Lord Kurosawa's palace.
He would slip through the snow
In a bright silk kimono
When cherry blossoms were falling.

Reflective Dodo paused
And stopped. He saw his whole life
Pass before his eyes.
He saw the cat innards
Red on white snow. They were
Neat and fresh
Like the clean tatami mats laid out
For the visit of the Shogun.
Sweet and ripe.
August plums in a lacquered bowl.

Did Dodo see too clearly?
Did he feel too deeply?

Afterwards he would write
When the starlight fell
Through open shoji panels.
He licked the falling snowflakes
From his fur. His cousins waited for him
In the Northern palace.

"Dodo the Cat" was published in *Ravens Fleeing Darkness*, no. 10 1976.

REMARKS ON NARRATIVE:
THE EXAMPLE OF ROBERT GLÜCK'S POETRY

There is a story being told about you . . .
MARX, CITED BY J.P. FAYE

1

If nothing else—but there certainly is a great deal more here—Robert Glück's offering of narrations attracts attention as storytelling. The stories and poems present themselves to us as a series of developments of narrative possibilities in poetry itself. As has now been apparent for some time, the poetry of the '70s seems generally to have reached a point of stagnation, increasing a kind of refinement of technique and available forms, without yet being able to profit greatly from the vigor, energy and accessibility that mark so much of the new Movement writing of gays, women and Third World writers, among others. Ultimately this impasse of poetry reflects conditions in society itself. In the meantime, however, poetry's consciousness of itself in relation to society can often be more progressive and open to new awareness when it takes the form of a critique of its own poetic forms.

2

Robert Glück's narratives seem to me to be just such a critique of many recent formalistic tendencies in poetry, particularly the new trends toward conceptualization, linguistic abstraction and process poetry. These various orientations appear as a refusal to be heard socially, that is, to speak to any real audience. Thus the function of the poem often seems to continue the autonomous Modernist sense of the poem's existence on the page, and only there. Counteracting some of these tendencies, Frank O'Hara in the '50s and early '60s, and then some of the poets in New York—Ron Padgett should be mentioned particularly—began to integrate narrative material as a technique to constitute the poem again socially. Robert Glück's poems seem to come from, and be a development of, this countertendency to prevailing Modernist practices. His poems in this respect bring out a strongly judgmental or juridical aspect of this narrative function in a tradition which up to now has not adequately or politically appreciated it.

3

I say 'politically' because I think this is the real meaning behind the confusing narrative disguises that these poems often take on. They find it satisfying, for instance, to keep a running commentary on themselves— the metatext that is spoken from the present—while onstage appear conventional anecdotes, such as these narratives of someone's past, of ethnicity and family life. They are stories that mime a past as overheard by a mocking, sometimes cynical presence that seems to be manipulating them for its own ends. But when we think about it these stories may seem rather odd in other ways too. Sometimes they may seem to have an air of the slightly risqué, or else of the puzzlingly factitious or 'worked up,' but at all events of a certain rather embarrassing tone that for some reason appears to be assuming our complicity in its own slightly shady or seedy designs. We ought to be shocked of course, but we are not. These feelings clearly warn us—be on your guard, because these stories concern you. But the question is, how? For what is after all to be done with a set of stories whose every ridiculous conclusion is a vaudeville death? "Bobby, your mother has the face / of an angel and a heart of gold, / and you'll be sorry when she's dead." Certainly these stories are every bit as humorous as they are intended to be. But aren't they also in a sense compromising—to the extent that we find them as humorous as they say they are ?

4

If one of the concerns of a certain type of Jewish joke has been to reconcile the unreconcilable, then what is being narrated here seems to insist on an extremely unreconcilable side of things. "It cost XXX, but it was worth it, your uncle nearly *killed* me," says Aunt Sura. Of course—and we take it for granted—such a family life is not healthy. But that after all may not be the main point. Or we could put it another way. We might ask who the subject of these poems might be. And we might also ask who or what their object could be.

At the end of the "Mangle Story," for instance, we find that through some sleight of hand it is we ourselves who have become the narrator of the story, and through a linguistic ruse the subject of these stories has become only a conveniently transferrable function. And the narrator has become the object of a new narration being told—this time by ourselves. What the narrator seems to be claiming then is that it is the act of narrating itself that causes the narrative function to slip across the invisible bar of separation— from him to us. Thus at the conclusion of this anecdote he tells us that he "can only give (you) this story, which is the same as sitting with my back to you, half-listening." Are the narrator's claims to indifference sincere then? We suspect not. The narrator can hardly be indifferent if at this point the question for both us and for him is, who is the 'who' telling the story?— and how could we indicate this subject? Freud, knowledgeable enough about such matters to follow his 'dream-book' a little later with his 'joke-book,' thereby doubly accommodating the examples of wit from his own tradition, may be invoked here to tell us something important about the story he disclosed as the narration of a dream 'structured like a language'— and always taking place 'elsewhere,' as Lacan would later point out. For Freud the question of the narration is thus the place of the subject—the subject who is recounting that narration. It is to this question, the question of the location of the subject actually speaking these poems and stories, that we should now turn our attention—to locate, that is, that offstage 'elsewhere,' whose region, insofar as it constitutes conditions of reality, can now be called political rather than psychological. For it is only out of social conditions that the narrating imagination comes to be.

Conditions of reality operate in these poems and stories as a return to a social origin as well as to a destination of the narrative—ourselves as that 'audience' both hearing and producing these same stories. The narrative function reveals itself in the technical features which characterize it. The 'deceptive' ending, or ending of reversal, the rhetorical texture of a humor that makes us accomplices of a narrator who seems to claim that ethnic and family caricatures are indeed reflections of 'how things are'; or else ("The Body") the juridical and semantic usage of anger, acting as warnings or signals that the poems are partisan, and intended to have real effects on us—a judgmental viewpoint that declines to be 'objective' in any sense that would satisfy us. These devices constitute a transfer of the subject from a local determination in the speaking narrator to a more profound and generalized function which may be thought of as society itself, as it tells us the story that continues to constitute it.

These poems and stories, then, remind us of the actual, though unmentioned function of narration as a device for registering social meaning. They take on special importance, in my opinion, in clarifying our awareness of the relations of poetry to a material and social, or actual truth. They create the need for an audience—the sense of the narration as it presupposes a reception, and keeps in mind a destination. In a poetry such as this we can see both possibilities for present literary concern as well as signals for a future. A future that is certainly on the other side of our present writing, but one that may nonetheless reflect back to us some idea of what poetry and society might be in a place still to come.

"Remarks on Narrative: the Example of Robert Glück's Poetry" was published as the postscript to Robert Glück's *Family Poems*, (San Francisco: Black Star Editions, 1979). The essay was reproduced in *L=A=N=G=U=A=G=E* no. 10 and excerpted in *The L=A=N=G=U=A=G=E Book,* edited by Bruce Andrews and Charles Bernstein (Carbondale: Southern California University Press, 1984).

GAY LANGUAGE AS POLITICAL PRAXIS:
THE POETRY OF FRANK O'HARA

Recent evidence suggests that the work of the New York poet, Frank O'Hara, is now on its way to becoming part of the American canon. The barriers to its acceptance have largely fallen, and the work of this poet of the 50s is now in the process of being assimilated within the educational system as an important event and text. For all intents and purposes the work of this poet has become legitimate.

A satisfactory account of the critical acceptance of these once ill-reputed poems, however, is not likely to be found within the official discourse which is producing it. A demystification of the critical discourse about these poems may in fact require rethinking some of the current directions in text formulation. Raising the question of O'Hara's sexuality, largely repressed from critical discourse to date, may for this reason help us point to some strategical shifts in recent canonical perspectives and suggest in the process some of the changed social realities which such a discourse often masks. Indeed, serious discussion today seems to agree that the question of sexuality is long overdue on the agenda. Attacks on ERA and the women's movement in general and setbacks for gays from Dade County, Florida, to Eugene, Oregon, have gathered momentum and reached a focal point in what might be called the rise of a new fascism. Questions about the relation between capitalism and everyday life become more and more insistently a subject for both theoretical inquiry and practical concern for those whose basic commitment is to the structural change of society. Today social progressives can ignore these issues only at the risk of jeopardizing the whole left-progressive movement. Committed literary critics will want then to consider the unspoken assumptions of current text formulation in order to more clearly understand the mechanisms involved in literary attempts to rewrite basic social antagonisms.[1]

---

1 My understanding of textuality has profited generally from the work of Barthes and Derrida, but more usefully I think from that of René Balibar and Fredric Jameson. Jameson's lectures at the first Summer Institute of the Marxist Literary

I

Critical discussion of O'Hara's work, however, has only recently become widespread. Following his death in 1966, O'Hara's work was relatively unknown outside a rather small group of literary and art-world people. Since then this poetic work has slowly become known and received at popular and academic institutional levels. For some time this poetry was considered unacceptable because of its imputed qualities of superficiality and frivolity. Now however, O'Hara's poetry shows signs of acceptance and legitimation on the basis of the same qualities that earlier resulted in its exclusion from the canon. In effect, O'Hara's work has come to be considered "textual" as qualities like textual "surface," playfulness, and "painterly" immediacy have become valorized critically, reflecting an increasing ideological shift toward versions of a text-philosophy originally found in Barthes and Derrida.

Let us take a short look at the critical reception of O'Hara's work. When *The Collected Poems* was first published,[2] the review in the *New York Times*, viewing the collection as good light verse, spoke of the poems as "entertainments" or "gossip"[3] rather than serious poetry. And except for a single phrase cited from one of the O'Hara poems—"the fierce inventories of desire"—there was no reference to the sexuality of the poems. If there was any connection between the "entertainment" or "gossip" aspect of the poems and their qualities as "inventories of desire," that connection was not one, apparently, that had to be noted.

Group of the MLA, during the summer of 1977, have been particularly helpful to me, as were the discussions of what is now the fifth section of this essay. I would also like to acknowledge an indebtedness to two other lecturers at the Institute, Terry Eagleton and Stanley Aronowitz, for presentations I often found myself recalling in preparing certain difficult sections of this paper. In general, in the stimulating environment of this Institute I found a great deal to draw from, though, indeed, much to struggle with too.

2 Frank O'Hara, *The Collected Poems of Frank O'Hara*, ed. Donald Allen (New York: Knopf, 1971). Hereafter cited in the text as *CP*.

3 Review of *CP* by Herbert A. Leibowitz, *New York Times Book Review*, November 28, 1971.

In the following year, however, critical discussion first got solidly underway with an important article by Helen Vendler appearing in *Parnassus: Poetry in Review*. The Vendler article gives critical approval to O'Hara's poetry as a description of contemporary life which represents everyday life as a perceived succession of unrelated events, taking note of O'Hara's characteristic "absence of... syntax" as the pivotal issue to be dealt with. "We cannot," the Vendler article concludes

> logically repudiate ideology and then lament its absence (though Stevens made a whole poetry out of just that illogic). O'Hara puts our dilemma inescapably before us, for the first time, and is, therefore, in his fine multiplicity and his utter absence of what might be called an intellectual syntax, a poet to be reckoned with, a new species.[4]

Earlier in the article Vendler had already made clear that such a lack of intellectual syntax refuses both maleness and ideology, seen as conflated, and proposes a kind of anti-logic of its own:

> The wish not to impute significance has rarely been stronger in lyric poetry... Such a radical and dismissive logic flouts the whole male world and its relentless demand for ideologies, causes, and systems of significance.[5]

The disadvantage of such a formulation, however, is that it displaces to a concessive afterthought the specific meaning of these observations. Vendler clarifies that meaning in the following parenthetical remark:

> We may regret the equableness and charm of our guide and wish him occasionally more Apollonian or more Dionysian (the sex

---

4 Helen Vendler, "The Virtues of the Alterable," *Parnassus: Poetry in Review* no. 1 (1972): 20.
5 Ibid., 9.

poems aren't very good, though they try hard and are brave in their homosexual details), but there's no point wishing O'Hara other than he was.[6]

Sexuality does come into question in at least some of the poems, then, though these poems "aren't very good," and the sex is a matter of "details."

Interestingly enough, however, by the time the Vendler article appeared, O'Hara's poetry was already beginning to be known within the community of gay men. For many gays, O'Hara's poems expressed an awareness of gay language and social life, and the poetry itself was fast becoming an occasion for community discussion of internal and external problems in gay newspapers and magazines.[7] This discussion of O'Hara's poems within the community, however, was effectively passed over by the official criticism. O'Hara's poems became a language without syntax, or entertainment and gossip. But not gay language. And the sex poems are found to be "not very good."

Another strategy for dealing with the sexual question can be sketched out by briefly reviewing what might be called the "pre-critical" discussion of O'Hara—articles and essays, mostly by other poets, that appeared in the late 60s immediately before the Vendler article. These articles and essays of the poets may be seen as "pre-critical" because they function as putting on notice the institutional critics who will follow them that the O'Hara corpus should be considered susceptible of those rereading and rewriting operations that would formulate it as a legitimate "text." To be sure, the poet critics of this time were certainly aware of the need to create an initial audience for O'Hara's work. For a general public a poetry that was thought superficial or frivolous would probably be considered no poetry at all. The

---

6 Ibid., 20.
7 Marjorie Perloff, *Frank O'Hara: Poet among Painters* (New York: Braziller, 1977), 3-4, refers to an article appearing in the now defunct San Francisco *Advocate*. (Other and more accessible articles and notes on O'Hara's work can be found in early issues of *Gay Sunshine*.) For a review of some of the pre-criticism of the poets and academic criticism of O'Hara's poems, see pp. 1-18 in Perloff. See also note 15 below.

historical task that confronted these poet critics was to make the O'Hara poems really available for the first time as serious poetry, to massively legitimize the work in such a way that any potential misconstructions of the poetry could be avoided or even refuted before they were raised. O'Hara's poetry then would have to be provided with some kind of credentials. It has since become clear that these credentials would be the poet's modernism.

Of the essays of this period, Bill Berkson's piece "Frank O'Hara and His Poems" stands out as the pioneering effort. Setting O'Hara's work in a modernist context within an appropriate visual lay-out (two photo reproductions of O'Hara portraits by well-known contemporaries of the poet), Berkson's article details the poet's connections with the American and French modernist traditions with a wealth of allusions to a number of the central figures in that movement—Stein, Williams, Satie, and Cage in music, and David Smith (citing O'Hara's monograph on the sculptor); mentioning too O'Hara's familiarity with the French poets, especially Reverdy and Char (O'Hara did translations of several of their poems). Qualities of language in O'Hara's poetry that might otherwise seem "inappropriate" for serious poetry are seen as particularly relevant because particularly in keeping with declared modernist aims—the attempt to break up the perceived unity of the poem, for instance, in favor of a more process-oriented approach. Thus, "No one of his poems is closed-off or exhaustive,"—and qualities like "lavishness" and "glamor" are approved. The "diffuseness" of the poems becomes "positive and vital," and though "each poem is in some part excessive," as a whole the poems are like Williams' work in that "they make supreme logic *together*."[8] Other poet critics writing on O'Hara about this time include Paul Carroll, with a validating concern for what he called the "impure" element in O'Hara's poetry[9]— those makeshift or improvisatory aspects which will be treated more comprehensively by Berkson; Richard Howard, with an existentializing

---

8 Bill Berkson, "Frank O'Hara and His Poems," *Art and Literature* no. 12 (Spring 1968).
9 Paul Carroll, *The Poem in its Skin* (Chicago: Big Table, 1968).

approach that concentrates more on the "glamor" of the O'Hara legend[10]; and finally John Ashbery, in an extended presentation of O'Hara's links with the French influences of Dada and literary surrealism (introductory essay to the Donald Allen *Collected Poems of O'Hara*). These other poets fill out and extend Berkson's initial modernizing interpretation.[11]

What then of criticism proper, or academic theorizing criticism since Vendler in the later 70s? Two important trends may be noted. The first relates O'Hara to the influences of the "Action Painting" of the day in an attempt to see the poem as "object."[12] And another and increasingly important trend, related to the first but more theoretical, reads O'Hara in light of French text-philosophy. The landmark discussion here is Charles Altieri's 1973 essay, "The Significance of Frank O'Hara,"[13] in which the O'Hara poems are legitimized as a Derridean "text." Noting that his discussion is based on Derrida, Altieri refers to a recent essay by the French writer elaborating the notion of *jeu* and discovers that the values of the O'Hara poems are essentially those validated by contemporary text-

---

10 In addition to the essays cited, during the late 60s and early 70s many biographical and personal notes on O'Hara and his circle began appearing. Most of these short pieces have been collected in *Homage to Frank O'Hara*, edited by Bill Berkson and Joe LeSueur, (Bolinas, CA: Big Sky, 1978) a special book-length double edition of the magazine *Big Sky*, nos. 11-12.

11 Richard Howard, "Frank O'Hara: 'Since Once We Are We Always Will Be in this Life Come What May,'" in *Alone with America* (New York: Atheneum, 1969). Interestingly, Howard notes in passing that the poems can be considered "accounts of Frank O'Hara's activity insofar as he belongs to a collectivity," describing the language of O'Hara's poetry as "newsy, fretful and of course *entertaining*" (Howard's emphasis)—though he lets the hint drop at that.

12 See for example Charles Molesworth, "The Clear Architecture of the Nerves: The Poetry of Frank O'Hara," in *Iowa Review* no. 6 (Summer and Fall, 1975): 61-73—the most intelligent example of this tendency. Citing Marcuse, Molesworth observes that in the context of these years, "O'Hara's poetry takes on the prospects of the perfect expression of a post-industrialized world: it is the highest poetic product of commodity market capitalism." One wonders, however, how such an argument would account for the specific sexual dimension of this poetry. An extension of the market capitalism viewpoint itself?

13 Charles Altieri, "The Significance of Frank O'Hara," *Iowa Review* no. 4 (Winter 1973): 90-104.

philosophy. What kind of "presence," Altieri asks, is it that the O'Hara text affirms? First and foremost, he answers, it is a presence "stripped of. . . ontological vestments," the present as a "landscape without depth" and with "no underlying significance of meanings to be interpreted." The language disruptiveness of the text can only refer us over and over again to itself alone—not social practice. Altieri sees the specific qualities of the O'Hara metaphor as much like what he calls "camp," though by means of a rewriting or recoding operation the social-linguistic value of this aspect of O'Hara as a *language practice of gay men* goes unnoted, and what remains is a kind of universalizing arbitrariness or language "playfulness" that is characteristic of textuality as such. But arguments of this sort are fundamentally unsound. The universalizing project of text philosophy supposes a language with neither meaning nor social site—a language which does not exist, except perhaps for text-philosophy itself.

Of these several stages for dealing with the repressed sexual content of O'Hara's poetry, the current strategy of text-philosophy, then, seems the purest and most programmatic in its removal of language from questions of historical context. This refusal has both a form and a content. Its content is the suspension of biographical-social investigation. And its form is the repression from the critical discourse of an antagonist sexual language in the poems.[14]

---

14 In O'Hara criticism the biographical question has remained the cutting edge of critical approaches because it cannot seriously be raised in O'Hara's case without at the same time formulating it as a sexual or sexual-political question; hence its repression. To assess the hostility to such antagonist sexual questions in general one can note, for example, the characteristically emotional responses of most academic reviewers to the recent publication of Simon Karlinsky's *The Sexual Labyrinth of Nikolai Gogol* (Cambridge, MA: Harvard University Press, 1976). Karlinsky's work was attacked by George Steiner as a particularly distressing example of the recent tendency to introduce partisan or polemical viewpoints into areas which should be the preserve of objective scholarship. George Steiner, "Books: Wild Laughter," *New Yorker*, February 28, 1977, 99-102. More recently, in a lecture sponsored by the Department of English, University of California-Berkeley (March 1978), Steiner has suggested a remedy for this kind of confusion: a return to theological criteria for literary judgment. We ought at least to commend Steiner for the forthrightness of his declaration of allegiances.

In the remaining sections of this paper I would like to show that the critical repression of this antagonist sexual question is in fact a repression of a politically oppositional language. The literary artifacts of this oppositional language in O'Hara's poems must be seen against the backdrop of the literary oppositional movements of the period, but more importantly, in the social context of gay community life. For it was significantly in the post-War years that gay men first began to feel themselves a cohesive group, and with group needs. An investigation of the social practice and language of these poems then is not meant to be of merely "historical" interest. Rather it is an attempt to comment on and extend the interested struggles of gay people today. And it is in this context that I raise the historical question of Frank O'Hara's sexuality.[15]

---

15 In the preceding discussion my remarks about the O'Hara criticism have been directed toward showing the stages of its development as an instrument of text formulation, that is, as a vehicle of the theoretical process in which the O'Hara texts have been submitted to the several rereadings which have allowed them to become acceptable or usable in the schools and at higher levels of the educational system.

This "theoretical" phase, however, has shown some signs of giving way to a more "practical" or expository phase. Marjorie Perloff's book, I think, marks out just such a stage. With majority critical opinion now apparently inclined to accept the O'Hara text, the principal task of criticism at this point seems to be consolidation, or specifying the agreed-on conclusions in as effective a way as possible for the school system. Perloff's book does this intelligently, concretely developing the major theoretical points about O'Hara's poetry to recent structuralist views of text and surface, and about O'Hara's central importance as a cultural figure of the period of the late 50s and early 60s. Perloff makes O'Hara's poetry for the first time accessible and in a real sense "teachable"—a reminder that the function and meaning of text can also be "for use in the schools." In a recent review of this book in *Gay Sunshine* Rudy Kikel remarks that Perloff ". . . is concerned to establish a 'tradition' in the light of which O'Hara will find acceptance by an academic establishment, because a teacher herself, she gives us ways in which O'Hara can be 'taught.'" Kikel, it should likewise be noted, remarks on the significant absence of a discussion of O'Hara's sexuality as such and wonders if in this context "the fully subversive nature of the poet's contribution can be appreciated." Rudy Kikel, "The Gay Frank O'Hara," *Gay Sunshine* no. 35 (Winter 1978): 8-9.

II

A few remarks about the meaning of language as social practice—or more precisely, praxis—might be helpful at this point. The work of the Soviet language philosopher V.N. Volosinov pointed the way in this area, showing how Marxist theory might be helpfully applied to language study. In *Marxism and the Philosophy of Language*, first published in 1930, Volosinov laid the groundwork for future social investigation of language, noting that "Individual consciousness is a social-ideological fact," which "takes shape and being in the material of signs created by an organized group in the process of its social intercourse."[16] Rather than expressing individual consciousness, language, as Volosinov observed, actually is that consciousness—materially, and as the effect of group interaction. The domain of ideology, as Volosinov put it, "coincides with that of signs. They equate with one another. Whenever a sign is present, ideology is present too. Everything ideological possesses semiotic value."[17] Language *is* consciousness; what it expresses is social interest. As the material being of group ideology, it thus registers in its minutest details the changing historical features of the group producing it. In this sense then language is neither "arbitrary" nor meaningless; nor is it inert or already given. Volosinov's understanding of language as group praxis thus lays a foundation for understanding the stakes involved in critical attempts to repress antagonist languages in a text. For when a dominated group registers its language praxis, it registers its struggle. Indeed, it registers it against the attempts of competing or dominating groups to repress that struggle.

But at this point we must construct a more sophisticated model to deal with problems, not foreseen by Volosinov's analysis. The experience of the Third World has raised questions about language split in group life; it has become historically evident that a new linguistic-cultural problematic

---

16 V.N. Volosinov, *Marxism and the Philosophy of Language*, trans. Ladislav Matejka and I.R. Titunik (New York: Seminar Press, 1973), 12-13.
17 Ibid., 10.

is shaped when oppressed groups find themselves under the necessity of speaking not only (or only partly) their own language but the language of another, dominating group. The language of an oppressed group in such circumstances tends to become a *coded* language—whose opposition is expressed only in "deformed" or distorted fashion. The relations of colonized groups with their colonizers in the final and breakup period of global imperialism give us a classic case in point. The task of analysis then becomes one of giving an adequate account of the (masked) oppositional content of these coded languages and of then tracing the historical stages by which such groups become able to speak their own language or languages without disguise. The language of these groups now develops as an expression of a political practice and, on the site of each individual within the group, fights out the battle against the dominating group linguistically as much as politically. The linguistic-political oppression we must now consider is thus a double relation—external with respect to the oppressor outside and internal with respect to his presence within. In the work of Frantz Fanon these mediated relations come to the fore and have been developed as a significant theoretical advance. Fanon's *Wretched of the Earth*[18] is exemplary in describing the situation of language split in such cases. In Fanon's view, the language-cultural situation of the native-born intellectual is privileged because it is the intellectual who sums up the divided experience of the group as a whole; he or she is the specialized site of competing language practices. Speaking not only his or her own language but the language of the imperialist oppressor also, the intellectual produces a kind of text in which the oppressor's language represses his or her own by rewriting it. Such a dilemma then is both personal and existential. Its solution calls for a violence experienced as both literal and figurative. The violent act, collective in its structure and meaning for Fanon, is nevertheless lived psychologically on an individual level—in the immediate awareness of each oppressed man or woman that he or she is "setting to rights" an unbearable situation against his or her oppressor.

---

18 Frantz Fanon, *The Wretched of the Earth*, trans. Constance Farrington (New York: Grove, 1968). See especially chapter one, "Concerning Violence."

The act of violence is first of all an *exterior* one, essentially for Fanon the act by which the faceless North African brings him or herself into being for the first time by making the French colonizer an object. In this way the native-born man or woman, who has existed before "as an animal" in a colonized awareness, first shapes his or her own humanity. But violence is also *interior*. In this sense and on a more figurative level, it is especially the intellectual who is "colonized from within" by interiorizing the cultural and linguistic codes of the oppressor. Educated and divided by the oppressor language and culture, the intellectual is the exemplary "site" of competing codes and cultures. As a figure for the oppressed group as a whole, the intellectual must now be seen as a kind of text that requires a violent reversal of the codes that constitute it. In heightened form the intellectual lives out the cultural-linguistic struggles of the group as a whole.[19]

Analysis of oppositional texts, following this point of view, will then be an analysis of the concrete ways in which opposition, in spite of its textual repression, disruptively and violently continues to assert itself. It will be an analysis that explains languages as the praxis of a social group, the outcome of a historically situated, materially located group interaction. It will be an analysis that supplements and specifies Volosinov's. Indeed, more recent social language investigations have begun to verify Volosinov's radical insight—that the language of a group gives that group's consciousness in its developed and developing forms. A number of sociolinguistic studies[20] have made us more aware of the violent, oppositional nature of

---

19   But as for Fanon himself, doesn't he continue to "speak French?" And how is such a fact to be accounted for? Though the question should be raised in the larger context of the national liberation movements of the time, it is important to note in passing that such a question has formal, stylistic dimensions that locate it in rhetorical forms of appeal characteristic of a classical *lycée* tradition. And if, for example, the mode of argumentation often specifically recalls that of Sartre, it is noteworthy that Sartre himself presents *The Wretched of the Earth* with a preface addressing the work to its French readership as its properly intended audience.

20   Among recent social language studies I have in one way or another found helpful are the following: Robin Lakoff, *Language and Woman's Place* (New York: Harper and Row, 1975); J.L. Dillard, *Lexicon of Black English* (New York: Seabury Press, 1977); edited by John J. Gumperz and Dell Hymes,

the language forms of oppressed groups, and Fanon's text—as a rewriting of an oppositional language so that it becomes for the moment more "acceptable"—will alert us to the disguised or coded nature of such an opposition and to the indirect ways in which such an opposition is bound to be reflected and refracted. The consciousness of the oppressed group will be expressed only in distorted forms, but in these forms we will read its oppositional content.

The gay language reflected in O'Hara's poetry can be located, I believe, in such a theoretical context. As the consciousness of an oppositional group, however, this language often resists recognition. To the extent that an oppositional group feels itself powerless, or on this side of a revolutionary praxis—and this certainly was the case with gay men in the 50s—the oppositional content of its language inevitably is "coded." Black "spirituals," for instance, are now often seen as a form of coded opposition for the Black community in the nineteenth-century South. And gays in the decisive formative period of the late 40s and 50s have felt a similar need to resort to linguistic disguises. Such disguises, however, were often in complicity with quite different needs of the dominant group.

To be sure, the coding model cuts both ways. The coded nature of the gay language of the post-War period expressed a need for self-preservation and concealment on the part of the gay community—for a linguistic

---

Directions in Sociolinguistics (New York: Holt, Rinehart and Winston, 1972); Joshua A. Fishman, ed., *Readings in the Sociology of Language* (The Hague: Mouton, 1968), and "The Sociology of Language," in Thomas A. Sebeok, ed., *Current Trends in Linguistics* (The Hague: Mouton, 1974); Basil Bernstein, *Class Codes and Control:* Volume 1—*Theoretical Studies Towards A Sociology of Language* (London: Routledge and Kegan Paul, 1972); William Labov, *The Social Stratification of English in New York City* (Washington, D.C.: Center for Applied Linguistics, 1966), and *Language in the Inner City: Studies in the Black English Vernacular* (Philadelphia: University of Pennsylvania Press, 1972); René Balibar and Dominique LaPorte, *Le Francais national: politique et pratique de la langue nationale sous la Revolution* (Paris: Hachette, 1974) and René Balibar with Geneviève Merlin and Gilles Tret, *Les Francais fictifs: Le rapport des styles littéraires au francais national* (Paris: Hachette, 1974)

For an excellent bibliography with remarks on several of these works and others, see Alvin W. Gouldner, *The Dialectic of Ideology and Technology: The Origins, Grammar and Future of Ideology* (New York: Seabury, 1976), 64-66.

defense against the threat of dominant group penetrations. On the other hand, coded gay language also had the effect of preventing the recognition of an oppositional content of gay speech, on the part of the dominant straight group. At the time this was probably inevitable; characteristically, dominant groups don't recognize the groups they dominate until they are compelled to do so. Thus, it is not unnatural that criticism refuses to *hear* gay language. For that language is in fact the structure of the dominated group's inadmissible consciousness—its material reality, as Volosinov would say. The language of the dominated group becomes inaudible, just as physical attributes, gestures, and mannerisms go unseen. At a certain stage of its development, the language of a dominated group is unheard.

The difficulty of actually hearing a language, or *locating* it, is sharpened and compounded in the case of a literary production. A text is the site of competing ideologies, and the literary piece produced by a member of a dominated group, in reflecting the consciousness of the oppressed group, also refracts and alters—or falsifies—that consciousness as its author produces it as literature. In a literary work the repressed language does indeed come to be heard, but in a distorted or problematic mode— ideologically reshaped by the dominant language.

How then can oppositional language of this kind be located? If, following Volosinov, every language practice is in reality a *praxis*, the question of the location of the language is one of locating its praxis, of putting the *text* into *context*. In the case of Frank O'Hara, this context refers us to the divisions of literary life in the immediate post-War years from the late 40s through the early 60s, and to the material and institutional settings of that literary life which made possible its literary productions—particularly its competing publishing and distribution networks, a praxis which will locate the dominant language of the poems. The non-dominant *gay* language of these poems, on the other hand, refers us to quite another praxis, the oppositional language practice of the gay community itself, in its historical period of formation in the late 40s and 50s.

III

Let us first of all turn to the literary situation of the 50s, which will locate the *dominant* language practice of the O'Hara poems. At the time, as we know, literary life and particularly poetry saw itself as largely divided between what was thought of as academic poetry on the one hand, and a new bohemian or beatnik poetry of protest on the other. This division in literary life was an important one in the self-estimation of writers themselves; it suggested that the alternative or "beat" writing was in fact a movement of real social opposition. But, as we will see later, such a division was more apparent than real. Both beats and academics were "establishment" in their solid connections with money and power and with the apparatuses of the dominant New York publishing houses of the day; for both academics and beats, the reigning "existentialist" mythology was to be reflected in the thematic and stylistic concerns of the writing itself. The beat and academic modes are more adequately seen as alternatives within the same dominant language discourse.

To gauge the passions generated in the partisan dispute of beatnik *vs.* academic, it might be helpful to recall that the beatnik poetry of the day was thought to be anti-establishment enough to have recourse to public legal action. And on three occasions trials ensued. In San Francisco Lenore Kandel's *Love Book* was put on trial, as Allen Ginsberg's *Howl* had been; in both cases the charge was obscenity. Then in Cleveland the poet d. a. levy was jailed and charged with reading a poem that advocated smoking marijuana. Generally among writers of the time poets like Ginsberg and Gregory Corso, together with the prose writers linked with them, like Burroughs, Kerouac, and the mostly non-writing Neal Cassidy were thought to be opposed in poetic practice as well as publically disruptive lifestyle to poets like W.S. Merwin, Robert Bly, Adrienne Rich, and Louis Simpson, as well as others like Delmore Schwartz, James Dickey, or Robert Lowell, considered establishment figures.

In John Ashbery's estimation at least[21] the terms of such a division ill-suited a poet like Frank O'Hara, who was as Ashbery put it, "too hip

---

21   In his obituary note on O'Hara, cited in Perloff, 12.

for the squares and too square for the hips"—a poet who was neither one nor the other. The terms of this opposition, however, probably ill-suited a number of the poets of the time. Of the beats, for instance, many had ascertainable connections through family or university training with privilege and influence as well as money.[22] Among academics, on the other hand, there were some, like Lowell himself, with what were for the day strong or radical political commitments, and certainly many with rather unconventional lifestyles. As for the "styles" of the poetry itself, one has seen a number of changes in the decades which have followed. So that the poetry of Ashbery himself, for instance, once classed with the beats, can hardly now be considered other than establishment, perhaps even academic. The later development of the poetry of Robert Bly on the other hand, first thought to be academic now often seems more beat in tone, as in the nearly Ginsbergian *The Teeth Mother Naked at Last*. But however qualified from an oppositional standpoint, the basic division between beats and academics does seem appropriate for organizing the various poetic conflicts of this period, particularly from a materialist standpoint. It refers us to new formations of American intellectual life in the post-War period.

What, infrastructurally, was this division all about? The developments of the market capitalism of the day give us a clue. The new consumer society had had a strong effect on university life, expanding its base with an influx of large numbers of new students and creating teaching jobs for a new class of intellectuals, "value-free technicians" of literary production, whose formalist and New Critical ideologies reflected the transformation and integration of the university and scholarly publishing into consumer society as a whole as rationalized instruments of production and consumption. Literature, in short, was becoming a commodity like other commodities.[23]

The academic poets from this materialist perspective were those who integrated themselves in a significant way into the university praxis,

---

22 See Donald Allen, ed., *The New American Poetry: 1945-1960* (New York: Grove, 1960), 427-452.
23 Noted in James E. Breslin's unpublished essay "The End of the Line: American Poetry, 1945-1955," 25.

through publishing and other economic connections, and with new features of poetic style that reflected the formalist New Critical ideology of the university. The beats, on the other hand, were those poets who for whatever reasons had to look elsewhere than to the official university praxis for the material base of their production and who, as a result, came to develop poetic styles that reflected the several alternative praxes of the day.

Among these alternative or non-academic praxes, some were of course "events"—like the appearance in 1960 of the Donald Allen anthology, *The New American Poetry: 1945-1960*,[24] an enormously successful publication that effectively united for the general public a number of often quite different poets and poetries as having a poetic practice opposed to the dominant and university practice. Published in New York by the "alternative" Grove Press, the Allen anthology was soon accepted popularly as a more or less definitive list of the bohemian poets of the day, an index to what was or was not beatnik writing. And for better or for worse, O'Hara's poetry was featured there prominently.

Beat praxis, however, can best be located materially—the Allen anthology that brought beat writing to the general public was, after all, an event, not an ongoing structure—in quasi-institutional networks of job and personal relations, complexes of book and magazine production, and so on, in material complexes that shaped a set of common poetic practices

---

24 The Allen anthology groups together in five separate sections poets now thought of as Black Mountain, San Francisco Renaissance, Beat, and New York School as well as another group with no special geographical designation, though in Allen's opinion the groupings remain "rather arbitrary." I group all these poets together as beat, or alternative, poets in order to contrast them with poets then thought of as academics. The "beats" properly so called, like Ginsberg and Corso, as well as the poets of the San Francisco Renaissance group, do not seem to have had such a strongly institutional praxis as the New York poets or those associated with Black Mountain. Black Mountain and New York seem more interesting to me because more strongly institutional in a material, organized fashion. Certainly the beats had a relation to social institutions in a loose sense, but with much less of a determinate material base of *site* for a writing praxis. Finally, it is well to remember that, whatever the "beat" influence was in the novel and other areas of writing (like Kerouac and Burroughs), "beat" poetry at best comprises only a few names—perhaps only Ginsberg and Corso, Orlovsky and Kerouac.

and gave these practices distinctive language features. The two most prominent of these institutional matrices were Black Mountain College, the experimental college in North Carolina newly reformed under the influence of Charles Olson, and the so-called New York School of poets allied with the art and art-publishing world in New York, centering itself around the personality and writing practice of O'Hara himself. Both of these complexes of production competed against the official university practice, at least as "alternatives" to the academic poetry.

The description of the latter group of poets as the "New York School" was originally a kind of insider's joke,[25] but has widely come to be accepted as an index of this group's common attitudes and aspirations about what was or was not acceptable in the language practice of poetry. Underlying these attitudes, however, was a socio-economic situation that related in a special way to the various art-related job and work connections of these poets. As a "conspiracy" of attitudes, friendships, and job situations, such an institutional network among New York School poets has been described by Virgil Thomson, for instance, as "American poets working for the Modern Art establishment, whether this is done as an employee of the Museum of Modern Art or as a contributor to any of the periodicals controlled by or perhaps connected with that Museum."[26] And this much can't be doubted: the social-economic relations of many New York poets at this time were largely determined by the dominant art-institutional life of the galleries, the art periodicals, and the art publishing industries as well of course in a special way by the Museum of Modern Art—with its extensive influence as a broker and dispenser of jobs for talented intellectuals and writers.[27] In these circumstances it wasn't unnatural that the writing of many of these poets had a great deal in common, and in many respects a common style. Nor is it surprising that the tone of the professional "art writing" of many

---

25 See Edwin Denby's account of the origin of this name as a double or triple joke, in Perloff, 195-196.
26 See Virgil Thomson's "Statement" in my edition of the Special Supplement, *Panjandrum* 2-3, 1973.
27 For a corroborative view of the power of the Modern at this time see Fred Moramarco, "John Ashbery and Frank O'Hara: The Painterly Poets" *Journal of Modern Literature* vol. 5, no. 3 (September 1976), 436-463.

of these poets should spill over into the poetic speech and language of their verse, giving it an infrastructural base. Such a tone might be called "institutional"—in the sense of a common set of economic and social interests centering around institutions for the production and consumption of art. The dominant language practice of O'Hara's poetry clearly reflects this art-institutional base—a base which, as we will see, expresses his several concerns as museum curator, writer for museum publications and art periodicals, and young poet whose first books were published by gallery presses. Later on we will look at this same museum-art complex in more detail and find important but submerged connections between O'Hara's life as a museum worker and his life as a gay man. Meanwhile however—to return to the question of language and poetic practice—we can note that O'Hara's position in the institutional art world gave him significant access to the alternative modernist culture of the day in abstract expressionist or "action" painting, making available to him an ideology which would eventually legitimize his work as part of the avant-garde movement.

It was Harold Rosenberg who first coined the term "Action Painting" (in "The American Action Painters," 1952) to describe that moment in painting when "the canvas began to appear to one American painter after another as an arena in which to act—rather than as a space in which to reproduce, redesign, analyze or 'express' an object, actual or imagined. What was to go on the canvas was not a picture but an event." As Fred Moramarco has recently noted, Rosenberg's formulation can be helpfully applied to explaining the goals of much of the New York poetry of the time, particularly that of O'Hara and Ashbery:

> If we changed the words "canvas," "painter," and "picture" in this passage to "page," "poet," and "poem" Rosenberg's perceptive statement can describe as well the situation in American poetry at the time. Just as American painters were experiencing the exhilarating freedom of discovering the act of painting as the "event" to be captured and frozen on the canvas, American poets were discovering, in the very act of poetic composition, the subject matter of their poetry.[28]

---

28 Moramarco, 438.

Moramarco is correct in pointing out the analogy between the two groups. Explaining things in retrospect we might say that the writing of the New York poets was a kind of *écriture* that didn't yet know itself by that name. To judge it by its declared intentions (at least in O'Hara's case), the writing of these poets was a project for self-referentiality: a textual project, an act or event that displaced the subject into an object produced, making the production process itself its own referent. In contrast to the writing of the academic poets, there was to be nothing transcendental in the modernist text of the New York poetry; nothing behind it or under it. Or if there was, no one cared to notice. From the standpoint of the New York poets the lines were drawn: action painting together with New York poetry on one side, academic poetry on the other.

Thus O'Hara attacked Lowell's "confessionalism" as a sort of concession to self-indulgence—bad writing that let him, as O'Hara put it, "get away with things that are just plain bad but you're supposed to be interested because he's supposed to be so upset."[29] Similarly, O'Hara's friend Kenneth Koch would take on Robert Frost—in a poem parodying Frost's tendentious symbolism, called, fairly enough, "Mending Sump." Poets like Lowell and Frost were bad writers, from this point of view, because their subject matter lay beyond the page. Articulating his own felt relation to the painting of the period and contrasting it implicitly with New Critical concerns for subject matter, O'Hara once noted, in reference to one of his own poems, that

> the verbal elements are not too interesting to discuss although they are intended consciously to keep the surface of the poem high and dry, not wet, reflective and self-conscious. Perhaps the obscurity comes in here, in the relationship between the surface and the meaning, but I like it that way since the one is the other (you have to use words) and I hope the poem to be the subject, not just about it.[30]

---

29 Cited in Perloff, 137.
30 *CP*, 497.

If the poem *was* the subject, it wasn't much like the New Critical or academic poem. Calling attention to these allegiances and caricaturing them, O'Hara would once sign himself in a letter to a close friend, "Yours in action art."[31] Clearly, O'Hara's sympathies and those of his friends didn't lie with the New Critics and their friends, the academic poets.

The publishing practices of the New York group of poets largely reflect this stance. In contrast with the academics, who published with university presses or established New York houses, the New York poets of the 50s themselves published either with the "alternative" presses like Grove— though this was rare—or put out their work more privately—O'Hara made use of art-gallery imprints—or else didn't really publish in any accepted sense. Donald Allen sums up the situation in the preface of *The New American Poetry*, stating that the poets of the anthology had as a rule

> written a large body of work, but most of what has been published
> so far has appeared only in a few little magazines, as broadsheets,
> pamphlets, and limited editions, or circulated in manuscript; a
> larger amount of it has reached its growing audience through
> poetry readings

thus insuring on the part of these poets the creation of "their own tradition, their own press, and their public."[32]

As a result the work of these poets—the New York group included among them—found only a limited general distribution; Allen Ginsberg, the exception, was not part of the New York group. Distribution was a privilege generally linked with publication by the established New York houses or the university presses, whose sales to libraries alone, if nothing else, would often guarantee a large press run. And it is these larger presses that were receptive to the established "academic" poets. Harcourt Brace,

---

31 Cited in Perloff, 497.
32 Donald Allen, *New American Poetry*, xi. See also Ron Loewinsohn's "After the (Mimeograph) Revolution," *Tri-Quarterly* no. 18 (Spring 1970), for an extended discussion.

for instance, was the publisher for Robert Lowell's *Lord Weary's Castle*, as well as the complete T.S. Eliot and important New Critical favorites like William Empson and Louis Simpson. Or again, the Wesleyan University Press put out Robert Bly's *Silence in the Snowy Fields* as well as a selection of other works by poets like Donald Davie, David Ignatow, and Donald Justice, all considered academic poets. These publishers gave wide distribution and national recognition to their poets; and in the case of university presses at least, often significantly underwrote or financed the books published.

On the other hand, publishing houses like Grove, Evergreen, and New Directions in New York or City Lights on the West Coast, though "alternative" publishers to be sure, compared with more important and larger houses like Harcourt, were nonetheless solidly commercial enterprises. And as it happens, they published, among others, Ashbery, Ginsberg, and O'Hara. Ashbery's *Some Trees* (1956) appeared with Yale— probably as establishment a publisher as could be found. Even O'Hara's poems were accepted for publication several times with *Poetry Magazine; His Meditations in an Emergency* came out with Evergreen and later *Lunch Poems* with City Lights. Such publishing data is suggestive and qualifies our estimation of the "beatnik" or bohemian poetries as really "alternative."

Such then is the general situation in which we should locate O'Hara's poetry when, in the middle 50s, he came to be known at least among other poets as an important poet of the day. At a time when poetry largely divided itself into two opposing camps with an "academic" or establishment supported poetry on one side and the "beatnik" or alternative poetries on the other side, O'Hara's poetic practice should certainly be linked with the alternative group; remembering as we should, however, that both academic and alternative poetries expressed, in a deeper way, only options *within* the general and dominant language practice. Indeed, if we were to look only at this dominant language of the O'Hara text—the language practice of the poetries we have reviewed—there would be no reason to think of O'Hara's work as a whole as any more "oppositional" than the work of the other alternative poets of the period—many of whom today, far from appearing threatening or disturbing, seem rather to be taking their places in American poetry as respected elders, the founding fathers of a now acceptable new poetry. "Opposition" then must be linked in O'Hara's poetry to a use of gay language.

IV

It is with good reason that criticism has repressed discussion of O'Hara's gay language practice. For this language practice is not simply "alternative" but, to choose another word, *oppositional*—having for its particular target male supremicist privilege, founded on the subjugation of women and effeminate men. And for this reason alone, gay male language is traditionally violent; the situation after all is *objectively* violent. In pre-assertive group conditions, as we will shortly see, the violence of an oppressed group usually internalizes itself. But such manifestations deceive no one; they remain objectionable even when masked or disguised as self-violence. Criticism then must reject the violence of this language as offensive to male privilege. And we may expect that as the crisis of international capitalism continues to deepen, and the opposition of oppressed groups on all fronts takes on increasingly antagonistic forms, critical discourse will react to this situation in an appropriate fashion—attempting to legitimize or co-opt the artifacts associated with these struggles by creating more sophisticated strategies for disguising the basic social contradictions present in the very language of these productions. For the question of O'Hara's gay language, as we noted, refers us to our own period—not his.

To disengage that oppositional language is first and foremost to remind ourselves of its violence and the importance of violence—as seen earlier in the case of Fanon's native-born intellectual—in the formation of group awareness of struggle.

In the early O'Hara there is a great deal of family violence,[33] obvious and usually easy enough to locate: victim against victimizer, ending in the

---

33 These poems and their variants are discussed at greater length in chapter 1 of my doctoral dissertation, "Frank O'Hara's Poems" (PhD diss., University of California-Berkeley, 1976), excerpted in *Homage to Frank O'Hara*.

death of the protagonist. Though in the following, and exceptional, poem the protagonist's reversal of this situation is notable:

> I ran through the snow like a young Czarevitch!
> My gun was loaded and wolves disguised
> as treed nymphs pointed out where the fathers
> had hidden in gopher holes. I shot them right
> between the eyes! The mothers were harder to find. . . .
> the shots hung glittering in air like poems.[34]

The poems aren't yet "gay language," though they do strike a note we should heed. Violent in the intent, to be sure, but also trivialized in a way that has yet to be explained. More typically the victim is the subject in these early poems, and frequently too the situation is a sexual one:

> Funny, I thought, that the lights are on this late
> and the hall door open; still up at this hour, a
> champion jai-alai player like himself? Oh fie!
> for shame! What a host, so zealous! And he was
> there in the hall, flat on a sheet of blood that
> ran down the stairs. I did appreciate it. There are
> few hosts who so thoroughly prepare to greet a guest
> only casually invited, and that several months ago.[35]

The violence is clearly linked to a sexual situation, but surprisingly enough as something like a casual inconvenience, as if the narrator finds it ordinary, even predictable. An inappropriate response surely, but a response we seem somehow invited to share. "I did appreciate it," remarks the narrator—assuming, one feels, that we ourselves would have such a response. And in fact the language becomes a coded accusation: it implies that the violence is our own. The trivializing function of gay language is rarely innocent.

---

34 *CP*, 60
35 *CP*, 14

Dominant view critiques of the "trivialization" of gay language have, of course, consistently refused the contestatory meaning of this language practice—irrespective of the increasingly polemical interpretations of gays themselves.[36] Trivialization is seen as a particular kind of humor that might be "anyone's": not the language practice of a specific, specifically located and specifically oppressed social group. What results has been a programmatic misinterpretation by euphemism. Thus in the O'Hara poems, as we have seen, the insistence has been to avoid a "sectarian," for which read gay viewpoint, and a concomitant emphasis on discovering a "universal" content of the poetry which would make it available to all.

Susan Sontag's 1962 *Partisan Review* essay, "Notes on Camp," is a landmark in this discussion, historically the first serious discussion of gay language from a positive viewpoint, and it should be credited in this regard. In Sontag's discussion, nevertheless, we see another strategy of assimilation at work—a strategy that understands "camp" as essentially an aspect of the *modern sensibility*. Gay language becomes innocuous or even good-natured, that is, non-antagonistic. "It goes without saying that the camp sensibility is disengaged, de-politicized—or at least apolitical," Sontag notes. Further, Sontag remarks,

> Camp taste is a kind of love, love for human nature. It relishes, rather than judges, the little triumphs and awkward intensities of "character". . . . People who share this sensibility are not laughing at the thing they label as "a camp," they're enjoying it. Camp is a *tender feeling*.[37]

---

36 Joseph J. Hayes, "Gayspeak," *Quarterly Journal of Speech* vol. 62, no. 3 (October 1976), has noted some of these polemical interpretations. Hayes' annotated *Language and Language Behavior of Lesbian Women and Gay Men: A Bibliography with Abstracts*, is soon to appear in the *Journal of Homosexuality* as a two-part series. It will be the definitive bibliography on the subject.

37 Susan Sontag, "Notes on Camp," in *Against Interpretation* (New York: Farrar, Straus and Giroux, 1966), 291-92.

From our present stand-point, however, such an interpretation can no longer illumine gay language. It does not contextualize that language as the praxis of a group. Rather, it is an interpretive rewriting procedure—and in fact a criticism. One wonders indeed if there is a place in such a view for the violence, the cynicism, and even the guilt that so often characterize gay language praxis. If O'Hara does write in a camp vein, such humor may have rather somber overtones, when understood as the lived group praxis of gays. Consider the oddly threatening function of the humor in a poem like this one:

> Is it dirty
> does it look dirty
> that's what you think of in the city
>
> does it just seem dirty
> that's what you think of in the city
> you don't refuse to breathe do you
>
> someone comes along with a very bad character
> he seems attractive, is he really, yes. very
> he's attractive as his character is bad. is it. yes
>
> that's what you think of in the city
> run your finger along your no-moss mind
> that's not a thought that's soot
>
> and you take a lot of dirt off someone
> is the character less bad. no. it improves constantly.
> you don't refuse to breathe do you[38]

At the back of his mind ("it's like Times Square at midnight / you don't know where you're going / but you know," says O'Hara in a later poem), a

----

38 *CP*, 327

gay man reading this poem may think with some alarm that this is what, after all, the possibility of "rough trade" might mean for him. Is the character less bad then?—asks O'Hara. No, it isn't, and it's still the possibility of violence. But "You don't refuse to breathe do you?" says another voice—closer to fatalism than one would have thought. Such a poem comes from a specific praxis, the praxis of gay men; but it is a praxis that often is disguised and so requires a "retranslating" on the part of the critic in order to recover the "original" writing beneath.

There are "clues" of course—gay usages or expressions, for instance, that will have greater meaning for gays than for straights, who may in fact ignore these clues. In one of his best long poems, "For the Chinese New Year & for Bill Berkson," when O'Hara says

> here we are and what the hell are we going to do
> with it we are going to blow it up like daddy did
> only us I really think we should go up for a change
> I'm tired of always going down what price glory
> it's one of those timeless priceless words like come[39]

The text of this passage is clearly one of anxiety about the Bomb, and a figurative expression for the "blowing-up" of American society, probably, as a monstrosity that can no longer be tolerated. O'Hara obviously did identify in some way with this end-phase of American late-capitalism, as he saw it ("as I historically / belong to the enormous bliss of American death," he remarks in "Rhapsody"). Yet such an anxiety may be "overdetermined" sexually. There is a subtext here which should not go unnoticed; the sexually specific phrase "words like come" may help to release to the reader the specifically gay content of another phrase, "I'm tired of always going down. . . ." The speaker is also saying, as it should now be evident, that he is "tired" of always having to be the one to satisfy the other person. Isn't he supposed to be gratified too? Yet because it still remains "glory," such a variant of his own sexuality seems to link up in the speaker's mind with

---

39 *CP*, 390

a kind of masochism, a self-identification of himself with the atomic destruction of all of society. Often, and especially in the later poems, such a self-identification will specify itself in a proliferation of suicide motifs:

> how can anyone be more amusing than oneself
> how can anyone fail to be
> can I borrow your forty-five
> I only need one bullet preferably silver
> if you can't be interesting at least you can be a legend
> (but I hate all that crap)[40]

To what extent is the construction of a gay subtext able to account for the tendency toward self-violence in poems like this last? It might be argued with some justification perhaps that the assumption of a gay subtext at this point is simply more or less useful according to one's ideological persuasions, that the violence in question could be anyone's—that it isn't necessarily a sexual political matter or the ideology of an oppressed group.

Yet here again it may be useful to draw on some of Fanon's insights with regard to the violence against self inevitable for an oppressed group in an historically "pre-assertive" situation. Speaking from his own clinically detailed experiences as a black psychiatrist among North African Arabs, Fanon stresses the historical inevitability in a pre-revolutionary situation that the oppressed characteristically internalize the violence of the oppressor, and that this self-violence manifests itself spiritually as well as physically: guilt, self-hate, and neurosis as well as unprovoked violence against others in one's group, rather than against the oppressor.

How does this apply to the situation of gay men in the 50s and early 60s when O'Hara was writing and when gays were clearly far from the later self-assertive phase that was to characterize Gay Lib in the 70s? It is after all the nature of classical gay humor—gay camp in the 50s, which tended to be pretty generally self-deprecatory—to be a repeating pattern of assurances to straights that the alienation felt in one's life as a gay person was at bottom

---

40 *CP*, 430

one's own fault, rather than the fault of the straight society that continued to benefit from the situation. More often than not, O'Hara remains true to the gay attitudes of this period, minimizing sensations of great pain and suffering with humor that neutralizes the seriousness of the harm done:

> Then too, the other day I was walking through a train
> with my suitcase and I overheard someone say "speaking of
>   faggots"
> now isn't life difficult enough without that
> and why am I always carrying something
> well it was a shitty looking person anyway
> better a faggot than a farthead
> or as fathers have often said to friends of mine
> "better dead than a dope" "if I thought you were queer I'd kill you"[41]

In this context too we can look at ambiguous feelings of self-worth in sexist or "drag" poems:

> I could find some rallying ground like pornography or religious exercise, but really, I say to myself, you are too serious a girl for that. . . . If, when my cerise muslin sweeps across the agora, I hear no whispers even if they're really echoes, I know they think I'm on my last legs, "She's just bought a new racing car" they say, or "She's using mercurochrome on her nipples."[42]

Or in the overtly sexual poems:

> My back is peeling and the tar
> melts underfoot as I cross the street.
> Sweaty foreheads wipe on my shirt
> as I pass. The sun hits a building

---

41 *CP* 441-442
42 *CP* 74-75

and shines off onto my face. The sun
licks my feet through my moccasins
as I feel my way along the asphalt.
The sun beams on my buttocks
as I outdistance the crowd. For a
moment I enter the cavernous vault
and its deadish cold. I suck off
every man in the Manhattan Storage &
Warehouse Co. Then, refreshed, again
to the streets! to the generous sun
and the vigorous heat of the city.[43]

Here relations of promiscuity are treated as if they could be satisfying or fulfilling. Situations like these suggest oppression turned inward.[44]

Postulating a gay subtext to these poems would help make comprehensible one of the otherwise rather puzzling features of the poetry: O'Hara's constant tendency to present symbols of deep and violent pain and then "contextualize" them, either turning them against himself in minimizing them or else by parodying his own feelings about the pain. The violence of the language of these poems is first of all a repressed violence, as if gay language were being *repressed* by straight language.

V

That such a language was felt as threatening and oppositional is clear enough at this point; and that it had to be rewritten in order to be critically legitimized. What is not yet clear, however, is how O'Hara himself aided and furthered such a project by creating an art or language artifact that

---

43 Frank O'Hara, *Poems Retrieved*, ed. Donald Allen (Bolinas, California: Grey Fox, 1977), 160.

44 Fanon's "Colonial War and Mental Disorders," in *The Wretched of the Earth*, 249-310, gives a detailed account of such mechanisms of "violence turned inward" in North African Arabs of the pre-assertive colonial period.

would be ambiguous enough to permit the later critical readings to repress or co-opt the antagonist gay language practice actually there. O'Hara of course was not only a gay man—but an art professional. And in this conjuncture we can historically locate the instrument that enabled the disturbing text of these poems to pass from an unacceptable antagonism as oppositional language practice to an acceptability within the discourse of art modernism. Let us return for a moment then to the question of O'Hara's life, and see how that life was itself a rewriting project, the repression of one praxis by another.

By profession Frank O'Hara of course did know and in fact had to know what the art-institutional language of the times was and how it worked. Besides being curator for the Museum of Modern Art, O'Hara was also by trade an art critic for the journals, a writer of important catalogs for the Museum shows, and on at least one occasion the author of a standard monograph on a major painter, Jackson Pollock. O'Hara was at the very center, as his friends have many times pointed out, of the institutional art-literature world of the galleries, the art magazines, and, of course, the dominating sphere of influence of the MoMA. He knew what the language of this interlinked group of interests and personalities was and he knew how to use it as well as anyone, or better.

In addition, O'Hara was also a gay man. At the organizational level in the art world, then as now it is largely a staff of gay men who provide institutional continuity for the magazines, the museums, the galleries, and so on, and give these institutions a continuing and recognizable profile. Inevitably in such a situation the language practice of gay men and the language practice of the art world itself, in its everyday speech, have often come to coincide or strongly influence each other. Such seems to have been the case in the New York art world of the 50s, where interests and contacts outside the work-place as well as the social life of the two groups often also overlapped. Gays in this situation were able to talk "art-talk" or "museum-talk" not only as art or museum people but also as gays; and art and museum people on their part could likewise "talk gay" irrespective of sexual orientation, as a kind of spilling over of job-related speech into overall speech patterns. Indeed, just as O'Hara's style may appear at first glance as simply "arty" or "chic," similarly the poetic language of many non-gay poets of this period often strikes the reader as "gay" in tone and stance, in apparent conflict with heterosexual content.[45]

The language practices dissimulate themselves and thus mask their places of origin. It is in this context that we must locate the O'Hara poems, once more recalling Volosinov. The text of O'Hara's poetry becomes a *site* of competing language practices—the dominant language practice of the New York art world of the 50s and the oppositional language practice of gay men. Volosinov has noted that a language becomes a dead language when it loses the "multi-accentuality" of its semiotic signs, so that these signs no longer serve as the "arenas for the clash of live social accents." But while the living language sign "always has two faces, like Janus, this *inner dialectic* quality of the sign comes out fully in the open only in times of social crisis or revolutionary changes."[46] On the site of O'Hara's poems, an oppositional gay language, so apparently interchangeable with the dominant language, is then disguised, and makes itself available to the repression of later critical discourse—so that only one language actually appears, the dominant art-institutional language. In the critical reading then both languages appear as the same, the dominant language of art-modernism. Thus O'Hara's "characteristic lack of syntax," the flippancy and the bias towards colloquialism, the aestheticist thematizations of "deco" literary styles, etc.—all are now instances of the universalizing language of art-modernism, expressions of the dominant art institutional and literary discourse of the day. And as for the language dimensions of the O'Hara poems that *can't* be fit into this scheme, they are either overlooked completely or else discovered to be "not very good." In retrospect, critical approval can recognize only the art-language aspects of this poetry.

To take up the question of O'Hara's art professionalism for a moment, it is important to note that O'Hara worked for the Museum of Modern Art at a historical period when the art object, as such, was coming close to

---

45 I think this is true of non-gay poets like Koch, Berrigan, Schjeldahl, and Padgett, all of whom were either themselves involved in the art world at some point or strongly influenced by the tradition in their development.
46 Volosinov, 23.

a completed objectivization as commodity in the "high period" of Abstract Expressionism. The relative importance of the use-value of the art object was certainly in decline, and the art object was beginning to mean above all a completed exchange-value as money. To be sure, one of the revealing signs of such a process was the remarkable rise in price of the art object itself, particularly the canvas painting, and the concomitant growth of profit potential for the speculations in the art market. The Museum could be expected to demand of its employees in key or decision-making positions an ability to grasp intuitively new historical exigencies that related to the changing policies of the Museum in situations that were then beginning to develop. So it is important to note in this context that O'Hara's family background was, it appears, middle or upper-middle class.[47] We learn from the poems, for instance, that O'Hara's family was at least well-off enough to provide a nurse for the children at one time, and apparently a horse for Frank, as well as advantages of private schooling and music lessons. And either because the family encouraged a sense of social ambition in Frank, or with the help of family connections, or perhaps simply because they could afford the costs of an education, we do know that in any event O'Hara ended up a Harvard undergraduate after two years of wartime service in the navy. At least for a while the family must have had enough money to be solidly middle-class.

Coming from this background O'Hara would probably have "understood money" quite well; he would have had a class background that allowed him to mix well at museum social functions, and he would have known how to implement ideological guidelines in new acquisitions, exhibitions, and so on. At the Museum of Modern Art at this period in its history, an ability to understand something about ideological matters

---

47 The important sources for biographical information about O'Hara are the poems themselves and short memoirs or anecdotal material (see note 10); though Donald Allen's "Short Chronology" (*CP*, pp. xiii-xvi) provides a helpful summary of O'Hara's work and education, dates of publication, etc. O'Hara's extensive correspondence has still to appear. A full-scale biography has been planned by the poet-critic Peter Schjeldahl, but "difficulties of access to archival materials make it appear that publication is not expected for some time" (letter, Peter Schjeldahl to Bruce Boone, June 21, 1978).

without having things explained must have been an important asset, perhaps even a prerequisite for advancement at the Museum. The Museum after all was for all practical purposes the Rockefeller museum. Co-founded, principally funded, and at this time still dominated and governed by that family, the Modern was in effect a family enterprise, answerable to that family alone. It was, as Abby Aldrich Rockefeller's sons are reported to have called it, "Mother's Museum."[48]

But if Rockefeller and other monied interests at some point in the 50s decided to underwrite the Modern Art movement,[49] including the new Abstract Expressionist painting, and to sponsor that movement through donations, purchases, and policy instruments like the Modern, the project could hardly have seemed unreasonable to them. As progressive as it generally and undoubtedly was, the Modern Art movement of New York at this time, in particular at its high point in Action Painting, must also be seen as a particularly successful instrument for embodying the late-capitalist, imperialist ideology of the time. Harold Rosenberg's articulation of the meaning of Action Painting—the canvas as "an arena to act in" rather than an object, an "event" rather than a picture—is, as we saw, a development of the modernist doctrine of self-referentiality; and, we may suppose, applicable to the general ideology of an expanding consumer society within the U.S. as well as the wider, imperialist goal of the consumerization of the Third World. The need for an analysis of such connections—more properly the job of art historians themselves—should at least be mentioned in passing.[50]

---

48 In the Rockefeller family it was Nelson, in the 50s, who interested himself in a particular way in the Modern and its new acquisitions policies—just as in the 30s it had been Nelson's mother, Abby Aldrich (Rockefeller), who had given impetus to the original idea and its implementation as the Museum's co-founder.

49 On the question of Rockefeller domination and control over the Museum of Modern Art, see especially Peter Collier and David Horowitz, *The Rockefellers: An American Dynasty* (New York: Holt, Rinehart and Winston, 1976). Also useful is Myer Kutz, *Rockefeller Power: America's Chosen Family* (New York: Simon and Schuster, 1974); as well as the impressionistic Russell Lynes, *Good Old Modern* (New York: Atheneum, 1973).

50 See Francis D. Klingender, *Marxism and Modern Art* (New York: International

It should not be surprising then that this global movement—toward rationalization of commodity exchange operations at a new level—would reflect itself locally in certain aspects of O'Hara's own work at the Museum, and in the form of job specialization. After a brief period at the front desk, O'Hara's job responsibilities became curatorial,[51] duties that involved facilitating the circulation and exchange of the art commodity itself by a descriptive inventory of new objects in the Museum acquisitions, as well

---

Publishers, 1945), for an attempt at such an analysis. Generally though, Marxism has still to work out a completed theory of mediations for problems like these. The historically progressive aspects of modernism in art and literature cannot simply be refused—and the example of Lukàcs is classical here. Nor however can Rosenberg and the bourgeois critics be accepted as adequate. How after all did the canvas *become* an "arena to act in" and why? Through what mediations can we trace the development of an American modernism as a necessary ideology of the consumer society of the day and a *de facto* instrument of U.S. imperialism abroad? Problems like these have not yet been worked out, yet we might briefly indicate the outlines of their *site*.

At the time, we can note, it had become increasingly necessary that the product to be consumed—art ideologies, or consumer durables and other goods—appear radically separated from any links to a visible and local production process. This means that such goods or ideologies, at a new level of completeness, would have to mask or mystify themselves as products of production and appear as having an autonomous existence. Thus, a Walt Disney movie must not seem to express local and specific U.S. values but to be the expression of an international cultural taste and humor—as Coca-Cola was imposed on foreign or other local beverage tastes, or in the way that American chemical fertilizers and farm tools have been marketed for profit everywhere without respecting different agricultural needs in Asia, Africa, and Latin America. Abstract Expressionism expressed a similar internationalism in art, largely denying its specific "American-ness," and asserting a factitious universalism in "human" values like freedom, courage, and existentialist meaning before the fact of death. Ideally, the work of art would express the same values everywhere, transcending national borders and local preferences to reveal a *nonspecific* humanness, like the ideology felt to be necessary for American market products. That the "arena" of the canvas would be conceived as a record of the art process that produced it was a way of mystifying the relation of *product to production*. In this sense process was not a production at all, or at least would not appear to be. What would appear would simply be the global possibility of the exchange, of the "self" *itself*, in some abstract mode.

51 See Waldo Rasmussen, "Frank O'Hara in the Museum," in *Homage to Frank O'Hara*, 84-90, for an anecdotal account of this aspect of O'Hara's life as recalled by a colleague at the Museum.

as cataloging art pieces already acquired for display locally or in traveling exhibitions. Whatever else he must have thought about his job with the Museum—and his perceptions of the art of this period seem to have been keenly knowledgeable and generous, always alert to the human dimensions of these works—O'Hara must, nevertheless, also have been quite aware that the work he was doing at the Museum was, at a social level, an impoverishment of this same human experience, an aesthetic production of the requirements of commodity capitalism. Catalogued and put up on museum walls, circulated from place to place, exhaustively described and analyzed, the art pieces O'Hara worked with would become—"against his will" he would say—fetishes, reifications of human experience and feelings, human productions alienated from their use-value. That is, art.[52] And in this regard O'Hara's thoughts at the end of his "In Memory of My Feelings" become illustrative of a profound contradiction:

> And yet
> I have forgotten my loves, and chiefly that one, the cancerous
> statue which my body could no longer contain,
>
> > against my will
> > against my love
>
> become art,
> > I could not change it into history
> and so remember it[53]

---

52 Among recent discussions of the ideological function of an art museum, one of the most interesting is *An Anti-Catalog*, by Rudolf Baranik and others (New York: The Catalog Committee of Artists Meeting for Cultural Change, 1977), available from them directly at 106 E. 19th St., no. 4, New York, N.Y. 10003. *The Anti-Catalog* focuses on the decision by the Whitney Museum to show the private collection of J.D. Rockefeller III as one of four Bicentennial shows. In an initial statement the artists note that they have "become increasingly aware that the meaning and real worth of their activities were directed and controlled by the market and its legitimizing institutions, of which museums are a major part." Included in the *Anti-Catalog* are important discussions on the social function of the museum in general ("Reifying Art Products from the Nexus of Their Social Production"), as well as several analyses of more particular issues ("Black Art and Its Historical Omission," "Looking for Women in the Rockefeller Collection," and "Why There Are No 'Great' Women Artists.")

53 *CP*, 257

O'Hara's art/writing practice is only established "against his will, against his love." It is time then to turn to the question of O'Hara's praxis as a gay man.

O'Hara's feelings about art as a museum professional interiorizes in some striking ways the attitudes of gay men as a group in the period. Gay men of course were entering into a period of growth and development as a social group, with an assertiveness that saw its recognition on a variety of levels, and the literary events of the time reflected this development. Baldwin, Ginsberg, Capote, Burroughs, and other figures were creating in one area or another a public recognition of the existence of gay men as a group for the first time. To be sure, an institutional infrastructure was also developing—a praxis, though, whose internal contradictions marked out certain limitations in advance in gay community life. For if bars, baths, and other institutions brought gays together, that much was certainly to the good, a stage of socialization that contrasts strongly with the largely isolated or individual experience of gay men in the pre-war period. But these same institutions also exploited gay men both financially and sexually. And most important of all, gay men characteristically interiorized the commodity relation thus given as the defining meaning of sexuality itself. Thus promiscuity, self-rejection, and the reification of the sexual experience as a series of "numbers" or "tricks"—expressions whose referent is clearly the language of prostitution—often brought the commodity relation to the center of gay self-experience. Indeed one's whole life might be experienced from within as a commodity relation—whose essential meaning would then be a kind of counting operation or extended inventory. An additive series. To a perceptive art professional like O'Hara the inventorying and additive nature of the fetishized sexual experience in the gay culture of this time may well have been a metaphor for the commodity relation of the art world itself, so that a reified sexual experience from this point of view would contain the meaning of the fetishized, self-referential art object, itemized, counted, and continuously exchanged. Or was it the other way around? Is it art that contains the meaning of sexuality—or sexuality the meaning of art in these poems? Such a question brings us to the heart of our inquiry, the text.

VI

Here we have a precedent in our inquiry. Recently the question of women's language has been raised by Robin Lakoff. In *Language and Woman's Place*[54], Lakoff has demonstrated that the traditional language features of women's language express and structure continuing assumptions about the position of women in society, and that "the kinds of 'politeness' used by and of and to women, do not arise by accident; that they are, indeed, stifling, exclusive, and oppressive" (83). Lakoff's analysis, however, has been criticized by some feminists as an a-historical treatment of women's language that fails to document new developments in women's language as well as aspects of traditional usage that might now be seen as "oppositional" in at least a germinal way. Further development of a social understanding of women's speech has much to gain, I believe, by taking this critique seriously. Gay language research too should be critiqued along similar lines so that past stages (like the language of O'Hara's period) can be seen as integrated and surpassed by present day language practices.

How then, to return to the question, is O'Hara's language gay? If we ask a gay man, the simplest answer to this question would probably be this: that O'Hara talks gay. That is, he *sounds* like a gay person when he talks. There is an accent on conversation as chatting, an enjoyable and "unserious" social occupation much like gossip. In fact O'Hara seems like other gay men talking, only more articulate—unexpectedly startling or even brilliant, but much like any gay man who talks with others within the community of the period. Such a response is important. For to find out whether a given language belongs to a community, we have ultimately to query its speakers. We ask them if that is the language they speak or have spoken in the past.

In looking at O'Hara's language then let us first of all look at a certain tone, recognizably gay and linguistic for gay men themselves, as in this for example, the often quoted Lana Turner poem:

---

54 Robin Lakoff, *Language and Woman's Place* (New York: Harper & Row, 1975).

Lana Turner has collapsed!
I was trotting along and suddenly
it started raining and snowing
and you said it was hailing
but hailing hits you on the head
hard so it was really snowing and
raining and I was in such a hurry
to meet you but the traffic
was acting exactly like the sky
and suddenly I see a headline
LANA TURNER HAS COLLAPSED!
there is no snow in Hollywood
there is no rain in California
I have been to lots of parties
and acted perfectly disgraceful
but I never actually collapsed
oh Lana Turner we love you get up[55]

The tone could be called a little silly, even superficial. It is a tone that is non-moralistic, often ironic and sympathetic at the same time: a way of speaking that indexes the historical language use of gay men. It can be called a "trivializing" tone. Characteristically, as in the Lana Turner poem, it functions as *a displacement of connectives*. It proceeds paratactically. In the poem itself, events, observations, etc., are simply enumerated: "I do this, I do that." Its prototypical connective is the non-connective "and." Similarly we can note that the poem often just exclaims, and then passes on to another item; the displaced meanings must be construed from a context. Or again, the identity of "you" (line four) is left unspecified—displaced to the (contextual) situation of those who already know. Ultimately this displacement is a declaration of non-seriousness of intent. It implies, as we will soon see, that connections might be dangerous.

---

55 *CP,* 449

We can compare this language tone in O'Hara's poem to that of certain other artifacts of the period.[56] Take for instance this little poem-graffito, a kind of wistful complaint jotted down by the underground movie star and comedian Taylor Mead, as an entry in what he called his Amphetamine Diaries:

> Taylor Mead Taylor Mead
> that's all I hear all day
> long it's like a train carrying
> me somewhere only we
> never get anywhere
> interesting more than a
> second and the scenery out
> the window stinks.[57]

Or this confidence from a diary of Ned Rorem's:

> Unfortunately Margaret Truman is the same age as I,
> and I must go through life being the same age as she.[58]

This language echoes a practice that was also O'Hara's. O'Hara's appreciation and familiarity with such a language is evident in a number of ordinary situations, like the obligatory letters to friends that continue a valued relationship at a distance. Here for example is an excerpt from a letter written to his roommate Joe LeSueur, while O'Hara was traveling in Europe as part of his job as curator for the Museum of Modern Art. He is describing with obvious appreciation a party in Rome, where

---

56 Joseph J. Hayes (see footnote 36) glosses certain of these trivializing dimensions, noting the adversary relationships implied by them, in a gossip column citation from a Los Angeles bar tabloid, *Data-Boy*; it is in non-literary artifacts like this that one comes closest to finding a language "informant" in my view.

57 Taylor Mead, *Taylor Mead On Amphetamine and in Europe: Excerpts from the Anonymous Diary of a New York Youth*, vol. 3 (New York: Boss Books, 1968), 7.

58 Ned Rorem, *Paris and New York Diaries* (New York: Avon, 1970), 45. (Originally published by George Braziller, 1966.)

I met a terribly nice photographer who is a marquis... and a great camp named Guidarino Guidi who has some of the zest (and the manners) of John Myers and screamed when meeting me, giving V Gassman quite a shove, "Frank O'Hara! what are you doing here! where did you get him Plinio? I am your translator. I am making you famous in Italy. Everyone loves your movie poem. I did it so brilliantly because it is exactly like my childhood. Is it exactly like your childhood? Never mind, I'll kill that Bill Weaver for not telling me you were here, he claimed to be a close friend of yours! He is? well he's no friend of mine anymore. My dear, so do you know Charles Henri Ford?[59]

And so on. The trivialization project of this language, however, has a marked sense of urgency; for on the horizon of this discourse is the always immanent possibility of disaster, a peril that implicates each of its speakers collectively, as a danger common to all. This project is in fact a buried narrative; it conceals a destination. In the context of the O'Hara poem cited above it becomes important that Lana Turner actually "get up"; in encouraging her, O'Hara encourages both himself and unnamed others who might be *like* Lana Turner in important respects to persevere, to keep on existing, at a bare minimum at least to live. Likewise, if the train carrying Taylor Mead is, as he notes, carrying him "somewhere," that destination becomes a warning indexed in the hodological space of a scenery that "stinks." It foregrounds a danger point. And isn't the photographer-marquis of O'Hara's letter to Joe LeSueur in a similar situation? He is after all, as O'Hara tells it, prepared to "kill" on account of a failed introduction. And as the extremity of his situation is signaled linguistically, it gets *circulated* by O'Hara in his letter to LeSueur as a meaning that belongs to the community. It then remains for Ned Rorem's brief "confidence" to indicate the danger at its limit—in the empty passage of time that anticipates death itself. Gay language is a trivialization that speaks and hides its catastrophe in relation to a future.

---

59 Frank O'Hara, *Belgrade, November 19, 1963* (New York: Adventures in Poetry, n.d.), 3.

The displacement is strategic then. And like the original meaning of storytelling itself, as developed by Walter Benjamin in his essay "The Storyteller,"[60] it attempts to work out solutions to catastrophic problems faced by groups as a whole. From this viewpoint the trivialization of gay language is the opposite of the commodified trivialization of newspapers and reports—the serial items and "faits divers" which Benjamin shows, in the same essay, to be without meaning and so without residue, exhausted by their simple consumption. Formally suppressing the connections between things, the trivialization of this gay language becomes a ruse whose intent is to disarm the intelligence of the "other." It thus *relates* rather than *describes*. In anecdotes, verbal witticisms and stories, it is language functioning to give counsel to the collectivity.

The anecdotal and other narrative techniques of gay language are not in fact "literary"; they are not "art." Like gossip and other "low" functions of language, they may recall an earlier stratum in history, a pre-bourgeois time. For at its inception in medieval town life, as Benjamin tells us, storytelling arose as a *group* activity of "giving advice"—against some danger threatening the community. This unifying threat, Benjamin continues, was perceived variously. The inscription *ultima multis* on a town-hall clock in Spain, for instance, understood this threat in a religious mode ("the last hour for many"). Or the group story could perhaps be related pedagogically, as in the *Märchen* or fairytales, helping to socialize the community young by giving examples of a human capacity to work with natural forces rather than against them, or at least not be defeated by them. It is a collective dimension not unlike this that functions in gay language as a kind of buried narrative. It is foregrounded in O'Hara in a particular way, and it helps account for a sense of a life lived as continuously imperiled and unfulfilled in its essential social needs by virtue of membership in a community whose existence is always in question:

---

60 Walter Benjamin, "The Storyteller," *Illuminations* (New York: Schocken, 1969).

In Bayreuth once
we were very good friends of the Wagners
and I stepped in once
for Isadora so perfectly
she would never allow me to dance again
that's the way it was in Bayreuth. . . .
now if you feel like you want to deal with
Tokyo
you've really got something to handle
it's like Times Square at midnight
you don't know where you're going
but you know

and then in Harbin I knew
how to behave it was glorious that
was love sneaking up on me through the snow
and I felt it was because of all
the postcards and the smiles and kisses and grunts
that was love but I kept on traveling[61]

In this poem we can grasp the deeper meaning of the "lack of syntax" in O'Hara which criticism has attributed to the universalizing projects of art-modernism. "Lack of syntax" in these poems is buried community story.

The connections are repressed, they remain implicit. And if the narrator states that he "stepped in once / for Isadora so perfectly / she would never allow me to dance again," the community understands: "perfectly." It has ears to hear its own praxis. In the language practice of the dominant group, the narrator's assertion can only seem "disconnected." An aporia of meaning functions, an antimony, a meaningless babel. For what man could *speak* like this and still *be* a man? Yet the speaker is a man, not a woman; his statement therefore cancels itself. Criticism both understands and does not understand the connections at this point—

----

61 *CP*, 401-402

"it's like Times Square at midnight / you don't know where you're going / but you know." What position then can the dominant language take with respect to this other language? *Aures habet, et non audiet*: the schizophrenia of the dominant discourse is necessary for its own survival. But the paratactic language of the community also benefits the community itself. Opaque and transgressive with respect to the outsider, the connections of the discourse are constituted for the community as the news of a praxis—its continuing project of self-renewal after each experience of disaster. Thus the paratactic function, set up in the O'Hara poem as a lateral migration from city to city or person to person becomes a homology for the community's project to move through time to some safe place in the future. "That was love," says the speaker, "but I kept on traveling." With this self-defensive measure the community speaks itself for itself, and not others.

To ask if a particular language practice is gay language practice is then really to ask if that language practice calls up and relates, or narrates, a community. The speech acts of gay men are not always gay speech acts. To locate this difference we can compare two poems—one from the mid-Fifties by O'Hara and another by Allen Ginsberg from the mid-Sixties. Though both poems are written by gay men and both are "about" a gay bar, the Ginsberg poem will be shown to be non-gay as a language practice and the O'Hara poem, on the other hand, gay. We will read the following Ginsberg poem, "Chances 'R'":

> Nymph and shepherd raise electric tridents
>   glowing red against the plaster wall,
> The jukebox beating out magic syllables,
> A line of painted boys snapping fingers
>   & shaking thin Italian trouserlegs
>   or rough dungarees on big asses
>   bumping and dipping
> ritually, with no religion but the
>   old one of cocksuckers
> naturally, in Kansas center of America
>   the farmboys in Diabolic bar light

alone stiff necked or lined up
>dancing row on row like Afric husbands
& the music's sad here, whereas Sunset Trip or
Jukebox Corner it's ecstatic pinball machines—
Religiously, with concentration and free
>prayer; fairy boys of the plains
>and their gay sisters of the city
step together to the center of the floor
>illuminated by machine eyes, screaming drumbeats,
>passionate voices of Oklahoma City
>chanting No Satisfaction
Suspended from Heaven the Chances R
Club floats rayed by stars
along a Wichita tree avenue
>traversed with streetlights on the plain[62]

against this poem of O'Hara's, "At the Old Place":

Joe is restless and so am I, so restless.
Button's buddy lips frame "L G T T H O P?"
across the bar. "Yes!" I cry, for dancing's
my soul delight. (Feet! Feet!) "Come on!"

Through the streets we skip like swallows.
Howard malingers. (Come on, Howard.) Ashes
malingers. (Come on, J.A.) Dick malingers.
(Come on, Dick.) Alvin darts ahead. (Wait up,
Alvin.) Jack Earl and Someone don't come.

Down the dark stairs drifts the steaming cha-
cha-cha. Through the urine and smoke we charge
to the floor. Wrapped in Ashes' arms I glide.

---

62 Allen Ginsberg, *Planet News* (San Francisco: City Lights, 1968), 109.

(It's heaven!) Button lindys with me. (It's
heaven!) Joe's two-steps, too, are incredible,
and then a fast rhumba with Alvin, like skipping
on toothpicks. And the interminable intermissions,

we have them. Jack Earl and Someone drift
guiltily in. "I knew they were gay
the minute I laid eyes on them!" screams John.
How ashamed they are of us!   we hope.[63]

What audiences then are conjured by these respective languages? Or to
put it another way, who is speaking? For the question of the "who" is the
question of the discourse itself. Who does it address itself to, and what
community does it speak?[64]

The Ginsberg poem, we are tempted to say, shows a certain kinship
with what Sartre has called "the spirit of seriousness." And to be sure, the
speaker seems painfully distant from the scene he describes. The terms
of the description are hardly friendly, and the gay men dancing are "fairy
boys," "gay sisters," with "no religion but the / old one of cocksuckers."
Such a language characterizes the viewpoint of the dominant "other"—an
outsider. The speaker observes rather than participating in the scene, from
a juridical standpoint that echoes the terms of male supremacy. Thus "the
music's sad here." But perhaps that's because the gay men described are not
really persons but types. They're "farmboys in Kansas" or "Afric husbands,"
and dancing, they shake "thin Italian trouserlegs." This mythic containment
("Diabolic bar light," the "ritual" or "prayer" "illuminated by machine eyes,
screaming drumbeats") has the added effect of reinforcing the oppressive

---

63 *CP*, 223-224
64 I dealt with this question in my "Afterword," in Robert Glück, *Family Poems*
(San Francisco: Black Star, 1978). In a still unfinished longer work I treat
this question more generally, as it applies to the broad spectrum of recent
minority and oppositional movements in the United States, contextualized by
liberation struggles still going on as well as by the development of communist
oppositions in the Eastern Bloc countries of actually existing socialism.

discourse of official psychiatry, condemning the participants to a lifetime unhappiness of their own making. For indeed, whatever the ecstasies of this infernal pastoral ("Nymph and shepherd raise electric tridents / glowing red"), the "passionate voices" "chanting No Satisfaction" are damned souls. They can at best look only to eternity ("Suspended from Heaven. . . rayed by stars") for release. The poem finally becomes a non-narrative spectacle, a moral tableau perhaps—of universal types, lost souls seeking their salvation. Speaking from outside the community he describes, the speaker speaks another language, a *dominant discourse*.[65]

The speaker of the O'Hara poem on the other hand from the outset speaks as a part of the community. He speaks its language as a story that unfolds in time, not eternity. He thus names names—Joe, Button, Ashes, Dick, and so on. Everything becomes frivolous, trivialized. If the dancing became "the Dance" it wouldn't be fun anymore, so it's just the "lindy," the "two-step" or the "rhumba." The language practice makes itself the community's. "Yes! I cry, for dancing's / my soul delight. (Feet! Feet!) 'Come on!'"—and—"Through the streets we skip like swallows." And the rhumba becomes "like skipping/ on toothpicks." The connections are subverted, because it is the community itself that will make them. The poem develops itself then as a series of actions. The problem is stated at the beginning with the narrator at home with some friends, bored, "restless." What to do with the evening still ahead of them? Somebody's lips mime

---

65 John Tytell, *Naked Angels: The Lives and Literature of the Beat Generation* (New York: McGraw Hill, 1976), 229, citing the following Ginsberg verses from an early poem called "In Society":
> I walked into the cocktail party
> room and found three or four queers
> talking together in queertalk.
> I tried to be friendly but heard
> myself talking to one in hiptalk
—makes the point that "behind the subject of the poem is Ginsberg's discomfort with his own homosexuality." Perhaps. It seems to me, though, that it is more a question of Ginsberg's defining reluctance to be politically homosexual. The question is objective and a question of praxis, not "subjective" in some privatized, psychological sense.

an answer: "L G T T H O P?" Let's go to the Old Place. And they're off, though a complication is suggested. Jack, Earl, and "Someone" don't come; we wonder why. Then the bar scene ("Down the dark stairs. . ."). The action is articulated in the series of dances and "interminable intermissions." Finally the earlier conflict is resolved when the three who didn't come show up after all: "I knew they were gay / the minute I laid eyes on them!" The evening seems successful by the end of the narration. But the catastrophic potential of the initial situation—the refusal of three of the men to come along—is only surmounted provisionally. For—"How ashamed they are of us! we hope." And we can be assured that the (guilty) shame of Jack, Earl, and Someone will be the occasion of still another story.

The gay language of O'Hara's period "trivializes" then by structuring a dangerous situation as community code. Such a language code, *a displacement of connections*, will be understood by those with a common experience; not by the dominant other, for whom it will be simply idle chatter with no meaning at all.

VII

Yet the gay community of O'Hara's period is gone. We have construed it from its artifacts—and among these the poems of O'Hara himself. And we have read in the texts produced by that community (or more accurately, "pre-community formation") a meaning of opposition that stems from a more politicized, later period. To be sure history itself has polarized these texts and, whether we like it or not, given them a partisan sense.

What then are the events of our own time which have politicized the situation? How and when did they take place? A new historical stage for gays may be dated from the Stonewall Riots of 1969. These events gave the gay community its baptism by fire. In 1969 after a particularly brutal police attack on a New York gay bar called "The Stonewall," street fighting erupted, squad cars were overturned, and a mass counterattack led principally by Third World gays, street queens, and lesbians successfully forced police back and out of the club area. Several days of rioting and spontaneous gatherings followed, and during this time the first militant gay political groups began to form. The Gay Liberation movement had been launched and was effectively underway. By the middle 70s, however, the gay movement had become less militant. The mid-Seventies became a time of organizational development and diversification. It saw the establishment of metropolitan gay community centers, the formation of campus student groups in larger colleges and universities, as well as the appearance of gay coffee houses and alternative meeting places and the first publication of polemical newspapers and magazines with a variety of viewpoints. The gay movement of this time saw a significant broadening of its material base and the establishment of effective institutional and political apparatuses—which were to prove invaluable in the struggles which followed. Those struggles are still with us, as the events of the past year and a half so dramatically indicate. They have advanced the community to a new stage of both political organization and militancy as a direct result of attacks from the New Right and the fundamentalist churches, and the electoral defeats beginning with the Dade County, Florida, defeat of 1977. Other defeats followed, and in the past two years a number of gay rights ordinances originally passed in the middle 70s have been voted down in Minnesota, Kansas, Oregon, and elsewhere. In the large cities violence against gays is on the upswing, and new electoral issues still remain to be voted on in many states; voter approval of the Briggs Initiative (Proposition 6) in California November, 1978 for example, would prohibit open gays as well as "sympathizers" from teaching in the state school system. Yet these reverses have also raised gay political awareness and action to a new level. The past two years have increasingly been a period of mobilizations, demonstrations and mass marches (on June 21, 1977, nearly 250,000 people marched in San Francisco against the Briggs Initiative and in support of gay rights); there have been a significant advances in the community for gay-socialist organizing and greater recognition by gay men of lesbian issues and co-participation with lesbians in decision-making in many new areas. Yet the situation remains serious, and without significant new links with labor, the women's movement and minorities, the gay rights movement may still founder. And there are contradictions within the gay community itself—principally those that pit a highly politicized leadership against the still lagging consciousness of the community as a whole. Indeed, the post-Stonewall gay community has actually seen its internal contradictions exacerbated rather than diminished—in the form of language practice as well as political practice.[66]

What then can be said of language practices in this period, and of the conflict in praxis that it registers in literary documents? Frank O'Hara's death in 1966, three years before Stonewall, may be considered to mark the closing of an era, the post-War period of a gay community-formation. Since that time, however, political practice has given gay language the option of openness. And in literary expressions gay language no longer has to appear in masked or "coded" forms as it did in O'Hara's time. If divisions in gay language practice have appeared then, they have been more a matter of internal rather than external conflicts. Yet these divisions may be worth considering; they express regionally the more general problems of minority groups, as they arrive at a stage of legitimation.

In the post-assertive period since Stonewall, gay language practice has developed contradictions that parallel language developments of minority groups elsewhere and of groups in national liberation struggles. Such contradictions may thus be of some interest for the development of social

---

66 The non-gay reader can begin to familiarize her/himself with the history of the gay movement (from its inception period in the mid-19th century, through its gay-liberation development of the past decades, to its increasingly socialist alignments of the past few years) by consulting one or more of the following books, pamphlets, and periodicals: John Lauritsen and David Thorstad, *The Early Homosexual Rights Movement: 1864-1935* (New York: Times Change Press, 1974); Jonathan Katz, *Gay American History: Lesbian and Gay Men in the USA* (New York: Crowell, 1976); Dennis Altman, *Homosexual Oppression and Liberation* (New York; Avon, 1973); *Magnus* (San Francisco gay socialist magazine); *Gay Sunshine* (gay-lib oriented, mainly cultural newspaper); *Gay Left* (British socialist magazine/newspaper); the newspaper of the French Leftist Le Groupe de Liberation homosexuel, politique et quotidien (GLH-PQ); "Toward a Scientific Analysis of the Gay Question," L.A. Research Group, P.O. Box 1362, Cudahy, California 90201 (pamphlet analyzing the anti-gay sexism of the sectarian communist parties, particularly the Revolutionary Union and the October League); *Lavender and Red Book: A Gay Liberation/Socialist Anthology* (includes excerpts from the previous entry and is usually available at movement bookstores); John F. Burnett, *The Meaning of Gay Liberation: an Analysis and Program for Action* (deals with current attacks from the right; available directly from 716 A Clayton St., San Francisco, California 94117, for 60c).

language theory. When Fanon raised the question of violence and of the necessary violence against the other, not only the other who stood outside (the settler) but also the internalized other within was to be overthrown in the violent act. The case of the colonized intellectual was exemplary in this regard; the community's language struggle was registered in its sharpest form on this site as a textualization of competing language-cultural codes. In political struggle the language-cultural codes of the oppressed group were to overthrow those of the oppressor and themselves become dominant. But such a reversal, according to Fanon, would also alter the very codes the community was asserting; and the language and cultural codes of the group would begin to transform themselves.[67] At this point the community has begun to polarize itself, developing internal conflicts. The advanced elements now formalize themselves as leadership groups over and above the community at large, and with interests of their own that inevitably conflict with those of the community they represent. This conflict can be located linguistically—in the struggle between the purer more politically progressive language codes of the leadership and the politically regressive but more socially oriented codes of the community as a whole.

Basil Bernstein's analyses of the function of "restricted" and "elaborated" codes (as class determinants) in present-day English society may help us specify this problem. For as Bernstein remarks, "These codes essentially transmit the culture and so constrain behavior."[68] "Elaborated" language

---

67 During the struggle for freedom, as Fanon saw, the youth of the oppressed group "may well make a mock of, and not hesitate to pour scorn upon the zombies of his ancestors, the horses with two heads, the dead who rise again, and the djinns who rush into your body while you yawn" (Fanon, *Wretched*, 58).

68 Basil Bernstein, *Class, Codes and Control*, vol. 1, 122. William Labov's critique of Bernstein's views can be found in *Sociolinguistic Patterns* (University of Pennsylvania Press, 1972). From Labov's standpoint Bernstein's restricted code seems to imply an inferiority of working class speech, particularly (in the U.S.) Black speech. Bernstein himself replies to this in the concluding chapter of *Class, Codes and Control*, vol. 1. One might also consult Harold Rosen's pamphlet *Language and Class: A Critical Look at the Theories of Basil Bernstein* (Bristol, England: Falling Wall, n.d.) and Alvin W. Gouldner's defense of Bernstein, and critical assessment of this controversy, in *The Dialectic of Ideology and Technology*, (New York: Seabury Press, 1976), 58-61.

codes, in Bernstein's view, are essentially the codes of middle-class and educated groups. Linguistically they tend to be analytic and individualistic, independent (to the extent that this is possible) of non-language contexts such as para-verbal aspects of speech like gesture and socially conventional behavior forms that imply solidarity with others. Non-concrete and non-specific, they become then the vehicle for typically abstract or theoretical discourse. "Restricted" codes on the other hand are seen as essentially the codes of the community itself, the social group as such; such codes characterize for Bernstein the ordinary discourse of the working class, and are opposed to hegemonic discourse. Relying primarily on the context of speech, with its conventionalized non- or para-verbal cues, these restricted codes express themselves immediately as a social solidarity. They are situational and cannot be understood outside of a *situation*. The gay language of O'Hara's poems is difficult to locate for precisely this reason; it is, in Bernstein's terms, a "restricted" language code.

The conflicting languages of post-assertive national-ethnic or minority groups can now helpfully be seen, following Bernstein, as a struggle between *elaborated* and *restricted* codes. Reflecting the contradictions of community praxis, the language of the advanced elements becomes increasingly a critical and political language—an elaborated code. And the language of the community as a whole, reflecting its newly won right to speak itself as it actually is or has been traditionally, now becomes a "restricted" code.

Within this theoretical context we can locate the contradictions of a gay language and poetry of our own period. The gay community, since Stonewall, has seen its own development of an "elaborated" and "restricted" language code. One of these has become politically progressive and critical of traditional community language and cultural forms, while the other is more concerned with a cultural-linguistic sense of the community as it is, or traditionally has been.

Here for example is a political poem from the San Francisco gay socialist magazine *Magnus*, written in what can be called a gay "elaborated" language—

Sex is not ours,
for, besides being counter-revolutionary,
monogamy is also unhealthy

and causes anxiety.
Nor could we be simply friends making
sexual experiments or
performing exercises in sensitivity. . . .
We eye each other
with suspicions of class-bias
and apprehension of a
premature proletariat leadership.[69]

As a language practice, the poem is clean and analytical, to the point of abstraction. Neither trivial nor frivolous in any traditional mode of gay language practice, it simply instructs. It is didactic. We might call it a love poem—*in the style of the tennis-court oath*. It is not far distant from terror. We can compare it in this respect with another gay political poem which, addressing itself to the community from its site in a gay-socialist publication, dispenses with even the perfunctory references of the first poem to gay affectional preferences, making its message to the community a generalized anti-imperialist warning—

Beware the dreaded
greedy
Anaconda
beware this snake
that strangles
with embraces
Chile beware
Montana   Arizona
its copper scales
its eyes of gold
and the hiss of its tongue
as it hugs[70]

---

69 *Magnus* no. 2 (Summer, 1977): 36.
70 *Hundred Flowers* (Eugene, Oregon, n.p.) (May, 1977).

The issue here is not whether this is good or bad poetry, but how such writing integrates a linguistic code. An extreme case, to be sure. Implicit in the language of these two poems is a stance that speaks *to* rather than *from* the community. Its real audience can in fact be only other highly politicized gay men, already conceiving of themselves as a leadership.

Not so, however, with the less progressive "restricted" stance of an opposing poetic practice speaking, from within the community, as a traditional language. In this excerpt from a Joe Brainard poem for instance there are obvious qualities of gay language as community experience in a popular or "restricted" fashion that makes the poem accessible to large numbers of gay men as their own and as a *common* experience:

> I remember when, in high school, if you wore green and
> yellow on Thursday it meant that you were queer.
> I remember when, in high school, I used to stuff a sock
> in my underwear.
> I remember "Queers can't whistle."
> I remember the skinny guy who gets sand kicked in his face in
> body-building advertisements.
> I remember how little your dick is getting out of a wet bathing
> suit.
> I remember daydreams of a doctor who (on the sly) was
> experimenting with a drug that would turn you into a real stud.
> All very "hush-hush." (As it was illegal.) There was a slight chance
> that something might go wrong and that I'd end up with a *really*
> giant cock, but I was willing to take that chance.[71]

Yet the poetic language of this poem is successful in invoking a *community* only at the price of removal to a past of nostalgia. And its success is limited from this point of view. The language of the poem does, however, remain

---

71 Winston Leyland, ed., *Angels of the Lyre* (San Francisco: Gay Sunshine Press/ Panjandrum, 1975), 25. Reprinted from Joe Brainard, *I Remember* (New York: Angel Hair, 1970).

a community language. Particularly because it is articulated paratactically (Vendler's "absence of an intellectual syntax"), and because it refuses to make connections between things. In this respect it is related to narrative.

The privileged role of this gay narrative, however, has recently shown signs of developing a more serious (and sophisticated) alienation than that of nostalgic removal in time. In this newer version of a traditional poetry, the narration of community relates simply a set of linguistic artifacts in which the community is invoked as the possibility of an individual erotic reverie of language itself. At the limit then, the traditional gay language style may become a production of language-objects to be consumed, and dream the community itself as an artifact. For example, in Dennis Cooper's poems (see following page), a sense of community is produced by referring to certain traditional *artifacts* of the community rather than to its own speech.[72]

Appropriately, these poems cite the language of movie magazines and Hollywood gossip. It is a language which, when consumed by gay men, is lived as an experience "always elsewhere." The pictures fulfill a similar function; they are derealized visual myths posing beside a gay American linguistic dream yet to be exorcized. This ideologically regressive language is still to be found in every shoddy movie theater and porn magazine in which gays are unprotestingly exploited in a commercialized, ersatz community experience. It appears in every alluring gossip column or movie magazine story about TV idols or punk rockers or other packaged artifacts. But it is a Utopian language that doesn't yet disengage itself from gay dreams.

Meanwhile other gay languages are beginning to be written, languages whose project is to be as genuinely communal as they are politically progressive. But for the most part they remain still inchoate and unintegrated, attempts rather than realizations—failed expressions of the unity of experience that only events themselves can bring when gay praxis has developed into another stage. In the future no doubt such a praxis will be seen as having begun in the events of the past year or two. When this

---

72 Dennis Cooper, "The Population of Heaven on Earth," *Little Caesar* no. 3, (1977).

future praxis develops, gay poetry and language will surely develop along with it.

Such divisions in current gay poetry return us to our starting point—to the writing of O'Hara himself. Gay poetry as developed in our period constitutes a lesson for rereading the literary artifacts of the past stages of development, not only of gays, but, I hope, for other groups as well. We would do an injustice to these artifacts if we only read them judgmentally—from an unmediated political viewpoint of our present time. Indeed, a body of writing or poetry like O'Hara's remains a richly complex and specifically literary mediation of ideology; a registration of the contradictions of his period which, as a moment of opposition "cancelled and raised," now makes our present experience both more comprehensible and more valuable. But neither can we, I believe, fall back on the ultimately non-critical procedures of past academic discussion. For if indeed O'Hara's work has now become "literary," we have little to lose and much to gain by rethinking the deeper, social meanings of the legitimation process itself.

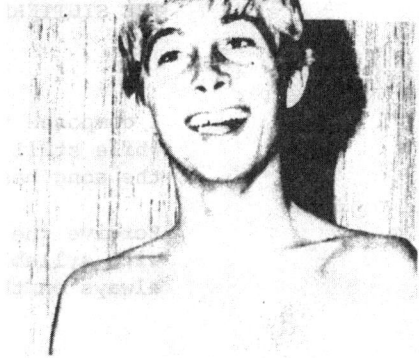

"I lie in my room most of the time dreaming of another planet so close I see the bristle of people on it. That would be greater than great! When I get lonely I lean out a window and fluff my blond hair. And the wolf whistles chase me back inside, slapping my happy head.

–Tom

"I sing and dance. I have the ability to make people laugh. At night I pack'em in the place's only nightclub and in the day play for free on the streets. "Haven't I seen you someplace before?" I ask, then make a face, and their cheers shiver the short blond hairs on my arms, my pay."

–Steve

"I'm the one in the shadows at Burger King waiting for an ideal girl. My Porsche boiling under my hands. I'm a looker so I can have anyone. The problem is to choose correctly, to see through her blonde hair and blouse to the true girl. Choosing wrong I'd blow two bright futures."

–Mark

"I'm the cynic. I also write a little. The world won't recognise greatness. They're obsessed with appearance. Now, I'm not knocking one of my assets. But there's more to me than that! Very annoyed, I rest my chin on my fist and look upset, to the delight of my friends."

–Jeff

"Gay Language as Political Praxis" was published in *Social Text 1* (Winter 1979). Dennis Cooper's "The Population of Heaven on Earth" first appeared in *Little Caesar* no. 3 (1977). It was cut and arranged by Bruce Boone for the first publication of this article, and is reprinted here with permission. Cooper's original piece includes two additional models.

TOWARD A GAY THEORY FOR THE '80s

What are the needs of gay men as we enter the '80s? And how are our needs different from those of the Gay Lib era of the late 60s and early 70s? Where do we go from here—and with what organizations, what forms of political or other activity? The analysis that follows tries to describe our present conditions as a community. It relates this present to past developments and to future ones as well. These future developments will be shaped in part by the forms of community action and political organization that we choose now.

WHAT IS THE AREA FOR ACTION?

The focus of the gay movement up to the present has been nearly exclusively on gay rights. This has meant a narrowing of our concerns to relation in civil society as individuals. As a result, gay demands have been reformist in nature. The gay movement continues to be shaped by single-issue causes and still has little long-term sense of direction. The consciousness of our movement as a movement is still a consciousness of "spontaneity."

As we see it, the principal focus of our energies at present should be the ghetto itself, the actually existing real collectivity of gay men. The ghetto is our community, and as such it is the only structure in and through which demands can be made and a consciousness developed which begins to transcend spontaneity. In this sense what we see as the main task of the gay movement is closely related to the community or action group politics that have appeared in a variety of locales during the past few years.

To develop a relation to the gay community then is to:

1. historicize our community and see it as a formation of the needs of capitalism itself, with, however, an objective or utopian content that remains in contradiction to those needs;
2. take as an initial and continuing point of view on community, the community's own self-experience and its stated needs;
3. describe the kind of organization that would raise community demands to levels that go beyond reformist needs to utopian and transformatory ones.

THE PRODUCTION OF GAY MEN

An adequate account of the formation of a specific social group of gay men has not yet been developed. We can, however, point out that within the capitalist era, gay sexuality and socialization have gone through a number of changes. In the 19th century for instance "gay identity" seems closely related to basic changes in family life centered around the developing nuclear family unit (Jeffrey Weeks, *Coming Out*) as well as to the formation of a characteristic of understanding most basic phenomena, including sexuality, as part of a total applied-knowledge system (Foucault, *History of Sexuality*) that categorizes differences. As a result, through the 19th century and into the early 20th, gay men were conscious of themselves as individuals more than as a social group.

But towards the middle of our own century, gays began to develop more socially, and in the immediate post-War years of the late 40s and 50s the signs of this are recognizable in the formation of sizable big city ghettos in which the consciousness of gay men seems to take on more collective forms. But these same years also mark the beginning of the consumer society phase of late capitalism, and these two events seem in many ways closely related. In fact, the coming into being of the first real communities of gay men appears to have been possible only at a certain stage of capitalist development. At this time large numbers of gay men first began to find ghetto life not only attractive, but necessary, and so moved from rural and small town environments into the large cities. Once there, we developed and were developed by a set of characteristic institutions, bars, bathhouses, etc.; the net effect of these institutions was two-fold. They provided partial satisfaction of gay sexual and social needs on a collective or group basis and they shaped a specific type of commodity consciousness that was to link gay men to the needs of a consumer capitalist society.

But what were these capitalist needs, specifically? In much of recent thinking about the advent of consumer society (Baudrillard, *The Mirror of Production*) an emphasis has been placed on a strategic shift within the formations of late capitalism from a characteristic relation to commodities primarily as use-values to a new relation, on the part of consumers, to these same commodity items as exchange-values. So, it has been said, in advanced capitalist societies it tends to be more and more production as a code of representation rather than a particular commodity product that is consumed. In this way of thinking, late capitalism in its consumer society phase is marked by an emphasis on the sign function of commodities and on the power of these sign commodities to create an autonomous meaning system by more and more referring only to other signs or each other.

In order to accomplish this shift, capitalism is forced to create something like a set of specialists or experts in sign production. New attention must be paid to the sign as a value and a corresponding sophistication developed in the ability to discern and discriminate among meaning in everyday life. Within this perspective we can see gay men not just as people with a certain gender designation but with one that is historicized in a particular way. Gay men, in this way of thinking, would be something like the specialized group in late capitalism that functions as a general producer of signs. We are produced, to use capitalism's own metaphor, to produce signs.

What are the advantages of this point of view? First of all, to formulate the question in this way relates our construction as gendered subjects at a given period of time to an underlying economic structure, and our sexuality can now be thought in a determinate way as a function of the society producing it (us). But this way of raising the question also enables us to deal with the actual perceptions of homophobia which displace its general awareness of the commodification of private life onto its most visible victims in this area and in this way helps back the wider social recognition of our emancipatory potential and at the same time impedes an effective self-recognition of this potential even in our own community.

We can also now begin to talk about truth content of certain gay stereotypes and see in discredited stereotypes a refused but liberatory possibility about the spectrum of gender choice, since what is disavowed in these stereotypes has a great deal to do with how we really are, and how we are both like and unlike others who make gender choices. On the one hand we seem to have much in common with women in being socialized, from an early age and in a more intense way than other men, toward nurturing functions and to a heightened attentiveness of the personal or private. But we are also socialized like men. Expectations are formed for us, on the basis of our sex, that encourages and demands the development of skills oriented toward society at large, toward an impersonal or public world, rather than to family life or parenting. In short we become men, but men oriented toward a particular pole of male possibilities, a special set of capabilities and strengths. And to the extent that we shape ourselves around nurturing and personality needs, we make job choices that reflect the development we have. Choosing ourselves, we also determine the jobs we will have later. Yet the opposite is also true. Our jobs choose us, because the society of our period needs these jobs filled.

Homophobia begins to speak at this point. Gays, it points out, are produced to fulfill the purposes of an inhuman and alienating commodity capitalist society (*Two Local Chapters in the Spectacle of Decomposition*, Chris Shutes; a recent homophobic pamphlet). But the defining bad faith of homophobia lies in failing to proceed to a future truth: that each of the other gender designations is produced to fulfill equally alienating functions. They are equally deformed. Such a realization remains fundamental to any claim for a Freudo-Marixst thought today. Lacanian interpretation, for instance, however it remains practically homophobic and sexist, is a programmatic insistence on the construction of a social base in understanding all sexuality and its meaning. This is the correct transcription of its slogan, The Unconscious is the Voice of the Other. Beyond Lacan in Freud himself, the basis of political Freudian thought had been laid in the theory of infantile bisexuality.

All this comes down to a single truth, with which any analysis of gays and the gay ghetto has to begin. If we have been formed by society as gay men, we have also been formed for the social purpose of what we are calling "living in the ghetto". Our task at this point is to understand what "living in the ghetto" might mean, to understand its basic contradictions. Only in this way we consciously work out our transforming potentials in order to construct a future.

CONTRADICTIONS IN GHETTO LIFE

Strange as it might sound, what we need at this stage of the analysis is an ability to think about certain developed aspects of commodity life in a positive way, as making demands on capitalism for the reorganization of society according to human needs. What ought to be taken seriously is Marx's dictum about new forms of social organization first being prepared and coming to have a certain existence "within the womb of the old."

To be sure, these positive, utopian aspects of ghetto life are in actuality inseparable from deformations of community life. They are the other side of the coin. This is the basic truth of homophobic perceptions. Rightly or wrongly, what seems threatening here are of course the twin and interrelated "problems" of promiscuity and commodification. It is this aspect of things that our allies, women or particularly lesbians, point out to us. How then do these arise as distortions of our social and sexual needs? Or to phrase the question a little differently, don't the deformations of the gay ghetto arise as advances of capital into areas from which it was once excluded? The area of the private and the personal above all. Gay sexual relations in a ghetto context are often repetitive and unsatisfying and take place in an exploitative commodity environment. Bars, bathhouses, after-hours clubs and so on function more or less on this principle. Additionally the cultural life of the ghetto, or received assumptions we make about each other, tend to misshape gay sexual needs in characteristic patterns by isolating and fetishizing sexuality as if it was separable from related human needs like tenderness, intimacy and the development of ongoing relationships. But all this is obvious and in itself doesn't go far in understanding the meaning of a gay community life. Positive developments in ghetto life, if less obvious, for that reason need greater clarification and more explanation. And they need to be discussed by the community itself because, in the strongest way, they mark the transformatory potential of a gay collectivity to influence the development of future socializations and societies.

An adequate theorization will show how the distortions that are most characteristic in our community also hold, from another point of view, the deepest promise for new, utopian social forms. These two aspects of the community are the poles of a single contradiction. But what are the potentials for a future? Three perhaps stand out as particularly important and interrelated. First, gay sexuality and friendship represent the possibility of conceiving physical and emotional intimacy beyond the historical deformations of family life and relations between men and women now fixed as constitutively oppressive. Gay sexuality, from this point of view, has a liberatory status that contrasts with the instrumental deformations of other sexualities. To a greater or lesser degree, these other sexualities both serve male privilege and impose an ideal of reproduction that represses self-development. Second, as a possibility of physical intimacy built on the relation of equals, gay sexuality represents a qualitatively new potential for the development of human friendship in a natural form, where friendship and sexuality may come to be merely deepening awareness of the same phenomenon. Third, gay sexuality, particularly as it comes to be more and more influenced by feminism and the women's movement, can be seen as an important force in raising the historically neglected questions of subjectivity and affectivity. Up till now these questions have been at best underdeveloped by Marxism and the various Marxist movements. Recently, the undeniable strength and importance of the women's movement in Western democracies, as well as the gay movement, has led most Marxist movements to rethink their assumptions in this area, as mass demands are now being made from the first time for more satisfying forms of subjectivity. The women's movement and the gay movement are raising this question for the first time as a political question and, in a politicization of what was previously considered only "personal," have the greatest possible liberatory potentials. The real danger, however, remains: such potentials, if neglected by the left, are inevitably coopted and defused by neutral or even reactionary movements like historical existentialism, the current French New Philosophy or the contemporary youth culture movements. "There is a greater need today for types of relations within which more subjectivity and more sentiment can find expression, in which affective conduct is taken more into account." (Jurgen Habermas).[1] "But, for the first time there are communities built on sexuality, not on a sexual act, but on the feelings and a whole way of life of sexuality" (Amber Hollibaugh).[2]

---

1 Jurgen Habermas, "Conservatism and Capital Crisis," *New Left Review* no. 115, 1979).

2 Amber Hollibaugh, "San Francisco Lesbian and Gay Men's History Project," forum on the May 21, 1979 riots in San Francisco).

For gay men, as we noted, this community takes on the contradictory, commodified shape we are calling "the ghetto". Positive and utopian aspects of community only exist today as commodified. But commodified how? Not "in general," but in some very specific ways. The commodification that characterizes the gay community takes place as a general demand for the introduction of subjective relations into the public sphere itself. The ghetto, even in its commodified existence, constitutes a demand for integrating the private into the public sphere, for a way of thinking about the private as the public for the first time. The liberatory potentials of the ghetto take this form. It is revealing for instance that gay men are rarely interested in commodities that do not reveal a personal, or private dimension of things. This interest on our part helps explain a conventional association of gays with certain areas of the semiotic industry, various arts, fashion and so on.

But can we begin to explain this phenomenon in terms of our socialization? Earlier we supposed a close relation between the consumer society phase of capitalism and gay men as specialists in the production of signs, a social grouping whose particular function is to deal with the semiotic, with signification in the most general way. This helps explain why there is a particular set of jobs that we find ourselves as gay men gravitating to. It allows us to see, for instance, why we are generally and characteristically "over-represented" in communications, service jobs and jobs dealing with the public, language skills areas, education, personal services and so on: in short, the areas stereotypically associated with us. As gay men we produce signs because we have chosen ourselves or been chosen for nurturing and personal relations, usually considered areas of specialization by women (Ulrike Prokop, "Production and the Context of Women's Daily Life"). But unlike women, gay men have not been socialized to be parents, housewives or sustainers of affectional relations in a family on an unpaid basis. Instead our gender designation as male means socialization of these same affectional and nurturing skills to a public, official area rather than to a private one. We are socialized like men, because we are designated for a job function in an official area. But since the jobs we choose are those associated with nurturing and the affectional life (that is private and subjective aspects of living), our characteristic job functions as gay men become perceived as the commodification of what has been traditionally thought of as non-commodifiable. Thus, even before we come to the ghetto, we have been socialized to a certain relation to commodity that characterizes the ghetto. The development of the ghetto in this way reflects our own development. This relationship to the personal, through commodity, must be demystified and deconstructed so that it can be allowed to develop new, liberatory, and more social forms.

The starting place for this development should be an investigation of the positive insights and feelings we already have, as a group, about the ghetto. We know for instance that the ghetto serves as a place of refuge from exterior violence directed against gay people, and that it's a place of relaxation. And if it's a place for the satisfaction of sexual and social needs, it's time to ask about the positive nature of these satisfactions (Guy Hocquenghem, *Homosexual Desire*), and not simply condemn them as "commodified." Likewise we know that certain ghetto notions like glamour, the cult of "stars," or cultural nostalgia are signs of the historically important potential for gay men to express, communally, the sense of a subjectivity. As a community too, we give an important if not central place in our lives to questions of love and sex. (Alexandra Kollantai, ???????)
[3] This aspect of our lives should properly be seen as emancipatory in its potential toward a future. Finally, we should know how to value the superstructural and cultural apparatuses of our community. We should see the positive role that language has taken in forming the community, and how historically a gay language has functioned as an oppositional discourse and as the location of an objective demand for non-instrumental values in society at large. And finally, we should see institutions like the bars as critical locations for the development of a new politics. Recalling the function of the Black Cat bar in the 50s historically, of the Stonewall in connection with the birth of the gay liberation movement of the 60s

---

3 Editor's note: This appears as is in the original pamphlet, with multiple question marks in lieu of a source. [. . .] Kollantai (1872-1952) was a Russian Communist Revolutionary. Boone's oblique reference here may refer to one of Kollantai's many texts of the Revolutionary period, for example, "Sexual Relations and the Class Struggle."

and of the Castro Street bars in the May '79 riots we should realize the pivotal importance of the bars in developing a continuing gay politics in the future.

In dealing with contradictions of ghetto life, we should mention at least in passing two other phases of the problem: our relations with each other on individual basis within the ghetto, and our relations with the "outside." In our relations individually inside the ghetto there are serious problems that can no longer be overlooked. In a general way, these have to do with the status of our relations with each other as often transitory in nature, with the necessity of developing more positive orientations of support, affection and tenderness toward each other and of making more room in our lives for affective relationships that are not defined so exclusively in sexual terms. On the other hand, we should note positively the special value we tend to place on friendship, the characteristic gay male openness to new experiences on an immediate level and our comparatively strong dislike for instrumental relations to friendship. With regard to our relations as a community with "the outside" it is important to note that our struggle is still taking place at a fundamental level, that we are still fighting for the right to exist as a community. With the electoral reverse of the past few years and the construction of public discourse of homophobia in the Bryant and Briggs campaigns we are begging to understand how much still has to be done in the dialectic of legitimation and socialization that the gay movement has begun. Our status is still that of the outsider. As a collectivity our social being is not considered, nor are our personal qualities. We are defined as those who are not part of the larger community. This discourse should be defined and confronted. It recalls classically a mechanism that has been historically put into effect against other outsider groups (Sartre, *Anti-Semite and Jew*), and it is not in our own interest to ignore it or to indulge in the wish-fulfillment that legal and moral "tolerance" is any adequate goal of our movement. We should realize that this is the time when we must press forward to make social demands that are radical enough to help bring about the basic restructuring of society as a whole.

WHAT IS TO BE DONE? SOME TASKS LIE AHEAD

Following this analysis, with its emphasis on the central role to be played by the ghetto itself in a new gay movement in the near future, we can point to three or four particular areas that ought to be considered likely places for action on the part of a new gay organization: the area of work within the unions and the unionization of the bars and so on, relations to community institutions like community center and gay health clinics, and the whole question of institutionalized violence.

1. THE UNIONS AND UNIONIZATION.

An effort ought to be made to assign priority to this area; it is perhaps the principal area for work to be done at this point. The bars, bathhouses etc. ought to be unionized in stages with great stress laid on the questions that have to do with the specifically gay, and gay community, aspects of these institutions. Here we mean health and safety areas, at the beginning of any such campaigns. The bar owners, whose official ideology as gay entrepreneurs has always been that they are there 'to serve the community' and that their institutions are in fact community institutions, should be taken at their word and be forced contractually and with other pressure to recognize both in principle and concretely the rights of employees, first of all, but also of customers and community, to co-determine policy as well as implementation of policy in these same areas. It should be further recognized that health and safety doesn't mean simply adequate measure of fire protection, cleanliness etc. but also a co-participation by employees and customers in other areas relating to comfort and a more human-social environment, noise level of juke boxes and stereo systems and so on. Unionization should definitely also come to terms with the (specifically) gay questions of sexism and sexual harassment on the job of employees by employers, of racism and ageism in hiring practices and so on. Furthermore, a definite long-rage goal of unionization should be to promote the demand for a greater, and real, responsiveness by the bars to the general needs of the community. Bars for instance could set aside at least one or two days a week during the daytime for community meetings, political groups who need a central meeting place, community oriented afternoons of entertainment etc. They could also function far more effectively as communication centers for the community, with large bulletin boards listing community events and political events of all kind. And last, bars should eventually be levied a certain percentage of their profits for community benefits, community and employee boards should be empowered to have access to accounts and books and to make decisions accordingly on what monies should be assessed for activities the community finds important. Naturally the bars will resist all of these demands, but in the process of making such demands and beginning to struggle for them the community will become far more politicized.

On the question of the unions themselves, internally, caucuses should be formed in all unions with gay membership to any degree at all and demands should be made for specifically gay needs, job protection, etc. In a particular way this would apply to unions with a significant gay profile, such as librarians, etc.

2. COMMUNITY CENTERS AND GAY HEALTH CLINICS.

Financial demands should be made on the municipality in an organized way for fulfilling these needs of gay people. Medical schools should be forced to integrate aspects of gay health care into their overall curricula. In the gay community centers that are already set up, gay men should demand greater attention to the use of these facilities for the needs of women, women's evenings etc.

3. VIOLENCE, INTIMIDATION.

This is an area that is absolutely central to gay life. Educational and agitational work should be done in the community with regard to violence in the following areas:

 a. youth gang violence on the streets generally, in the cruising
  areas, parks etc.

b. police violence as historical and as continuing, on the individual level and at a mass and institutional levels, raiding of bars, homes, increased arrest levels in recent years.

c. harassment, both police and legal/juridical; questions of blackmail; intimidation and surveillance.

d. the function of violence or murder; how it is a systematic tool of repression; how it has a long and continuing history; how it is a function of the maintenance of privilege and how, in this way, it relates to the question of a pervasive violence against women, the third world and finally, the working class: state power; individual terrorist murder, political terrorist murder (the toothpaste scrawled on the mirror with the message "Fags must die. . ."); relation of all this to the discourse of graffiti that presents us with the threat of death.

e. relation of interior/exterior violence, the question of violence within the community itself; relation of violence in the community to demands for changing the male socialization process; linking this with women's anti-rape struggles; reform of sex/gender instruction in the schools; how concepts of gay "violence" get ideologically and legally exploited, instead of being seen as the interiorization of the violence of straight society against us; parallels of "self-violence" on the part of Black people, women, etc.

AN ORGANIZATION AND AN ORGANIZATIONAL ACTIVITY

Against this theoretical background and with an awareness of the need to implement action, the need for a new and appropriate organization becomes apparent. How would we describe such an organization?

Implicitly the theory and practices just outlined critique past and existing organizations as either reformist on the one hand or ultra-left on the other. Organizations, mainly gay lib in orientation, that are most evident in mass work, the marches, demonstrations etc., are also those that tend to have been coopted to reformist goals: gay rights generally, single issue causes etc.

They promote little long-term awareness of possible future developments of our movement organizations and have only a limited consciousness of our links with other liberation and class struggles. But on the other hand there is a critique to be made against left-sectarian and gay left-sectarian political organizations as well. This critique must be made on the grounds of a generally instrumental approach to the gay movement that has failed to recognize our specificity. Such organizations generally have seen little need in principle for an autonomous gay movement. As a result they have characteristically pressed for the integration of gays as a group into the working-class struggle and into the working-class political organizations or parties. Effectively this would mean the dissolution of any autonomous gay movement as such, a demand which would only be a disaster as far as gays are concerned. Our critiques must be made against the liquidationist and instrumentalizing approaches of the sectarian parties too.

But how would a new organization such as the one we are proposing see itself concretely? First of all it would recognize that it would have a limited term of usefulness, probably a decade or less. Secondly, it wouldn't attempt to be a mass organization. It would rather be a small group of socialists and socialist-oriented gay men whose commitment lay in strengthening and consolidating an autonomous gay movement toward greater long-term consciousness (and toward an awareness of the eventual need for convergence, first, with other liberation groups, and then with a future communist movement) on the terrain of educational and agitational activities in the ghetto itself, and organized around the actually felt needs of members of the community as they express such needs. Such an organization would have the highest respect for the self-experience of the community and would organize in areas like those we have already described. It would work through community organizing activity work to raise community consciousness to an ability to see beyond reformism. It would, however, never attempt to "recruit" either for workers' organizations or for political organizations.

Such an organization would need trained and skilled persons willing to work on a variety of educational tasks in a variety of areas. These areas would include: demonstrations, posters, tracts and other educational activity that linked up our movement with feminists, union organizing etc., low-key social and cultural events like dances, clubs and so on, information booths and speakers bureau, films and film discussions, forums on local events, etc. High priority in all this would be assigned to relations with the women's movement, the workers' movement and the third world.

There would be an important place in this organization for theoretical work, particularly relating to the areas mentioned as well as elaborating historical questions relating to the gay movement and formulating a theory of the ghetto in more detail. To implement work of this kind we would see the need for a theoretical journal and on a more informal level, a newsletter. Conferences might be convened when useful and we would take for granted an exchange of all materials produced.

An organization of this kind could exist locally and autonomously, but there isn't any reason why such organizations should not have close connections with each other from city to city and region to region.

San Francisco, October 1979

POSTSCRIPT, JANUARY '81

A year and a half passed since this was written (after talks with and suggestions from Alex Wilson and Robbie Schwartzwald at the 2nd Marxist Literary Group summer institute, 1979), and I now feel its possible deficiencies in two areas. First, the analysis comes close to suggesting that the conditions of the gay community are a simple "function" or "expression" of capitalism—an economic reduction. I'm not happy with the objection but don't know what to do with it right now. Second, the proposals, or program, should have been more adequately developed. This I agree with and would add that the need to form coalitions, particularly with minority communities, should have been stressed more strongly. In spite of these two criticisms, I hope the pamphlet may have some usefulness in furthering discussions among gay activists about where our movement is going.

"Toward a Gay Theory for the '80s" was published as a mimeographed pamphlet, typeset by Terry Ludwar (Vancouver, February 1981).

WRITING, POWER AND ACTIVITY

1.

Modernism, particularly in its completed forms in recent trends in poetry, can only be understood and validated, partly or wholly or not at all, insofar as these same trends represent a specifically utopian moment in language. Charles Bernstein's essay on "The Dollar Value of Poetry" reminds us of this. "Social force," Bernstein says citing Simone Weil, "is bound to be accompanied by lies." Poetry then can refuse to be in the service of capitalism by being "untranslatable," "unparaphrasable." In a commodity society, we might say, poetry can refuse an exchange-value to make itself available as use-value, or to use another term, text(-uality). Recent trends in poetry can be described as the attempt to deny this commodity aspect of language.

How far should we go in this project? The question is not simple. It implies that the project is historically conditioned, and developmental, and that at a certain point it will have to be thought through again when objective conditions change. In the last analysis the reciprocity between what writing *is* and what it *ought to be* becomes a question of what writing actually does, that is, politics. To judge from a plurality of practices like that of this magazine, the imperative to formulate writing questions politically is recognized more and more widely—and what is more important, by poets themselves. To place ourselves in this discussion then in the last analysis seems to be to ask how writing can relate to revolution, that is, class and liberal struggles. But not in any simplistic way. What is at stake here is the ability to give full play to the two poles of instrumentality and self-referentiality. Until the present, though, it has been generally assumed that it is the second of these poles, the self-referential aspect of language, that ought to give writing its self-nature and legitimacy for others.

But it is hard to imagine how this question, phrased in just such a way, can avoid having an eternal, once-and-for-all aspect to it. Posing the question in this way, one doesn't so easily arrive at history. If indeed a utopian content were the only criterion of what a useful and acceptable writing has been or continues to be, finding writing that didn't embody that criterion would become a difficulty interesting only to the most incurable of scholastics.

Maybe we can sharpen this question by rephrasing it. Is it possible to imagine a modernism that doesn't assimilate itself into the project of symptomatic reading? That is to say, into a humanism. But what about the struggle then? Taking sides? Being *parti pris*? Or are these concerns out of date in our formalist era? Of course one assumes they are not. But *if* they are not, it's hard to see how they wouldn't be instrumental concerns. If all literature expresses and embodies a yearning for a non-alienated future, it isn't clear in the balance how aspirations for participatory writerliness—a readerly praxis—do not end as subjective improvements that may become indispensable to reaction itself. This possibility poses a useful limit case. For it once more foregrounds the political.

Literary history is in a sense the enumeration of past consensuses of this problem that are no longer seen as viable. Romanticism and the cult of the artist. Symbolism and alienated utopia. Modernism and the fetishization of language as product. Described in this way, however, the trajectory is one that grows increasingly melancholy. In each of these stages literature has more and more radically narrowed its rights to the public participation in the ongoing construction of society by itself—inseparable from power. A profound disjunction that has proved favorable neither to power nor to literature. Yet both continue to influence each other, fascinate each other, and their uneasy attractiveness seems to register the uneven development of revolution itself. This specific inability to think writing as power at one and the same time then comes to have a name. It is false consciousness.

2.

So perhaps we can start again and understand writing, poetry, as developed in our time as a *critique of power*. Such a critique—a denigration or disavowal—can now be usefully described and evaluated from a political-historical perspective. The refusal of the moment of power in the transition stage to socialism becomes objectively regressive or even reactionary as the refusal of contestation. Simultaneously, though, this refusal names the utopian content of a later period. But in the transition to this later time—communism—critique of power takes on the positive meaning and no longer functions regressively. It becomes instead the means of expediting a passing over to the era of history proper, to the dismantling of the state and its apparatuses and to the first general realization of a human social life. The legitimacy of writing as a critique of power then stands or fails in relation to its historical timeliness in utopian struggles. In periods when legitimate demands are given utopian formulations, the anti-instrumental character of this kind of writing gives it a definite progressive function. In an era of class struggle, however, when political demands take on instrumental complexion, such a writing may come to seem less useful. At this point writing may often become propaganda. Yet there are strong indications from our own time that the model has been broken down and that these either-or formulations have been simply bypassed.

This is the dilemma. Modernism's alliance with terrorism and disorder has become irrelevant precisely to the extent that communistic or utopian possibilities have begun to make their presence felt in collective, durable political formulations in objective associations with the working class. And to that degree that these new utopian forces make themselves felt politically, writing is to that extent forced to rethink its abdication from power. By a consensual removal of itself to the margins of the public sphere of commodity production—in order to privilege utopian demands for use-value—writing historically founded its notion of self-legitimacy on a reintegration in the communist future. But what if in a variety of regions and in germinal form that future has *already* begun to make its appearance in the advanced capitalist countries in the West?

3.

All this of course is to speak once more of the cultural revolution, and to ask again if any legacy remains 10 years after Maoism, May of '68 in Paris, the anti-war days of the '60s and Counterculture, and the Prague Spring. . .

What has happened? In 10 years objectively anarcho-communist forms of political organization have sprung up and proliferated wherever one looks.

Feminism and the gay movement, ecology and anti-nuclear movements—in Europe and in this country both—power issues on a municipal level, consumer and tenants' movements, the large-scale prison movement and so on—a whole spectrum of liberation organizations has now arisen. Their impact has been to raise issues in mass political organizations, such that their solution is not possible within a program advancing a demand for socialism alone, but only on the basis of one making radical demands *beyond* that—to communism, in fact.

Within this perspective one might legitimately ask if the solution of writing and writers can still remain what it has been programmatically—that is, a political absence validated by the notion of a critique of power in an autonomous writing area. Early in the 19th Century this was the concordant reached between writing and society, an agreement according to which society's writing practice was from then on to seem something other than self-expression. But if this agreement is now seen as renegotiable, we will need another conceptual model in order to do it. For writing's renunciation of instrumental values in regard to language will continue to imply the negotiation of an attempt at power as long as writing and power are seen in a relation of mutual exclusivity. If, in other words, writing must always be either on the side of utopia or on the side of instrumentality. And if—more radically—class and liberation struggles are to persist in regarding each other with stares of non-recognition. In this case surely writing would remain exterior to power, and power to writing. But what if the situation were to change? What if at a certain point in history, class struggle were to begin to have a doubly implicated relationship with human liberation struggle? And what if human history had begun to think socialism and communism *globally* and *at the same time?*—and here the work of Rudolf Bahro might be seen as dramatic indicator of these very possibilities. If one were to be able to think the situation in some such way as this, one could also conceive of the possibility of some collective intellectual work existing on its own behalf. Rather than instrumentality for another, writing's relation to power would then be self-expression. This new model would have profound implications for the norms and forms of writing as now practiced. For writing's 'eternal,' or unreflected, premise has been that the notion of writing for another and that of writing as a commodity are in reality one and the same thing—an understanding that has made modernism possible. But let us suppose for a moment that the situation has changed. Let us suppose that this binary description is no longer adequate to the course of events. Writing now grounds itself in an *interior* relation to power. It becomes a self-expression, and a group practice. With this supposition writing's past is simply the series of discrete moments, salvageable enclaves or testimonials to what is still to come. Its present on the other hand becomes the collective intellectual practice one is engaged in at any moment. Writing would not be separate from whatever one does as an intellectual—in the body of those who both think and act, and who stand in a certain tendential, final relation to the Modern Prince. That is how this reality might be mapped in the present. And here one can already see certain points of possible focus. There are probably very ordinary or predictable areas like work in mass or sectarian organizations, critical and educational outputs, the construction of political narration or what-have-you. In all this play would be supposed. This writing would be instrumental in a new way, certainly, but never in a sense that didn't say 'we' that wasn't freely willed. It probably wouldn't get along with commissars.

Naturally one supposes that this writing has begun and that it is only a question of locating it—and that each can begin finding it in her life or his. It is impossible to assume that this writing has not already begun in places one visits each day. Writers, in this view, are simply people engaged in teaching, political organization, community work and liberation groups, and so on—in fact in normal activities we are already engaged in. This is the opposite of modernism and écriture. Above all, a writing like the one I am supposing accepts its relation to power. It knows it has no other choice. But in this it feels tremendously exuberant, at the thought of the possibilities opening before it. And it knows too, it is embarked.

"Writing Power Activity" was first published in $L=A=N=G=U=A=G=E$ no. 9/10. (October 1979) and was subsequently republished in *The $L=A=N=G=U=A=G=E$ Book* (Carbondale: Southern Illinois UP, 1984).

WRITING'S CURRENT IMPASSE
AND THE POSSIBILITIES FOR RENEWAL

In contrast with the socially conscious writers of the 30s many of us who are left or left oriented writers today see ourselves as historically advantaged. We make comparisons and assume we've benefited. Current attitudes suppose that our marxism is 'objective,' while theirs was a kind of belief, quasi-religious in tone. Yet it remains an odd situation when left writers do not see a kinship with other left writers who preceded them. It's more than likely that our rejection of this earlier age is made possible by a symmetrical ignorance of ours, a reluctance to challenge our own assumptions about writing and thinking, our own belief systems. We acknowledge the political activity of that earlier age willingly enough, but we're less generous when it comes to their writing style—a crude literary Stalinism, we suppose. From Granville Hicks and the middle-class Communists or fellow travelling highbrow critics to Mike Gold and the John Reed proletarians, most of the left writers of that time seem uncomfortably tainted with the serious political errors of 'illusionism,' 'psychology' and 'reductionism.' Sartre himself in the late 40s would condemn socialist realism for these same qualities—while making sure to acknowledge the need for commitment. But these literary assumptions may need a re-examination at a new level. As we begin the 80s, there are indications that something has gone wrong for us and that the left modernism of the last decade has painted itself into an increasingly constricted, academic corner from which it has yet to emerge with any new claims to relevancy.

Many of the dominant ideas about what writing should be stem from Sartre's old opponent, Roland Barthes—received ideas about writerly autonomy, textuality and the values of pleasure, for instance. It's important to note this source since a context is provided in this way historically. Such a genealogy can begin to lay the problem out, and we can see what these principles once stood for. What was at issue then—in the structuralist debates—was the basic explanatory power of historical thought. Especially in the exciting and pace-setting sciences of anthropology and linguistics there were growing indications that the human or social sciences would have to jettison their traditional causalist pre-suppositions and assumptions just as surely as physics and the physical sciences had done. As the awareness of these developments reached the literary arena, it was clear that here too assumptions were being made that would have to be challenged. At the center of the controversy arguing against Sartre's dictation of a committed or goal-oriented literature was Roland Barthes. Literary assumptions changed, and Barthes became de facto leader of the new structuralist theory and practice. Under Barthes' influence, writers began criticizing their collective past. Structuralism showed how the links between any historical past and our ways of thinking about that past are tenuous at best or non-existent. All this was applied to literature. Perhaps the past was even a kind of projection we made from our own standpoint; but if so, a committed writing became problematic in the extreme. Writing had to assume these connections in order to be politically and morally effective—so that now the whole edifice of an engaged writing was seriously called into question. It appeared that events could act as witnesses only afterwards, when they could be called to the stand and asked to give narratives, tell stories. From this new way of thinking a new writing practice developed, one that accented language values in literature and writing's pleasure aspect, one that devalued writing's purposefulness. This is the writing we know as ours. In it writing's previous goal-orientation is fully cancelled and writing accepts itself as a production of micro-occurrences and short-term destinies.

The reasons for this are not difficult to understand. No one loves a bureaucracy anymore, and writing a proletarian novel these days would in many ways be the equivalent of joining a sect. For many socialists the writerly scandal of bureaucratic deformations involves events that cannot be dismissed without discussion—Czechoslovakia, Cambodia, Afghanistan and so on. These events have called into question the bureaucratic stage of socialism; they imply the need to rethink marxism in the direction of democracy. For left writers now there is, as a result, a growing intuition that the search for a new writing must unquestionably include feminism, democracy and the acceptance of the erotic as basic assumptions, without which a left writing project would inevitably fail. Left writing today, it appears, must not simply further socialism, but must also criticize power, and if possible do both together. To the extent it succeeds, it registers a gain, becoming necessarily anti-authoritarian, pleasure-loving and non-dismissive. So doing, writing mirrors the era. It advances to an historical stage and in an historical direction of some promise.

But a left writing of this description has failed to materialize. It remains what ought to have been attempted rather than what really was tried. Instead of both criticizing power and furthering socialism, the writing which did eventuate from the late 60s—our writing—has concerned itself far more with the critique of power than with an advocacy of socialism—bracketed as too 'thematic,' concerned with content. As a result, our left writing of the 70s has had its characteristic deformation. It has become 'textual' at the price of abandoning any specific political tasks. As techniques of randomness have come to characterize this writing project, its social functions are no longer clear. In its intent our writing of course remains transformative, but in its practice it has become—alas!—integrative. Our project's self-definition of itself as science has cut it off from any real and public feeling life. It's doubtful whether left modernist writing can be called 'left' any more. But shouldn't this be a cause for dismay—perhaps even alarm? For if our writing is no longer to have social effects, why do we write? These questions are urgent ones, I think. They involve understanding our origins first of all. They also involve understanding our current situation in politics and society.

How did the left modernist project first begin—and what were its goals? A beginning in the discussion might well involve a more frank assessment of modernism's relation to the Bolshevik Revolution. It ought to be candidly noted that modernism's ties with Revolution seem closer retrospectively than was the case at the time. If there was an alliance involved, it was more with anarchist, experimentalist and workerist trends than with more orthodox statist and Leninist currents. On any balance sheet of the modernist movement, it is true, we would have to note modernism's characteristic anti-capitalism—but in some way qualify it too. For the question of modernism's ties with fascism in other countries remains a sign of its unequal development. Certainly the various modernisms took their several paths, from futurism in Italy to vorticism in England to formalism in Russia and the young USSR, etc.. In its last development, modernism has become a writing practice familiar to us in our own time and country as a deconstructive practice, a systematic attempt to demystify and come to terms with language as a commodity force. This is the variant that is now the *koine* of left writing. As a trajectory, it has shape and curve—and we can describe it. It is a writing that has historically stood in opposition to the alienation and exploitation of human and language resources by the modern state. It can be described as anti-capitalist but not always in a benign sense, given its sometime fascist connections. Above all the modernist protest and project has been structurally anti-bureaucratic; its most typifying demand has been for a return of basic emotions and perceptions to a grounding in human experience and an attack on statist substitutes for this in deformed language and in the extension of the control mechanisms of industrial discipline into broader currents of social life. For modernism, Bolshevism—and sometimes fascism—seemed in this sense 'anti-capitalist.' Both denounced the alienation of previously untouched areas of social life by bureaucracies with totalizing goals. But in this development modernism's links with the working-class have been tenuous. So that modernism—even in its left modernist, committed variant—has remained basically utopian in character—an expression of hopes, a collection of protests and documentation of spiritual distress in capitalist times rather than a program for meeting needs, expressing the demand for social change.

But it's appropriate to think of a modernism that might be more successful. One with perhaps a more genuinely popular character. We might think of a modernism with community and collective dimensions for instance. Might this not be a modernism too?—only one perhaps more readily adapted to social struggle. The determinant element in this might well be the intensive effort to give the forms and codes of community and collective life a transformative shape with topical or local signification—with thematic 'content' in other words.

As an aspiration of course the idea, as applied to modernism, wouldn't exactly be new; and its roots certainly would go back to the 30s in our country. For what was critical for large scale left writing practice then—irrespective of how inept or unrealized—was the effort to give precisely this transformative character to group speech at every level, from broad-based community codes to the sophisticated, technical codes of the intelligentsia. The writer's basic connection had in some way to be with group life. Naturally the reasons for this varied. But for nearly a decade writing in the United States was colored in some way or other by this basic orientation.

And in this sense the left writers' movement was much closer in spirit to Russian modernism than the original modernism was to the socialist realist movement that followed it. In spite of organizational or Party ties not even the crudest of the American writers (Gold would be a good example) were ever bureaucrats in any literal sense. But that of course is exactly what the Soviet writers were. In America—unless you were the editor of the *New Masses*—you weren't on anyone's payroll and you didn't stand to benefit from any advantages that might accrue to you from a State. Soviet writers by contrast might hope not only for rewards but for advancement—into an apparatus, etc. The reasons of opportunism for a writer's association with the Communist movement in this country were slight or non-existent. Not that there wouldn't be neurotic or other rather unattractive reasons instead. But by and large and historically in the American left writers of this period there was a compelling aspiration, a real need to relate to the group life of the times. And at least for a short time during our literary history that need often superseded personal ones.

The drawbacks of the period remain drawbacks of course—and needn't be rehearsed again. There are on the other hand definite lessons to be learned from these literary predecessors. Preeminent among them is the practical lesson. Inside the Party or alongside it the intellectuals and writers of the time quite simply *had* to learn certain organizational skills or would have been of no use in advancing the causes and social movements they chose to support—and they very quickly did learn these skills. They propagandized and polemicized. They formed commissions and investigated. They attended congresses, they issued reports. This activity set the tone for an era. What practically resulted was an increase in a mass awareness that society was divided along class lines and—a bit later—a more urgent consciousness of the need for a 'United Front' against fascism. Many writers participated in these struggles only briefly—and with real contradictions and misunderstandings—but what they gained for themselves, for however short the period, was a relation to the life of ordinary people, their deepest hopes and aspirations, to the large American society from which historically they had excluded themselves. For the first time—if there were precedents they were weak or half-forgotten—American writers were in a real, not a factitious relation to the masses of their fellow Americans. Writers had come to be in good faith and were once again part of society. This one overriding fact must have meant a great deal. To judge from the plethora of memoirs from this period, when writers wrote with social goals at the time they felt themselves alive, many of them, for the first time. I think it would be difficult to overestimate this feeling. To the extent that the left modernism of today feels itself discouraged, academic or tangential to current life, it must to this same degree stand in marked contrast to that earlier time. A relation to life is all-important for writing. The writing of the 30s for that reason has valuable lessons for us—as we begin with some confusion to face the 80s.

Now it is not altogether true that our own period remains ignorant of the problem, and certain trends in left modernism have begun gradually to recognize the existence of this critique. This has come about mainly through feminism and gay writing—as writing that 'criticizes power' as well as contains expressive political dimensions. Thus in some segments of the modernist movement biographical and autobiographical modes of writing now seem interesting—but in an abstract way. Even textual writing has itself begun to gravitate toward biography, narrative even. Again, there is the special place for criticism in left modernism. Here we can see politics appearing, surprisingly, as theme—that is, a technical discourse of specialists lending the text a certain worldly cachet. These correctives unfortunately are hardly radical. They allude to social life but do not express it, and their politics remain abstract.

Though there are certainly qualifications and reservations to be made, the earlier aspirations of left writers for a relation to social life once more makes the need for 'Americanism' in our current writing goals not only thinkable, but desirable. The writing of the 30s becomes a paradigm. This is true whether the left writers in question were 'proletarian' or 'middle class' in their backgrounds, and it becomes critical as the decade wears on. After the so-called Third Period of Communism (1928-1935), the restricted and aggressive marxism of the post-Lenin years gave way to the broader, alliance-minded United Front era (1935-1939). Shortly after the 7th Congress of the Communist International, the American Party began to open its doors to popular, Americanist and radical currents— and in not too selective a fashion intellectuals and middle-class writers now associated themselves with what seemed in many ways the leading movement of the times, a progressive movement that fought for the rights of workers, expressed the yearning of most Americans for a better national life and—perhaps most important of all—led the anti-fascist struggle, at least until the Hitler-Stalin pact.

In time, however, the Party's Americanism became dubious or discredited. After all, how far could one go? Granville Hicks' 1938 *I Like America*— written while Hicks was still in the Party and presumably expressive of the Party line—brought the uncomfortable problem of patriotism to the fore. It remained for Earl Browder, the Party's General Secretary, to take the line to its logical—but still surprising—conclusion. 'Communism is Twentieth Century Americanism,' Browder had announced, and in 1944 at Browder's urging the Party was dissolved, to become the 'Communist Political Association.' Two years after, Browder was read out of the Party, after publication of the Duclos letter. But the damage was done. The Party's revisionism brought it and the Left with it into a troublesome disrespect. As the New Left was later to wonder—in the 60s and 70s—to what extent is the Party, as historical representative of the American left, still to be considered revolutionary? To what extent is this a result of a turn toward 'Americanism,' or populism?

But the limits of Americanism were revealed in writing as well. Additionally, the implications of the Moscow Trials and other unsavory aspects of Russian statism were beginning to make themselves felt. Writers began to leave the Party in droves; fellow travelers retreated once more to their private concerns. Many even ended as anti-Communists—John Dos Passos, Howard Fast and others. Others still, the Trotskyist sympathizers like Edmund Wilson and the *Partisan Review* group, were to become the Liberals of the Cold War years. Objectively these desertions from the Communist movement may be justified; yet the phenomenon remains a disturbing one—in spite of the Stalinism and revisionism which may have been its enabling cause. The swing toward Americanism on the part of the writers of this period was important as a corrective against the formalist currents which had preceded it. As the Communist influence on national life began to ebb, these writers followed suit, retrenched and took up their mostly private concerns. From the vantage point of our time it's difficult not to conclude that the ideals to which these writers had committed themselves were in some way inadequate from the beginning. Their ideals were not just Americanist—but Stalinist and authoritarian as well.

A fair review of the literature of the time can hardly avoid the observation that it was, in fact, through and through authoritarian, sexist in its implications and blatantly homophobic. This is, in addition, not an unfair critique of the Left to which it was allied. The problem of the writing of the period may even be seen, for simplicity's sake, as the problem of the CP in this period. Like the Party, writers felt themselves in a sort of double relation to the masses. They were part of this large grouping and expressed it, but they were also above it, leading. And to the degree that they became the 'leaders' of the writing movement of their day, these writers, like the Party 'leading elements,' were drawn to authoritarian satisfactions. In the absence of objective self-interest in allying themselves with the Socialist movement— and writers and other middle-class intellectuals were notorious for joining the movement for reasons of idealism or self-sacrificing humanitarianism— it would have been difficult or impossible not to have expected these writers to compensate for real considerations with some concessions to pretense or bullying. Or this could become something like pedantry. "Oh, we could preach sermons on Sunday," Earl Browder remarked of writers allied with the Party, "but for the intellectuals every day was Sunday." But in a sense this was natural. For these intellectuals and middle-class writers lacked any organic connection between the collective interests of their own and working class interests. But questions as to whether this situation might have been otherwise are probably speculative. The period was what it was.

The important exception was the United Front, which Dimitroff had proclaimed at the Seventh Congress. In this struggle against the terrible new movement of Germany, Italy and elsewhere, there was a great deal of self-interest for writers. They had direct—visceral—reasons for struggling against this movement, and every day the reasons became clearer. With an awareness of events then taking place in Germany and elsewhere intellectuals instinctively knew that a successful fascism would make the continuation of their pursuit of a life choice as intellectuals or writers difficult if not impossible. Their choice of themselves and fascism, they realized, were mutually self-exclusive. Additionally, many of these same intellectuals and writers were Jewish. And on that score clearly they had if possible still more urgent reasons for combatting fascism and allying themselves with a Communist-led United Front. Here at last was an *organic* relation to the progressive movement on the part of intellectuals and writers. With a United Front politic, motivations of guilt, self-sacrifice and so on were temporarily suspended. There was no need for such motivations. As a writer you were fighting in your own interest.

This 'organic' exception to the typically idealist relation of writers to the left movement of the 30s gives us a clue, I believe, to the re-evaluation of the period for our own purposes. Left writing in that time can be said to have been successful to the extent that it had organic—rather than idealistic—relations with the left movement as a whole. Empathy is not, and was not, enough. As an intellectual or writer you have to speak *as a leftist* from that viewpoint, from the viewpoint of the intellectual and writer. Otherwise the characteristic faults of your writing are likely to be those that typify the left writing of the 30s—a too frequent pedantry, moralism or authoritarianism.

The left writing of our own period ought to question what its own best interests are. If it does so, it may well see that its intellectuals have a continuing interest in the critique of power. That struggle of course will still target language commodification as its special enemy. But aren't our interests wider here than we have suspected? The fight against language alienation, it appears, is only a part of the story, one instance among many in the ongoing fight against the relations of subalternity.

"Writing's Current Impasse and the Possibilities for Renewal" first appeared in *Open Letter* 5.1 / *L=A=N=G=U=A=G=E* vol. 4, edited by Bruce Andrews and Charles Bernstein (Winter 1982).

LANGUAGE WRITING:
THE PLUSES & MINUSES OF THE NEW FORMALISM

It's not that the current Language Writing movement doesn't succeed on its own terms. It excels on that terrain—abstraction, language experimentation and so on. But it isn't what you would call an *engaged* writing and as a moment it suffers from some serious defects for this reason. And for the same reason, it gives you the feeling of being rather distant from life. It's as if the genuine intelligence you feel there ends up eluding life, not participating in it or embracing it.

The most recent issue of *Hills* magazine (a double issue, 6/7; 36 Clyde St., SF, CA 94017; 217 pages, $5) is a frustrating and dazzling example of this—intelligence of a high order, but misdirected. The *Hills* issue is given the title *Talks*, and the talks collected here—performances, lectures, and informal chats—are the relatively unedited transcriptions from Bob Perelman's local 'Talks Series,' begun in spring of 1977 and still continuing. It's a substantial and comprehensive offering by itself, but since only 11 of the 29 talks that were given are reproduced here, there probably will be more volumes of 'Talks' later. Those which are presented are diverse in viewpoint but characteristically abstract.

The first thing that should be said is that this abstraction is probably a good thing. The 'Talks Series' has been quite influential and stimulated theory discussions, where often anti-intellectualism has been the rule. The 'talks' reproduced aren't fussy either. There's one place in the anthology that I positively dislike, by William Graves on Pope, but aside from that there aren't any that are 'academic' or frivolous. They are serious attempts to develop a common writing project. Characteristically, it is true, they resort to technical ways of saying things and probably that is objectionable in a public format. The objections to 'obscurity' are more serious because I think they are really political ones—but I'll go more into this later. The implication of these charges is that there is too much elitism in these writings and that if the Language Writers want to be political, they should make their politics deal more with the actual world. It's not that you can't do theory, according to this way of thinking, but you have to make your theory have actual consequences. So what *is* the theory of the Language

Writers? The virtue of publication of these *Hills Talks* is to explain that theory as comprehensively as possible.

It's quite interesting that Bill Berkson's talk starts things off, since Berkson hasn't particularly been known as a Language Poet. It gives you a sense that whatever this 'Language Writing' is, it isn't just confined to Language Writers. It's a general direction in writing. Right from the beginning in Berkson's talk what's noticeable is the keynoting of technical aspects in writing. Berkson stresses the idea of talking or talks as almost a new genre or at least area of experimentation. He illustrates this rather provocatively with a commentary on a Frank O'Hara letter to him. This gets compared with the anecdotal pieces in O'Hara's poetry—poems like "Biotherm" and "Second Avenue"—as examples of 'talk' concerns. A discussion period follows this talk, as is usually the case with this series. Here the idea surfaces that 'you can talk about anything, everything is OK' and that O'Hara is the great example of this. Then there's a demur from Erica Hunt, who questions this as self-indulgence. Unfortunately this objection doesn't seem to get developed as far as it should. Can a person *always* 'say what they want, when they want to'? in other words, doesn't language have consequences (think of the recent controversies over racist and sexist films like *Windows, Charlie Chan* and *Cruising*)? What should have been happening in this discussion was more explicitness, more directness, about the consequences of these various points of view. One example of a movement towards this directness was a recent writing panel at 80 Langton St., where the problem of the social implications of role models came up—Erica Hunt speaking in favor of a normative approach and Kathy Acker taking an 'Autonomist'/anarchist position. It is this sort of discussion that should happen more often.

This reminds me of a moment in another discussion, the one after David Bromige's talk on "Intuition and Poetry." Bob Perelman raises an interesting question about consequences in language by bringing up the limit case when writing *has no social responsibility at all.* He's speaking to the poet Michael Palmer:

> Michael, I wanted to ask you: Are there examples of writers whose intentions are perfectly clear who you can still read?

> When you really dope out the intention does the writing cease
> to be interesting to you?

This isn't a dumb question, and there's a lot at stake. But somehow this question gets dealt with more and more abstractly as the discussion continues and other poets involve themselves. It gets to be technical. The question becomes whether a writing "intends" or not toward a person's own life. Well, of course it does! Only this way of phrasing things is just frighteningly selective because it remains so silent about the social origins and social goals of writing.

Yet it's interesting to me that it's Perelman—among many other poets there—who raises the question in the first place. He's the Language Writer that seems most intuitively aware of social dimensions in things (though Ron Silliman is in a more abstract way). And it's Perelman whose poetry I like the most. I think it's quite good. It's larger and more complex than most of this writing, tangibly sensitive, quite beautiful.

And actually this last quality troubles me. Beauty has become problematic, it's difficult to know how to behave in its presence. Reading Bob Perelman's work, his poetry at least, gives me satisfactions I can't express except in doubtful forms. "A sweet singer," "an inspired lyricist!"—in short, suspect exclamations of another era. I liked his earlier *Braille* (Ithaca House, 1975) and the new *a.k.a.* (Tuumba Press, 1979) but mostly the *7 Works* (The Figures, 1978). Something in this poetry is close to the life of *things*, not their explanations and to that extent, I think, is something that doubts the Language Poetry program.

Still, Perelman, whether he "is" a Language Poet or "isn't" one, seems to be the one who comes closest to thinking about history as a problem in— and of—his poetry. I think his phrase "road tones" is something like a sense of purposefulness in things ("hodos" is road, so this is what "hodological space" really means in philosophy). In a poem of the same title he says of these "road tones":

> In the prime of their loveliness
> they fall from the aether into
> books. They are mistaken

for one's own hands, and are used
freely from one generation to the next.

These are new feelings in language formalism. When the poet Frank O'Hara tried out this position it became outright modernism and the "unrecapturable nostalgia for nostalgia" once evoked in the period of "In Memory of My Feelings." But I think Perelman is up to something a little different. O'Hara's fear was that modernism would lead to death, his hope was that it wouldn't. For Perelman on the other hand, it's as if modernism is *already* how you have things. So the only tack you take is to write about them as if they were all absent. And then—only then!—it all gushes back again, hot and heavy. You can have it all again, the heavy syrup, the songs, the love, all of it. Including Keats.

Of course in this stance there's something to make you a little giddy—and that is planned too. Ironic vertigo—a text/metatext operation liberally sprinkled with perfumes. But it's a spectacle or show, and you can't participate. Loving what he presents, Bob Perelman wants you to see it's factitious, or made-up, and that you shouldn't want it to be more than that. Accept it. Here's the little white lie he wants you to understand at the beginning of his prose piece called "Autobiography"—

Everyone keeps shouting in my ears. But rest assured, dear Papa, that these are my own sentiments and have not been borrowed from any one.

They *have* to course. And that is the point. They're borrowed—from some mythical storehouse of language treasures of the past. The images, language fragments, feelings, structure, everything. That's why there's this sadness and humor, letters of a "Persian" at a distance from his native clime. Sometimes the quoting is even official. If you open *7 Works* to the first page you find out that "Vienna: A Correspondence" is taken "mostly from the letters of Mozart and his family." Bob Perelman does pastiche as well as anyone I know. That's what makes me uneasy—the meaning gets produced as, well, 'afterlife.'

And what about narrative in Perelman's writing? Here my uneasiness mounts by leaps and bounds. It's a "buried narrative" with quote marks around it, so you don't mistake it from human life. Not surprisingly, it's awfully funny and sardonic. If a little like Krazy Kat, this for instance—

> I name the things after the words that sponsor them. He normally knew little of the depths below daily consciousness, except for what the shifting weights and tones of the immediate senses never fail to lay out over long periods drifting across the whole thing. I'm afraid I didn't catch . . . He fell off a log.

—there's also a directness like Marx parodying German philosophy with a feeling for home truths. "He fell off a log." Well, he *should* have, with all that philosophizing! In *a.k.a.,* from which the above is taken, this crisis of representation—for that is what it really is—gets taken to extremes, and for the first time the actual magnitude of the disaster is glimpsed. It's global. There isn't an aspect of narrative that isn't entirely subverted, and storytelling becomes a convertible function on the capitalist model. So pronouns exchange for pronouns, tenses for tenses and so on. What's being said about narrative is this—things don't come from other things, they just follow them. You can tell your story beginning where you want. Now all this is very beautiful and very sad and more than a little true, I think. But it also misses some real basics in human life that everybody has. After all, we should sometimes be angry, eat and drink and take pleasure without a surfeit of thinking, and in the end face death without too much fear. And that is missing.

Yet I think Bob Perelman should take a great deal of credit for *knowing* it is missing and trying to do something about it—a position I don't find in other Language Poetry. Perelman for that reason remains the most intelligent writer among them. The rationale for his poetry occurs in a theoretical piece of his own included in the *Talks* anthology called "The First Person." Using the language of French structuralism Perelman's essay is an attempt to deal with both the social and the individual in life fully, to the neglect of neither. In technical terms this turns out to be the famous distinction of Ferdinand de Saussure's between *language* and *parole*—language as an abstraction and real talking, or "language" and "speaking" as Perelman says. Like the structuralists before them many of the Language

Writers are a bit suspicious of the *parole* side of things and seem to prefer the *language* aspect. And this naturally means you will tend to be abstract—rather than concrete or historical. Perelman puts himself squarely on the fence in this debate. He wants to have both sides—in tension. In this sense he cites Creeley and Gertrude Stein as prototypes. He admires the way they give expression to these two aspects of language, creating antagonisms and then—hopeful antinomies. Pound and Olson he finds mostly problematic here (I never liked them much myself), and O'Hara seems to be mostly a success story. William Stafford (Perelman does an analysis of a tendentious poem of Stafford's called "Travelling Through the Dark") is the appropriate whipping-boy—a horrendous example of what goes wrong if the speaking side of language is emphasized to the exclusion of the abstract side. Academic illusionism is what happens when poetry's *artifacted* nature isn't constantly apparent.

At the end of the essay Perelman makes the transition to his own writing. He wants a kind of tension between both these sides of language, playing off one pole against the other. But he remains doubtful it can really be done. Answering Barrett Watten in the discussion period after this talk he remarks—

> What I was trying to do here, and it can't be done, is to identify—and any writer does this—is to identify with the language in your head, which you can't do, because it's not any identity.

Barrett Watten represents a more straightforwardly abstract pole of Language Writing, and his essay on "Russian Formalism & the Present" is probably the most informative of these talks in its historical dimension. Watten's intent is to legitimize Language Poetry as an extension of Russian Formalism. For this perspective he lays out the Formalist project in some detail. Russian Formalism, he shows, was a program to deconstruct the illusionism of language at that historical stage, using a pedagogy of shock to disabuse people of the myths that words were "equal to" things, that language could ever "represent" reality, and that bourgeois ideals like the sense of self or identity could ever actually be found. The Formalists, Watten points out, wanted to show us how language as it exists is deformed and commodified, how it suits the Capitalist system all too well.

So far so good. Only what is Watten saying about our own era? Like a number of other historical answers it is akin to, defamiliarization or ostraneine was a call to see things as they are, rather than as they are names. In this it's related to Rimbaud's systematic disturbance of the senses, Blake's cleansing of the doors of perception, Brecht's alienation. Words used in new ways can have a certain shock value, a negative charge to upset normal ways of "seeing" what we think we see. And according to this line of thought, the program of defamiliarized language use becomes political to the extent that we then will no longer put up with the mass social deceptions. Watten's example is the gas line crunch of the 1973—how it points up the non-relation between the images we had for this experience and the crisis as it was actually lived. "We don't believe our senses," he asserts, "the level of automatism we have to deal with is of an order of the Formalists would not have believed. The necessity for techniques seems absolute in the face of this fact." An absolute necessity for techniques? To me this seems a dubious statement on several counts. Does it mean that taking state power should no longer be on anyone's agenda? That if we use words rightly society will change by itself? But most of all Watten's assertion seems idealistic, giving precedence to language over concrete action in constructing a new social reality.

And here Watten goes on to make a parallel that seems even more misguided. "The Russian Revolution," he says, "was a period of total reorganization, so that anything one did was a political act in itself. That's close to the design potential of the self-evident word. There is a near identity between Russian modernism as the most extreme and typical case of modernism and the invention of the Russian modernist state."

One ought to be pardoned at this point for drawing in the breath and doing some serious thinking about this. Hard questions are in order. Is Watten suggesting that Russian Formalism helped to bring about the October Revolution? If so—how? And how close is the parallel between the Russian society of that time and our own U.S. society? Even in *that* society, was it Vertov's filmic atomism that stirred people to action—or Lenin's old-fashioned prose? So what's helpful—montage or narration?

And what about the experience of most of the left-sectarian political parties both here and in the other developed countries of the West? Should their strong historical distaste for most forms of modernism be written off without comment? The upshot of all this, to my way of thinking, is that the once acclaimed linking of modernist cultural forms with leftism now appears as a historical vestige instead of a current solution to problems in the United States. It's not an answer but a turning back of the clock. Theoretical people, in my view, should be looking toward what is actually happening here in our own time—developments like Black writing, women's writing and various kinds of movement writing for example.

But if Watten is the historical scholar of the group of Language Poets, it is Ron Silliman who is its creative theorist. That at least is what one feels on comparing Watten's piece with Silliman's essay in the *Talks* anthology. Silliman is as scholarly as Watten, but he pushes things to a practical edge in a way that Watten doesn't. His theory seems more closely aligned with current practice and so more creative. To be sure, he is generalizing about what might be called the 'hard-core' Language Writers—poets like himself, Barrett Watten, Kit Robinson, Bruce Andrews and, I think, Clark Coolidge. But in the most basic sense it is a theory about his own recent work, *Sitting Up, Standing, Taking Steps* (Tuumba, 1978), *Ketjak* (This, 1978) and *Tjanting* (forthcoming)—why he writes the way he does. An apology or explanation.

I haven't particularly cared for this practice, but it's only fair to say something about it before going on to the theory, which I often like. Silliman's is a poetry that is a meditative empiricism like this O'Hara-esque ("Second Avenue") segment from *Sitting Up:*

> Color films of dead people. Burned out buses among blackout dillweed, Military Ocean Terminal. Deer fetus wine of China. Pigeons in the eaves of a Queen Anne's Tower. All tones of identical length.

as well as a dreamy generation of minimal units like this from *Ketjak*—

Revolving door. How will I know when I make a mistake. The garbage barge at the bridge. The throb in the wrist. Earth science. Their first goal was to separate the worker from the means of production.

Other poet critics have drawn attention to specifically language-oriented aspects of this poetry (and in *Language* no. 8 Steve Benson reviews Silliman's reading of all of *Ketjak* at the Powell St. turnaround last year) usually pointing out its structure of agglomeration—12 paragraphs growing from two words ("Revolving door") to a paragraph chapter almost 46 pages long, repeating or rephrasing old material and adding new. Some of this is educational in intent, I think ("Their first goal. . ." etc. is a political statement in addition to anything else it is), and with Silliman's work more generally it is a didactic side of things that can hardly be underestimated. He illustrates his intentions when he cites this line from *Tjanting* in his *Talks* piece—

Someone called Douglas. Someone called Douglas over. He was killed by someone called Douglas over in Oakland.

—to show "how meaning shifts as units are integrated into successively higher levels." There's little left to guesswork though there is a tilt in favor of sound.

This approach strikes me as abstract. I'm not altogether gratified by poetry that is openly educational toward me without consulting me first. And what about the human dimension? I don't think teaching people a hypothesis is a good enough reason to write poetry—unless it gives everyone a significant increment of pleasure. Otherwise what you have is studies—'etudes.' But pleasure comes in stirring up emotions, someway or other telling a story. That, it seems to me, is what the best women's poetry does now. Judy Grahn, or Tillie Olsen in prose. Here language isn't illusionistic but it does speak about the world, politically, and gives us pleasure in the process.

Yet there are people who like Silliman's poetry. In another place in the *Talks* (the discussion after the Bill Berkson talk), Silliman notes in passing that he doesn't write poems. "Maybe I write poetry," he says to explain an earlier matter, "but I don't write poems." This reminds me of a sense of scale in Silliman's work that I think has to rephrase the question of pleasure. Scale in Ron Silliman is sometimes positively Russian, reminiscent of the block-wide-and-long epics of Mayakovsky. Or it's American in its aspirations to sheer largeness, a scope that whether you like their poetry or nor, speaks in Whitman, Sandberg and William Carlos Williams. What's to say about this? I mention it for the sake of fairness. You have to read Silliman's poetry at some length, but there is a kind of pay-off—a build-up of sound and image, a sense of rhythmic complexity that is luxuriant, fascinating and undeniable, the pleasures of scale. As I say, I don't care for it, but read for yourselves and see.

I have fewer reservations and am more attracted to Silliman's critical writing—though this isn't to say I have *none*. In the first issue of *Renegade* magazine, Ron Silliman talks about the kinship of Walter Benjamin and French structuralism. I'm not sure as I go along with this but I think I see what he's talking about. I do have one big objection. I don't think Benjamin's Zionism is anything other than absolutely constitutive of his thought—and that brings in political and mystical considerations that make it awfully difficult to see him as a sort of 'proto-structuralist.' But be that as it may, Ron Silliman is a terrific prose critic, and his "Benjamin Obscura" positively bristles with intellectual and political energy of a very high order. Where the run-of-the-mill journal criticism of Language Writers is often guilty of incredible excesses of self-indulgence and a paucity of intellectual themes, Silliman really has something to say. He has actual *content.* And this should make you want to read him.

Silliman's essay "The New Sentence," while technical, is probably the most rewarding piece in the *Talks* anthology. If you want a definitive explanation of what Language Writing in its hard-core aspects is all about, read this. It sums up the purest elements of the Language movement of the late '70s.

Beginning with a fascinating summary of past theory on the sentence, Silliman's essay starts its provocations. All of theory to date, it turns out, has been simply an *evasion* theory, and this comes in large part from Saussure's paying more attention to the systematic features of language than the actual talking aspect of it. These are of course the same coupled concepts we met with earlier in Bob Perelman. Only instead of being called *language* and *parole* or language and speaking, they will now be called "the paradigmatic" and the "syntagmatic." Silliman cites Roland Barthes and tells us that:

> History has seen the movement from a syntagmatic focus to a paradigmatic one, and. . . a break has occurred at a point when some critical mass—not specifically identified by Barthes—renders it impossible for units to continue to integrate beyond grammatical levels, e.g., the sentence.

In other words the whole process of *making connections* in a language has become characteristically difficult, problematic, in modern times. Silliman doesn't disagree. But he wants us to realize though that this specific inability to make connections is characteristic of modernist and experimental writing, it isn't very applicable to popular writing where narrative is the strong feature. And so it happens, says Silliman, that the poles of paradigm and syntagm "have become more and more identified with the limits, respectively, of high and low art." This means that popular or low art, so-called, by continuing to emphasize connections, gets to be an art of narrating, or telling stories. High art, on the other hand, or what we call modernism or experimental wiring, objects to the illusion features often associated with narration and attempts to take narrative apart, or 'deconstruct' it. What is left is called a 'text'—and doesn't any longer refer to anything outside itself. Thus you have, so to speak, best sellers on one side and experimental modernism on the other. The *Thorn Birds* vs. *Tender Buttons.*

This is a very interesting and intelligent argument, I think, but there are some substantial objections to it. I will get to them in a moment. In the meantime I want to ask if we should continue to assume that modernism has been entirely progressive in a *political* sense? Barrett Watten's earlier argument as well as Ron Silliman's present essay implies that the question needn't be raised, because it is obvious that modernism has always been a Left-oriented phenomenon. But that's not accurate, as a little reflection will show. It's certainly true of Surrealism and Russian Formalism, or it for the most part anyway. And in this country too there have been individual modernists we can be proud of from their sense of political responsibility— one would name Zukofsky or George Oppen. But far too often modernism has taken a more sinister direction—and there is evidence that this is at least equality a tendency. In France, one of the greatest, Celine, was an outright fascist. And by the '30s many of the ex-Surrealists had become extremely questionable in their attitudes toward nationalism and Catholicism, including Reverdy, one of the best. In England there's the rather irritating example of Wyndham Lewis, the leading modernist writer there. There's Pound's Jew-baiting and fascism and you can look at Eliot's record. One could certainly recite the names of modernists who did better by their consciences, perhaps make a case that they were more 'purely' or essentially modernist. Matters get terribly complex here. But you can't just assume that modernism equals progressivism.

And as for popular art. Well, there are schlock best-sellers to be sure. There are movies, comics and other commodity mass-artifacts. But there's also popular *literature*. It is popular and it is narrative, and there's a tradition of it. Steinbeck's stories champion rural working people in the time of Great Depression. Mike Gold's *Jews Without Money* is a literary classic, and it's both funny and idiomatic. Upton Sinclair was as good a muckraker as he was a melodramatic storyteller, and Jack London was a fairly good Socialist Realist even before there were Commissars. And so on. But the point is, there does exist another, and non-modernist, tradition. And it's important that it's there because it sets a narrative precedent to think about. It's worth considering because it had a mass base and was politically progressive. It is a counter-tendency to the modernism of that era and can be learned from.

And the present? Where are the descendants of modernism on the one hand and popular narrativity on the other? The *Talks* anthology gives us some answers to these questions. The points of view represented differ, sometimes significantly, and there are greater and lesser degrees of a language orientation here. But the net impression the volume gives you is this—in our time it is the Language Writing movement that is carrying out the modernist program, in some ways more radically than Stein herself.

Once again Ron Silliman suggests why in a remarkable discussion of Gertrude Stein and the French prose-poem tradition. In Silliman's reading, Stein carries on the tradition and develops it further, yet finds herself stymied at a certain level and unable to proceed beyond. Setting herself a minimalist program she takes the analysis of larger units down to the paragraph but no further. It is the paragraph rather than the sentence that is the minimal writing unit for Stein because Stein correctly perceived that without an organization of writing around paragraphs you have no emotions, no intentionality, because paragraphs, not sentences, are the literary equivalent of speech situations. Thus Stein never achieved a writing based on sentences since she was in at least partial complicity with the referential world. Here the implications of Silliman's analysis have become clear. He is advising a clean break with that world, a world of meaning, the world of emotions, the world of cause and effect. In short, with everything but the world of language considered formally.

This, I think, is the cause of much of the antagonism toward Language Writing on the part of many other groups in the writing community. Let me put this quite plainly. If you take away people's emotions, their ability to tell stories and their capability to deal generally with the outside world, you are really not going to have much of an appeal to several significant groups. Blacks, Latins and other racial minorities for instance. Most feminists and politically oriented gay men for instance. And it all likelihood political people generally.

Probably this is self-evident but it has become an issue in the writing community recently. There have been a number of letters to *Poetry Flash* regarding this issue and the outcry over the glaring underrepresentation of women and minorities in the latest distribution of NEA grants has certainly increased the feeling that formalism is a *political* issue. An insistence on meaning, on one hand, is often seen as linked to demands for social change.

In a poem titled "Response to L=A=N=G=U=A=G=E," Karen Brodine has put it this way—

It's true I want things to mean
It's true I mean things
to change, in a driving force, a pressure

in your life, then write about that you must.
directly, urgently, before too late. [not verified]

Some Language Writers are aware, often acutely aware of these objections. Rae Armantrout tries to deal with some of these objections in the first issue of L=A=N=G=U=A=G=E magazine in "Why Don't Women Do Language-Oriented Writing?" "Women need to describe the condition of their lives," she asserts, adding that "this entails representation." But this is true, I believe, of other groups as well. It seems quiet unlikely, for instance, that a person could deal adequately with racism, or oppression based on class or realities of prison life, say, in a formalist language. According to its program anyway, Language Writing refers to itself rather than the world.

I'm not sure whether I see signs of change in all this or not. I would certainly like to, since I consider Language Poetry one of the significant developments of our time. So much real thought has gone into it, so much concern and insight into the commodified conditions of language in our everyday life. Some of it is even poetry I like a great deal—Bob Perelman's. And Silliman's critical prose would be hard to match for intelligence and a sense of commitment to social change. But still, I need something more than this. I need a literature that will help bring on social change.

One last note. And it is indicative, I am afraid, that none of the three I'll mention is really central to Language Writing, and that this may well have something to do with gender, sexual orientation, race or all three. I want to say Fanny Howe's piece strikes a positive note with me. It's called "Justice" and speaks language whose content, referential often enough, seems more open to the world—

That the governing tongue should be honest, like *no private property*, the way Marx summed it up.

This language may be Catholic mystical in its forms but it's progressive in its content. One thinks of Archbishop Romero's forthright stands before his assassination. The writing gets too theoretical sometimes, but there's always something to think about.

And I'd like to mention Erica Hunt. Hunt doesn't have a piece of her own in these *Talks* but distinguishes herself when she does speak—in the discussions and occasional remarks—for her intelligence, good sense and ability to take a dissenting position when that is called for.

Last, a word about what may be the most *curious* piece in this *Talks* anthology—Steve Benson's strange performance called "Views of Communist China." For his performance, Steve Benson recreated his own apartment temporarily in another poet's flat, moving in furnishings, decorations and so on. At some point, he says he considered himself a tour guide for the audience. Excerpts from a book on the People's Republic are read by Benson and Bob Perelman. Then a lengthy discussion ensues until the performance closes with a quoted dialogic interchange, apparently from the same book. In the course of his performance, Benson discloses truly intimate feelings with what appears to me as a sometimes alarming openness. And perhaps inevitably, another poet present for the discussion takes advantage of this vulnerability. At this point the discussion is not at all edifying. It seems cruel on the second poet's part and even had overtones of homophobia. But I have a second reservation about the piece. How can a subject as serious as "Communist China" be treated like a fantasy? For much of the piece the subject seems to be dealt with so figuratively that it seems lacking in respect for the real China of more than 500,000,000 real people—with a history that ought to elicit that consideration more readily than seems the case here. The tone seems to imply once more that Language Writing refers to itself, not the world. Yet at some point in this piece one realizes that there is an equation being set up between, oddly, what Communist China *is* and what one *feels*. The performance ends with Bob Perelman taking up the book to read a long narrative passage about visiting the apartment of an older Party militant. Perelman and Benson take, respectively, the voices of the narrator-interviewer and a young girl.

Perelman: What do you want to do as an adult?
(pause)
Benson: Whatever the Party needs, I will become.

Perelman: She stopped for a moment and stood motionless, and then, a radiant smile of beautiful straight white teeth.

Well, I like the gay aspects of this scene. But it makes an odd ending.

"Language Writing: The Pluses and Minuses of the New Formalism" is a review of *Talks/Hills* 6/7 and first appeared in *Soup*, no. 2, edited by Steve Abbott (Feb. 1981).

A NOTE ON *LA FONTAINE*

Bob and I had been working on some ideas for new ways of doing narrative and we wanted to collaborate on a translation. So for two or three nights a week for a couple of months I'd go to Bob's for dinner with a rough French translation of one of La Fontaine's fables in hand and we'd just play around with it, throwing in our own experience and adding or subtracting I guess randomly, until it was ready. We believed classics like LaFontaine should always be disrespected, just be brutally used for your own purposes, mutilated and mixed with impossibly related contemporary experiences, without rhyme or reason! We "threw in everything but the kitchen sink," but mainly I think a lot of homo stuff and some politico-philosophic essays. It's amusing to disrespect anything, especially a classic that has bored people forever in their school years, though sometimes, yes, as an offbeat approach, we did find ourselves being more straightforward, though naturally even then, still with hallmark perversity. It was tons of fun. After all what's better than working with a good friend?

"Note on *La Fontaine*" was written for this volume.

SELECTIONS FROM *LA FONTAINE*
by Bruce Boone and Robert Glück

TRANSLATIONS/ALTERATIONS/LA FONTAINE

Does La Fontaine patronize his animals? There's always this rush through the details (but in our translations we've altered that some) so he can *use* them. Back in our own century we're more at the home with this word. Friendship, family, love—there's not much among us that can't be exploited. So who are we to rebuke Joyce Haber when she calls her book *The Users*? The high gloss cover shows, well, a cigarette being ground out by a bejeweled hand. Hollywood has come a long way from animal stories like the *Fables* or the *Stories & Tales,* hasn't it? Otherwise where would our writers like Joyce Haber be? You could think of others I imagine.

True, he wanted to identify with them. He wanted to go back to those forests and waters he inherited. He might have been in charge of them, like his dad before him. But the list of these alternate lives goes on. For instance, he could have stayed with the Oratorians and been a priest, taught dirty little boys their ABC's and wiped their noses. An inventory of ghostly might-have-beens. Instead, he pleased a brilliant Court (sometimes) and wrote aslant about money and power. Dying, he repudiated his earlier convictions. Blasphemy had gone out of style. Throughout his worldly life we'd love to think he still valued these animals, was true to his childhood loves, his sense of wonder.

What happened was different, but not altogether. As most of us know, a writer's ego is deep and complex. Here's Montaigne, an admired predecessor and writer too, thinking out loud. 'What do I know?' Is it so dumb a question? There are worlds out there, he continues, terrifying worlds a-whirling and a-whirling, like our egos. The common mind sees but the outside skin, while inside—ah horrors!—the cogs, the wheels! We join our friend La Fontaine in answering: The fox, the lion, the goat and the lamb, what chance have simple animals like these? Suppressing his better part, animals, La Fontaine takes the path of self-advancement; he joins the bourgeoisie. To save his soul, he makes a stipulation—'I'll show things as they are.'

La Fontaine thinks he is smart. Since he has shown us how rotten society is, nothing else is required from him. Should he join the Revolution? Why, he thinks, everything I've written has been for the Revolution. They have such peasant mentalities, why don't they understand this?—and so on. When La Fontaine excuses himself this way, we ought to turn our heads to spare him. We're not all Otto Rene Castillos, Meridel Le Sueurs, John Reeds. If nothing else than from self-interest, we should be more kind.

On the other hand kindness is not ignorance. That should be kept in mind too. Our author's viewpoint is social darwinistic—nature red in tooth and claw. Which he called a cat and mouse game. There are feathers flying and bits of claw or blood. As things settle, you see there are some hens missing in the coop. In their convent, the nuns who were raped know that the joke is on them, they've been used and thrown away. Tant pis, says M. de La Fontaine—the monster.

Should we return to—dogs, cats, mice, pigeons, lions and geese? These keep coming back; they remind me of something—what selfishness might be in another time, without cruelty, exploitation. It's beyond knowing. Now foxes in waistcoats speak verse.

A MUTILATION (FUTURE APPEALED TO)

'Now here's one I like!'
Or—'Stop me if you've heard this,' but
this story's the exception. It's
vouched for by Science and actually
happened. You judge.

A tree is cut down on account of age—
too much rot. It's the owl's hiding place.
Inside they find
spiders and nasty bugs of all kinds,
lizards and of course mice. The mice
have huge gluttonous tummies and no feet.
Why? Our learned owl's plied them
with grain; he's forced nutritious seed
down gullets and mutilated their little legs.
Why not admit it? this bird reasoned.
Here's what happened. He hunted them.
When caught, they'd escape. The owl's
distressed. For a remedy, he cripples them.
Fine! Now Mr. Owl
can perch at leisure. His larder's
full. Eat them at once? Heath problems
surely follow. One by one then. He's
on owl Easy Street now. Lessons? This
bird's prudence and ours are the same—
and intelligence often comes in small
packages. Why do the Cartesians continue
their blind speculations? This bird's
a piece of clockwork, cog and wheel and nothing
else? Learn from a philosopher with more
to teach—Nature. Nature's your true guide.
'Eat 'em when you get 'em—or they
run off. Too many? Pack 'em in the cooler.'

My judgment's harsh?
Wasn't the era? Think before condemning.
The lucky ones of the century ate the
lovely Duchesse pears, the best there were.
We breathed clean air, took walks. Our
writing hasn't been surpassed. Our poor
were easily forgotten; we never knew them.
On my deathbed I thought of the Estate
rather than Heaven. My last Will was this—
Read my poems.

BOOK 12 #5

A young mouse, poor, no experience
in the field, believed imploring
and giving reasons would convince:

Let me live
—a mouse
of my size
and upkeep—
do I burden
this house?
Do I starve
the innkeeper
and his wife?
A grain of wheat
feeds me. A nut
fills me up—
look at
my ribs.
Don't you want
this meal to get fat
for Messrs. Vos Enfants?

Thus the trapped mouse parleyed with the cat.
The other says:

Is this a discourse for the Old and Powerful?
Cat and Old, pardon you? Hardly.
Descend to your death. Go to the nether world.
Die. And for this defeat
harangue the Spinning Sisters. My kittens
will catch plenty of mice to eat.

He pauses, cleans his chops. His fur's plain
brown, set off by a gold button and a bit of
velvet. He shuns rings and wears jewels only
on his shoebuckles, his garters, and his hat,
which is trimmed in Spanish needlepoint
and topped with a white plume. He turns to us
and says:

As for this fable, here's the moral that applies:
Who flatter themselves, believe they can have everything?
Mice.

A vaguely abstract person once called on death. 'Death,' quoth he, 'how attractive you seem! Why don't you come and end my sufferings?' Death, the 17ᵗʰ Century *gentilhomme*, stood at the door and walked in. 'Eeek!' squeals that abstract-type person. 'Take away this dreadful thing. Keep away, Death; Death, don't come closer!' Then there's the great philosopher Maecenas who said this—'Deform me, ravage me, make me stupid as a Scythian, make me armless, legless and sightless. But please don't take away my sweet life.'

La Fontaine seems a bit troubled by these stories. He remarks that they lack something. A friend tells him he should be more concrete, so he adds this. An itinerant collector of wood was weighted down by his bundle. Trudging along his gloomy way he finally reaches the door of his miserable hovel. He slips the bundle from his shoulder and considers life's sorrows. Has he had any pleasure since coming into life? He's been poorer than poor—the dregs of the earth. Sleep, bread? He's hardly had any. Then there's soldiers, creditors, taxes, king. No end in sight. So death doesn't delay when he's called. 'Death,' says the man, 'just help me rearrange this bundle. I won't keep you a moment.' An ornamental flourish concludes:

> We call for death—
> but there's still breath.
> 'I'll survive, I'll survive!
> I'm alive!'

The Duchess having died, says St. Simon, they took out her heart and put the entrails in a reliquary urn. Then at high mass people began to notice a peculiar odor. The service was interrupted with a loud report which sprayed the contents over the whole chapel. In the ensuing rush for the doors, a number of our elegant court ladies were trampled. The King led the rest to safety.

Aesop was in a quandary. He was well known for his cleverness, but how would he get out of this? Figs are brought for lunch, then stolen, and the Phrygian slave is suspected. Speech difficulties first hindered, they say— then saved. Can a mute accuse those who accuse him? Insult's added to this injury. He's so ugly, it's said, only his face tells the truth. When strong men see him, they doubt themselves—women flee him. As the laughter dies down, here's La Fontaine getting at a serious business of drawing morals. 'But the badly shaped bottle held rare wine,' he tells us. Next the masterful exposition—generations of sullen French schoolchildren will sit glumly through this on generations of sullen stone benches. Aesop, it seems, defended himself. He had them bring in a bowl of warm water and put two fingers to his throat. What followed, did. The ground in front of Aesop is covered with—only warm water. Then Aesop makes signs for the steward and other servants to be brought in. The others follow suit and then it's the steward's turn. He does the same, and in the pool of water on the floor are the barely digested figs, still pink in color. Everyone marvels. What a wonderful story!—a rationalist's miracle tale. Will the wily La Fontaine vouch for its truth? But—he protests—it's enough that the story is charming!

Lack of common understanding is so interesting that who would bother with harmony? That lack's most resonant expression is formalism, which the two squirrels, the two mice, the two cats, the two goats, the two wolves, the two lions who wrote this book love, but not more than they love you.

Sincerely? Oh Reader, we need no other proof than your regal impetuosities, your ardent and lively temper, the intelligence, courage, and magnanimity which are your unfailing characteristics. We venture to provide you with certain tales. These fictions are a species of history in which no one is flattered. There is no protection under which we could place them more illustrious than your own. The taste and judgment shown by you in all things, together with our desire to obey you and ardor to please you, have made the whole world your admirer. We no longer have need to consult Apollo, the nine Muses, or any of the deities who dwell on Parnassus. Nature has endowed you with every gift which it could bestow: skill in adjudging intellectual things; also knowledge of the laws which govern them. We see you as a conqueror of whom one could say yet more fitly than of Alexander that you are about to hold a Parliament of the Universe.

Court life has got me thinking. If we're poor in middles we explore edges, manners, names, the tense space between gestures. Isn't it like a fairy tale: a hanky flourished too daringly, an incautious solemnness when the king tells a joke, and you are relegated to the outer darkness. A survival instinct says the world is not a very safe place. An alligator could eat you; still smiling for the camera you back off a cliff, contract a tropical spore, choke on a fishbone. So be careful, be ready, be calm, be strong, be sensible. Carry a jacket when you go out. That's received wisdom. Still, imagine a world that applies, touching close as the night when we generously fold ourselves into each other's bodies.

I blame equally those who take on themselves to praise, and those who take on themselves to blame, and those who merely amuse themselves, and I can only approve of those who seek with tears.

The lion reached the end of the line; despair and old age reached him at the same time. It's an abuse to promise what can't be delivered—to kings or anyone.

He sent out messengers to each species for their doctors (each has its own) and they arrived from every locale. The fox excuses himself, no explanations. The wolf slanders his absent comrade. (Courtiers—stop destroying yourselves!) His Majesty commands them to smoke out the fox. He comes, and knowing the wolf is behind all this he says:

> Sire,
> Let not a hardly sincere report
> Misrepresent my absence at court.
> I was on a pilgrimage and made a vow
> For your health, using the journey to kowtow
> To professionals and experts in the field.
> I consulted and consulted. You can be healed.
> You only lack heat—a long age slayed
> it in you. Apply the skin of a wolf flayed
> Alive, still hot and smoking. This cure's
> A tonic for failing natures.
> Monsieur Wolf will provide, from
> The goodness of his heart, your robe-de-chambre.

The King tried this advice: Monsieur Wolf is flayed and dismembered. The monarch wears him and sups on him.

• • •

At last, the fruit taken after his soup bloated his stomach, dulled his digestion and took the edge off his appetite for the first time in his life. The King had never known hunger; however late circumstances sometimes delayed his dinner. I heard him say several times that his appetite was whetted with the first spoonfuls of soup, and he ate so prodigiously, so substantially, and so equably morning and evening that one never tired of watching him. Such quantities of water and fruit, unrelieved by spirits, turned his blood to gangrene by diluting it. It was further thinned by his nightly sweating, and this was recognized as the cause of death at autopsy. His organs were all so beautiful and healthy that it can safely be said he could have passed the century mark. Most surprising of all were his stomach and his bowels, which were twice the length and volume of an ordinary man's.

. . .

Courtiers, in your career nothing is forgiven.

I blame equally those who take on themselves to praise, A stag loved himself mirrored in a fountain, the beauty of his antlers: 'My right profile, my left profile, my forehead rises aristocratically to the rhododendrons, the purity of, the nobility of, the loftiness of, the heightened reality of. . .' He murmured, 'Stunning craftsmanship, remarkable achievement.'

and those who take on themselves to blame, Then the stag noticed his spindly ankles retreating in the depths. He could hardly look at them! 'The proportion's off! I hate my feet! Never in the history of the universe did noble qualities conclude so trivially, basely, vilely, contemptibly, abjectly, what a disgrace.'

and those who merely amuse themselves, 'You never wanted other than Romantic stories of the knights of the Round Table etc., but this of course merits your perusal. My obligation—to season them so they can in their fashion please you. Yours—to praise my intentions even when they fail. And if you find the account to your taste, perhaps afterwards you will read others, more serious.'

and I can only approve of those who seek with tears. Bang!—The report rings out. Does M. de la Fontaine look up apprehensively from his writing table? The servants have worn millenarian smiles all day. Strange. And the stag breaks for the forest, followed not too distantly by foaming greyhounds and hunters. At every step he's more and more appreciating his feet which have not deserted him even though he had given up on them. He's also beginning to view his antlers as rather superficial. He thinks to himself, he thinks to us, 'Topic sentences without paragraphs, pennants without a victory, no, worse, burdens weighing me down, tangling me in the bushes.'

One day La Fontaine is trying to think of a new subject, one that won't rock the boat. Sex is definitely out for him, since priests and hypocrites have got him condemned before. Should he try the theme of friendship? But when he praised the high dramatic art of Champmêlé, didn't the snickers come fast and furious? Still, La Fontaine thinks it's worth a try: It's clear there have been successes with the topic. Shouldn't I add my name to the list? Cicero writing his sublime *De Amicitia* in ancient Rome. What a wonderful piece, so lofty, so respectable! Aside from the *Orations*, he'd deserve praise for that one effort. And Montaigne!—writing in the quiet Gascon countryside about a friend who died young. Now the words come back. 'In the friendship whereof I speak'—the passage still moves me—'our souls mingle and blend in a fusion so complete that the seam that joins them disappears and is found no more. If pressed to say why I loved him I'd reply, because it was him, because it was me.' A writer of stature, of genuine worth!—thinks La Fontaine.

The king grows more repressive every day—and the court goes along with him. Apparently, the times have changed. Isn't it a mark of wisdom for the writer to reflect those changes? Maybe I should write about the delights of passion restrained for instance. Or I could always picture the charms of philosophical discourse—that's quite popular too. Here La Fontaine pauses and jots down a few thoughts. 'Two friends,' notes the writer, 'they're both virtuous, both have blameless lives.' 'Well, it's a start,' he thinks encouragingly. 'I wonder how the two might look? Should one be older and the other younger for instance?' But here the canny Frenchman scents danger—he's on the alert for trouble now. 'Yet with a difference in age, they think of sex, invariably,'—and he resolves for them to be equal in years. 'Just to be on the safe side,' adds La Fontaine, 'I'll have them talk philosophy day in and day out, I'll make them perfect gentlemen.'

So now the subject of his poem's decided. What about a complication? And doesn't every poem have to have a moral?—introduction? And then the ending, the most important of all. He weighs the choices. Then: I'll choose a debate form, I think, it's really the style I love best. And when their contest is ended, I'll have them appeal to us: Reader, which of us two was the better friend? Deferring to their betters in taste and understanding, they add: You decide! My plan's an excellent one, thinks La Fontaine confidently, and I might as well be frank about it, it's one more proof of the genius I'm famous for, my glory.

But now it's time for La Fontaine to get down to the nuts and bolts of his story. He has to choose this or that detail at every point in the plot, at every point in the diction he has to select one phrase over another. But that's what a writer's art consist in—enlightened choices. So La Fontaine decides: One friend will be upset, but I won't reveal exactly why. He'll wake up at night, run to the other one's house. The second friend will ask: Have you lost money? Take this purse—it's filled with drachmas. Did you fight? I have my sword—let's go right now. Or are you suffering because of love? Why don't you take one of my servants then? To all this the first friend will have one answer: Thank you, he'll say. I dreamed you appeared to me. You looked a little pale.

La Fontaine is a book-length collaboration with Robert Glück, published by Blackstar Editions (San Francisco, 1981).

"STONED OUT OF MY GOURD":
A REVIEW OF DENNIS COOPER'S
THE TENDERNESS OF THE WOLVES
(THE CROSSING PRESS, 1982)

On the cover of his new book *The Tenderness of the Wolves*, Dennis Cooper's image looks out suspiciously, his back against what's possibly an art gallery. Given the extraordinary title, tilted perspective and film-noir looking shadows, you probably wouldn't be off-base in thinking of this picture as werewolf-ish. Is sensationalism OK? ("A lit match would Tinkerbelle down," says the voice-over in Cooper's story "A Herd" and then we notice the body, there on the ground, doused in kerosene.) Dennis Cooper is one writer for whom being inflammatory pays off in a big way. Glamor and control are the hallmarks of this writer. From your first encounter with him you're aware of this strange/morbid/fascinating etc. preoccupation of his, with *image* (in the whole spectrum of meaning of the word). You see it there for you, and as you do, it distends and fills out, grows murky and disturbs—

> He stood alone in the shadow.
> His hands and his shoes jutted
> out of the dark, with some dope
> smoke. The rest of his body was
> vague but exact, like a hologram
> glimpsed through thick glasses.

—as Cooper says about himself in the first poem of *Tenderness* called "There." And if the poem isn't about Cooper himself, it is about an *image* of his.

Not yet 30, Cooper has, among experimental writers, a reputation for work that's both solid and sensational. His ability to produce a writing of quality that's paradoxically both innovative and accessible, makes him attractive to younger gays, to New Wavers, to writers and artists and others. You could say Cooper has a lot of "crossover" appeal—in many directions at once.

His life itself has indicated some of these interests. At one point Cooper was a punk rock musician. Then he made experimental movies. Currently he's been showing a flair for the organization and even business side of writing. He's a successful editor and publisher (*Little Caesar* magazine and Little Caesar Books). As director of the Beyond Baroque Poetry Series in Los Angeles for several years, he's almost singlehandedly turned around a definitely unremarkable and moribund L.A. writing scene—making it at least competitive. And if Cooper tends to startle you with the virtuosity of these successes, that response might in turn suggest something about the aggressive seductions of writing.

The glamor of this writing could be called its advertising—as in a Brian De Palma movie. Its cold neon surfaces and ingenue textures don't claim to do a lot for you healthwise. They want to grab your attention. Cooper's sensibilities are quite post-modern in this sense. All the visual flak—high and low art allusions, smoky sexuality, pushing of dreck and commercial values—help to make the writing self-conscious, not superficial. There are no false promises here. Nothing's delivered but the hard edges, and that's a guarantee of integrity.

So we watch outtakes from a life. Through a haze you get what it's like to grow up a rich kid in L.A.—the dope, sex stuff. Cooper's feelings are so incredibly distant! A patchwork map of California from 20 miles up. The thin air is so heady; it lessens pain—

> Mark and I take the new space ship up.
> The wind wants it.
> We pop like toast from the earth's atmosphere

—as Cooper says in a piece called "Space Case," from his late 70s chapbook, *Tiger Beat*. Numbness and a sense of scale go hand-in-hand here. The disadvantage naturally is that you are not on the planet any longer. Curiously, this will substitute for lost feeling—life is fun, free-play and flexibility—quite human qualities. In his earlier work, the problem Dennis Cooper developed was—how do you tie utopian qualities like these, securely, to a real but inhospitable (planetary) surface? Cooper's writerly answer to this, all along, has been to tap into legend.

So, from earlier excursions into the first person, in *The Tenderness of Wolves* Cooper removes himself more frequently to the third person. He tells us for instance in "There" that

> ... punks, jocks,
> everyone watched him, pictured
> him sprawled at a desk, clothes
> torn apart by ulterior powers,
> his sneer smudged with girls'
> kisses, boys' wet red fists.

Apparently, legend means a lot to Dennis Cooper—though particular legends can be discarded one after the other. In the case of the above poem it happens to be the Rimbaud legend, distanced by throwing in a lot of suburban brattiness (spoiled rich kid genius nastiness), but it could be anything. And at least in formalist terms, or technique, this use of figure on an empty ground puts Cooper squarely in the most vanguard, post-modernist company—Julian Schnabel and the neo-expressionists in painting, and Robert Glück and Kathy Acker in literature. As a spinoff, it gives Cooper's work chic. Legend is the figure on an empty ground.

Cooper's choice of such techniques is hardly arbitrary, but clearly conditioned by attitudes about how you should act if you are to survive in the world. His allegiances are first to brains, then emotions. Implied is a perception that this is the modus operandi of society itself. Winners know this, misfits and losers can't. Should this social touch-mindedness be applied to art, too? It's not a question that needs arguing, for Cooper. "It was my favorite film," he says in this introduction to *Tenderness* (speaking of Alain Resnais's film *Providence*), "it held the right combination of smarts and emotion—starring the first, with a cameo by the later. When I established myself as an artist ... I'd do something like it." Even pleasure itself, from this viewpoint, gets to be defined differently. In one of the sex poems of this collection, "No God," Cooper tells us about going out cruising, finding someone, a guy that looks like a shadow. He'll go with him. "Like me he's just moving further away," Cooper explains non-judgmentally. The only ones who aren't stupid wrecks are the few with consciousness. The rest in society are just undead.

But consciousness like this can never be sure of itself, unless others confirm its objectness—by watching, by being subjects. And that's where a very peculiar character called God comes in. In one piece, the long narrative called "A Herd," God looks down from his heavens on the grisly doings of the mass murderer Ray, with something approaching serenity. In another, "An Aerial View," God is a sort of artist—he's called a "dilettante." Dispassion about human life and death is his key signature, and the buried narrative suggests that's what a writer is like too. With a terribly short attention span and lots of cool. God's folkloric. A doper; an old man with a *Texas Chainsaw Massacre* sense of humor. Cooper's portrait of him in "An Aerial View"—

> His lips are lava which has cooled,
> His mind as wild as the tree tops,
> as dope touched to match, breath

is as sardonic as it is envying. For a final number? The trickster just disappears!—"drifts slowly away like a freighter unloaded of all its cargo." As an answer to the problem of the subject who guarantees you, God's been put on hold—or maybe self-destructed. So the problem apparently still stands.

As I mentioned earlier, Dennis Cooper used to write in a lighter vein, but even then—if you look back—there were elegiac qualities that pointed to this more serious, more philosophically-oriented future for him. There was something like love this called "Billy McCall's Summer 1979," from *Tiger Beat*—

> you are willing to sleep now,
> unafraid of missing something.
> you are going to be rude forever.

—about a 22-year old who thinks, now at his "peak," that "drugs were a pretty good game. / school was worth it." But in the disavowal of the disintegration to come—

there are no signs of death
in you, only energy
and pleasure controlled

—isn't there a more urgent sign of its actual presence? There's a good-bye
look, once loved by Chandler, another L.A. writer.

But for now that look is still (mostly) present by its absence. Instead
there's a high-spirited, manic type of fun, a payload of obviousness that gets
you high like nothing else in your life. It's a love of fantasy. So, in the poem
"David Cassidy Then" Dennis imagines winning a date with the media star
on The Dating Game. A breathy, hysterical emcee announces their prize to
the dazed pair, turning to the star—

"David, we'll be flying you and your date
to . . . Rio de Janeiro! You'll be
staying at the luxurious Rio Hilton
and attend a party in your honor!"

Later the poem shows terrific sex (Dennis eats out David, David obliging
with a great consciousness of his own worth), and then comes the obligatory
publicity appearance for David's fans. While cameras "angle to get David's
sheathed body," Dennis knows the real truth

. . . "This is David,"
I say, smelling my face like a corsage,
and pull him close, stoned out of my gourd.

—that this sex bouquet is indisputable evidence that he's really David's date.

Tiger Beat was followed by Idols, Cooper's major book until The
Tenderness of the Wolves. What Idols did, essentially, was completely map out
the territory that Cooper would then treat more analytically in Tenderness.
Idols finds Cooper just getting high on sheer exuberant possibilities—
syntax, lexical items, themes, imagery—the elements of a world that will be
unmistakably his. After Idols we'll be able to recognize his catalog of riffs,
shticks, a sequence of John F. Kennedy Jr. poems, postcards of the young

Kennedy on his way to manhood. Another series has as its subject matter a bunch of hustlers, models and second-rate media stars of rock and kids' magazines. Then there's the beautiful series called "Boys I've Wanted," lyrical portrayals of classmates from other days. In *Idols* we encounter the world of desire, and it doesn't matter whether it's for commodities, celebrity, fame, sex or whatever. And if we don't have to worry yet about desire's deeper meaning(s), that's OK. There's a lot to be exuberant about in just what we do see. I

> dreamt of taming him
> with my body, my mouth
> so wet he would drink from it
> like a kid does a hose
> when he has been running all day
> and must stop, must drink

says Dennis in a breathtakingly perfect portrayal of sexual longing called "Mark Clark." "My skin tattooed there," Cooper said in "My Type," on the picture, the image, of an old lover

> its mind as set as
> Danger's, says, Dennis
> plus Mike forever.

Tenderness takes us to the deeper, darker meanings. Both subject and object are now torn loose from their former moorings in context. The object of desire tends to become more and more an "image," or fantasy, while the subject becomes the colonizer of that image. And this is, I think, the meaning of Dennis Cooper's long piece, "A Herd," at the end of *Tenderness*. Other sections of the book deal with exploitation as their basic theme. Sex-exploitation, commodity-exploitation and the exploitation a writer might practice on his "material" (i.e. people he uses in his work and, from another point of view, his readers too) are revealed as tendential murder. The story "Dinner" shows one man literally using up another one sexually and then throwing him away. And Cooper as narrator does exactly the same thing with a prostitute his friends "buy" for him in "For My Birthday." In the story "Lunch" there's an implicit equation between what an artwork is and murder. A performance artist (apparently) with a tape recorder and a distanced attitude goes around making tapes of his friends' voices. Then finally—"Jack checked off a list in his notebook. Four down and fifteen to shoot. So far it was going well."

But unlike the anti-porn people, and the anti-sex moralizers, for Cooper it's also important to tell of the satisfactions of the commodity world—to insist that distorted satisfactions are also real, and shouldn't be dismissed. There's one moving example he gives in a poem called "Being Aware," a sort of mystical monologue of a street hustler, who's clearly headed downward—a loser. When tricks are with him, older men, usually, who just want to use him, he dreams of his past. "Hey, Dad," he exclaims achingly, "it's been like this / for decades." Then comes the matter-of-fact reversal. "It means tons to me," he thinks.

But even with these qualifications, Cooper's frightening last word is "A Herd." Accounting for nearly half of *The Tenderness of Wolves* in actual length, "A Herd" is a long narrative with several parts and often coinciding viewpoints. Everyone has a story to tell about the central fact of an(other) young man's murder, beginning with the mass murderer, Ray. Mother and father of the young man, the murder victim, high school friends and sex-friends, even God they all get into the act. It's a weird story all together. A crazy guy wants to kill kids so they'll finally become *objects* for him. Of course mother and father just don't understand—behind their eyes they are only Ozzie and Harriet. Too bad for them. God might understand, but he's out of the picture—he doesn't count. As for the kids? Maybe. Maybe in a confused sense they know, but even that's not certain. But Ray knows, the murderer. He's heard voices—like Joan of Arc—and he *knows*. And at the end, chaining up the boy, before the explosion of sadistic violence, he looks for the "idol's look," as Cooper calls it—which he can't find. He grows weary in these situations, but when a boy dies, Ray gets his prize. And

> [...] with the facial expressions dulled and in place, Ray would
> gradually find that the kid brought to mind some ripe child
> whose hit songs were stuck on the radio, whose visage beamed

down from most billboards. Then what Ray had done took on meaning—

as, I think, Dennis Cooper's somber book does too. These hard-edged meditations on the meaning of commodity society bring us close as any poetry to a confrontation with the meaning and structures of our own lives.

"Stoned Out of My Gourd" was first published in *Fuse* (Canada) no. 6, vol. 4 (Nov/Dec 1982).

KATHY ACKER'S *GREAT EXPECTATIONS*

What's involved in a performing art of the text is a relation to an audience, which means feedback. Joan Rivers jokes about being seen by three stagehands between costume changes. One throws up; the other two become homosexuals. This makes national headlines. Everybody either approves or disapproves.

Like Kathy. She has all these voices or personas or whatever coming at me from all sides and I can hate it (them) or love it (them), it doesn't matter. Just react. Sylvère Lotringer, editor of the chic terrorist magazine *SEMIOTEXT(e)*. Steve Maas (I hope I've got his name right) and his crummy/glittery Mudd Club. Rosa who writes them letters. Cynthia who fucks Propertius. I can hardly IMAGINE the disgusting/sophisticated/wonderful New York that's being purveyed under the guise of ancient Rome. Or else we're in Egypt and talking with Anwar Sadat. And Kathy says apropos of it-hardly-matters-which of these made-up locales, "A bones-sticking-out cow is dragging a cart by glittering religious objects past a dead murderer"—to see the scene. There's no time, as she keeps insisting, things just are—so everything's everyplace. A pastiche art, and it's not a formalism, or if it is, isn't Ashbery, has the obviousness of being tarted-up—a little Proust, some Dickens, oh maybe a little trashy Victoria Holt—a cosmetic art in short. No relation too sacred to blab about to her readers. Sole requirement: a response.

So to spill your heart out, guts, anything: to spill the most intimate secrets of one's personal life out there, and see these surprised-looking figures emerge—sex, money, ghosts from a family closet (for instance suicide). It sets you back on your heels. A horribly inhuman and completely inappropriate (2 diff. criteria) family funeral scene where everybody's asking who ripped off the family's *800 shares of IBM*, with *you did, you little bitch*, the answer implied, to the protagonist. Two words come to mind to describe Acker, shameless and brazen, as in this from *Great Expectations,* the letter to Rosa's (Kathy's) (ex) boyfriend Sylvère:

> This serves you right. I told you this was going to happen. Now
> that I've spent last night fucking you, I'm in love with you. I'm

writing these few lines to give you the news and the news isn't good. A few minutes ago the cops arrested me for stealing a copy of *SEMIOTEXT(e)*. You keep talking about how you're making Italian terrorism fashionable: isn't my ass here in New York worth at least a penny to you for every dollar of Italian terrorist ass over there?

Consider what's happening beneath the flashy surface though. Sylvère in real life is getting his due in more ways than one. His magazine *SEMIOTEXT(e)* gets free ink—publicity. By the same token it's implied that Lotringer is really another jaded entrepreneur, selling anarchy for U.S. dollars. If not actionable at least this isn't complimentary. What, we have to ask ourselves, is Sylvère's take on this? Hasn't a real-life person (Sylvère Lotringer of New York City in this case) been insulted? Kathy starts to plug you into a *reading dynamics* of her book: the effects of her words on her people have to be constantly factored in. She makes sure her text isn't autonomous from the world.

Further implicated in NAMING NAMES: community. There has to be a related group that actually cares about the dirt you're dealing—and not just the abstract group of those-who-have-the-$5.95-to-buy-a-copy-of-your-book. I think this is at least part of the reason Propertius occurs as a character in Kathy's book. He—and others, like Catullus—are extremely interested in the relations they have with a group that knows and cares about the gossip they're retailing. That's ancient Rome. Where everybody who's anybody knows each other. New York's similar for Acker: the glamor of artistic competition. Catullus's book was called *Odi et Amo*—I hate and I love. In Kathy's book gossip helps articulate the society of artists, writers, others in New York with an interested relation to the first two. And this aspect of naming names is certainly a post-modernist tendency in Acker's work.

The countertendency is the moralism. In fact Acker's tendentiousness is actually structural. She NAMES NAMES and then tells you why she just did this. First give them a little narration, then give them a little philosophy. What philosophy? Well, that naming is the key to life—and life's problems. It's the constructedness of naming—or language as a phenomenon—that's so obnoxious. Maybe then by naming enough of these names, repeating and so running through their obsessional content enough you can get free of them—I hope! A person approaches the real by naming, eventually to become indifferent (maybe). You can numb yourself. But further: underneath names is the problem of phantasies, people themselves (ego), the articulation of a supposed real thru images. This last, incidentally, can remind a person of Jack Spicer, in its elevation to the lynchpin of a person's methodology of (poetry) writing (remember the constantly expressed desire to be "independent of images" of Spicer and in the *After Lorca* prose sections?)—though Acker's work fronts the *emotional* quality of these images. And in all this Kathy's work proposes not as some knowledge-for-its-own-sake or episteme (objective science) but as ethics—I'm doing all this thinking and writing about the thinking so I can maybe, if I'm lucky, be less unhappy. For Acker this writing is urgent.

The program (therapy involved) is the process (writing). Even the worst images (ones that have the most power to hurt), if repeated often enough, lose some force. The protagonist in the middle of a long s/m dialog: "I'm doing everything I can to understand. / I'm doing everything I can to control. / I'm doing everything I can to love (name)." "BLOOD SEEPS OUT OF ONE OF THE GIRLS' CUNTS WHILE HER LEGS ARE SPREAD OPEN"—followed in her book by the most emotionally neutral, bland stuff you could find—"Hatless, wearing practically no makeup, . . . dressed as she is in a very full wool tweed little boys' trousers and a box-cut matching jacket." This gives you the effect of primal therapy; at the end you feel like a damn dishrag. But it's the *effect* of therapy. No one expects a cure; least of all Acker. In spite of repetition of the most violent images one after another—there's no progress. At the beginning Kathy had invoked the idea of changing her relation to the image ("picture") of her mother. "I have to forgive my mother for rejecting me and committing suicide" and all that forgiveness will "transform need into desire." But at the end there's a full admission that the "only anguish" Kathy knows is from "running away," and the initial project of change seems an illusion. The last words are "Dear mother" (before "END," last page), and that's all. No full stop, but a comma ending this book, marking the cyclical aspect to things. Desire present only as a machine to run on names.

Isn't there a religious sensibility here? The impulse that, because there's too much pain in her life, makes Kathy *scream* I trust most. Then there's the other side, the voice or impulse which keeps suggesting—aren't violence and stupidity just like muscle spasms? To break their grip, push into them. Comedy, of which there's a lot in Kathy Acker, is just a stop-gap to reconcile mutually opposing, finally irreconcilable viewpoints:

> WIFE (entering their wall-to-wall carpeted living room): But you can't leave me. It's Christmas.
> HUBBIE: This is my vacation. I worked like a dog all year to keep you in trinkets and furs. I want to do what I want for once in my life and it's Christmas.
> WIFE: You're gonna desert us on Christmas! You louse! You lousy louse! Mother always said you were a louse and, besides, she has more money than you! I don't know why I married you I certainly didn't marry you for the money. (Starts to sob)
> HUBBIE: Stop it, dear. (Doesn't know what to do when he sees a woman crying. It makes him feel so helpless.) The children'll see and think something's the matter.

—and this comedy, an unbounded appreciation for your own and other's stupidity, becomes a dead end. Between the lines—a fatalism. A belief that karma makes the world happen, a belief in IMAGES, NAMES. Is there a covert plea for some kind of Buddhism? Why do people act like they believe that these images and names are what they purport to be, and can't we be deprogrammed some way so we hurt less? Questions *Great Expectations* nags us, teases us with. Acker is very sincere in raising issues like these in her religio-philosophical meditative sections, but it should also be pointed out that the high tone of seriousness they imply provides an ideal cover for the (for me) much more interesting (and morally unimproved) scandal-mongering sections. Which is where she makes her real breakthroughs.

What Acker set out to do (to judge from a whole body of other work from *The Adult Life of Toulouse Lautrec* to *Kathy Goes to Haiti*) is to cross modernism with the life of the feelings. In the process she discovers she's in conflict with a basic tenet of modernism (the autonomy of the text, écriture), since the book she writes inevitably—and more and more—keeps slipping off the page. The sense of scandal and invocation of real people comes from a need to deal with emotion, and to the extent the text has become increasingly disconnected from life, extreme measures are obviously called for. These extremities plug into Kathy's Buddhist series I've just talked about—DESIRE/PAIN/SCREAM. If they scream (you, me, anybody), you've made a connection and are dealing with life once more. Pain, the emblem of life—you know you're not dead.

At a time when production of emotion had become problematic for literature, a writer might search for ways to reconnect (rather than disconnect) signifier with signified and so start the flow of actual (rather than simulated) emotion. Names of people implicate these people in the sequence desire/pain/scream of the book. They pin down, as anchoring points, the dislocated signifiers, attaching them to signifieds—or more exactly, they stop the field of signifiers from continuously sliding on the field of signifieds. This forces, allows, the entrance of the/a REAL.

Take the case of Sylvère. There's some obvious sense that now, with the publication of Kathy's book, the ball is in Sylvère's court, and that our participation as readers has been factored into this dynamic. The book becomes one event in a series that's ongoing through certain people's histories—and has for that reason less of a privileged status (ontologically) than the (classical) commodity book. In order to effectively provoke Sylvère, Kathy needs an audience—us—so that Sylvère will lose face, or seem to, if he doesn't react to Kathy; because of us, her readership, just *ignoring* Kathy isn't any longer one of Sylvère's options. How does Kathy bait him? First, she represents herself as behaving sluttishly toward him—giving us to understand his sexual mastery of her. Second, she excoriates Lotringer as a moral bankrupt—he sells anarchist ideals for money, in her opinion, pretends to be what he isn't. Does Acker take this public stance to get Lotringer to come back to her to make him know what he's missing in no longer having her? To get revenge? Does she want to simply use him for his name value to make us buy her books (and, somewhere not too deep down, have critics write criticism about her), exploiting his personal history with her for career goals? It doesn't matter; her motivations are as complex as a summary of *Les Liaisons dangereuses.* For good reasons or bad ones, Acker has made substantive innovations in the idea of narrative-writing (formerly a.k.a. "novel"), has integrally linked this with the idea of altering social life by what you do. And as it has since Burroughs's proposal of a "virus theory" of narrative writing, aggression seems a necessary part of the project. Break some eggs, in other words. When writing historically recontacts the real, it's usually up against it first and foremost.

Sontag, Erica Jong and others just give Acker an opportunity of upping the stakes. Doesn't our pleasure, as readers, depend very much on the knowledge we have of the actual social relations involved? So Acker factors in this performance aspect, firmly emplacing her book in the now. "Dear Susan Sontag," writes the plainly faux-naive Kathy/Rosa, "Would you please read my books and make me famous?" A pert miss who closes with this dubious compliment to the famous critic—"I understand you're very literate, Susan Sontag." Hoping Kathy won't take a spill on this high wire, we await the next installment. And maybe Sontag *will* make Acker famous. Or maybe, outraged by Acker's liberties, Sontag will do her worst—and just ignore Kathy. We'll wait and see as we'll wait and see what (if any) response Erica Jong will make of Acker's scathing "Hello, I'm Erica Jong," in which she tears the former feminist (now commodity writer) limb from limb, making her the idea of a sell-out. Names in Acker's writing are key. Structurally they make the closure of the writing impossible. Meaning is generated from outside the book.

Finally, there's the personal revelations about herself, family wealth, attraction to s/m, the terrifying fact of her mother's suicide. Or—in a lighter vein—the missing 800 shares of IBM stock and disastrous family funeral in which Kathy seems to be suspected (by the rest of the family) of walking off with it. Or her anecdotes of being afraid her boyfriend wants her money. "Is my lover trying to get my inheritance," she wonders out loud to us just before the Clifford/Seattle section starts. Later another lover (I think) will snarl out an insult about her "grandmother's capitalist hoard" and so reinforces this money preoccupation. I think Acker is trying to put herself a step ahead of us, anticipate us here. Who would reproach her at this point? She's blabbed so much about that family money of hers that you're bored by the subject and would obviously never dream of criticizing her for their ill-gotten gains. Same with the rest. Isn't Acker's purpose in advertising her interest in s/m for instance—or else the scary event of her mother's suicide, another example, to *disarm* us in the dialectic between her and us? Now that everything in Kathy's personal life is all spelled out, frankly, we're hardly in a position anymore to be able to blackmail her. So Acker's maneuverings go essentially beyond Confessionalism or New York School making of confidences, beyond therapy into writerly choices. Relations with readers structure themes, not the other way around. As a result the formal status of this writing can only be described as novel. Acker's intention is to strip bare the motivation (usually concealed) that makes literature serve personal ends, reintroduce notions of subjectivity into (post) modernist writing.

"Kathy Acker's *Great Expectations*" first appeared in *Poetics Journal* no. 4, edited by Barrett Watten and Lyn Hejinian (1984).

GEORGES BATAILLE:
A FAVE "NEW" WRITER AND HIS VILE BOOKS

I find lust an emotion indistinguishable from anger.
—JOE ORTON, BEFORE BEING MURDERED
BY HIS LOVER (DIARY ENTRY)

As for me, it's the wind of death that sustains me.
—MADELEINE, THE INCESTUOUS MOTHER
IN GEORGES BATAILLE'S *MY MOTHER*

I like the purity of Georges Bataille's work. Uselessness, purposelessness, rancor—that makes me think of gay style in the 50s. This is odd since Bataille is—was—completely heterosexual.

But you'll admit his perspective's perverse, and it's my hope he'll appeal on this basis. Think of yesterday's great gay heroines—the Judys, Blanches, Tallulahs: Was it for beauty alone they were loved? Bataille's values—uselessness, waste, kink—turn into sheer loveliness, extravagance. If it doesn't cost, what's it *worth*?, asks this apologist for the darker side. His considered wisdom: Suffering or human loss (he calls it *anguish*) isn't just a stage toward what we want; it's what (all along) we desire most.

An example of how this works is *My Mother*. Everything about Madeleine is so stagy—so affected—especially her *language*: Isn't this a person deeply concerned with the biggest questions of life? Will it surprise you if I say that Madeleine's a monster? Here's a sample of her twisted perspective:

> Vice in my view is like the mind's dark radiance which blinds
> and of which I am dying. As I debauch myself I sense my lucidity
> grow.

Now Madeleine's no hedonist or vulgar sensualist. She's on a spiritual journey. She perseveres where her deepest and most crying sexual needs (incest, lesbianism, being a procuress for her son) take her, and this is ultimately to suicide. She goes from strength to strength, as the Bible says; and we're unstinting in praise.

So bless Madeleine and those who, like Bataille, stand for a commitment to the theatrical, to a deeper understanding of the ability to express, go outside ourselves:

> If we didn't know how to dramatize, we couldn't get out of ourselves. We'd be isolated, compressed. But a kind of rapture— in anguish—leaves us on the margin of tears; and then we lose ourselves, forget ourselves, communicate with an ungraspable beyond. (*Inner Experience*)

A place of dreams, the childish, the animal? Opposites don't just attract, they really *meet* in this place, since, as Bataille says:

> There exists on the contrary an affinity between: on the one hand, carelessness, generosity, the need to brave death, tumultuous love, suspicious naiveté. On the other, the will to become prey to the unknown. ("The Notion of Expenditure")

Too poetic? Bataille didn't *intend* his writing to be taken this way. He once proposed human sacrifice as a way out of the disaster zone that was French politics and economy of the late 30s. In Bataille's beautiful writing you can forget—though only temporarily—that he had in mind a critique of late capitalism where death, he thought, is as meaningless as life. The accent's on language.

To take up a more practical question for the moment: "Who is this Bataille and why haven't I heard of him?" As opposed to the kudos he has received for his writing in his own country (France), why the delay in recognition for him on our side of the Atlantic?

Bataille died in 1962, and at about this time the French decided to rank the work of this professional librarian (his on-the-job-hours were spent in France's Bibliothèque Nationale; his specialty, coins) with that of the other world-class writer of the day, Jean-Paul Sartre. Now, this is definitely odd, since during their respective lifetimes (which almost overlapped) Sartre was considered the more innovative of the two giants; it was assumed his writing would have the most hard-hitting impact in areas like philosophy, literature, politics, economics, sociology etc., for generations to come. Today people consider Bataille to be the pioneer, the one with the most power to stir radical perspectives. Are Bataille's thoughts on the importance and value of sexual risk-taking one of the reasons? What caused the changeover?

For one thing, Bataille's thought is closer to anarchy—nearer in spirit to the counterculture movement of the late 60s. Bataille's writing supposed that political and personal change couldn't be separate—a principle Sartre gave lip-service to but balked at, subordinating private to public, subjective to objective. Bataille's interest in sex was primary; it was essentially an encounter with the imaginative or terrifying. The popular appeal of this was reflected in the slogan of the French student rebellion of May of 1968—"All power to the imagination." Would a philosophy that was sexually permissive, if not downright liberating, appeal more strongly to gays than one that was essentially silent or repressive on sex matters?

Whatever judgment future generations make, it's clear gay men were among those most active in pushing Bataille's writing. It's not hard to suppose that gay intellectuals saw in the pro-Bataille movement a straw in the wind, one indication among others that the thinking on sexuality in Western life was about to loosen up, undergo some change for the better. In any case, Michel Foucault, the "out" gay philosopher-critic, promoted Bataille as a significant influence on his own thought as well as being the harbinger of a new era. "We owe to Bataille a large part of what we are," Foucault writes in his preface to Bataille's collected works. Gay critic-writer Roland Barthes also attributed to the older writer a pivotal influence in the development of his concepts—*ecriture, texte, jouissance.* There's a perception of common interests going on between gay males and Bataille.

What about women? Do Bataille's aspirations, his stress on the role of violence, even when it's consensual violence, put him into a serious conflict with feminist women? There are two schools. Some French feminist critics, like Julia Kristeva, point to Bataille's liberating stance, which accents the "sacred" or "violent" aspects of sexual need and leads us to the sphere of "nonexclusiveness" and "the abject"—meaning older layers of human emotion and reaction. Kristeva says that historically these layers refer to the flexible ego-boundaries of the mother-child relation and to the greater capacity of women to identify with others. But isn't Bataille part of a whole patriarchal discourse we're trying to get rid of?, asks Benoîte Groult, meaning porn. Critics like Groult protest: Bataille wants us to become animals—that's exactly what we're against. These critics join with those of the current (U.S.) anti-porn movement. Robin Morgan, in *Going Too Far*, says:

> Today, I can affirm my mother and identify with her beyond all my intricate ambivalence. I can confront ersatz "sexual liberation" and its pornographic manifestos for what they are—degrading sexist propaganda.

Bataille and his image of violence. He's *for* it, since it helps break up *this* world, bring on the next. Like Madeleine, Bataille's character in *My Mother*, Bataille is, as Sartre once said, a "new mystic." In *L'Expérience intérieur*, for instance, Bataille describes the world he's aiming for as one where "self" is "no longer the isolating, isolated subject of the world but a place of communication, of the fusion of subject and object." In order for that to happen, for "animality" to return to us, something always had to *crumble utterly*—and isn't the name and image of that process death itself? So death, according to Bataille, is always the *repressed other* of sensuality and is what makes erotic experience a "voyage of discovery" (Madeleine again). The slogan Bataille popularized to show this: "The erotic is assent to life to the point of death" (*Erotism*).

An S/M image then? In spite of there having been few visible signs of a French S/M community in Bataille's day, I'd give the question a yes, if I could qualify that assent from him. Like most philosophers, the practical tends to stymie Bataille. He's strongest on words; he doesn't know how to bring about in a *physical way* the world he's proposing. Bataille's interim solution is curious. Philosophers, others, should write books with appropriate images that, at some time, will lead to a new world.

At this point I'm happy to oblige Bataille. Here's my example of an image I consider moving. It's from *The Story of the Eye*, the earliest of

Bataille's porn books (1928). In it, two vicious French schoolchildren bump off a pal of theirs. With great sexual excitement, they watch her die from asphyxiation. It's not the description of the actual killing that thrills me, but the portrayal of the tableau that follows. Suddenly the whole scene is elevated in a frenzied way to a rapture that's almost religious in tone, by a death (reports the narrator) that leaves us as onlookers—

> blind and, as it were, very remote from anything we touched, in a world where gestures have no carrying power, like voices in a space that is absolutely soundless.

Don't these narrations of Bataille's have something in common with the non-sexual accounts of Don Juan's exploits in Carlos Castaneda's books? The point in both cases is, as Don Juan says, "to stop the world."

One last question: Is Bataille's lyrical, demanding writing about to spill over its cult status barriers?

The *People* magazine audience may not be ready for Bataille yet, but university readership has shown an enormous interest in the French writer's theories. Big-name (*Semiotext(e)*) and lesser-name (*Raritan, Discourse*) academic publications have been busy printing up Bataille's critical articles. Will the still unavailable Bataille appear soon? Of the untranslated books *Inner Experience* is probably most important. A major collection of early (economic and political) writing is due next spring (*Visions of Excess*, translated by Allan Stoekl, University of Minnesota Press). As far as Bataille's pornography goes, there's no longer a lack of solid appreciation for *that*. When *L'Abbé C*, the last of Bataille's sex novels to appear in English, was finally published in 1983, the *New York Times* gave it a ringing endorsement. Bataille's dirty book, *The Times* found, was provocative and stimulating, and contained the seeds of a new sexual ethics, philosophy.

Doesn't Bataille's transgressively-minded work *offend* anymore? Experimentalist writers like Kathy Acker, gay writers on the cutting-edge like New York's Dennis Cooper or San Francisco's Robert Glück, say the opposite. Bataille's impact on these writers takes the form of a sense of the beautiful as a mix of silence and aggressiveness. In his last collection, *Elements of a Coffee Service*, Glück details sex scenes of Aztec human sacrifice, eroticized as reverie. He has this to say about Bataille's influence on his latest book (*Jack the Modernist*, to appear this fall): "Bataille's useful because he dares to take us to the limit—he takes sex and death to the boundary where language falls away. That's where I want my writing to be." These writers seem to ask with Bataille: How can you find respect for values of immediacy and "animal life" without a sexual-cultural-political *violence*? But what would that new world of animality look like—I wonder—and how do we get there?

"Georges Bataille: A Fave New Writer and His Vile Books" first appeared in *The Advocate*, no. 400 (August 7, 1984).

PERCEPTION OF A BODY AMONG WRITING'S PARTS

Do the parts make up the partners? Should Bataille's, or Foucault's writing retrospectively be seen as complementary, irrationally opposed, not condemned to solipsism? For Bataille there's the seduction of the pathetic—being a lonely human being, dark night of the soul, etc. But this is also a firm intention, on the part of loneliness, to burst, do away with itself—no, the self—once and for all, as he points out. In *Inner Experience*, this results in frantic cancelling operations:

> Suppression of subject and object. The only way not to end up with possession of the object by the subject. That is, avoid the absurd rush of the *ipse* [Bataille's word for personal, individual consciousness] that wants to become everything.

Bataille the typical tormented modernist? The assumed stance of rationality in Foucault contrasts this. Light on the Dark. Clarity. He, Foucault, writes about how royal power started up institutions like the clinic, the madhouse, or the prison in the West for instance. There's a perspective on cultural necessities being dictated, and it first suggests—then explicitly states—that your emotional life isn't yours, that it's a historical function organized for somebody else's benefit. Not timeless, any more than writing or subjectivity is. "That sexuality," Foucault says in *The History of Sexuality*, "is originally, historically bourgeois, and that, in its successive shifts and transportations, it induces specific class effects." In this play, Bataille as Dark, Foucault as Light, there are questions for me about my being Dark for the sake of Light, aren't there, as a writer? Or the opposite. Light for Dark.

What I mean: What are the politics of trying to serve two Masters? How is it done? If like most writers I want to be a weird person, would my desire to undermine the state of things weaken or end up reinforcing the first desire? If writers want to get under your skin, don't we also just want to be ourselves? Kathy Acker's stance in *Blood and Guts in High School* is to lay these two sides of things side by side. To each position you give yourself wholly. So first there is the repressive side emphasized. Writers must be responsible people, mustn't they?

Once upon a time there was a materialistic society, one of the results of this materialism was a "sexual revolution."

Followed not too long after (in the language of Hawthorne's *The Scarlet Letter* as pastiche) by the volte face, hope springs eternal, a new day.

TEACH ME A NEW LANGUAGE, DIMWIT.
A LANGUAGE THAT MEANS SOMETHING TO ME.
Hello, Hester. Would you like to go out to dinner with me?
HAWTHORNE SAYS PARADISE IS POSSIBLE.

The body, as language itself? A cloud appears:

Dear Dimwit,
I'm so scared that I'm not thinking anymore. I want to do whatever I can to make you happy. If you don't want to fuck me, that's OK. If you want to fuck me once a month like you do all your other girlfriends that's OK. I'll do anything so I can keep knowing you. I think you're the most interesting man I know even though I'm scared of getting hurt by you.

It darkens, and it rains again. Ugh, back to Square One, isn't it?

Dear Dimwit,
Now you're gone from my life. You're not here. Go fuck yourself 'cause I hate you. I know you don't need me. I hurt. I'm stupid.

One way of being a writer—a way of writing for Kathy—is political. First you do one thing, then another.

I do Dark, then I do Light. The first is a "bursting apart," it's *non-meaning*. The context is its meaning, a narration. The perils come in, or seem to, if, of the two, the lineaments of the face of the first aren't revealed by looking at the second—and the other way around too. Dark averts the always possible threat of boredom, the status quo, system. Light gives you the vision to see the target in the first place, *articulates* it. Jack Spicer's aphorisms for instance (*Textbook of Poetry*) have as their point the making clear of these dilemmas. A troubled balance.

> Nothingness is alive in the eyes of the beloved. He wears the clothes wherein he walks naked. . . . I can write a poem about him a hundred times but he is not there. I have no words for him.

Which, on Spicer's most airy days, isn't that far from Shelley, neo-Platonism, praise of abstraction. The more intellectual the writer (in a radical sense the more the writer a writer) the stronger, more evident lies the danger to turn your back on the Dark that is your starting place. Hence Foucault, here, in his later career (*The History of Sexuality*)—

> Let us not isolate the restrictions, reticences, evasions or silences which all these procedures may have manifested, in order to refer them to some constitutive taboo, psychical repression or death instinct.

In fact the opposite is true, thinks Foucault at this point. Without his own sudden, untoward death, would Foucault have taken his distrust of subjectivity (sexuality) to a rejection of sex as such, the Dark?

> What was formed was a political ordering of life, not through the enslavement of others, but through an affirmation of self.

And as Foucault moves farther down this road towards a more secure emplacement of *self* against the backdrop of common sense, Bataille's the more attractive. A writer *begins* with the messy, the ugly, the kinky—where else would you go, who else is obligated to take you in?

Bataille's deficiencies in realizing social concerns put the brakes on my budding admiration for the Dark unqualified. Here's an exemplary rant of his. Fascism is nearly a corner unturned, as Bataille joins his fathers in this reasoning / unreasoning expression of the "hatred of poetry."

If you want to get to the end of humanness at that point you'll have to *force* things. The contrary—a poetic nonchalance, a passive attitude, disgust for the virile reaction, which is decisive: literary decadence (a fine pessimism). The damnation of Rimbaud who turned his back on the possible he obtained to recover decisiveness intact in him. The access to extremity has as its condition the hatred not of poetry but of poetic femininity (absence of decisions, the poet is a woman, invention, words, violence). To poetry I oppose the experience of the possible. The question isn't contemplation but a "tearing apart." Nonetheless, there is such a thing as a mystical experience that I'm talking about. (Rimbaud was one of its adepts, but without the tenacity he later put to good use in trying his fortune. His experiment had a poetic issue; in general, he was unaware of the simplicity that affirms passing wishes, without a future in literary history he chose womanly evasion, the esthetic, involuntary, uncertain expression.) [*La Haine de la poésie*]

Bataille's assumption that men and women have fixed positions in the play of subject and object not only disqualifies him on this score but weakens your confidence in other areas. Foucault's the more farsighted. OK, blow things away if you want, he seems to be saying. But he cautions—doesn't the explosion, rupture, even the collapsing in on itself of things it's apparently been the prime aim of modernism to promote—doesn't all this take place in a *situation, context,* inevitably? Bataille wanted a dark that was unknowing—but unknowing takes place against the backdrops of a particular time, place (in this case—France, early part of the century), doesn't it?

"Our Color is purple, or lavender," my first lover affirmed, intensely whispering to my avid and puzzled young ears the forbidden litany of who we were or might be. "No one knows why this is, it just is," handsome Vonnie said, her lips against me like the vibrant breasts of birds, her voice timbered as also song, her words like half-remembered ballad or blues lyrics that sounded stranger than English describing fragments of a story neither of us could recognize. She taught me the words of Gay life; she could not tell me what they meant. She wore a ring on her little finger as a badge of her Gayness, and the first thing she bought for me as a love and Gay-entry token was a slender silver and turquoise ring for the little finger on my left hand. She could not tell me what this had to do with our love for each other and our decision to attempt the difficult task of living together as lovers instead of taking the socially ordained path of marrying men, a continual pressure we were subjected to by every person we knew. Except other Lesbians.

That's the opening of Judy Grahn's *Another Mother Tongue*. I like its emphasis on story, on narration. How else would a young person find her way to the Darkness of being lesbian but by twisting—both herself and the things she lived with—into stories, badgering, beating, pushing, pulling this way and that till they gave up their meaning finally? What I mean to say here is there is some "ornery" aspect to the perverse. You twist the Dark till the Light comes out.

Once I envied French culture for the respect it gives writers, but now feel its limitations, the strengths, contrary-wise, of this culture, ours. If it's not the wisdom we're driving at, as writers—why continue high-flown claims, not go beyond them? Poe, without Grahn's sense of collective or group life, has equally the sense of magic of the later writer, which, as he intimates in one of his stories-on-stories, "The Imp of the Perverse," is the heart of his art—

We have a task before us which must be speedily performed. We know that it will be ruinous to make delay. The most important crisis of our life calls, trumpet-tongued, for immediate energy and action. We glow, we are consumed with eagerness to commence the work, with the anticipation of whose glorious result our whole souls are on fire. It must, it shall be undertaken today, and yet we put it off until tomorrow; and why? There is no answer, except that we feel *perverse* . . .

So is this self-destructive? Immolation? Bataille calls it expenditure—*la dépense.* The positive erodes, no thanks to god; so we only have ourselves to think of in this regard, thank you. Against self-interest, in Poe's story, the narrator confesses. He's a murderer. What compels him to tell this tale? Is the narrator awaiting a day of execution? He's in jail, everything said is a flashback. Writing pushes out the boundaries of things, oneself, in "generosity," "masochism." Is political commitment even part of this? César Vallejo's death, Good Friday, extending a Communist commitment to death, suggests possibly yes. The hallmark of Frank O'Hara's writing is a gift of self to friends—a potlatch, Bataille-style. So how far does the pendulum swing before you return to side-one, where writers beguile.

Take Dennis Cooper's style in "My Dad." It's so "self-reflexive." It's a good example of the backlash inherent in a writerly stance of being "pro-Dark":

Paul Petersen sang "My Dad," his '64 hit, on *The Donna Reed Show.* He did so stage-left, in full view of Carl Betz, his dad in that scene, in those days. Now it's '83. Feelings for dads aren't so simple. Simping his heart out, Paul Petersen sat on a theatrical trunk, very still. A still of it hangs in the National Archives. He chimed out the number. His father had done him a favor. He was his papa's favorite after he had that hit. That's why he sang it.

Things got back to normal. Carl Betz was Judd, for the Defense, then died of cancer. A friend of my friend Lee's friend Nick's father. We all felt sad, said a few words for him. Paul made his peace with show business and joined an insurance firm. "Now there is a man." That's what he sang to his dad (indirectly), Carl Betz (more directly), and my father (most indirectly). "My Dad" directed my life in this fashion. I fashioned dad out of nothing: a few lyrics, catchy tune, picture sleeve, a vague mental image.

Paul's changed. First, the cute young jock with a grateful dad. Then, a salesman with moustache and gold record. Still sees Elliott Gould on occasion. His last friend in the whirl of the business. I feel for him. Paul was feeling me out when I heard that song, but don't get the wrong vague idea. He was a dish but he didn't deliver. He was his daddy's boy, sat in that shadow.

My dog shat on my copy of Paul Petersen's "My Dad." Now it won't play. Makes a lousy mirror. "Look in me, Pop," the lyric was saying, "see yourself?" When I heard that tune yesteryear I saw Petersen sit on a trunk on a darkened stage in a TV show named for his (quote unquote) mother. Neither loss of his contract, nor lack of reruns, nor black of set, nor back of his jeans, nor *I Dream of Jeannie*, nor "Little Drummer Boy" (my favorite song, after "My Dad," of course) coaxes a lump to my throat like that sensation of love three times removed when Paul Petersen sang his smash to Carl Betz, who I'll bet was emoting a storm, i.e., "popular fiction."

Friction on the set! Giant TV star egos! An ergo remembrance that flickers out then the insurance man sings in a voice that's no longer his own. The one way back is a tune like a tomb. But "My Dad"'s in there! Carl Betz, dead. Paul Petersen, doll. My feelings, dulled. Donna Reed, dowager. Shelley Fabares, *Dynasty* (ABC Wednesday).

Shelley's survived. Her song "Johnny Angel" a cult hit today with ironic and sentimental young fags. But I forget what she said about boyfriends whereas I parenthesized what Mr. Petersen felt for his dad, played it over and over. I covered its tracks and now "My Dad" will never locate me out here. It's lost in a kind of grate, as in "frazzles the nerves" when you listen. It's forgotten, verboten. And I am alone among friends thinking backwards, a ward of its barely there message of pride for a thing that's died.

Putting the dark into brackets—as Cooper's sophistication does here and as Poe's did in another way, calling into question the death he ends his stories with, taking away with one hand what he gives with another—is a way of paying tribute to what's kept back, the impulse toward that. "Being the staggering drunk" (Bataille calls attention to the *price* involved, *obstacles* that present themselves on writing's journey) "who slowly, little by little, takes his candle for himself, blows it out, and with screams and in fear takes himself at last for night" [*Inner Experience*].

I add this: In the only photo that's been located of Bataille, he's staring back at you with this incredibly weird smile. Anxious isn't the word. How innocently do you think Bataille wrote the smutty literature for which he's famous? When everyone's always ending up being torn to pieces, eaten with such zeal by the other characters, you half imagine the point's to make you, the reader, the main cannibal. Bataille's twistedness covers the pages as an appeal as much for disapproval as endorsement. In a famous article ("A New Mystic"), Sartre fulfills Bataille's expectations by censuring Bataille's real childishness—the last line of his essay reads, "The rest is the business of psychiatrists."

To me, Bataille's expressions of *transgressing* (law, order, whatever), taken historically, say as much about Western Culture's specific lacks as they do about "eternal" values of philosophical meaningfulness *vs.* its deconstruction: i.e., what crosses your wires. Could there be by any chance—my hope!—a place where the two coincide?

> The most merciful thing in the world, I think, is the inability of the human mind to correlate all its contents. We live on a placid island of ignorance in the midst of black seas of infinity, and it was not meant that we should voyage far. The sciences, each straining in its own direction, have hitherto harmed us little; but some day the piecing together of dissociated knowledge will open up such terrifying vistas of reality, and of our frightful position therein, that we shall either go mad from the revelation or flee from the deadly light into the peace and safety of a new dark age.

Of course this passage from one of H.P. Lovecraft's stories can't help but be read now as much in a spirit of camp as in the one of stark terror which it was intended to provoke. It's so prophetic! In spite of the racism and social phobias that his stories typically imply, H.P. is Bataille's transgressive *match* in a comprehension of the power of Dark at a level of the body. The perspective begins in the town he was born in, lived in most of his life— Providence, R.I. What sarcasm in the name!—since the perspective, once opened up, seems by turns to twist, to go on out where the mushroom cloud goes, the cloud of unknowing, a light shining from the historical beginnings of the Western Enlightenment, it sometimes seems—now brighter by far than a million, million suns. Dark imposed on Light—*vice versa.*

We have mixed feelings in everything we approach. Is it important for an anti-nuke activist, writer Robert Glück, in this case ("Night Flight" in *Elements of a Coffee Service*), to write seduced by, seductively of, forces he's also made it his point to oppose, later, with the guarantee of a body (his own)?

> I thought, "I haven't been remembering my dreams," and with that my morning dream returned. I told it to Bruce. I dreamed I was dying. I cheerfully move beneath the vast dome of a hospital—the ceiling speeds and gleams like the inverted jewelry of a tape recorder. I walk up to a man suspended from the ceiling by his veins and arteries who tells me the meaning of life (which I forget) and then teaches me how to resurrect. (We avert our eyes even in dreams—even when I shut them I see a horizon line). I returned to life but then I went back and dreamed I died and stayed put. The bottom of the first dream gently gave way and the following dream occurred in its basement. I'm walking through a factory in the beautiful collective future of 2050. I'm in charge of converting matter into energy. I simply chuck matter through a porthole, a cool blue light spangles from inside and then a city has enough power. I feel a pleasurable impulse to put parts of my body through the window. It's slightly forbidden and intensely exciting. I start inconspicuously: little toe, little finger. Finally I ease in my whole body—a sensual rush—synapses diffusing—ejaculation.

This refusal—odd case of mixed emotions about the thing you have an intent to oppose—continues to puzzle me in an anti-nuke piece of my own ("Writing and an Anti-Nuclear Politics," in Bob Perelman's *Writing/Talks*), so I finally just built it in, made it part and parcel, to let everybody (you) see this too.

For gallows humor that comes close to stand-up comedy, a favorite of mine is Edward G. Robinson as Fred MacMurray's boss in *Double Indemnity*, telling MacMurray, the insurance rep, all the ways you can die accidentally. They're all down there in the tables, he tells him, in the actuarial statistics. Edward G. Robinson's at his best in scenes like this one, citing chapter and verse, ticking off on those plump fingers the categories of violence done to others. There's death by drowning, he notes, and death by falling from high places. There are deaths subdivided by location—by land, at sea, in the air. And death listed according to means—bathtub, auto accident, rope, shock. Each divides into still further subheadings, until at last you get this picture of a vast battlefield filled with severed limbs, crushed extremities, mangled bones. ["Hollywood Celluloid Nuke Madness"]

Is there a writer's dialectic of—first, I LOVE THE DARK, then no, THE LIGHT, then no, THE DARK, again? And which side of the fence do these belong to finally: diminishing planet resources, breakup of society we know, harms of racism, sexism, homophobia, etc.? Do they appear as Light, not just Dark?

So figure in this. In *Literature and Evil*, Bataille hardly has the same praise for Genet as he does for Baudelaire or Blake for instance. The problem is communication. The wonderful Dark does what it does when it opens out, *is* that going out. But don't make a mistake here, says Bataille—communication isn't the same as information at all. In a situation of information, sender and recipient remain unchanged, just what they were before the process. This is the blip blip blip of the phone line. But real communication causes alteration of both sender and recipient—nothing's the same as it was before. The problem with Genet's writing, thinks Bataille, is—there's no *communication* (with us, readers). He doesn't really *give* anything. Writing should be sacrifice. In contrast—far from communicating, but writing such sentences become smokescreens. Bataille is the figure of frigidity. Does Bataille's anti-Genet polemic help explain why good political writing doesn't try to *use* ("instrumentalize") you, but gives to you of itself enough to be "twisted", a little Dark? What are the mixed attitudes about death communicated by the following, for instance, so pragmatic at the outset, but containing too a deep *respect* (Ntozake Shange's "crooked woman," *From Okra to Greens*)?

> the woman dont stand up
> straight
> aint never stood up
> straight/ always bent
> some which a way
> crooked turned abt
> slanted sorta toward
> a shadow of herself
> seems like she
> trying to get all in the
> ground/ wit the death
> of her
> somethin always on her
> shoulders/ pushin
> her outta herself
> cuttin at her limbs
> a wonder she cd
> stand at all/ seein
> how she waz all curled over herself

So my question is can writers develop images of this doubleness? A way the not-meshing of parts and not-meaning of the words, sentences, and larger units of your discourse can be faithful to their mysteries, that is their non-meanings, or Dark aspects, and at the same time, by some mysterious process, to see the body rise again. This is my hope.

Charles Bernstein's borrowing of Mary Shelley's use of the Golem story shows that, necessarily, when pieces come together, there's always going to be something left over. Which is, to my mind, another way of asserting the indispensableness of this Dark. Be as scattered, as disjunct as you like. But isn't beauty something other?

I propose Dr. Frankenstein's creation as a central image for a poem because, in the blasé sophistication of the humdrum, there is all-too-great a willingness to domesticate that which is beyond our control and in so doing cede that measure of responsibility we can assert. . . ["Blood on the Cutting Room Floor"] [unverified]

Frankenstein's monster glows with this lovely perverseness. If the initial violence of the creation of this monster has been forgotten by most, who would prefer to forget about it? *We* can't. The monster's *heimish*, comical face is a result. To forget or forgive, both so equally impossible. Wouldn't both be insults, still more violence, etc.?

> Monsters and metaphors arose
> From human necessity. The period
> Ends the sentence by force.
> "When the lightning hit the house,
> It gave the apparatus a boost,
> And gave me the power,
> To turn the page of a book!"
>
> Elaine went a little too near the lake
> And her geiger counter went crazy.
> Monsters spent the next five minutes
> Lumbering out of their element. The brush
> Feels its way through the light.
> ["Mature Ejaculation" in *Primer* by Bob Perelman]

My perverse parts are my partners, they are plural. The whole *greater* than the sum of its parts. Bernstein again:

> When you put bits and pieces of language together you get more than the sum of the parts, the process resembling Dr. Frankenstein's stitching together pieces of flesh and engendering not dead matter, not an abstract arid and random collation

of parts, but a simulacrum of human being and a being in its own right. this is the story of the poem, its internal narration, as the kidneys and liver and heart narrate the body's story. . . [unverified]

So it's my very own body, a very large hope.

"Perception of a Body Among Writing's Parts" was originally prepared as a talk, given at the Foucault Conference, University of California, Berkeley, 1985, and subsequently published in *Jimmy and Lucy's House of K* no. 4 (June 1985) 31-45.

BRUCE BOONE INTERVIEWED
BY CHARLES BERNSTEIN

CHARLES BERNSTEIN: In recent conversations, you've spoken about the "dark." Do you think that there's an absence within the discussions on the Left, whether or not they involve art or literature, of an acknowledgement of the "dark"?

BRUCE BOONE: Yeah. I think that's what's holding up any kind of theoretical and practical and actual organizational development of any effective Left in this country or any developed countries.

CB: Explain what you mean by—and how you account for—this absence of dealing with the "dark."

BB: I think the real reason is historical—actually Charles, I think that the real reason is the one that everybody intuitively feels about the Left. The Left is the offspring and progeny of the Enlightenment. The Enlightenment is, you know, exactly what it says. It's the victory, the total victory, in the sense of totalitarian victory, of light and of the forces of light. Which means rationality. And which means repression and which means all these other things counterposed to which is the Dark. People are basically going on that heritage but they can't basically do anything other than cosmetic change at present to account for the opposite, the Dark.

CB: Isn't there also an association of concepts of the Dark with a kind of bad romanticism—which is the reason why parts of the Left might have problems with it? Because of the association of occultism, the seeming refusal of principles that would allow for an analysis of oppression, rather than revealing oppression as sensually embodied in aspects of our benighted times.

BB: That's a mouthful, Charles. I think there's several factors. Um, let's see how will I, one of the things Fred Jameson talks about a lot, and that I think makes a lot of real smart sense, is his perpetual analogy (I don't think it's an original one but he takes it farther) between modernism and political vanguardism. They're both, the underlying concept of both is that you carry the standards, there's a small group that's actually quite elitist. There's a small group who understands things in the case of Lenin's thinking. This is a group of shoddy petty bourgeois intellectuals who bring the word of the gospels to the benighted lower classes. And in the case of modernists it's like architectural modernism . . . you make an enclave in which you do something which is far more human than the present world allows. But the vocabulary, the language, the syntax in general, of the present world, doesn't in its debased form permit it. I think that that modernism is still the underlying political thinking of political people and so the refusal to acknowledge Dark is related to some kind of arrogance. It's an elitism which is anti-democratic essentially or authoritarianism—the word you use in your article in *Soup*.[1] One way Dark can return to politics is through an absolute refusal of authoritarianism, and at this point the political name for what's starting to develop both in politics and language is something very close to the word anarchism or anarchy. As a way that the left ought to be going further in the direction of anarchy. And Marxism itself ought to be letting down its hair in that direction. And that would be the specific political name or description of the kind of thing that starts to take account of that Dark.

CB: You're suggesting by this an anti-Leninist . . .

BB: Oh sure!

CB: Marxism?

BB: Oh yeah!

---

1 "Socialist Realism or Real Socialism," first published in *Soup 4: New Critical Perspectives*, ed. Bruce Boone (San Francisco: Soup, 1985) and collected in *Content's Dream: 1975-1984* (Los Angeles: Sun & Moon, 1986).

CB: Give me some history, in terms of writing or art, as well as perhaps political thinking or writing, by which you would trace a lineage for this new anarchism. This multicolored, rather than white or positivist Left, orientation.

BB: Well I think one of the things that's very interesting and I found this out in the course of doing the article on Duncan for *Ironwood* is that of all the places in the political spectrum in the early part of this century through the 30's it was only the anarchists among Trotskyites, anarchists, communists, uh social democrats and so forth, it was really only the anarchists who had any understanding of gays and what that meant. It goes from bad to worse after that. From Trotskyites to communists to concentration camps where they shoot gay people and so on. Which is still an issue if regimes call themselves Marxist and usually are a bureaucratic type. So I think that's a very interesting fact. Historically where does anarchism come from?

CB: Can you give me sources, examples of writing that seem to you to touch on, or mime, some of these negative capabilities?

BB: I think that there's sort of like two or three major strands in writing and I think that they're very interesting. I was thinking about that last night because they kind of parallel each other without really knowing it, so to speak. One of them is philosophy and there you get kind of a genealogy. You start in the West with maybe Nietzsche. There might be some people before but Nietzsche was the first one who was really a bad boy. I mean, he says, I'm going to be naughty. Or you know in the words of Eartha Kitt, "I want to be evil." Okay, that's Nietzsche. That comes and then goes to Bataille who I think is a greater figure. Bataille totally works that out and it's a process, from my point of view, which is well known, I think, that Bataille appreciation is only beginning; it's really going to be a complete revolution when it gets here. I think it's going to displace the structural stuff at the University when it gets here cause it's the immense understanding of it. So you got Nietzsche, Bataille and then Bataille's disciples who didn't necessarily know him, by the way. I'm not talking about Leiris and people like that in the 30's. I'm talking about Foucault and then Derrida, both of whom announced publicly on many, many occasions that direct derivation from Bataille. In fact, Foucault in various places says everything I am I owe to Bataille. And there's a very famous essay on Bataille which traces Derrida's own thoughts, by Derrida. So you go through this and then the post-Derridians, you get people like Deleuze and Guattari and/or Michel Serres, with his "parasites." It's similar. This whole French stuff talking evil but also noise and the communication, which is another way of saying "evil," I think, so this whole philosophical . . .

CB: You're not equating the Dark with evil here are you? Or are you? I understand the "dark" as an image (like in that song Lil Green sings, "Romance in the Dark"). So I also mentioned multicolored as another antiwhite, antipositivist image. That would allow for shadows; or be simply an alternative to "white" as the concentration of all the colors, including the absence of color that is black. Something to get us off the focus on a white image of white, in the sense that you have it in Poe.[2] That which is pure positivistic accumulation. Hegelian accumulation. But now evil would seem to me to be too much of a nodal point within what is really the spectrum of the nonwhite. Or do you think it's more of a key focus? Because if so, you're going to sound more Manichean than I would suspect you are.

BB: I sound partly Manichean and want to sound that way. Remember I'm living on the West Coast. The immediate heritage for us is the Spicer people and Spicer circle. The Manichean sense is very explicit in Spicer, Duncan, and Blaser.

CB: Maybe this is why you thought it would be interesting to be interviewed live from the East while being in the West?

BB: Right, a nice dialectic. [laughter] I think Nietzsche and Bataille both say evil is the word for this. I don't think so, I think Dark is better, I think

---

2 Edgar Allan Poe, *The Narrative of Arthur Gordon Pym* (1838).

they're roughly equivalent. They say evil is the best word, but remember evil is the word that applies to the current state of Christianized Europe because there isn't another word in the vocabulary system right now, but it's too easy an opposition. There are pluses and minuses. Bataille's or Derrida's evil is like a sheer negativity in the most blank sense, not a positive negativity in terms of Christian Europe at this time. We don't have another word for evil. Now it's important to be aware the word evil has limitations other words like Dark might not. Beyond good and evil, Nietzsche's idea. Evil is closer to that than good is in terms of Christian Europe. So I like evil okay, but with the qualification I myself now prefer to say dark. Dark isn't as theological sounding.

CB: Okay, you are still, in answering that question, talking about parallel strains. But you can't mention in the same breath some of the names you have mentioned without at the same time acknowledging that they have fairly opposing perspectives on the very issue that you're talking about.

BB: Yes. This is all philosophy. There's a whole other strain which is schlock literature, obviously. Okay, one of the reasons is because of the political configuration now and in French history. There's no real important native schlock tradition in France. The science fiction and the horror and the other kind of mass writing I'm interested in, is in the Anglo-American tradition, especially in Britain and especially in the U.S. In France, the whole thing is missing as a popular tradition on which to draw. They are sort of forced to be thinking out of the abstract and out of high class tradition like philosophy, so you get Bataille, Derrida, etc. But here in the U.S., we have this other tradition I call mass writing or genre literature, or whatever which is commercial in nature. It's mass market.

CB: What kind of genre fiction are you talking about?

BB: I'm talking about everything—from Mary Shelley [who] is still pretty high class when she does *Frankenstein*. Time progresses. By the time you get to *Dracula* in 1897 or so you've got almost a century of weird English misfits.

CB: Are you talking about Gothic?

BB: Gothic. First came Gothic. Then came Arthur Machen and the Little People hiding behind the dunes in Wales and living underground and all this kind of stuff which is literature of the inflamed weird imagination. And this is a very very strong thing, it's very very *new*. I'm just beginning to understand what a completely wide and deep tradition there was of this in England. Of course it's in this country, but not as strong.

CB: You don't mention, although I mentioned it in passing, Poe, and the interest of Baudelaire in Poe. Baudelaire's *Fleurs du mal*. How does that fit into your—?

BB: A really great point! Um, the uh, one of the interesting things about American literature is that it's already very early on tied in with high literature much more closely than in France, but even more closely than in England. I think that's absolutely right to say Poe is a good example. I mean he starts three genres, at least, at once. He does the detective and mystery story, "The Purloined Letter," he does sheer horror. You know, my heart stopped in "The Cask of Amontillado."

CB: And science fiction of course . . .

BB: *The Narrative of Arthur Gordon Pym.*

CB: Which revolves around an image of the Dark, of contradiction of black and white. In the end, Pym arrives on a completely black island—the people are "jet black," the land is without "any light-colored substances." *The Narrative of Arthur Gordon Pym* is about the descent into Dark, literally into black. Yet the final image is of something beyond the veil of darkness in which Pym finds himself after escaping the island. It is of a larger-than-life shrouded human figure, with a complexion of "the perfect whiteness of the snow."

BB: The all-colored atheism at the end which is white according to Melville, that's his phrase, "The all-color of atheism." So that's interesting. The strength of the native Anglo-American tradition in schlock writing which isn't there on the European continent on the popular level. That strength is testified to by its early entrance into high writing like Poe's. And of course Poe isn't the only one. He was just a very dramatic example. Hawthorne is less dramatic but to me a more cogent and convincing example, at least as good as Poe. Hawthorne is more to the point for high writing because he's so allegorical and the whole meaning of allegory. But then you have this whole tradition and Lovecraft is a person I'm immensely influenced by. And Lovecraft is a schlock rewriting of Poe if you read him. It's tacky and scary and stupid but taking a lot more chances because it's schlock. Then you go on and in the same New England there is this direct genealogy to Stephen King who I'm also very interested in, and he traces his writer's genealogy to Lovecraft on through him back to Poe.

CB: Did you know that King is enormously influenced by Williams? William Carlos Williams?

BB: Explain that because I don't know it.

CB: I can't explain it in terms of reading his work which I don't know. But he showed up at the Williams' centennial conference in Orono, Maine, last summer and professed a great admiration for Williams.

BB: Hum.

CB: I don't know what the meaning of this is. It's peculiar when you're talking about parallel strains. Now what King would see in Williams, I don't know.

BB: All I can think of is Williams' last recorded work is from *The Paris Review* interview where the interview goes on and then there's this footnote at the end which says he died shortly after. His last recorded words are he gets up at the end of the interview, goes to the blinds. And he's sort of a hobbling old guy at this point. He goes to the venetian blinds, pulls them down and looks out, turns to the interviewers and his last words are, "There's a lot of bastards out there."

[laughter]

CB: The parallel strains, you're saying... so now this is the second parallel strain, which you've interworked a little bit with the high and the low in American and British literature, which we could pursue at some length, but I don't want to lose the overall thing that you're saying. What are the parallel strains that you're suggesting here?

BB: Parallel strains. Well, in the second one don't forget to throw in all the movies which have been done so wonderfully in this country, all the science fiction movies and horror movies from the fifties on, especially. Okay. Philosophy is the first big strain. You have your pulp or mass or schlock or whatever is the second parallel. The Europeans were working this out at this very abstract level because there wasn't any accessibility for them to any really popular stuff having to do with evil in Anglo-American countries. Now the third is high writers of mystic and magic and the Other World, your Spicer Circle, Duncan, Blaser, and so on...

CB: Think also of Lansing who has such an interesting, specifically in the Dark...

BB: Gerrit Lansing?

CB: *The Heavenly Tree Grows Downward*, and more recently, *Analytic Psychology*. A lot of his concerns have been with the occult, for example, but within a poetry context. He also writes about his concern for nonheterosexual metaphors.

BB: Nonheterosexual?

CB: Right. Nonheterosexual, that is to say, various images. Cause he's not, I think it would be a mistake to say that he was interested in only homosexual types of images, as far as tropes and so on. I think he feels that the heterosexual imagery in and of itself is a limitation related to Western philosophy.

BB: Yeah, it is.

CB: That we have to get beyond to something more polymorphous and androgynous. I think androgynous is more what he talks about but he's also very interested in black magic and things like that. He's also written some important essays. "The Burden of Set" is an essay which relates to some of the things that you were talking about.

BB: Where do you find those?

CB: Some of it was reprinted in *Caterpillar*. It was originally in his magazine, *Set*.[3] Again, he is more in the kind of Duncan-Olson tradition of being interested in various heterodox lore. But I'm wondering if you can see that as a parallel strain?

BB: Exactly. In fact, that is the third strain.

CB: For instance, in "The Burden of Set," Lansing writes "European whiteness is a sepulcher & European consciousness a museum." Then he writes, on the "sexual image": "All is permitted. Change in the Heavenly Female Power. As equality of the sexes swings around, the biochemical basis of the old differentiation is shifted. This doesn't mean everyone will be queer, but as new magnetic centers astrally arise in men & women the scope of both amativeness & adhesiveness will be prodigiously enlarged." He goes on to quote from the fragments of Berosus that "We can trace a Babylonian genesis from which was later derived both the Hebrew & the orphic (later the Platonic) myths about the original bisexuality of the first

---

3 Available at EPC Digital Library

man, Adam, male-female, from whom the opposites were later separated & polarized by the male-female god. Under the permissions, man will be able to find in woman more the original wholeness, & woman in man . . . The work of Renovating Intelligence." And so on. You know it's kind of a Duncan . . . it has parallels in Duncan. I wonder how you feel about that. It seems overly mythologized, perhaps.

BB: This is getting within that and I think that that's definitely the third strand where this stuff is working out. This kind of poetic, occult oppositionalism in high literature, high poetry itself that has come to be. But I do have some critiques and I think that you put your finger on one of them when you talked about myths. There's a tendency when you get in the occult to forget that you're dealing with a set of metaphors in one tradition which has historical roots and is rather dated because the vocabulary and images are fixed early on and were fixed in ways that aren't necessarily always applicable right now. That's one of the reasons for returning to mass pulp and pop because that gives a vocabulary working right now, whereas with a lot of the occult and stuff it's a past or dated one.

So one of Stephen King's most important ancestors from another point of view is not Poe for him but Ray Bradbury, cause in the field of horror, Ray Bradbury was the first guy who really put this stuff which used to be Gothic trappings and you know, old timey European kind of degeneracy stuff, and he said it in completely totally American terms and geographies. So Stephen King picks up on this, actually does it one better, so you know Stephen King is as American as vomiting out pizza from your mouth.

[laughter]

I mean, he's really completely contemporary. There is this sense that what Stephen King did in his own line of the three lines, I would like to see other people doing, such as maybe myself, with regard to the occult stuff, but in high writing. I'd like to kind of rid it of strict adherence to a terminology which I don't think fits any longer. And so if there is one critique of the Duncan/Spicer/Blaser that would be it, although Spicer is least susceptible to that criticism. He's the one of those three who . . . one of Spicer's really great genius things is he begins the change that Stephen King did thoroughly for horror. Jack Spicer does it within this tradition of occult mystical high writing.

CB: How would *The Shining* or *The Dead Zone* work in a way that would be politically useful to a reader?

BB: Okay. I was just having this exact conversation with Michael Amnasan at Small Press Traffic yesterday when I dropped in, so I can say it very clearly, it's fresh in my mind. Uh, we were talking about *Tjanting* by Ron Silliman, and I was saying, "Well, what do you like about this Michael? Is it beautiful?" And he kind of paused and he didn't give me a straight answer. He said, "Well, I like it as a whole. I really like it as a whole." And I thought about this and let it sort of sit for a while and I thought, well, I think that's a good thing to say. It's a sense of wallpaper writing. Wallpaper writing, which has to do with John Ashbery too, or a lot of people. It's like when you just plug in minimalist music, you get this buildup, increment, the accumulation. You don't ever say this paragraph is absolutely splendid. Or it's a little off the mark and sounds a little weird, cause it's the whole thing, the product sense, so I agreed. If you carry this product sense, is somebody like Stephen King something like a, what do you call it, cyborg? Because what you have is something like a . . . what do you call it, a cyborg? Like being made half of a machine and half as a person. Is that a cyborg? Think of the kind of beings in Borges' descriptions of Chinese encyclopedias. I mean, you could just have different kinds of things, you have different kinds of beings at the epistemological plane. Okay, so if you were to take this notion of product, and apply it to sort of a Borges tree, or different epistemological planes, all being united in the most absolutely outrageous way, you have, for me, Stephen King. Because with Stephen King you have at least five different epistemological planes, none of which are comprehensible without reference to the other. The first is mass, or schlock, or genre writing. You can have any kind of mass writing to a certain extent, but that's only the beginning of Stephen King. There are references to other aspects of his writing, such as his own criticism, *Danse Macabre*, when he writes about the horror tradition in America in films and other horror books than his. Now there are references back and forth, there is the whole thing of the immense number of interviews he gives, and these are all constituencies that sort of carry out a kind of a common project that I see. There is the criticism *on* Stephen King, which is always elucidating his life. When he wrote *The Shining*, when he was in Colorado at that hotel, this is really the hotel, and we can see this. And this was when he got married to Tabitha, and he puts this reference to her, you know, and so on. There's also, like, parallel things that link up; Stephen King's novels properly talk to each other in the same way that I would like *my* books to talk about Bob Glück's books by putting in references to them and vice-versa. And they also talk to the great horror writers of the past. The characters in *Salem's Lot* actually quote, they cite Shirley Jackson, *The Haunting of Hill House*.

Stephen King's books talk to each other by setting up a sort of Faulkner Yoknapatawpha County mythology, where there's these phony, made-up names. Towns in the state of Maine, which don't exist, they only exist in King's stories. But *Salem's Lot* is the name of one of these towns. First it's in an early story, then he refers to it, like in *Firestarter*. The guy is driving up the turnpike, and then he sees the road-signs for the turn-offs, and one of 'em is "Salem's Lot," or another is something else, which is a real town. So you have this Borges principle of the real and the unreal together. Then talking of books among themselves, that's there too. A woman in *The Dead Zone* refers to an earlier King piece. Then you have the interviews talking *to* the books. In *Danse Macabre* he discusses his books. So, this is a sort of a mass production package where I would also see Ron's point of wallpaper principle. A product. Don't look at any one particular line someone writes. I see this in Stephen King, carried out on several different epistemological planes. The most important is audience relation, let me just say two words on that. The audience relation is like *Dynasty*, the TV show, is created by the fact that viewers write in to the show's producers. They say what they demand has to happen according to their point of view. For instance, this guy Armistead Maupin, who's a popular gay writer, wrote *Tales of the City*, wrote this long indignant letter to *The Los Angeles Times*, saying, if Steven [Carrington] is gay (Steven is a character on *Dynasty*, the gay character), how come we don't see him being gay any more since he's married? We don't *see* him going out with boyfriends any more. What *is* this, is Steven gay or is he *not* gay? The producers of *Dynasty* felt called upon to answer that in a formal reply saying yes, he is gay. And notice they say he *is* gay, not we *consider* him gay. It's a question of real factuality. And then they say, he's not only gay but you will see, in future episodes. Well, this is all talking about a writer/audience relationship. Which, in Stephen King, comes out very, very strongly also. It's parallel to Stephen King. I wrote a ten-page letter to Stephen King, in which I said Stephen, I think you do very good when you do this and this, but you still have something to work on when you do this, and I gave him further strokes for that, and so on. And either he was going to answer it or not. Most likely not. But the fact is he writes in such a way that he solicits this. And he goes on, to some extent I think, when he writes *Danse Macabre*, his book of criticism, not a novel. He says well, hey guys! This is real fanzine style audience dynamics. He has this persona, like a beer drinker, a bit of a slouch, and so he talks a bit like that, he says Hey guys! It's fanzine talk. He tells his probably mainly male readership, write in, and tell me if I got some of this stuff wrong. I do the best I can. But you write in and tell me where I got any details to what I'm saying wrong. And then people *did* write in. In the second edition of *Danse Macabre*, he talks about what they said. He says you know, I was really out-to-lunch on that, boy was I wrong, because in fact, it was in 1949, not 1947 when the movie *Zombies in Outer Space* for instance appeared, and I just got that wrong. It's like *Dynasty*, in other words, and there's an influence.

CB: You're getting yourself in deeper it seems to me though, especially when you use an all-encompassing term like wallpaper writing. Whereas, in fact, what you and Silliman do is structurally different. I wouldn't describe it as wallpaper because it's not a question of absorbing the wallpaper and saying I want to see more of this pattern or that pattern. Like "space music," which is I suppose a popular form of music, *Music from the Hearts of Space* kind of thing. . . in which you're enveloped by a single albeit slightly shifting harmonic sound. Even Phil Glass I would consider to be more in line of the equivalent of what you're talking about by wallpaper. Whereas what you and Silliman seem to be doing, as different as you each are, is actively interfering with the perception of the continuous wave—

by intervening! Ron, through the use of arithmetic and other patterns which make themselves manifest, and make the reader conscious of how the structure is being generated. And you, by actually intruding into the narrative, interrupting it. This is a crucial difference, and this is odd to even have to say because it's so obvious. The difference is that in *My Walk with Bob* and *Century of Clouds*, as well as the *La Fontaine* book for that matter, you break in. You interfere. You make the very kinds of comments that you're making now, within the context of the book. It would be as if Stephen King made some kind of the comments that you made in your ten-page letter to him, or that you're making now to me, within the novel, and talked about its links with the high and the low European, to French philosophy, and so on. This is what makes your work in fact not wallpaper, and that seems to me a very important political break from what you're talking about in King, which, as much as you admire, it seems to me by your own example, you must feel is inadequate to actually make those links. Because the problem with *our* culture is that it passively is able to absorb an incredible amount of material, that is, it literally contains the Dark, in its interstices, in the shadows . . . everything that we need to know that would break us out of the spell that we're under is present, but made inaudible and untouchable by the hypnotic force of media-sized wallpaper consciousness, in which the depths of darkness are, as by optical illusion, transformed into surface decorations. And you might even say, theoretically, if you read an issue of *The New York Times*, it will tell you a lot of what you would need to know, to analyze the society and even find ways to change it; but that is because it is between, or under, the lines, it gets absorbed subliminally, and never is brought to consciousness. What you seem to be interested in doing, in a different way than Ron, but in that sense similarly, in a structural way, is to force these issues to be brought to consciousness, and to be dealt with. And not to let everything sort of fade into the background, so the overpowering rhythm and beat and drum drive obliterates any ability to respond and act.

BB: Let me try and formulate what I mean in a sort of weird sense, that um, I thought of recently. That sense is that what I would like my art to be and anyone's art, in some way, is a communication with the dead. Now, if you have that phrase, to communicate with the dead, you can stress either communicate or the dead. Popular writing stresses communication, Stephen King, the sense of his fans and fanzines directed him in a community like *Dynasty*, the TV program, okay, there's communication for you. On the other hand, modernists, modern writing, and a lot of writing that was generated by your own magazine *L=A-N=G=U=A=G=E*, and, uh, some of the *L=A=N=G=U=A=G=E* anthologies and so on, stresses the necessity for crossed signals, so for a deadness. There's a negativity I would say, a canceling operation. Now, it's very obvious, and this tradition of, that's been around your magazine, for instance, has made it very clear to people that the relation called communication that goes on in the current writing or culture situation, is a debased one because it's a commodity one. It's really a *transmission of information*, not a real *communication*. So the way to deal with that is negativity, canceling. Now, it would be my ideal and hope to have a canceling and communication at the same time. This is a bit of a paradox, because, on the face of it, they seem to be terms that exclude each other. So part of my going back to these three strains: philosophy, the schlock writing, and the occult high poetry in the American tradition, like Spicer, is to try and put them all together in some way to try and make sense of how you can say I want to communicate and yet the people I'm communicating with are dead. The communication mediated by this falsification is always a commodity. So there's no way, we're trapped. I think the last time in history when you could really stand upon an enclave which was *not* a commodity, but defined itself as *true*, was the old-time Beatnik days. Jack Spicer refusing to have any of his works copyrighted, thinking that Duncan was a complete sell-out and jerk because he published with— was it New Directions?

CB: Yeah.

BB: Anyway, Duncan would publish with big New York publishers is the point. He was a sell-out for Spicer. Now New Directions wasn't that big at the time, but . . .

CB: . . . It's not that big now, in some ways . . .

BB: . . . No, but it's a *commercial* press! Now the Beatnik times are the last times you could have this idea that there are places in the country, either geographical places or places in the heart or any other definition of places you can *retreat to*! As if on a Utopian island and stand aside from the commodity deck which defines everything else.

The last time reality permitted you to think that way is probably the fifties or maybe the sixties at some point. By the end of the sixties, it's just no longer permitted. Everything is commodity. A writer starts out as a commodity from the word go, with grants and everything. The Baudelaire quote from *Fusées*—"What is art? Prostitution." . . . he says. I love that.

CB: I wonder if . . . is it that the historical situation has changed or is it simply that the analysis is deeper? On the one hand, there are plenty of people now who would want to claim that same "Beat" position of authenticity. On the other, the bad faith of the claim to authenticity that a certain kind of writing occupies an authentic place as opposed to a commercialized, commodified, "rhetorical" position—may in fact have been exposed before 1950 by a number of writers, some of whom you've mentioned, some of whom you've not. So I wonder, in a way, because you're saying it's not possible to do now, why was it, in fact, possible then? Wasn't that really a problem in the '50s too? Doesn't that remain a problem of some of those writers you speak of?

BB: Well, I think that's theirs, I think it goes back to an analysis of economics. The thought that there's another stage of capitalism.

CB: That changed from 1955-1975?

BB: At some point after World War II. It's hard to localize this, but that there was a change that meant a post-war development of commodity capitalism at some point which meant an emphasis on consuming. Which also mean that capitalism then, that the bottom line of that was capital realized it's markets in the obvious way were diminishing to a point of fewer returns, in America at least, and there would have to be new fields to colonize. One of these fields, the most important one, the heart, or subjectivity, sex, emotions. You have this immense push, and part of this can be figured by the image of the girl smiling in a bathing suit on top of a car selling it . . .

CB: That image is from the '40s.

BB: It thought it could colonize these new areas, and I think that, you know, it didn't happen automatically in 1946, was a slow process. That's why there are these people in the '50s, the Beatniks, trying to hold onto that Utopian island. I think that essentially, at some point in the late '60s, there was a completed thing, where emotion and subjectivity and sexuality and religion were effectively . . . this colonization is more or less complete by the '70s, early '70s. And also the colonization of writing. So that you can't have the image of the writer as a clerk or religious figure or a prophet, like Ginsberg had, that's not possible because you're a complete commodity as a writer by some point in the '70s. You start out as a young professional.

CB: But I think you're in a way being too easy on that, saying that there was a *reason* for them to have that view, the Beatnik writers. Theirs probably wasn't that deep a view and I think that the reason that Duncan and Olson, and so on, wanted to dig into that heterodox tradition of Western and non-Western learning was to find something that wasn't just a kind of a created space of subjectivity, which was claimed in that kind of almost anti-intellectual way, but to see what was *under* that. I think that kind of mining, even though it did perhaps end up in a certain kind of highly reified sense of learning, reifying the "ancient" to a degree that removed it, was actually a more interesting response to that situation than simply saying that you could, by sheer will, create a good faith subjective space that was somehow more real—and everybody else was fucked up. This goes back to your thought about the choice between communication and cancelling communication. My own perspective on that would be that the idea of communication itself, especially "mass media" kind of communication, entails a cancellation of communication. That when one wants to operate outside of principles of mass communication—you know, operate out of a desire for noncommunication—but that rather communication, as it has generally been practiced, has been sabotaged and . . .

BB: Yes, I think you have to reveal that . . .

CB: So I don't know . . .

BB: Well, language writing classically reveals this by "fucking up the text" to put it crudely, making it a *détournement*, altering it, let's say. Okay, then, you're detouring the text and you cancel the meanings in some way . . .

CB: Well, I think it depends on who you're talking about again, with a generalization of that kind. You know that kind of writing is multiplicious. I think you could also be talking about a richer mining of the field of meaning and communication rather than a cancellation in any degree. In a way, you're *cancelling cancellation*. That would be what would interest me, let's put it that way.

BB: There's a certain cancellation historically in the '70s that proceeds at the level of the page that has as its model the text. The cancellation involves things that refer, bounce off of each other on the page in the text itself and that's *ecriture*. Now the cancellation that I'm more interested in has to do with the dialectic of communicate/cancel that happens between the audience and the reader and the recipient of the message that goes out there, um, and I think that's for me the things I'm interested in, which is aggressivity and negativity.

This is how *sadism* of the writer comes in, vis-à-vis the reader. The specific mechanism is psychological. One of the things that's important for Acker is her relation to an audience. That relation is a very aggressive one and that's why it's important. That's how the commodity level of the package she's putting out is taken account of or recognized . . .

So, for me, more important than the cancellation of the message on the page is the dynamic of cancellation and aggressivity, which is a psychological term for the way this is coming out. The way that proceeds with regard to the people who are out there reading, the readers. But there definitely has to be an *erotic* dimension of this (*not* neurotic, but erotic) and the reason there has to be an erotic dimension is because we'll have to make the people *like* what's happening. If you say buzz off, bozo, they're not going to buy your books and the message won't only be canceled, it will never happen in the first place. That's to put it bluntly. So what you have to do is you have to create a dynamic of negativity that's erotic. The erotic part guarantees the continuing of the message and the communication keeps on going on. The sadistic part of that is when the negativity is revealed as negativity. There's just a big explosion in people's faces, in your audiences.

CB: When does representing stereotypes or repressive images of human beings, or representing relationships among human beings in sexist or racist images, become problematic? Given that it may be erotic...

BB: Can you give me an example?

CB: Well, given that it may be erotic to your point of view, it may be aggressive, it may be gripping. When does it become so primarily involved with reinforcing those attitudes that you want to put a stop to it? How far can you go?

BB: I think there has to be consent.

CB: Well, since we're talking about writing... I assume we could be depicting scenes which don't involve consent.

BB: No no no, there has to be consent between the *reader and writer.*

CB: Right; I understand that. But let's talk about a nonconsensual situation.

BB: When it applies to the reader and the writer...?

CB: That are being described...

BB: Or when it applies to someone else than the reader or writer?

CB: Right.

BB: In other words, take H.P. Lovecraft, he's a racist among other things. He's a wonderful writer but the other side of his coin of weirdness is racism. And one of the ways he conjures up weirdness during blood curdling mess horror, he says I was in Providence or some other old city, or he creates an old New England village and gives you the picture of non-WASP New Englanders, the foreigners with their deformed faces, their hideous languages and so on. He mentions words like Aryan and he was really into a racist mythology. I think that's a real thing but does not apply when he's bad-mouthing other groups like the Fiji Islanders. Or, well, he doesn't like any nonwhite people. Non-New Englanders he thinks are just foreigners, even Irish and Italian. They just seemed really weird to him and foreign from his New England viewpoint. If he was addressing them and he bad-mouthed them in the process of also charming the birds out of their trees, that would be one thing. But no, that's not it at all. He's charming the birds out of other New Englanders' uptight bigoted trees. So what's happening is you have this. It is *not* a dialectic of sadism/masochism. It is not a dialectic of negativity of eros. It *is* a dialectic of exclusion, pure and simple, and that's where prejudice comes in. Where the isms come on like racism or sexism or stuff. When you portray something where you want somebody to get off on . . . when you're going to act like a person who's going to make other people submit, when you want to dominate your reader, you've got to make sure that they're consenting and you have to build in the eros factor. There is or has to be a love underneath is what I think it comes down to. You have to really love them and you have to really know that and it has to be kind of a spider dance of love, and that's not happening when H.P. Lovecraft is badmouthing Fiji Islanders and other non-white people. Now the same thing with women when you come to sexuality. I would say Kathy Acker is a great example because. . . and Dennis Cooper's a great example because they are talking always in the family so to speak. I think Kathy Acker, because she is a woman, has the right to talk about women and has the right to kind of prick-tease, if you want. Dennis Cooper, since he's talking to and about a context of gay community. Dennis's community comes out of gay community, and so really this is a dialogue that's taking place in gay communities. So, the kind of exploitation and turning other people into objects is happening, there's a degree of consent there that you're talking about. Now, if other people talked about gay men that way, I wouldn't like it. Does that begin to answer the question?

CB: I'm curious about how this line is going to be drawn—that an image done within the context of the gay community, which seems derogatory toward gay people, exploitive sexually, is okay. It's as if the identical page is going to be okay done by one writer and not okay done by another writer. It's like a kind of extreme reader reception theory that you're advocating.

BB: Just as Jews can be anti-Semitic, or gays can be homophobic, and black people can be racist about black people—I can't think of an example, but here's a negative one. Dennis Cooper. He's not homophobic but has some weird stuff in the gay department. There's a distinction for you. I hope there's no homophobia in Bob Glück and myself. I think that's one of the things that's very much on my mind and on Bob's mind.

CB: So is homophobia irrespective of who writes it, that you can tell by reading it, not . . . ?

BB: Part of the way you can tell if something is one of those things is its location or non-location in the community. That's one part. But that won't give you all the answers.

CB: What about problems within what is deemed to be erotic, what is found to be erotic, as actually expressing ingrained, exploitive, commodified kinds of impersonal behaviors? That people are schooled into, or behavior modified into. I don't see that critiqued in what you're saying. How about art in which we're not released from this kind of behavior, we're simply given new instances of it, even if there's love or nonlove involved. It's as if there's no way out of a vicious cycle. The sexuality and eroticism may well express the most insatiable kind of commodified relationships in our society. That instead of putting us in touch with liberating kinds of impulses, anarchic impulses, they may, in fact, be very much regulating and controlling mechanisms? It seems to me again the difference between what you're *saying* and what you actually *do* is that you intervene in your own writing to make this kind of critique that I'm suggesting. In *Carmen* you go on for four or five pages, or ten pages, and then you do some kind of discussion. There's a release, a Brechtian moment there, that comments on the other thing and this suggests a Utopian impulse in your writing. But whereas a lot of the other things you're saying here suggest essentially a dystopian perspective.

BB: Yeah...

CB: So I'm confused. I see where you're interested in that material as source material, but I also see how you constantly want to transform it, when you're actually doing it yourself. Or when you're talking about it, or in your critical writing. And yet you seem, when you're talking about some of this material, not to find it as problematic as I'd imagine you would from having read the critiques of those impulses in yourself as displayed in your own texts.

BB: Part of my writing has to do with an identification I feel strongly in myself as "post-modern." Opposed to "modern." And, for me, this has to do with the um, the fact that every text has to have a metatext commenting on it, which is what I think you were referring to. The languages that are around today to work with are all we have, and you can only speak in your own language, after all. You can't speak a foreign language that you don't know. It seems tautological, doesn't it? But I think it's worth saying. Now, what if the languages you have are completely debased? As they are. I grew up in a commodity society, I speak commodity language. That's a debased language. The only way I can deal with that, my way of dealing with that is not detournement, but is this idea of metatext as opposed to text. You say something, and there isn't any other way that exists, than to say that thing just as you said it. But then you perform this step-back operation and you *comment* on it. That's the only way you can deal with the fact that all the languages that are given to you speak right now in this culture and this day are debased ones.

CB: Right. But this type of perspective, I would call it, rather, polyphonic or polyvocal, or as is now more current to say, dialogic (though I think "dialogic" has problems with it since it suggests a kind of two-way conduit of communication) . . . anyway a polyvocal or polyphonic kind of writing when one text comments on or speaks to the other text and so on, seems to me, to try to reach a deeper kind of communication that's not assumed to be able to be contained within a single kind of genre or focus or frame.

BB: Except I don't feel so polyphonic. Polyphonic to me means like the basic Roland Barthes idea of text as a bunch of strands braided. I think what's really important is, you have to get another idea of standing back and being at a new reality level. In other words . . .

CB: I think you're closer to dialogic . . .

BB: . . . the idea of frames almost like Erving Goffman. . . . supposes you make your whole, there's language and there's meta-language. And in meta-language you take everything you said as only one vocable, and the current language. Now that's very different from, you know, just weaving different strands of voice in a kind of creative babble, which is what polyphonic suggests, and what Roland Barthes suggests. And even what I think dialogic, if the word refers to Bahktin, uh, usually expresses. They take Bahktin's wonderful descriptions of the carnival as being kind of a creative babble of voices. Well that's different from presupposing the writing is one text and, like Borges, you step back, and you completely colonize . . .

CB: But you want to give some kind of a fulcrum authority to the second voice, and the difference is I think when the writing is read that one simply has, in your case, two voices which is the reason why I say dialogic, not polylogic. Dialogic in the sense of the one voice commented to or talking to another. You want to say one is "meta" and one is primary; I'm not sure that distinction matters in a certain way. You want to give a certain kind of authenticity to the commentary, but everything you're saying about manipulation, the eroticism of the experience and so on, suggests the reader simply will absorb what you're saying in that duration sequence that is given. And the authority that you want to give to what you're calling the meta-language, which I would say is the second voice, doesn't hold up, because it is simply another kind of charge, another kind of rush, that makes that voice, you know, leap from the page into the ear. And that it's constantly repossessed by the overall weave of the book, even if there are only supposedly two strands in the book. Of course there's a lot of strands that you don't control, that come out. And I would say that there's many in your work that make it more "poly," which is to say there's the philosophical, there's the political, there's the interest in the genre, the fiction, there's the autobiographical strain which is separable from some of those other things, even though it may be the integrating trope. So all of those things you may in fact *try* to manipulate to come together, but one can pull them apart.

BB: As far as I know, the terms you're using refer to something that happens *in* the text but don't refer *between* texts. They don't refer to a reader content or community for instance. Bob Glück and I refer to each other and each other's writing in our books. There's a "horizontal" connection. "Vertical" would be, I'll say in *Carmen*. After I finished *Century of Clouds*, Jonathan told me that the anecdote that I had told them was incorrect so on that basis I decided I would actually *say* that in *Carmen*. So the two books will be linked that way, and I will say something like, "Reader, do you remember when I said X in *Century of Clouds* or *My Walk with Bob*?" And then I will say that I was wrong there, that the truth really is, etc. That's the first point. The second is something like uh "biographical" . . .

CB: Autobiographical . . .

BB: Autobiographical, yes, what that means . . .

CB: What interests you about that? What's the difference from a reader's point of view between the autobiographical and fiction?

BB: Yeah. You know the story about *Moll Flanders*? That Defoe made up his book to *look like* it was the real person, Moll Flanders, talking, and the people bought into that idea? And that's why they bought his books. But that there was sort of a let-down when they realized this wasn't the case and there was a sort of a hoax . . .? Well, I was thinking of this and reread "The Custom-House" introduction of Hawthorne recently and I was immensely struck because the problem that he sets up is an autobiographical input. In reply to this he says, "I'm a modest person. I don't really go along totally with self-revelation." So how is he autobiographical then? In "The Custom-House" introduction to *The Scarlet Letter*, he is bringing up "autobiographical" as a *problem*. What he says is he couldn't write *The Scarlet Letter* until he had left the Custom-House, the physical place. It was in the Custom-House that he found the piece of cloth that is a real or scarlet letter, and a short narration of about 10 pages that's the basis of *The Scarlet Letter*. There's a biographical basis there. Not autobiographical. But he says that he couldn't retell the story, write this until he left. First fate had to take a hand and Hawthorne had to get kicked out of the Custom-House by a change in political administrations. He says he felt decapitated or dead. Which is very interesting. And then that deadness sort of extends on to the whole Custom House situation and he mentally says he sort of kills off the people. He says, "I can't even remember what they look like anymore! They're fading from me, getting further and further away, those Custom-House people. So now if I can write about that I must be dead too. I'm making everything *so* dead that now as a matter of fact my family, which has lived in Salem Mass., for four generations or eight generations, is now going to move out. I'm going to move out of Salem, with them." Imagine! "I'm announcing this with this book, I'm cutting all the ties." I think there are two things that are happening. He's wanting to *ground*. The way I take autobiographical or personal in writing is it's a way of *grounding* your speech so it doesn't float away or become a fantasy. The people in Defoe's day were afraid Defoe's book, once it was revealed as not to be by Moll Flanders was just *that*! Fantasy!

If you contrast the autobiographical, not with scientific writing or personal writing, but with fiction in the old time sense of something . . . that's a cheat and fraud, made up . . . then you see the real point to autobiographical. Spicer saw this too. It means you ground what you're saying. It's sort of a continuation of Black Mountain when they referred to "locality" or "polis." Or something like that.

I think that when people read something, the only way it really means something is if the words in some way can be *verified*. One of the ways they judge what that is it takes place in your actual life. But they gotta really be sure of this. You gotta show them, and then it's grounded.

CB: But isn't that a rhetorical trick?

BB: Not for me. I want to tell real stories with real names. This is where I think I relate to Kathy Acker. She puts down the name of somebody like Susan Sontag. Well in real life somebody could actually go to Susan Sontag and say Susan, isn't this really awful, what Kathy Acker says about you? Well, so I say about Bob Glück or if I mention Bob Glück's book in a book of mine, you can actually go into the world and check out what I saw. Take Jonathan. Now I don't say Jonathan's last name but you can presumably find Jonathan and look him up and say Jonathan does this tally with what Bruce says about you? You know there's a principle of verification. It's like nuclear arms tests.

CB: Yeah. But what happens if Jonathan says that it has no relation. Bruce just made it up. Just like the fact that a lot of people who read this will think that you spoke to me on the phone rather than that you simply made up my questions and your answers?

BB: Well, wait a minute. If they know they can go, if I give somebody's real name, if it's really clear that Bob is Bob Glück and when Bob mentions me it's really clear that Bruce is Bruce Boone from book to book—there is a principle of verification built into that type of thing. That's different from Joyce Carol Oates.

CB: But that reader isn't really going to check out whether these things actually happened or you made them up. I'm not sure what difference it really makes . . .

BB: If you put real people in, they have the option to reply. Sylvère has the option of saying something in public about Kathy Acker.

CB: But people can be mentioned and invoked in a way that they can't reply to, in a way that in order to reply it would just get them in deeper, or would further misconstrue the situation. I mean my limited experience with having my name invoked in various public contexts is such that I realize that even when the things that are said are patently misrepresentative, there is no easy way to respond. You can't really set the record straight. Because once something is said, regardless of what you say, you have to respond to the fiction that's been created. And in responding to it you may wind up giving more credibility to the fiction than if you simply pass over it in silence. Or you will just create another kind of alternative version of the truth that you want to have. I mean the newspapers are the best example of the fictional, ideological fiction, that's created everyday. In the New York *Post* or New York *Times* "real" people are being quoted as saying "real" things, which they may or may not have said, which may or may not in any way be accurate to what they're saying, which many of them have no recourse to correct. I mean that's what people always criticize about the newspapers. It has the veneer of being related to real people who could conceivably sue the paper like Ariel Sharon has just sued *Time*. Here is your great instance. Ariel Sharon suing *Time* for actually printing something that was essentially correct. Am I going to be sued because of what I'm saying that *Time* was correct even though it's adjudicated that is was wrong? Probably not. But . . .

BB: I would like to invoke my sense that I started within that communication with the dead and that this has two parts. And the "dead" part contains the negativity, and the "communication" part contains the eros. Well, when I put somebody in the text I treat them like an object that's not only an object but a commodity. I commodify them and I do them, I'm aggressive, that's the sadistic part. I, and this bothers me, at a very deep level I can purvey a very, very intimate story of my breaking up with my lover Jonathan, my ex-lover Jonathan in public. It's true I sent him everything I wrote just like I sent stuff to a certain David that I'm

BRUCE BOONE • 197

mentioning in a David story included in *Carmen,* and got his okay. And I changed things for Jonathan because Jonathan said to change them and this isn't right or I would rather not have this there or add this or whatever. I do that and I send it to people and it comes back. That's only the sort of a minimal level of human relations I think.

CB: But that's a matter of *politeness* in a sense . . .

BB: Wait wait!

CB: Yeah.

BB: Politeness is *human*!

CB: Sure, I agree that if you're going to do that, your approach is the right way to do it, but what . . . ?

BB: What we have is a situation that even though I go out of my way to do all those things which I don't think everybody does, and I think your New York *Times* situation is the opposite. People aren't doing that in the New York *Times* in the newspapers. Well, nonetheless, what I still have is I've commodified these people. I've commodified my then love for a certain person and relation. So how do you deal with that, that's the communicate. The communicate is the eros.

CB: Let me . . .

BB: Wait . . . That's the communicate and the communicate is the axis of eros which is reaching out and touching somebody and making contact and asserting continuity underneath difference. The other side is the aggression and negativity and that's the side that recognizes that in spite of your best efforts in fact you are taking place in a commodity medium. And that is the aggression. That's the importance of aggression or negativity and is when the metatext level . . . when I take cognizance consciously of my own scruples about how this is happening in spite of my best efforts and because

I am actually putting this person in a book which is equal to a commodity. Does that . . . ?

CB: Yeah. In fact, well, you're preempting my question which was severalfold. Which has to suggest that the difference between what you're doing and, for example, the kind of Beat claim of authenticity which you were criticizing before, is that you are not hiding behind the authenticity of autobiography, although you were not being totally explicit about that. It seems to me in reading the text versus hearing some of the things that you were saying, up until your last response, it seemed that autobiography was being endowed with the ring of some kind of final truth. Rather than that you have used autobiography, real names, in a sense to suggest their own narrative construction, their own fictionality, their own—to use your term—commodification. And there's no way to unmake commodification by retreating to the personal or to the autobiographical, but that one has to see that the commodification enters into all descriptions, all narration, and all aggression; that you must in your work counter the aggression with counter-aggression or negate the aggression.

BB: So there's a negation of a negation going on?

CB: How many frames you're willing to allow . . . as where we talked about the idea of dialogic versus polyvocal, that there is the situation and there's the frame of it. But it seems to me that when you negate the negation you allow for a much more multiple kind of regress than simply point/counterpoint/countercounterpoint, each of which had its own positivity in aggression. Negation in our society is always aggressive. This is also something I see acted out in your writing. I'm not saying this isn't there. I'm saying it is there. But not necessarily accounted for.

BB: This doesn't go on to infinity, though; it's not an infinite retreat . . .

CB: Oh, I didn't say that. I said multiple.

BB: Okay . . .

CB: Multiple meaning more than two, is what I mean. More than two.

BB: Well, I think that's true.

CB: You tend to work in twos, I think.

BB: I think that writing, my idea of writing is that it's something that I saw later described by Robin Blaser as doubleness and I like that term although I'd been thinking in those directions before I read Robin Blaser, especially the work of his middle years.

CB: But to be aware of the doubleness is itself . . .

BB: The opposition we've had so far is like the dead end versus communication. The point for me if you always have to be doing *both* those things at once. Where a person gets into trouble is that they fail to do both at exactly the same time, simultaneously. One of the reasons I like Baudelaire is he's always aware of this doubleness. Here's the quote. "The immense profundity of thought in ordinary locations: holes hollowed out by generations of ants."[4]

CB: I didn't know that one.

BB: Well, Baudelaire has this real strong sense of doubleness, sense of eros and aggression taking place at the same time. In his relations with his girlfriend that was always fronted. The scandal of Baudelaire's love life is that those happened at the same time, so for me Baudelaire is really a wonderful example of a doubleness of what he was doing.

CB: Well, let's change the frame here. I have a couple of different kinds of questions. Why don't you describe what got you interested in *La Fontaine* and how exactly you did that translation?

---

4 Charles Baudelaire, *Fusées* [*Rockets*] (1867): "Profondeur immense de la pensée dans les locutions vulgaires, trous creusés par des générations de fourmis."

BB: One of the ideas I liked about Stephen King is his relation between many different aspects of his output as a totality. The interviews, all the different things. One of the things I always want to do is have interviews relate to criticism, relate to narrative, relate to poetry, poetry I've done, make all these things bounce off each other in ways that ask that somebody take them as a whole. There's a principle of complex being or multiple ontological aspects that takes place in *La Fontaine*, the book Robert Glück and I did together. The idea we wanted to do is we wanted to break up just a plain text and have it clear you're going always from translation to criticism and back again and throwing in the kitchen sink. So we put in excerpts of our favorite novels or favorite English-language poetry—Wordsworth, Marvell. We bring in, you know, different classics of English literature and actually quote them and stuff that make a certain pastiche level which makes a creature that's like a griffin. It's made up of ontologically different parts. I think that that's the spirit when we did *La Fontaine*.

CB: How did you work on it as a collaboration?

BB: Well, one of us said to the other one uh, everybody in a writing career is careerist oriented, and one of the things you notice about writers of the past is that they all at some point along the line do their translation. They do their diaries, their letters, they do their novel, their plays, they do their criticism. They also do their translation. So one of us said to the other, well, we should do our translation. So that's how it started. What we did is just every Sunday over breakfast we'd go over versions we'd made of certain poems. I have a little bit more French than Bob so I would usually start with an idea or poem that I liked and come with a kind of an initial sketch. We'd talk about whether it was worthwhile doing it or not. Most of the time we did it. And then maybe Bob would take it for a while and then the next Sunday we'd talk about his version or work on it and do a little more or change it together or it would go to me and then I would rework it and then it would go back for mutual discussion and changes. Sort of like that, with a lot of coffee and conversation and uh . . .

CB: Were you always working from the original French or did you consult the different translations? To what degree were you interested . . . ?

BB: I thought it was a bad idea to look at any other translations. Bob might have. I don't know. He might have looked at Marianne Moore, but we both remarked that we didn't really like Marianne Moore very well.

CB: What kind of reaction did you get to that book? Since it was a different kind of book than your others, and at the same time, a somewhat radical concept of a translation. Did you get people saying—how could you interrupt La Fontaine? What is it that you're doing?

BB: Well, of everything that I've done and maybe even Bob's done I think that's the one that's got the most almost totally affirmative response. I can't think of anybody who said anything negative or negative things. If they were said they would have to have been behind our backs!

CB: Have you thought about doing translations since doing that book?

BB: Yeah. I've been thinking about Baudelaire, but he's so incredibly difficult not to turn out a kind of standard school product. That's one of the reasons why he's so attractive. Plus the fact I find with Baudelaire, he just gets more and more interesting and attractive all the time. A lot of it is doubleness and the other side of that is negativity and aggression.

CB: If you did a Baudelaire, for example, would you be interrupting the text in the way that you did La Fontaine's, or would you try to render it in a straighter way? Would you be more attentive to homophonic issues, that is to say, keeping sound and syntactic structures homologous?

BB: One of the basic reasons why I have never started anything isn't for lack of time although that's an important one, it's more like I still don't quite, it's immensely attractive but I really have to figure out some way of avoiding the trap of ending up with a flat translation which I would not want to do. It would have to be radically different but I would not like it to take place like *La Fontaine* did and I don't know yet so I haven't started doing that and I may not ever.

CB: Let me switch gears again. You've done a lot of critical writing. I wonder what you think of that question of the style of that writing? Are you interested in writing essays, and so on, to the same degree that you are interested in writing the kinds of work represented by *Century of Clouds*?

BB: I think I'm equally interested in writing essays, but I'd like to have some balance. I want that to be the only one thing. But again the same principle of creating a being of mixed ontological parts is pivotal.

CB: In the criticism? In the essays themselves?

BB: In the essays themselves.

CB: Because I think a lot of your essays actually don't suggest that completely. You've written some shorter pieces which are fairly straightforward even, you know, partisan and content specific, getting forward a particular perspective. Other pieces have been kind of considerations of various neglected . . . I'm thinking of the O'Hara piece for example . . . neglected aspects of considering a poet's work. It seems to me that in the essays you sometimes tend toward a more straightforward, less mixed genre, approach to thinking.

BB: Yeah. But I would rather think of it as the way the mixed genre stuff takes place on a spectrum. It can be more or less obvious, and this is determined to a large extent by the place of publication and how much I can get away with.

CB: Right.

BB: With some publications you have to almost smuggle in the difference and the non-criticism stuff.

CB: Do you feel as I do, a stifling environment in publishing essays, that places that publish them are conservative in terms of what they accept?

BB: I firmly agree with you. I think that that's one of the limits on essay writing that I'm beginning to feel so even if I wasn't going to be finishing *Carmen* it might make me want to put an end to essay writing in the future. It's so hard to smuggle in other stuff. The easiest place I've found so far is Kevin Killian and Bryan Monte's *No Apologies*. Because it was so unknown I had more leeway and I could define my own terms a lot more, so I could be a lot more free-wheeling. I think that an example would be Duncan, the Duncan essay, the long Duncan essay in the Duncan issue of *Ironwood*. The short Duncan essay is coming out soon in the January-February St. Mark's newsletter. In the one for *Ironwood* I was real conscious I had to almost conceal the mixed genre stuff. So even though I quote Bob Glück, for instance, and I refer to conversations in graduate school, I had to really really work to make that flow smoothly. In terms of the essay and actually I would prefer to flow roughly, so to speak not smoothly. I would like those breaks to be more apparent but I was working in terms of a kind of context which only allowed that stuff to take place at the lower end of the spectrum. So I am kind of, it's so hard to work into smuggling the stuff. That essays are getting less attractive to me.

CB: Would you mention a couple of your essays which you feel most exemplify what you . . . ?

BB: The Robin Blaser essay in *No Apologies* no. 2, the anti-nuke essay reprinted in Bob Perelman's *Writing/Talks*, the New Narrative essay to be out in *Poetics Journal*. Those are favorites, I guess.

CB: Of course, this is quite an interesting problem. I.e.: conservativeness. If it's in a nonliterary publication then they just . . . anything that has any interest in the way writing of the essay is being done, the way the narration or exposition takes place, is stigmatized as *literary* and therefore not acceptable except as a poem. And not the kind of poem they're going to read either. In contrast, the literary magazines more sympathetic to an open form are primarily read by other poets. This tends to parochialize the activity and the insight of the people writing about political and social issues in more open forms. Because you can't get them into places like *Social Text* or *New Left Review* which remain essentially conservative, or even reactionary, in their policies toward style, despite the fact that they claim . . .

B B : *Social Text* isn't reactionary. They printed one of the most free-wheeling essays I've ever had, which is the Jack Spicer one which is littered with typos by the way . . . I'm supposed to be talking about Jack Spicer in it and end up talking about Steven Spielberg and throw in gay sex in the back room, talk about myself and it's all over the page. I'm surprised, actually. Well, maybe this surprise of mine that they printed it sort of matches your fear that they're sort of conventional. But at least there's some exceptions. I mean that was one big exception to me.

C B : Yeah well . . .

B B : But *New Left Review* and these others are completely academic and more often right field than *Social Text*.

C B : In terms you mean actually of their style?

B B : You could more easily get into *Social Text* by far than into *New Left Review* or *New German Critique* or you know something like that.

C B : It's not that *New Left Review* doesn't publish an enormous number of very interesting pieces, but they limit the kind of range of discussion by prescribing the form in which they allow the discussion to take place.

B B : Right.

C B : Which seems to be a problem. I wonder what you're thinking . . . I know some time ago you were quite interested in the question of writer's organization or writers organizing. What's your current thoughts about that?

BB: I was, I have some differences with the kind of writer's organization that has come to be and it didn't quite fit my idea as to what that would be. I was less concerned with a professional organization in terms of professional self-advancement than I think legitimately the current writer's organization that's been organized is. Their model is a union.

CB: You're thinking about the National Writers Union.

BB: Yeah. I think something more, okay put it this way, let's invoke E.P. Thompson's great essay, "Notes on Exterminism," which is the most interesting anti-nuke essay I've ever read. His basic thesis is that the sort of union that's in the U.S. is locked into a conflict which transcends either one of them as ideological system. So it's not exactly an orthodox Marxist viewpoint and is probably more interesting for that reason. Well, his concrete suggestion in that is part being locked into these dilemmas is being locked into institutions with no way to get out of them as institutions. It's sort of a micro-political rather than macro-political viewpoint. And for people who want to make a difference he says that the conflict among people that will help break this armaments race cannot take place in government-sponsored organization levels. It has to be grassroots or micro. And so he sort of makes this proposal which is now out there floating, which I've thought of for a long time now, which is that writers and other cultural people who are interested in disarmament and other issues of saving the planet can get together on their own. Well, I would think of any kind of writer's thing more in directions like that. The possibility of making contact with creative people or artistic people or cultural people in the Soviet Union. How could you make that work?

CB: Within the present situation, what kind of organization do you think writers could be involved with that would be of some value?

BB: Right now I'm feeling disheartened. Partly because of this illness. So I feel weak. So this is my own life. But partly there's a sort of an ideological vacuum now. People have retreated so there are yuppies now. People feel a vacuum in thinking and they're dormant. And I feel that way too. I don't feel any helpful ideas on that front that you mention.

CB: What kind of writing would you like to see proliferate in the next few years, within the prose/poetry communities?

BB: There's a lot of interesting writing and writers that I see coming up here, Kevin Killian and Dodie Bellamy are two that are very concerned about that. Kevin writes basically, he has an article on *Dynasty* for instance which is kind of schlock oriented which I like coming up in the *Soup* magazine I'm editing that's coming out. Dodie Bellamy is writing a vampire novel. That's the sort of direction I'd like to see.

CB: What other writers are doing things that are of great interest to you right at this moment?

BB: I am utterly enchanted by each new Bob Perelman book. That's one. Bob Glück's *Jack the Modernist* which is going to come out, I guess, this fall is enthralling for me. I think it's a further light-year's advance on stuff that's already really great that he had done on *Elements*. I think that the most interesting thing that I would like to see in all this converging on is schlock, or genre writing, converging more and more with the higher type theories. I mean sort of like in the sense the two opposite ends of the spectrum. That I think is interesting. How can they be got together? That's really where the zap, the fertilizing and the electrical and sparkle, of Americanness at its best seems to be going now.

CB: That seems like a good place to stop.

This interview was conducted over the phone and first published in the first issue of *Ottotole*, edited by Mike Amnasan (Fall 1985).

DARK QUEER SUITE

STEPHEN KING POEM

"Gai" exists but boisterous too: God. Some ex-hippies
in the movie I saw at the Castro with David. *The
Big Chill.* Near-to-chunky William Hurt. Glenn
Close a real love. Kevin Kline. JoBeth what's
her name. *Now* like my neighborhood, 24th St.

To wake up in the night and a flash (I do this
all the time actually) tells you my god there's
a *nuclear war* on! If there's visitors to the
planet or rubble of it in 2020 and there's anything
left they'll wonder why these poems, ours, rhymed
language with "nothing." Señorita Presidente, whined
Baudelaire to his bitchy girlfriend, *ta t*ête, *ton geste,
ton air.* Just glitter and breathe. Ice.

It grids at this point, affection's
the invader. Space shudders, orgasms of some Other
World come out, they're gism. Vampires in
the old US of A? The piece of flesh crawls.
Let the sombitch *be,* Jed. Hideous infantile giggling.

That back of his, covered with hair, creative? Mr.
Idiot of dreams's sitting on his back porch, droolin'
or dreamin'. World out there's a-shiver with ideas
said Baudelaire leaning out his balcony, wrinkles brow,
is there a comparison maybe? Like all those long and
solemn ... huh! ... can't remember how it ends till
the sucker *finishes,* says he. Three Mile Island
short circuit, right? Breadlines, right? A Grenada.
Bag that.

Dearest, I'm writing this to let you know sincerely
that the brightest light we saw last night on lush back
skies was wallpaper. Just Steven Spielberg. I
hope that's OK with you, babe. As my sentences
become more irreversible they are revealed as just
bridges collapsing—and I hope *that's* OK too. What
can I say, really now? Ribs, peach cobbler.
When the children come in for dinner, doesn't just
about everybody? When you find some good advice,
you let me know. Keep in touch, honey. You know I

"Teeth brushed very well" in a too bright voice. Oh
girl, look at *yourselves* in the mirror. Try to
keep saying yes, I think it helps. Sex, anger,
trophies. Little things to put in quotes. A
social syntax. I'm short on recommendations,
long on fear. Keep the circuits open, that's all.

Shambling up to you on the road, ugh, all covered
with . . . what *is* it Charlie, *gore*? Wriggle ears,
make face. Looks like something botched
at McDonald's. Irate townspeople. "Why don't it
go back where it came from?" It can't. It
wants to say I'm just a big reflection of
you, you know. Right now it doesn't have
words because we don't have words. The
big black uglies come in and I just stare. Black star
spreads its fearsome light. Oh, too cold.

I love my man. On this piece of velvet
what's pleasanter than twinkly lights.
In my absence I don't compare hot breath.
The blistering limbs keep plastering our
walls. Against this determination are
three. The mind's the body, spirit too.
Soul's irreducible. A finishing with the
quest for mastery in the pumping of iron.
My wish is the gods grant you a long and
happy, Thor 3. This was to kiss, salute.
Same to you sincerely, Atem bar Akatan.
We grossly ignored the doubts I told him,
my plan to teach. Without resolves or
resources, I told him, these asteroids
continue to whirl. Where they have limbs,
our pride's bolts. Look from that porthole.
The spears of light that are thrown down,
ache in. Boisterous freedom's my
only delight. Be loving you too, true.
Emblazoned on the foreheads were stars.

JOHN WIENERS, AMERICAN POET

To be propelled by doubts is violence,
voices. When the light's not on, the dark.
Where we go for sex gleams in the bushes.
Forms of it accumulate like mushrooms. A
place of crossover. In this or that
invaders gleam so handsomely. Not bilateral
not ours but a radial symmetry. The male
householder seems hostile, I saw him there,
many legs and arms, inattentive. The voices
sweet statistical like bats flying,
ones you saw in the basement. Strange!
Don't look for us in the attic, dear, they
mock and cruelly chime. No one's a bozo,
are they? You're on the other side, ahead,
like him. These shoes spattered by gauze.
Messy spores drift down from stars,
Philosophical, I see in doorways. Shapes.
That I see. Stars unwind. Being him.

PULP TERROR

Start to eat pastiche and you'll eat it
in shame. Listen to the apparent goodness
of these grave accents. I'm never with you
when the erotically inclined reader across the
hall listens to you, I promise. The breath has
to leave. Like the Safeway hamburger on
the gory trail. I go. What's inside and is
marked with a red color is outside only the gray
you know always. Meat ashes, their love meat.
Closed shutters repeating classroom instructions.
The hand's ripped shockingly from the eye. Tongue
from mouth. O Altitudos. Suffer. Refuse to
sneer. Give back their boasting to the animals.
The inability humans have is the most merciful thing,
says H.P. Lovecraft. It means you can't correlate
the contents of your own mind. This is a sight
to follow, having read it in a book. The dead
rise. Stars blotted out. Come, Spirit, come.

LOVECRAFT

Twist the little normalcy with words.
The sentences, new letters gateways to faces.
With an older woman's love my own's compared,
blackened. The stale echoes of bimorphism
that don't provide Providence. These
stretched out are models, crack. In the
blood find no ichor. This indescribable
glug glug glug isn't a speech, remember
it's sounds. The rubble reformulates itself
above, alien aircraft, huddling. Remove
this from us, we beg. What part of me is
heard at a distance? In this ruined meat
palaver, message of hope, never gain
lifted up from the page. How these bright
trumpets quicken me as anyone! The bathetic
moaning bellow. Here I am, the unearthly
light when animal tissue is heard to
decay. Dead Cthulhu sits in his dream house,
R'lyeh. Ph-nglue mglw-nafh Cthulu R'lyeh
wgah'nagl fhtagn. Sister to complicity
is his brother, sound. Every premise
his promise, black heavens' milky spawn.

Dark Queer Suite appeared in its entirety in *Mirage* no. 4 / *Period(ical)* no. 127 (San Francisco, February 2006). "Stephen King Poem" was first published in *Mirage* no. 0, *Prospectus Issue* (1985). "John Wieners, American Poet" was first published in *Mirage, John Wieners Issue* (1984). All issues of *Mirage* were edited by Kevin Killian and Dodie Bellamy. "Pulp Terror" first appeared in *Semiotext(e) USA,* no. 13 (New York: Autonomedia, 1987).

LETTER TO STEPHEN KING,
THE HORROR WRITER
MOST OF TODAY, TUES. NOV. 20TH, 1984

Dear Stephen,

Without being guilty of any insulting intent, I hope I can call you that—though I may have to leave "Steve" to such later time as may or may not develop. But "Mr. King" seemed just hopelessly off base.

The idea of being able to use somebody's first name is actually related to something I like best about your style and is the main point of this letter. It first "clicked" in *Danse Macabre* when you said in the later edition I'm reading how you did get a reaction to the invitation you extended in the first edition (you pointed out how completely unlikely it was for anyone writing about all these old movies, books etc. to get all the details right—and suggested readers write in and tell you when you fouled up, getting this or that wrong in some story or whatever), big enough (several hundred letters?) but not *too*, not overwhelming. I liked it a lot that you'd incorporate the corrections of inevitable mistakes you'd have made into your new version (you credited someone whose name I forget with helping you sort out all this stuff and check it out so the rev. ed. 'd be *right* where the 1st ed was *wrong*!). But mainly I liked it that this whole approach seemed to testify to some idea you had of being able to reach the reader, make contact. Didn't the reader count then? Without getting preachy about it (I hate it when writers *nag* at me; but if they don't have any raison d'etre above and beyond making a buck, I feel they've let me down), you put across the idea you really *cared* about the reader. And part of that seems to come out a lot negatively. There's something that's half way a plaint, half way a boast in the writing of yours that I've read that oddly, I think, corroborates this intuition of mine. The writer figure, Ben, in *Salem's Lot*, gets feedback *for miles* from the townsfolk; they tell him his writing has really meant something to them (put a little *magic* in their lives, is what the gist of it is), they give him the strokes he really deserves, a recognition he's in some important way lacked, though, from the people who are set up by society to give "official" recognition to good writing when they see it—the critics of "high" literature! And let me just say that I really agree with this not-too-subtle hint on your part to (some of?) the official writing establishment that they've really erred in their official estimations of how *good* Stephen King's writing is. It's as if they can't see further than their nose (as my Mom'd say). How come? For myself, I think the reason for "high" writing's inability to see the obvious fact of the incredible importance of your own writing has to do at least partly with the elitist nature of any kind of official criticism. It's a familiar stupidity. Writers who are read by literally millions just can't be any good, can they? Though what's odd to me is some of the same people who will dump on a Stephen King novel will say (not that you're doing the same thing; but I do think there's something comparable in the fact of both you and him capturing some essential aspect of the time we're living in right now) how great Stephen Spielberg is. It's as if because both S. King and what's-her-name (which has slipped my mind and it occurs to me ((uncharitably)) to wonder why) who wrote *The Thorn Birds* do the same thing, don't they, since both are shlock writers (that word isn't a pejorative for me, but if it is for you, then you can substitute the phrase "mass writer" or "commodity writer" if it sounds better). But as I say, all that's just one level. And it's a pretty vulgar objection, which is to say an objection at the level of the lowest common denominator—why isn't this person, Stephen King, given panels and conferences at the Modern Languages Association annual convention?

So agreed. You don't exactly write like Franz Kafka. Is there another reason people (a lot of the high critics, I mean) don't credit your writing? Here's where it gets interesting. For me anyway. Since I think what's really great about your writing is your *relation to the reader(s)*. Now I think it's possible I may be getting into hot water with you at this point, since what I got (mostly from between the lines of *Danse Macabre*) is that you think what the really good thing, what you ought to be recognized for in your writing is the basic fact you can *tell a story* as well as about anybody today. Well, OK. But I think that for you, if you think about it, that's really all mechanics. It's the *why* that counts. How come you've *learned* to tell a good story??? I think you've developed the skill of storytelling as an effective tool, essentially, to get into a relationship with readers out there (and here's where I think you start to zoom out of sight compared with the what you might call mass market generally, of whatever kind). Here's the kicker though. I think it's possible for the supposedly objective (who I admit doesn't really exist—so Mr./Ms. Objective Observer is going to look like Yours Truly's own sweet face in the mirror, when I get right down to it, I suppose—but my hope is if the interpretation I'm giving strikes any familiar chords in you, you'll give some serious thought to the other stuff I'll be saying in another page or so in this letter) observer to point out that in the reader/writer relation that develops in the reading of a S. King novel or piece of writing (I think this is pretty noticeable in the critical stuff, to judge from *Danse Macabre*), in comparison with a lot of other "mass" or junk food writing (tip of the hat to you, though you seem to mean the phrase as applied mainly to movies in your chapter on that in *D.C.*) there's a specifically erotic side of this relationship that develops that's the key to your art. In fact [it's] what makes it quote unquote more than itself as the junk or mass writing of its time, even as one of the best.

My friend Dodie (who, and I hope you won't cringe, is, as it happens, writing a damn good *vampire novel* right now!) is always telling me not to get carried away. And last night over pizza (on Castro St., at a pizza place with little "intimate" booths; though Dodie and I aren't intimate in any "sexual" way, I suppose I should say, so you won't get the wrong idea) when I explained this theory of the real or "deep" meaning of the writing of Stephen King as I have seen it to date (Dodie is the main person responsible for getting me to read you), Dodie didn't have any argument about the main thesis—the erotic relation. But—she said—I feel Stephen King is appealing particularly to *me*, as a woman. And I grant you—since the next step of my theory will be to say that the erotic relation to readers in your writing is a relation that applies mainly and specifically to men as your readers—I could be wrong in my feelings. Or Dodie could be right—but in a different way than she (or I) think(s). Anyway, I don't know how much thought you've given to questions of your relationship with your audience; but here is one reader at any rate writing to tell you I don't think it could possibly be anything less than absolutely critical/pivotal about all of your art. Let me put it in my best, most distanced Van Helsing bedside manner: it's what in your writing keeps them coming back for another *feed*. What's different from relations the classical Master of the Borgo Pass, lord of Darkness, has with his (own) victims? I think the real difference is the same as between rape and seduction. In other words: it's important to your dynamics that you want to *please*, not take by force. (Some examples of writers who do the opposite, i.e. want to dominate the reader, take him or her by force, whose writing, structurally-speaking, from the point of view of the reader/writer dynamics, shows traces of *sadism*: Sartre, John D. MacDonald, most of the hard-boiled detective school ((but not, I think, somebody so fantastically in love with the beautiful in *images*, as Raymond Chandler, and so ends up, in spite of the toughness, being actually rather courtly toward you as a reader)), etc.). Anyway you get the drift.

Now this (the male-oriented pleasingness of your reader/writer relation) is something I *feel* more than can in any way *prove*. So after just a couple of indications, I'll let the chips lie where they may on this one—and let you (I shouldn't say "let", I guess, since really who's a better judge than the person who's actually written the work) be the judge yourself. But I do think, whether you end up thinking I'm right or wrong on the specifics, you'll probably agree on the importance of the idea of audience relations for judging the actual *value* your books so evidently have for so many people, and why you manage to get such fantastic loyalties in fans (at least that I've noticed myself in so many people) as compared with X number of other mass writers who I'll have the courtesy and grace not to mention in the polite pages of this letter. My intent isn't to badmouth; if I don't like a writer, I just ignore them. There are lots of specific *spots* where you seem like you are really trying to woo the reader (the carrying out of the metaphor of the invitation to the dance in *DM* is just one place among many that, to me, says you are basically saying the main idea you have on your mind is a *romantic* one); but I'll limit myself to saying something about the language *code* or *codes* you employ as a writer as determining that the message you're delivering to us is in some specific way towards us as a male audience. (Have you ever read the influential English sociologist Basil Bernstein? He's pretty readily available in university-type bookstores in paperback and I'm getting the idea of this term "code," as well as the term itself, from him. His take is basically, the medium is the message; but specifically in "class" terms: i.e. speech or language that's highly abstract and analytical, Bernstein claims, transmits, *irrespective of content* (i.e. your content could even be that we ought to be smashing the state, comrades), a message that's middle (or upper-middle-to upper) class as far as its structure goes. Working class or lower class writing by contrast isn't analytical/abstract but is concrete and transmits this as a class value by stressing the community or large-group, rather than one-to-one or individualistic dimensions that analytical speech has. (Sorry about the scratched out stuff above, but I'm afraid if I stopped writing this letter at this point because I seem to have come to a fatigue level I might not get all my ideas out, which I really want to do; so I hope you'll forgive if occasionally there're a few x-ing outs and scratchy parts).

Anyway here's my idea. You've got a code in writing that's basically that of the male-dominated (and by male-dominated I don't mean that it's necessarily sexist; only that it's predominately male in composition, in actual numbers of people who belong) fanzine world. S. King is a lot richer, more complex and inspired than your typical fanzine, the correspondence that goes with it, the introductions to sci-fi books by friends of the guys who write these books, etc. But it seems to me like this or something much like this is really the bottom line, style wise, of the writing you do, the ideas on the world you purvey, etc. It's overwhelmingly, male-oriented. Sports metaphors. The specific knowledge that you take it for granted the reader will have that will make him another man, not a woman. And it's not even that the main characters have to *be* men; what about *Carrie*? It's just that, no matter what you're talking about, and to a large extent it's not even too important who's *doing* the talking, a male or female character, the atmosphere that's so thick you could cut it with a knife is a male-bonded one, guys from teenage up thru possibly mid-twenties or so, talking together safe in the knowledge that they are—and there are—just "the guys" in the group that makes up the audience. Now I don't happen to believe that doing this makes someone sexist (I think it could, but you'd be crazy to claim it *does*); and with you, what's noticeable is the places and times you go out of your way to try to counteract any impression readers might get that would lead them to conclude they could have "permission" from you to be sexist in your company. For instance when in *DM*, which I'm reading now, when you go out of your way to point up the sexist implications of the slip-ups of the movie in letting the "strong" heroine go chasing after the cat in *Alien*.

You state in *DM* at some point that horror writing is by its nature a defender of the status quo. For myself I don't believe this is, or has to be, the case. Either theoretically or when it comes to the case of your own writing. First of all, there's examples like the one I gave from your critical analysis of *Alien*. By politics I'd suspect (without having yet read any other critical stuff of yours than *DM*) you might have had some participation in the late 60s in the movement-oriented politics of that time and had for a time a pretty radical outlook on life; but possibly think of yourself as more or less of a "progressive" or even liberal at this point, as opposed to still being radical. Have I come anywhere near to guessing the political feelings you have? In any case what's really clear is that you want to be decent, not be prejudiced and if possible put in "cues" into your writing that make us readers just a little more liable, than not, after reading you to open our hearts to the claims of folks who have a legitimate gripe in this society and need our basic support. Example: the "good guy" role of the black cook in *The Shining* really stands out. He's not only in touch with his unconscious or whatever-you-call-it (sense of poetry, imagination, life forces), he's really swell as a human being, a real decent guy too.

So here's where I get back to the main point, which I hope I haven't got too far afield from: your relation to your readers. Now as I see it, that relation is code-wise both a male-oriented one and, in its principal tendency, erotic or romantic in its implications (the politeness and really-wanting-to-please). What do you think about this point? Because if you agree with me I'd like you to reconsider your (in *DM*) pretty unqualified assertion that horror-writing has got to be, in its nature, supportive of the status quo or the way society is now. Using buddy-buddy or male-bonding codes of the young fanzine or sf-reader type, there's a lot of homophobia in this wallpaper approach that I'd like you to reconsider. Example: how come gays have nearly always got to be referred to by the male-bonding straight guys, who are your main characters and (I think) *emotional stand-ins* for the readers themselves, as *faggots*? Stephen, I have to admit it. This really makes me, as a gay man who is also one of your devoted fans so far, *wince*! It really hurts me. And I can't help but notice that you really do try to do good by women, Jews, blacks, and others. Why the crummy ink about us gays? Here's a query you can ask yourself: how come I *don't* let these same sometimes regular-type guys who are my characters refer to women as "cunts" or black guys as "niggers" or Jews as "kikes"? I think if a writer allows his/her characters to be guilty of prejudice or distorted thinking, that has to be counteracted at some other place in the book or in some way that the author chooses so as the readers can't get the idea that this is really an OK attitude or one that can be countenanced. This example from the language the characters use can be, to an extent, paralleled and matched by selected plot developments. Now, again, it may be I'm wrong but here's how I read *Salem's Lot* for instance. You've got your good faggots and your bad ones. Only the problem is that with the character who stands in the spot that's emotionally designated (by the readers) as "good faggot" (the old high school teacher, Matt) we're given pretty firm indications that we can't be allowed to think the guy has an actual, real *sex life*! Matt's sort of a mysterious character 'cause 1) he's single and as far as we know never been married and, 2) in a "suspect" profession (English teacher who's also into drama coaching). He's also (I think) a little prissy. He's a hero alright and a good guy, I grant you that. But look what happens when a fag we can *approve* of (i.e., he's completely likeable and admirable) gets into a situation where sex *might even just possibly even in the imagination* (if the guy really is gay and has any feeling or soul to him) be a possibility: e.g. when he's in what's in fact a terribly intimate real situation, when Mike Ryerson's got nothing on but his shorts and is wandering around Matt's house like that; and Mike's not only been said already to be in his 20s and be a working class guy who works with his *hands* (using his muscles is part of this guy's job, since he's a grave-digger), but has also been described as a "good-looking guy." Is Matt supposed to be a "eunuch" or a guy who doesn't have any feeling left in his soul?! If Matt is going to be such a good guy type and also is going to be given the "suspect" signs of being gay, why not, in a good way, let him have a few sex feelings? Is Matt *not gay at all*???

Now this can be opposed to the "bad guy" faggot types: in the *Lot* that'd be the main vampires, that ghoulish duo, Barlow and pal. Everybody's (that is, to be specific the *men* in your novel) always wondering if these guys are gay (or—sigh!—faggots, as they say). Plus it seems a pretty sure tip off they've been living together a long time (centuries???); plus they're into, as a front operation, the antique business. So fags they are. Alas. There's a definite concession to homophobic feelings on readers' parts going on in the portrayal of this couple, as I'm sure a little reflection will tell you. Think of, by way of comparison, that hideous, *huge*, *beaked* (and I mean *huge* and I mean *beaked*, at the risk of unduly emphasizing my point: go back and see the movie to see what I mean) nose of Dracula's in the late Weimar/ early Hitler-time version of Dracula called *Nosferatu*. It doesn't take too much thought to imagine, at that peak-time of anti-Semitism, what the understanding of that nose must have been for German audiences of the day: so is Murnau to be criticized then? Well let's put it this way. If I was Jewish (I'm not; but for various reasons seem to be sensitive to the issue) the way that nose was portrayed might make me feel very *anxious*, given history.

Bear with me (you're almost at the end of this letter). If you're still reading this letter of mine and haven't thrown it into the garbage 'cause of being insulted at the suggestion you could use a little education on the issue of homophobia, I think I may have an even greater shock coming up for you.

So here it is. Your writing gets me hot. When it's at its best, it actually gives me a hard-on. Now note: the writing, I said. I have to admit, having seen you on that sort of terrible/wonderful commercial on TV (and even if you weren't straight, which you pretty obviously are), *you* don't do this to me: but your writing certainly does (when you really get going and are at your best, as I say). Not too much writing *does* do this for me. Baudelaire's, others' writing does it for instance. Four or five selected current "high" writers: Kathy Acker, Robert Glück, Dennis Cooper for instance (have you by any chance read any of them?). Anyway (and I'm not really sure I'm so unusual; if it turns out I'm the only reader in the world that this happens to this way, I'll be very surprised) your writing puts me into this incredibly delicious state I really like, which is actually physical (besides getting a hard-on when I read writing whose wavelength I'm really *on*, I sometimes get mild cases of sweating, or salivary gland activation or palpitations of the heart, etc. etc.—I'll stop at that, since this description is meant to indicate the *intensity* I want to communicate, not replicate the butcher's "organ meats" display at the supermarket). Anyway, my point is, a person could think of (good) writing that's not organized around the idea of a (or the) relationship with a reader (*the* reader/*the* readers). All surrealist poetry would be an example. 18th century poetry. The great Realist novels of the English 19th century. Academic poetry, American type, of the last 30 years, only *good*: like Robt. Lowell or, let's see, James Merrill—stuff that's basically high and dry and reflective. Then there's stuff (and this has always been my special love, I think, whenever it happens in literature, whether it's older lit., or current-type stuff) that's geared around *emotion*, direct talk to you as a reader—needs of *communication* is what I essentially mean. This is where you come in. And this, again, is where the intangibles of what I'm calling your late teens/men's club/boy-bonding system of writing (what I called your *code* a while back there) makes contact with my gripe about why don't you do better in your writing with us gays? The crossover between these two issues is the to me undoubted fact that the genius of your writing is in its charming wooing *sweetness*, and that this sweetness is surely directed mainly to this audience of (probably mostly) postpubescent men. Right or wrong, Stephen? Ok Ok!, there's *Firestarter* and *Carrie*; but as I said I don't think even there you've got—any more than for *hot horror wallpaper* style writing in general even when, *un*like yours it's not particularly immensely talented, as far as the code is concerned—anything other than *still this predominantly male audience*. So the upshot is (if I'm anywhere *near* being right in this thesis and it's the sweetness of your conversation toward other men that makes or breaks your talent) the question of how you treat gays in your writing, and do you really give them sufficient respect, is not unrelated to the gold lode of where your art starts becoming of *value*—and value that will put you up there in literary history, when the history of the literature of this time gets finally to be told, it's my opinion. Get my drift?

But of course all this is in a sense to talk about a or maybe *the* side of horror that rarely gets told; since it's precisely the side of horror—horrors!—that's *not* horror! And it's also to bring up a perhaps slightly screwy idea. Have I by any chance just crossed genre boundaries and glommed onto an idea that you, a master of generic discontinuities, might more rightly call maybe something like fantasy of some kind? (But I do remember your insisting in *DM* how ultimately unsatisfying any attempt to pin these things down is likely to be). What if horror has a (up-till-now-not-terribly-*developed*) reverse side of itself that has to do with human, or could I even say something like *religious* joy? in a sort of extended, hippy-dippy mystical sort of way is what I mean. I just re-saw *Close Encounters of the Third Kind* (as a matter of fact with Dodie), and I started thinking of this type of thing in relation to the child: who in Spielberg, as in in your writing, obviously stands for some kind of "privileged conduit" with those forces of the Beyond (I suppose I'm sort of an agnostic myself; though if someone started getting all Christian on me, I'd probably, just out of orneriness and contrariness, tell them I was a strict atheist) that are not just horrible and revolting and awful but have the potential maybe for something more, more like a kind of joyousness. I have the terrible feeling just now writing this that two days after mailing this to you I'm going to find what I'm saying here a bit sappy-sounding in retrospect—but there it is. Maybe joyousness isn't right—but the gloriousness of the powers of the imagination, would you buy into *that* then? Of course Spielberg is hardly as "dark" as you are. Still, there's some sense of parallel I get. Or am I just saying (I wonder) that I like some fantasy with my horror?

But the problem is, to the extent you're concerned that a writing—in this case your own writing—be, besides mass writing, also *art*, that you've got to think of some way, some guarantee so to speak, some enabling structural device of some kind, I guess I'd say, that'll insure that all this takes place on an adult enough level. That is—like I say—to the extent a person wants to be not just a junk food writer but more than that, an artist in whatever genre it is he or she has picked that the historical era he or she is in has put up for grabs! So my question is: are the child's shoulders (and this is picking up on your metaphor about how much weight the consumer of horror has to dead-press) big enough and strong enough to *lift* this? We're talking the power of your sweetness in talking to other men (ulp! I know I haven't exactly given tons of examples of what I mean by this: but can I refer in some payoff way to your *humor*? All those corny heh-heh jokes not just when you're more expansive as in *DM* but the humor that goes thru the novel-writing and sparkles with l-o-v-e, the real tenderness with which, and exactness of detail with which, that stand-in for all America, the Maine village, is described in your vampire novel ((I haven't read *Pet Semetary* yet; is it a vampire thing too?)), there's something there so *appreciative* of men talking to men, it strikes me, that it doesn't end up being "Hemingway-distanced" at all, but's really *decent* instead). But there are limits to this tender relating-to-men in your writing; and I'm wondering (tho this is somewhat of a shot in the dark since I've not yet read enough of your writing) if some of the unfulfilled potential to relate to the men who appear (to me) to be your (natural) audience is a possible effect of a displacement (and here's the gay stuff coming up again) of this potential greater relation to *men* onto the rather slender shoulders of the children? What do you think?

I realize I have my nerve writing this letter to you out of the blue; especially offering you my analysis unsolicited about your writing, the sort of mixed bag of problem and success I found there. But that writer/protagonist of *Salem's Lot* keeps coming back, and with his image, his questions and complaints as well: why aren't I better appreciated by criticism, why aren't I valued more like my real value? Anyway if any of this makes any sense to you or you ever want to write me back, I hereby withdraw my claims to a Dr. Van Helsing doctor designation and sign myself in civilian—

Bruce Boone

"Letter to Stephen King" is published here for the first time.

THE LAST *SOUP*:
NEW CRITICAL PERSPECTIVES

Criticism has an adversary relation to you and to the world—can it be celebratory as well? With this in mind, would writing have a carrot and stick relation? These essays strike out in several new directions and their common stance may be a demand for inclusivity at ever new stages. Meaning: language may not have changed much but can anyone believe pronoun lines are absolute? Can I-am-not-you be a relation, not just a separation? Textuality's inadequacies as a stance (my writing's only on the page) gets more evident all the time. The world's all around instructing that the ground shifts and doesn't stop for that motion; so the only idea left is the canny one of be flexible. One upshot : reader/writer lines are blurred, not forced in pre-given ways. Another: subjectivity and objectivity stop being a dichotomy and link up instead in writing, since that happens already in life. Suppose the theories of writing don't fit— then change them! Are "ecological" or amalgam theories of writing more sensitive to necessities of input? What's important is changing scales: languages. Otherwise—threats to vital collective aspirations will remain on the rise. Start small, give your writing its head; and it's likely writing will take you to some better place. And a more serious commitment to modesty is in order—since what could on the face of it be a more misguided idea, dangerous even, than the thought I am ever really *safe*? Can continued U. S. gunboat diplomacy or large-scale murder and erosion of life standards in Central America fail to lead to nuclear confrontation, other apocalyptic chemical-biological possibilities? To miss this is to miss the big picture. So the feeling of an interconnected subject-object world, as a view you start with, isn't always gratifying. On the other hand there's the, gasp, Future—which, to give intelligence and human love the credit it deserves as a motivating factor lies up ahead (that is: if there turns out to be an Up Ahead). And how beautiful it shines! This global millefleur of embracing stamens pistils lovely corollas of human veggie mineral etc.. Interconnection in their lifegivingness of interweaving forms of this planet Earth. Let's take the Great Leap Forward to the figurative Alpha Centauri! But then I want to *catch* myself. These wonderful aspirations have to be balanced with a more gravid reality principle. You keep your eye on the inspiring distance factor; but don't lose the trees for the forest! This two-foot approach to the idea of criticism redefined in American writing right now—one foot firmly on the ground and the other securely where aspirations are—is what I think of as a way to write criticism that crosses over to places people haven't considered. Psychological essay. Politics. An object and a thing like music. What have you. Hawthorne more to the point than New Criticism. Sade returns with his horrid 1,000 abominations and this turns out to be vastly more human than—the academicism of keeping one's distance and one's mouth shut—an AMERICAN POETRY REVIEW. Engagement counts, whether a former era's or our own. Can we do it? And if inclusiveness doesn't "include" turning around prospects of global Doom—why, if I can ask, did you become a reader/writer in the first place? If not to go BEYOND, I mean?

A worldly and hopeful essay by FERNANDO ALEGRIA opens up. An interrogation of responses from Latin culture to the example of Walt Whitman and his writing. Implicit in it is: can perspectives drawn from Lorca, based on negativity, enlarge ideas for gay community—what it might be? Then Neruda's reaction to the North American writer is looked at; his populist's agenda is treated with affection but wariness. Finally some parameters from Borges. Writers should be more modest, shouldn't they, since they're as much the person they're not in their writing as the other way around—or maybe, more reasonably, both at once? This shrewdness takes on more collective than personal applications with ROBERT GLÜCK's article—and gay is again in question. The idea is, what's the other side of being called a name? A disadvantage is certainly I'm reduced or made less than the complexity I really am. So can these pared down elements, sharp outlines, do anyone, the community, any good? Celebration, shining at the heart of our community, seems to require broad strokes. These minimal elements are our mirrors: we see ourselves.

Then GABRIELLE DANIELS takes up a community problem often shied away from—don't desired expansions of self happen most in the danger areas, places where community becomes plural? The backdrop to her question: OUR NIG by Harriet E. Wilson, the recently rediscovered novel by an American Black woman of the 19th century. To arrive at the meaning repressed by a hostile environment, look between the lines. And she does. There are also possibilities—greater solidarity than now exists between the women's and Black communities. Aspirations: scholarly notes.

RACHEL BLAU DUPLESSIS says look at what odd ancestors a person might have, particularly women, in the patriarchalist modernist writers. To take one of the best, Williams, as the starting point of your questions. The delight in them and in the perception of their writing text—what's by design left open structurally. But how to reconcile the encouragement with a less heartening understanding of the text as systematically sexist; what if his model for reader/writer relations is in fact rape? To make a deformed past useful again? Mixed reviews.

HONOR JOHNSON's essay: diary, a precedent and shape. Take part of a woman's life, something everyday like going to the bank. Are there indications you can see as a writer or artist? Compare this with assumptions built into culturally male oriented cinematic experience, put this along side of what you know about women's films, their writing, poetry. Make assumptions for openness and so on. DODIE BELLAMY's perspective often similar—but with a greater feeling for things' angularity. An evident humor makes you aware of what's left over—and the extra pushes you. She goes to the Roxie Theater to see Chantal Akerman's JEANNE DIELMAN. That's part of things too: occasion, audience, responses. The writer enlarges thereby, keeps on in her review. What's left? Anecdotes from personal life, an enigma from Jane Austen to Hollywood: if a woman identifies with her house, does she get smaller or larger by doing this? Boundaries; humor.

Everybody seems to complain about the bad side of porn—are there successes? DENNIS COOPER: *image* in porn extends your feeling-life; from risks perceived in it, subjectivity grows—emotions deepen. My satisfactions in male-on-male porn, the type I'm interested in, relates to telltale signs that [that?] actor up there does this for my benefit. The finer calibrations—being able to see this, the image of it—make for a dark trajectory. Is it like art? The subject matter of KEVIN KILLIAN's piece is another kind of darkness, delights of power, gossip. Is it OK for instance to ask, who is more eternal, Joan Collins or her persona, Alexis Carrington Colby Dexter? To have the taste of blood in one's mouth: to float, disembodied, partaking of both, between type and realization. Humanity's tribute to religion, implies Kevin. Then certainly within the million messages whirring and humming along America's uncounted telephone lines, he adds—talking to an ex-wife on the phone. Or where are we all headed, having sex in this bar then?

And STEVE ABBOTT. If modernism/postmodernism has no secrets, if deconstruction says *show your assumptions*—can writing that's about writing do this too? Discussions of current writers—"new narrative"— intend[ed] to demystify, mix easily with anecdote. Judy Grahn's poem, the occasion for wondering about his own mom's "talking to death." Or the concept of ambiguous borders brings up both: Kathy Acker's writing, a first visit to New York. At the end there are Joe's objections to what's seen as writing alienated from itself, so bringing the essay around again—the issue's connection, isn't it?

You hope this is the opposite of bullying. What CHARLES BERN-STEIN says is, if you start bossing people around so only your voice is heard—isn't that authoritarianism in writing as well as politics? To combat it, he says, accent play—in, through language. That plurality of voices. The famous openness. Talking to progressives he asks: if Stalinism's this idea's opposite, shouldn't we be in a hurry to get language and play back together?

How does language's dark or animal side come into the discussion then? The LEW ELLINGHAM/RON LOEWWSOHN interview, an interchange on Jack Spicer's life and writing, throws out many hints between anecdotal accounts of North Beach days. Spicer's ideas continue to haunt us. Assume your ability to make contact or go *beyond* (Spicer would have said: get messages from an Other World). Factor in loss: shedding light on dark. This dualist terminology runs all through the 3 economic-political-sacred essays of GEORGES BATAILLE, printed for the first time here in English. A split's presupposed. I go from one to the other, light and dark, across borders—that's what the "religious" had in mind before it got detracked. Bataille's ecological and environmental thought critiques limitations of productivist-oriented societies (Western). Bataille's sacredness: an assumption you make you're in touch with the opposite from you and not separate from it. X is a function of Y, as they say in math, and that's where we started in this discussion of New Critical Perspectives isn't it?—the interrelation of things? How they go together.

"The Last *Soup*: New Critical Perspectives" first appeared as the introduction to the fourth and final issue of *Soup* Magazine, edited by Bruce Boone, 1985.

THE TRUTH ABOUT TED

Ted didn't turn out to be what I expected. He turned out to be quite nice. But may I add a bit odd? Easily embarrassed, he would stare in impassive silence for long periods and then, properly encouraged with a solicitous nod or smile and polite question or two, become brightly loud and voluble. Earlier when I asked, Jonathan said Ted was straight, but Ted's brand of sociability really suggested something more like camp. Later, as I came to see him often in Jonathan's company, I wondered if Ted could be straight at all. Ted had the marked interests of a person who was gay, opera for instance. He hung out with gays almost exclusively. He looked gay and acted gay. He talked gay even. So why wasn't he gay? That was my essential argument to Jonathan, and after some time Jonathan gradually came over to my viewpoint. Yes, Ted was gay, whether he knew it or not. But isn't self-knowledge a matter of time? Let Ted do things at his own pace, Jonathan advised, he'll come out when it's time. Why be pushy? It's his life, after all, not yours.

So about the matter of Ted's sex life, Jonathan and I maintained a stance of polite non-inquiry vis-à-vis Ted. We limited ourselves to speculation. And in the meantime Jonathan and I broke up—we left our place on 18th St. In the city. I chose to go downtown, to what I have since recognized was a terrible little studio in the Tenderloin. Jonathan moved in with a group of musicians in the Fillmore, where he could practice and perform among kindred spirits.

We didn't stop seeing each other though—and we didn't stop speculating about Ted. Was he or wasn't he?—that was the question. If he was, when would he . . . ? and so on. I also discussed the matter with Bob. But at this point, since Bob had only met Ted once, and briefly, my discussions of the 'Ted question' with Bob became increasingly abstract and unreal—and began drifting further and further away from the real person Ted. For Bob and me, the issue of Ted's sexuality challenged our ability to come up with the right interpretation of signs generally. Ted was a test case of our hermeneutic proficiencies. I'd say, Well, Bob, at the opera last night, according to what I heard from Jonathan (that blabbermouth!), apparently Roy had a hot new item about Richard Bonnyng's boyfriend, and when he told Jonathan and Bernard about that, well, Ted just seemed all ears. So what do you think about that? And Bob would reply—sounds like he's gay to me, Bruce! Or I could take the devil's advocate position. Don't you think it could be a form of politeness?—I'd ask. Straight men can be polite too! Finally our Ted discussions became technical exercises, occasions for testing our skills as writers. We wanted to be able to verbalize our perceptions of life's ordinary events accurately, elegantly and truthfully so that other people would applaud us for our socially useful talents. Whatever else it was, Ted's 'problem' was grist for our writer's mill.

Not that this wasn't fun. The more complex and detailed (and superficial!!!) our discussion became, the more it seemed to draw out our deepest feelings. These feelings had to do with ourselves, with the community of gay men and in some odd way with the possibilities of human life, happiness generally. Talking about Ted became a way of talking about the things we cared about most—things we couldn't have talked about honestly and satisfyingly except as gossip. I can't begin to tell you how good I felt about this aspect of my life. It was wonderful in its own right. Yet I must also tell you this. I now believe that the good it represented was a limited one. Gossip and language—they do have their limitations. And I believe that even the gossiping we did about Ted was an illustration of this. Let me show you why I think so.

One favorite theme—because so incredibly rich—was Ted's non-stop ability to be embarrassed. His susceptibility to blushing, his capacity to be 'shocked'—over and over again. There were endless discussions of this. 'But that proves . . . !' I'd say. And Jonathan or Bob would reply, 'Not at all, it doesn't prove a thing. It proves the opposite. After all who's more worldly, straight or gay?' and so on. In the end each of these 'proofs' cut both ways and so didn't mean much—until a non-language reality could intervene. As it properly did, a little later. How it did is the story of those few phone calls I mentioned earlier.

The first phone call began like this. Jonathan had called me under a transparent pretext—information about a minor problem in the distribution of my book that he thought I should know about. So I knew Jonathan was up to something else. If any of you ever decides he or she wants to sail the inland sea of Jonathan's mind, I'd counsel you this. Be wary and mind your p's and q's, remember to navigate carefully!—I'd say. Do you perchance want to get to point B, now being at point A? Then with Jonathan go by way of C! That's my advice to you. With Jonathan directness isn't a good idea. So the day Jonathan called, I correctly followed my own recommendations—deciding to be patient and wait until Jonathan judged it was safe to get to the point. He had been at Cody's bookstore in Berkeley the other day, he said, with Ted, and had noticed copies of *My Walk with Bob* lying out on a display table. He decided I'd want to know how sales were doing and went over to take a look. All well and good, I thought to myself as Jonathan was telling me this, but what are you getting at? Jonathan continued. But one of the copies was definitely defective, he said. It had several missing pages, there might have been others. Jonathan thought I would want to know about this so I could replace the copies. I told Jonathan I was sincerely glad to hear that and would certainly make sure the damaged copies were replaced in short order, since Bob and I were planning to go over to Berkeley that weekend. I would replace the defective copies when I was there—but meanwhile, did Jonathan have any other news?

For reasons I couldn't understand, he seemed to want to continue talking about his afternoon in Berkeley at Cody's bookstore—with Ted. While they were there, Jonathan said, Ted started skimming my book in the hopes—he added—of finding some kind of gossip about people he knew. Like Aviva, Jonathan's sister. Or Laurette, whom Ted remembered from Jonathan's concerts and musical get-togethers. Basically, Ted just wanted to know what I would say about them. He finished looking through my story as Jonathan browsed in the Italian literature section. Later, when they had left, Ted told Jonathan he was a little shocked at the part in my story about the supposed new boyfriend that had come to Jonathan's concert on Laurette's arm. Did this mean, he asked Jonathan, that while Bruce and you were together you were seeing someone else—another man? Jonathan tried to explain things but Ted insisted on continuing this line of thought, resolute in knowing the facts whatever the cost. Now Ted hadn't read the whole story while he was in the bookstore, so he hardly could have realized that my narration of my feelings about Jonathan and language took place in a period of time that followed my breakup with Jonathan. Ted expressed his fears of Jonathan's potential 'adultery.' He became alarmed at the prospect that Jonathan might have been 'unfaithful.' Had Jonathan— Ted then asked directly—been seeing someone? The question surprised Jonathan. It didn't make any sense. Though ignorant of the facts of the situation, Ted's apprehensiveness remained genuine.

Illustrating his fears, Ted then told Jonathan an anecdote about a former room-mate of his, Ted's, who had just gotten back from New York City. The room-mate told Ted about having the best seats in the house while seeing "Evita" with a friend. But there was something suspicious in his friend's story, Ted pointed out. Ted attempted a roundabout way with Jonathan. The seats, he exclaimed, cost $50.00 each!—with the sense that this fact would speak volumes to Jonathan. When Jonathan remained clearly perplexed at this, Ted became more straightforward. By implication, he asked Jonathan, wouldn't that mean the friend was really more like a patron? When Ted asked his friend how in the world he could manage something so expensive, the friend had winked broadly and drawled—well, I just made sure to give him a real good time later on. When Jonathan came to this part of the story, I couldn't help but laugh. Jonathan was laughing too, it was such a completely ludicrous picture of what evil in the world might really mean. But Ted's own analysis was rather different from Jonathan's and mine. Taking the story at face value, Ted insisted that the dilemma was a real one. He was completely crestfallen by the cynicism it represented. Was this, Ted wanted to know, how people really behaved once they leave the protective environment of family and friends, when they take up life on their own in the big city? Was this what it meant to be an adult?—to be mature? As Jonathan repeated this anecdote to me on the phone and described the anguish on Ted's face, I felt waves of sympathy gushing up inside me. I felt a respect hard on its heels—then something like admiration. Didn't the story show Ted's first encounter with the Cash Nexus and his human horror before it? Didn't it show, too, by implication, Ted's high estimate of the opposite of this, a truly human and socialized way of behaving? For Ted's sake, I wanted to think so. But I had to be candid with myself. It isn't exactly, I thought, as though Ted has really been tested by life itself. And I persisted in this direction. Would Ted survive real trials? What would happen to Ted once he came out for instance? In gay life there would be two choices open to him. Forgetting idealism, he could become a shallow person and choose to live a life of fantasy. Or, deepening his experience of life with sex and the understanding of good and evil, he could become wise, strengthening his first idealism with power and adult comprehension. Which of the two paths would Ted take?—I asked. But until Ted actually did come out, wouldn't these possibilities remain academic? And Ted was certainly taking his time about it. The coming out, that is. But as Jonathan pointed out, it was his life, wasn't it?

As I told you, my expectations were for the best. But there was also the other side of the coin. What of Ted's well-known passion for Sir Walter Scott for instance? Would literary romance take him to, can we say, the community function of love, friendship and sociality? Or—and this alternative was equally possible—would Ted's Sir Walter Scott infatuation lead to a taste for superficiality, frivolity? To furbelows, to Offenbach for instance? (The prospects recede into infinity.) Well, history itself will be Ted's judge, I remarked airily.

But as fate would have it, the mystery of Ted's sexuality cleared up sooner than anyone imagined. About a week after my conversation with Jonathan, Bob called to remind me of our projected trip to Berkeley. It was time to see how our books were doing in the bookstores there. How many *Family Poems*, how many *My Walk With Bob*s should we take to Serendipity for instance? What did I think? And how many copies to Cody's?—our best outlet! There was Sand Dollar—but was it really worth going all the way to North Berkeley? Questions about the business end of our writing careers. Questions I didn't particularly want to deal with. Neither of us did. By default we were distributors of our own books, as well as being our own publishers, publicists and critics, reviewers, etc. We had chosen to go our own way in writing, not becoming part of the various 'schools' in our area, and the understandable consequence was that none of these schools was anxious to publish us. What would have been their interest in promoting our writing? But meanwhile Bob and I were pretty much on our own. If we wanted to be read, we would have to take on most of the drudgery of the business side of things ourselves. So we had become, in our own modest way, small time business men. I hastened to allay a guilty conscience with solacing precedents. Hadn't Rimbaud become a first class business person in Ethiopia?—I'd ask—forgetting for the moment that that was when Rimbaud stopped writing. And who—I'd continue rhetorically—was more spiritual in their innermost self than Rimbaud! Even the Pope runs a Bank of the Holy Spirit, I'd remind Bob. Was this what we had to look forward to in the future? Trudging from store to store, selling literature—heart to heart chats, transcendental yearnings of human nature, edifying counsel on politics—at $3.50 a copy! Not very edifying, is it?—I told Bob skeptically. Bob responded by pointing out that it wasn't very likely that this was what fate really had in store for us; we really did have better prospects than this ahead of us. And, anyway—didn't I have items of interest for him from other fronts? What about Jonathan's recent activities for instance? Bob had neatly segued us into another field of action.

If Bob was trying to steer our talk into less negative areas, I was certainly willing to go along with him. Our conversational energies were lagging. News of Jonathan might be a change for the better. Who could be sure anyhow? Maybe the ship of our changed fortunes was just out of sight over the horizon line, even now about to come in. How many literary committees and agents were at this very moment in furious competition to see which one could heap larger sums of money on us, shower us with high honors, traditional prizes, co-opt us with nationally distributed trade editions! To have continued our speculations about a future of poverty and lack of recognition would in fact, I realized, be tantamount to soliciting it. It would be the equivalent of declining another, better future—of rewards and recognition—substituting this one for the brighter one that we knew was actually to be ours. So why tempt fate, I thought, and turned to the subject at hand. Actually, I told him, there's quite a lot of news about Jonathan. Bringing Bob up to date on the topic of Jonathan's successes, I mentioned the concerts, critical acclaim, reviews and notices—then Jonathan's plans for the Bruges Competition. Then I mentioned Ted again. 'Ted!'—Bob said with alacrity. 'How that fateful name keeps recurring!'

As indeed it did. I had from Jonathan, I told Bob, a wonderful story of sexual realization—or maybe non-realization? depending on how you took it. And if the story doesn't improve you, I sad pertly—why, be sure, Bob!—it will amuse and delight you with its many knotty dilemmas and rare paradoxes, etc. You will certainly know more about the human heart by the time you are done. 'The human heart!'—mused Bob—'that dark and chambered place whose sere, ancient secrets. And what comes next . . . ?'

Bernard comes next. He was a lover Jonathan had had some time after Jonathan and I broke up. They had a relationship that lasted maybe a month, if I remember correctly. Then there got to be difficulties. So the romance part stopped between Jonathan and Bernard, but they continued to be friends. 'Sound like anybody else you know?'—I asked Bob. 'Sounds like everybody else I know,'—he replied. The friendship continued on the basis of what they had in common, I told Bob. For instance—music! Here I paused. 'Do you see? Do you begin to get the drift?' Bob allowed as he didn't. Would I be clearer please? Then—'Opera!'—I shouted triumphantly. You see, I proceeded to explain to Bob, Bernard naturally would begin to meet others in Jonathan's circle of friends. And just as naturally, especially those wonderful musical evenings of coffee and pastries and watching Joan Sutherland TV specials, wouldn't this group of friends include in a particular way, especially and above all—Roy? Don't you see it yet, Bob?—I asked my friend querulously. But Bob was getting restless. He asked me to come to the point. I wanted to be modest, but the glories of the thing were beyond me. 'The point!'—I fairly shouted. 'But it's Ted, isn't it?' I could hear Bob's heavy breathing on the phone, so I knew the first realization of the thing was already on him. It was all so truly wonderful! 'Such a simple solution can scarcely be imagined'—I commented. 'What,' I questioned candidly, at last beginning to be sure of myself, 'can be more appropriate . . . ' Bob sighed, 'Nu?' Then he had it fully. ' . . . than that Bernard, to put it simply, Bob . . . will bring Ted out!'

I heard Bob whistling softly in tribute to my daring. Then together we checked off the list of possibilities. Common friends like Jonathan and Roy for instance? Yes! Many. Common interests then? Uh huh. Opera and more opera! Well, how about a common age? You could say this was true— on condition that Bernard, being older only slightly, would sometimes get to be in the 'older and wiser' role, just to add spice of life. At the other end of the line, 5 blocks away in his house on Clipper St., I heard Bob's response. He weighed his words carefully. 'It adds up, Bruce,' Bob says to me calmly, 'and I think you've hit paydirt this time.' 'Well, it's darn nice of you to say it,' says I sweetly in my most straightforward Cybill-Shepherd-in-Taxi Driver voice. 'But seriously, Bob'—I continue—'it figures all the way around except for one tiny thing. A possibility is one thing, a marriage something else. A whole 'nother ballgame. Everyone I talked to—Jonathan, everyone!—agreed my calculations were brilliant; it was so clear, Ted and Bernard were to be the couple of the season. Logical and necessary, no? So I thought too. But we all forgot one thing which is after all maybe the most important.' Meaning what—asks Bob, still in synch with me, step by step in my argument. 'Meaning love, meaning chemistry, meaning whatever you want to call it.' Silence on Bob's end. 'When Bernard finally gets up his courage to ask Ted the big question, well, that's exactly the moment Ted chooses to slam the door right in Bernard's face.' More silence, Bob's breathing. 'And naturally, Bob, the explanation of this involves a bit of a story. . . . Would you like to hear it?'—I ask Bob. 'I think I would, Bruce,' says Bob.

Well, here's the story I got from Jonathan, I tell Bob. And the surprising thing is, it shows Ted isn't gay after all. Or that's the implication anyway. But the way things stand now, unfortunately, we may never know the truth. Remember Rashomon, that 50s Japanese movie where there were all these possible versions of the story and you couldn't say any one of them was the right one? 'Uh huh,' says Bob, 'it reminds me of Ed. You never know what version he would tell you. Ed was like the movies. Visual that way.'

'Here's the way this story goes, Bob. It seems several months ago Bernard and Ted meet for the first time, and—as Bernard later tells Jonathan—he, Bernard, was quite impressed with Ted, right off. Ted has the looks Bernard goes for in a big way. And too, Ted's smart, and Bernard likes that too. Then another thing, as it turns out, there was also their consuming and mutual love of opera.'

'That's a lot, Bruce—but do you think it's enough to build a relationship on?'

'Well, let me tell you Bob, according to Jonathan, this Bernard is one of life's go-getters. Every day, up at dawn with 100 chin-ups, that's for starters! For breakfast he has yogurt, just plain yogurt, that's all. Not even the kind with fruit on the bottom. Maybe a thin slice of bread, but never butter! Don't you think that's impressive?' Bob grunts a non-committal, 'un huh.'

On top of that, I continue, Bernard's learning how to be a court reporter and will probably make a lot of money in the future. In other words, I explain, Bernard's an eligible—a very, well, man-about-town. So Bernard has this bee in his bonnet—he just has to ask Ted out on a date. But first— as a kind of 'permission' is my guess—he decides to check in with Jonathan, he needs to see if the idea is viable in Jonathan's view, he and Ted being such good friends. Jonathan the prudent! He doesn't exactly tell Bernard yes, and he doesn't exactly tell him no. He just gives Bernard Ted's phone number, and that's that—more or less. Bernard gets going on his project right away. He calls Ted up that night. 'How would you like to get together after work sometime and have a drink or two with me?' But imagine Ted's consternation! Is this a formal invitation to go out with a man, just like women do? Ted's taken aback. What can he say? Being a person of good breeding, he doesn't know how to deal with Bernard's brashness. All this time of course Ted's supposed to be straight. But Bernard's assumption to the contrary is getting to Ted. He has to say something. So what answer does Ted give Bernard? Here's what he says, literally. 'I think you and Jonathan have something in common you don't share with me.' It's a strange answer, isn't it? Ted implies he's straight, not gay. But if it's what he implies, it's not what he says. So there Bernard is, right back where he started on square one—and Ted's sexual direction remains as unclear as ever. Altogether an enigmatic situation, don't you think?—I comment to Bob. We grow silent momentarily.

Bob deals well with silences. I think he supposes—correctly—that my silences have a life and meaning of their own, and if I drift off sooner or later I'll return.

I continued. I told Bob Bernard had been palpably upset by Ted's unfortunate remark, as much by the phrasing of it as by its substance. Could Ted possibly suppose he was being tactful with his dumb way of putting it? was the thing—whatever it was—that Jonathan and Bernard had in common a disease maybe? a joint checking account? a set of fine Lennox china? Bernard's dander was up. To put it bluntly, if Ted was straight his answer was insulting. And if he wasn't, well, why didn't Ted just come out and say he didn't want to go out with Bernard? Ted's answer seemed evasive and—coquettish. So here comes Bernard's counterattack. He's not going to suffer in silence. Nor is he prepared to see Ted smirking at him in the future!—even if this is, given Ted's sentimental character, a rather unlikely proposition. So here what our Bernard then tells Ted. He tells him, 'I'm not just interested in your body, you know, I'm also interested in your mind.' It was as if Ted was, oh, I don't know, a chorus girl, a starlet, anything. You get my drift—all the stereotypes of sexism coming out. Think of Marilyn Monroe reading Shakespeare. All the reporters crowd around thinking they gotta ask her opinions on the Bard or else they won't get an interview 'cause they're not taking her seriously. Does offense deserve counter-offense? Ted was certainly right to feel a little objectivized. So he just leaves Bernard dangling. Bernard extricates himself as he can. He makes a few more polite remarks for the record, hangs up. And that's it, I tell Bob. That's the story. Bernard and Ted are like most stories, they never really conclude. Just end.

Bob said that could be true all right because it reminded him of the time he and Ed went to Murray Edleman's workshop for gay couples. Wasn't that in 1974 Bob asked me—checking out my memory—or was it later? I wasn't sure, so I asked Bob if that was about the time I was in Berkeley with Jonathan. But Bob thought it was later. Anyway, he continued, this was a retreat—a time when you really face the issues of your life together. What happened was, each couple stood up and complained about this or that, whatever in their relationship. It was assumed you'd be better people for airing your dirty linen or nagging each other. When Ed's turn came, he said that what he wanted most with Bob was to feel he could go out into the world and do what he wanted to do and always know that Bob would be his home. Bob says he was really moved by this statement of Ed's. Bob told the group that this was one of the most beautiful things he had ever heard. 'I noticed,' says Bob, 'that everybody's jaws had dropped open when they heard me.' Bob says he's telling me this story to corroborate my own incomplete story of Ted and Bernard. 'It took years to understand that story,' says Bob. 'One of the many hidden agendas in the weekend was for me to learn how to assert myself and make demands. First I had to understand how selfish Ed was. That's when I realized what the open jaws meant.'

I thought Bob might be pulling my leg. Couldn't he change his mind about Ed again? I told myself I'd shelve this issue. What did I know about whether life concluded or narrations did? Wasn't it the same either way?

As events proved, it wasn't actually. About two months later I get an unexpected call from Jonathan. He says there've been some new developments in the Ted situation. Do I want to hear them? Naturally. So I get the details from Jonathan and pass them on to Bob at the next opportunity. Recently, it seems, Ted had been feeling like a show in the city. *Iolanthe*, for instance—one of his favorites—and by the Lamplighters. He phones Jonathan—doesn't everybody love Gilbert and Sullivan? How about going with me tonight? But Jonathan can't go with Ted that night, he's got a rehearsal. Ted's so, so, so disappointed. He's been studying all week long and it's a weekend! Doesn't he deserve a break in his work-week as much as anyone? Jonathan considers this. Sly Jonathan! He admits Ted has a point. You know, Ted—says J.—Bernard just loves Gilbert and Sullivan. Why don't you see whether he's doing anything tonight? Maybe he'd want to go along with you. Besides—continues J.—he mentioned particularly wanting to see *Iolanthe*. Well, what do you know? Maybe I should call up Bernard. Maybe you should, replies Jonathan. Jonathan the wise. Ted one of life's innocents.

So he does; they do. Go out, that is. Naturally it's a set-up. But it's in the best interests of all concerned. And a happy ending is predictable from the outset. So, after they see the show together, Ted and Bernard take a walk. What's more ordinary? They find a park bench. They sit down. What do they talk about? Who knows. But in my own mind I give them completely conventional lines. I make them say what couples have said to each other in such circumstances from time immemorial. 'I've admired you for a long time, you know, and I think you're really very attractive. 'I hope you'll forgive my being so anxious the first time you phoned me.' 'Isn't the park lovely tonight? There's a full moon and you can see all the stars.' Canzonetta sul aria. But you'll come, won't you?—says Mozart's count. Does he know? Susanna's as nervous as Almaviva. It's a *Marriage of Figaro*—in the distance you can hear the plashing of fountains. Not far away is Bernard's house, and that's where they plan to go. *'Donne, vedete s'io l'ho nel cor.'* Sound of violins, falling cadence. My only comment is this—God give them the night of happiness they deserve. People should get whatever happiness they can from life—because what else is the point. Of anything?—I conclude abruptly. That's it, Bob. The story of Ted's coming out.

On Bob's end, a short silence. 'I suppose that means Ted was gay all along. . . .'

'Obviously.'

'But the story still seems to lack something . . . you're not keeping something back, are you, Bruce?'

'Well, there is a detail. Though I don't really know if I should add it since it's so completely banal. It takes some of the magic out, I'm afraid. Anyway, here it is. A few months after Ted got out of college he went to the baths. One that was nearby. Does that interest you, Bob? And he got his first blow job. In the steamroom, it was. And for all I know gave one as well—though that wasn't part of what I heard. I wanted this to be a romantic story,'—I told Bob—'and here it is turning into a story about a quickie in a public bathhouse! How embarrassing! It's the opposite of the ending I wanted. There goes courtship, nice and slow, and spiritual. There goes roses. And what do you have, instead? A college blow job!'

Bob laughs, 'You have to let life define your stories, Bruce—instead of the other way around.'

I told Bob I'd think about this. And I did.

"The Truth About Ted (A Selection from *Carmen*)" was first published by exempli gratia (Berkeley 1984). Subsequently, the text was made available at X Poetics blog before being reissued by Summer BF Press (San Francisco, 2011).

AN EXCERPT FROM *CARMEN*
(A VISIT WITH ROY)

Next day I'm with Roy and his mother in Berkeley. Roy's going to the Soviet Union and he's so happy he's decided to give his mother lessons on the international political situation. But first we talk about his plans, how to get there. Should he fly to Riga for instance or maybe Warsaw and take the train. You would be with very nice people, only *Party cadres,* engineers and state planners coming back from their Baltic holiday. You'd be going first class in the grand style—like they used to do. The servers in their native Ukrainian dress wheeling huge, streaming samovars every afternoon at 4:00—tea on real china, fresh linen, napkins for everyone. But Roy says money's going to be a real problem, so maybe the train is out. He could possibly go through Helsinki though, take the boat-train. Now *that* would be a prospect to look forward to!—I tell him. Think about it. Coming in to Leningrad a-sparkle on the water like Venice, the Czar's Window on the West all golden and Italianated, shining in distance. Its art treasures. The summery Winter Palace. Nevsky Prospect. The green foliage cool and elegant in September heat. A veritable Faberge Easter egg of a city, right out of the pages of *Soviet Life!*—I exclaim. Roy laughs. Well, there actually will be politics, you know—in spite of everything! But I'm mistrustful. I assume the worst.

Roy's mother doesn't join in our jokes. It's a serious matter either way. A bit shame-faced, I say I agree. They didn't joke about it in the Arbeiterbund did they? Then Roy asks his mother, well, they're too *old* to remember, aren't they? How do you know it's not a *screen memory*—emphasizing to show he's being erudite. Look at the songs from Yiddishkeit for instance, Roy says. You'd say they didn't believe a word of it. There's our famous Jewish irony for you. Like all our songs, you have to make a face when you do them. "O zuk mir nit/ vo di fegel zingen . . ." Everyone laughs, including me. The argument goes back and forth between them, hard to tell how serious though. Roy's tack is to be scholarly; his mother's strong suit is indignant humanism, pleading etc.

The record's changed now at my request, though the *Carmen* will have to wait till this Verdi is finished. A new *Ballo in Maschera*—wonderful!

We'll all enjoy it. We talk about how the Met production did right by the gay character for a change—it shows the two friends as the redeeming axis. Or one of them at least. For the time being Roy and Iris have decided not to argue.

Ballo goes on and on, and I'm getting a little bored. Now why exactly did Jonathan like this one so much, I ask Roy. Oh yes. I remember and answer myself. Oscar's music is so much like the Offenbach that comes later. Isn't that it? Or is it? I'm confused again. Now Iris sees an opportunity to re-join the battle. "I'm so glad you like Verdi now, Roy, I can remember when you used to like Wagner. I remember that's all I used to hear from you, how wonderful *Wagner* was. You know, when I was young, no one would have Wagner in the house, it was Fascist music we used to say. Music for anti-Semites. Your grandfather had such a collection of music—oh he knew all the opera there was, and the symphonies too, he knew them all—and there was never a Wagner there. Not one. No Wagner in *our* house!"

The battle is on again, and Roy isn't slow to reply. He says that possibly Iris doesn't know that scientific criticism has shown that Wagner's music isn't really anti-Semitic after all, and that what they believed when Iris was young was a mistake, an over-simplification. He cites critics, learned scholars that just don't think so. Iris says that of course she didn't have the opportunity for an education like Roy had, but she does know what everybody said then. They said this music was against the Jews, and so everybody should be against it! Meanwhile I'm being completely ignored. I wonder if I should say something. Should I come in on Roy's side because he's my friend? Or should I help out Iris, since she's getting the worst of the argument. On the other hand, I tell myself sagely, I should probably just stay out of it, since it isn't my business in the first place, and besides it's too heated a topic. But I'm getting bored. I have to see Holly soon, we still have our walking engagement, and I'm already late as it is. But then again isn't it rude to leave in the middle of things? I hear Roy remarking very rhetorically that he never knew that Iris was so *Jewish*—he always thought she was a *secular* person. Uh, oh. But Iris has a ready reply. Well, she probably did get Jewish when Roy got so goyish. Uh oh, this should really stop, it's getting a bit sharp around the edges. Someone could end up getting hurt, including the "innocent bystander" namely me! So I politely clear my throat. Ahem! Is there, perhaps, just a little more coffee left on the stove? And could I have just a bite or two more of coffeecake . . . ? Roy and Iris stop and stare, and suddenly the storm has blown over. A flurry of politeness develops and a cheese Danish, the remnant of the coffeecake and a great display of solicitous entreaties and hospitable body language get lavished on me. I *have* to have some more coffee! Is that enough of the Danish, because there's more in the fridge I should know. And the *fruit*— which they completely forgot! Am I really positive I have to go off and see Holly? There's *plenty* here if I wanted a little lunch for instance. And so on. Iris and Roy are back to being Iris and Roy, I see. It's so terrible when friends are quarrelling. But when they stop it's like sunshine—the sun comes out after the rain. Iris's name, I think. Iris's name.

But before I can protest, Roy has put on *Carmen* for me, Maria Callas singing the title role. This is the whole reason I have come over, now I *have* to stay! I haven't heard the Callas and I do want to hear what Roy and Iris have to say about it, I'm gathering material for my *Carmen*, my next book. I have to stay a little longer, Holly will understand. I ask Roy a leading question, just to see what he'll say. I say some people say the famous phrase applied to Puccini's *Tosca* should really have been said about *Carmen*—the "shabby little shocker" someone called it. What does he think, I ask Roy.

Roy says he agrees. They were right at the Opera Comique to call it scandalous, he says, in fact it's *deeply* scandalous. Do I think there should be sensuality presented in front of a family audience?—I express uncertainty on the subject. Roy asserts he would have been deeply scandalized himself if he had been there on opening night in 1875. But how many quote marks are around Roy's opinion I wonder. Maybe he means that my question about the "scandal" in *Carmen* is a dopy question to begin with, so why treat it seriously. On the other hand Roy is decidedly serious about considering *Carmen* a very sensual piece, sexual even.

Then I want to know Iris's opinion. Iris says she always thought *Carmen* was like a musical, she didn't ever take it seriously. Roy's eyes begin to widen. She says it's just the music to hum along to—you know?—but you shouldn't look for too much meaning, I think. At least it isn't Fascist music!

"An excerpt from *Carmen* (A visit with Roy)" first appeared in *Tamarisk*, vol 5, no. 3/4 (Summer/Fall 1983).

NOTE ON *CARMEN*

Do you mourn aborted children? Not me. They are what they are. I don't cry. No tears please.

In what follows, you'll find two letters from an epistolary novel called *Carmen* that I worked on for a while in the 1980s. In it, a "sort-of-me" narrator writes to other writers in his San Francisco literary circle, hoping to integrate a specific community.

I tried this first in *Century of Clouds*, which moves in three concentric circles. These circles were intended as expanding versions of community, beginning with a religious community dating from the time when I was a young man, thru the hippie community of Haight-Ashbury during my twenties, and ending in a community of marxists, which I had thought of as a full realization of my desire for collectivity, kind of an apogee.

What about *Carmen* then? In this failed literary project, I tried to take the work of *Century of Clouds* to a "higher level," following up on community lessons by way of a drag-queen narrator named Orlando (thank you Virginia Woolf). Orlando was very gender fluid, emotive, gushy, and paranoid, to boot. But out of cowardly fear, I abandoned it. I just caved, thinking—ohmigosh, this is way too far out!, and out of cowardice, I dumped this work into the garbage can of history. Dear Orlando, Dear Carmen, so sorry! Would that I had been more courageous!

"Note on *Carmen*" was written for this volume.

THREE LETTERS FROM *CARMEN*

Dear Megan,

Do paranoid types like ourselves hear them, the screams I mean, like those birth-defect people in SCANNERS overhearing spiteful conversations about themselves from clear across the restaurant floor and deciding to punish the perpetrators with a ray-zap and a smirking innocent face? In our own restaurant on Castro Street it's reversed, and we're the enemy looking down on those poor defenseless still wiggling pigs in a blanket and seeing your (and my) non-flappable expressions over coffee and orange juice. Was your breakfast partner this morning Jody Foster—and are you lamb-like enough really to become Jody Foster? Is it Orlando's fate written in the stars to become another Jody Foster? Orlando's still thinking about his/her nighttime straight-man visitor. Is a strict vegetarian diet of eating only burritos like famous vegetarian DENNIS COOPER to be Bruce's own destiny? Meanwhile I'm backsliding. Sometimes the spiritual world just makes me want to scream. On the one hand, at breakfast I turn pale hearing secret screams of pigs in blankets that nobody else in the restaurant can hear. Does that make me crazy? But on the other hand, when Dodie and I go to Grace Cathedral, home church to Timothy Archer in THE TRANSMIGRATION OF TIMOTHY ARCHER, my favorite Philip K. Dick novel, we unsuccessfully strain our ears to hear silence among well-heeled Anglican New Agers babbling nonsense. Could it be the spiritual world is only available in PARTS? Hopeful to reconnect in death with a son who in life he'd been a bad father to and who killed himself because of this, the actual bishop Pike—in the novel called Tim Archer—optimistically sets out to the Holy Land on advice from a fake medium to find his dead—suicide—son. Search teams find him days later face up in the sand with a happy look on his puss. Was he stupid or smart? I am so tired of hearing screams. Jody Foster has nothing on me. I want them to stop.

Neotony. What does your body look like all dehydrated and turned to leather if the desert preserves it? Does it look like those Cenobites described by Clive Barker in his novel of flayed people coming back from hell because they want new skins? Chic Orlando and Megan, two enlightened citizens of the enlightened community of letters, consider the perils of meat-eating over IMITATION bacon at Megan's house three months earlier—which is way before Jody Foster's SILENCE OF THE LAMBS. It's the other one, Anthony Hopkins' Hannibal the Cannibal who downs people's kidneys with fava beans and KEE-ANNN-TEEE, as he says. I wonder if I'll like him in HOWARD'S END. The spiritual world must be very mixed up is all I can say when confused with VEGETARIANISM like Mr. Hopkins'.

Jody sets out on the trail of a serial murderer to quiet a violence remembered from her youth. If the slaughtered lambs don't shut-up and keep silent, won't she just go crazy? Sorry Jody. With a message like that, don't you just love this movie? But the killer's naturally this wigged-out cross-dressing fag, complete with mincing poodle. MEGAN, is that what the American public imagines homos are like? In the end of course another cross-dressing homosexual is slaughtered, with his faithful poodle dog alongside, killed by FBI agent Jody on behalf of a blood-thirsty public that demands drag-queen victims, like its parents did before it in PSYCHO and its older brothers/sisters enjoyed seeing in still-great but still homophobic Brian DiPalma's DRESSED TO KILL. Am I projecting my own squeelings onto the pigs in the blanket? I wonder if imitation-soy-extender links are really THAT bad, M? Your own little lamb, your own unborn, seen thru ultra-sound, its tender skeleton, at that age, already bouncing around, is that what you said the doctors told you they call the BUNGEE PHASE? I imagine all the little lambs in the world—what about the mothers that say goodbye to these little lambs? Fail to embrace vegetarianism? Yes or no?

If in the carnival of the flesh the lambs are silent, how to stop self-promotion gossip, malice, slander in a writer's world? Don't we all have dirty hands? And speaking of career complaints, when is KATHY gonna come thru with that blurb she promised me for my next translation, QUINGARD'S ALBUCIUS? As I agree to dish KATHY, aren't the dead literal pigs on the platter looking up at the live human ones?

Of course being the dead, we are still alive as writers, though in another way than what we thought. Yesterday when browsing in the library, I read of this quote unquote "DAIMON" that appeared to 1st century philosophical great APOLLONIUS OF TYANA, who was sort of the competition to Jesus in the religion business of that era. Later in his MAXIMUS letter Charles Olson seems to think a lot of himself too, since he takes that name from the one used by the tutor of Apollonius—but otherwise I can't tell you the significance. There are a lot of dead white men in the world. Someday I will be one too. Anyhow this oracle that appears to APOLLONIUS the famous wonderworker and mystic Buddhist-type of those years, tells him SHOULD ANYONE WANT TO EMBRACE MY WAY OF LIFE, HE MUST RESOLVE TO BANISH FROM HIS BOARD ALL FOOD THAT ONCE BORE LIFE. I admire the oracle for its seriousness about vegetarianism of course but would it be equally serious about capital punishment?

(Apollonius is on record as condemning a couple of executions.) Would the oracle feel that the spiritual path required of you not only a certain self-betterment but also participation in the political processes of your day—the marches against racism and imperialism and sexism and homophobia for instance? And for that matter—I would like to ask the oracle—would it disapprove of the violence of writing? What tears the lambs of the world apart limb from limb more than writing? Does the beauty of writing cancel out the violence it indulges, putting one word after another, ripping apart the seamless garment of silence into screams that we hear as readers?

I can't make up my mind if I hate the fakery of the other world and love the violence of WORDS or just want to make interesting letters, with really no opinion on the subject. Would I go to bed with someone just to have something interesting to write about even if they don't do all that much for me, sexually? The number one interest in the Jeffery Dahmer case for the citizens of Milwaukee was the CANNIBALISM angle, not the serial killings. Are we writers as stupid as these ordinary people then? Letters from the so-called Ascended Masters came down thru a secret hole in the ceiling to announce the universe's personal endorsement of writer Madame Blavatsky and her organization. And why did somebody as smart as my creator MRS. LEONARD/AKA VIRGINIA WOOLF believe it when the stars told her she was a piece of shit and should go drown herself? And hey! Look at that name—Woolf—what does that tell you? Writers have to eat meat, it says to me—the name means a carnivore. Woolf. I'm sick of trying to be spiritual and anguished. I just want to join the human race. Though something wants me to continue to be a writer, that may not be possible. Megan, name me even one writer we both respect who's not basically a predator.

Your semblable and soeur/frère, ORLANDO

Dear DAVID,

Dear heart, at the DARIO reading the other night at A DIFFERENT LIGHT I wondered WHO ARE THE BIOLOGICAL FEMALES HERE? The masks we wear are too firmly attached not to need, they say, a certain VIOLENCE to disclose what lies on the other side. VIOLENCE IS INFORMATION they kept saying. All the sentences seemed to scan all right but when it came to the images there was a blurring that took place that reminded me of something missing. In Dario's TERROR IN THE OPERA and SUSPIRIA the blue is on the verge of eternity and the red remains the color of spilled blood like the sleeping animals roused in DENNIS COOPER's MISSING MEN. It is a question of gels. The artifice involved in taking out certain in-between parts with a knife, for instance. VALERIE taught us that, didn't she? The parts extracted are not necessary. REPRODUCTION is at best a debatable proposition that all too often consolidates the worst aspects instead of opening the door to the more EVOLVED and NECESSARY parts of our nature? The CHRISTIAN DESERT SAINTS of the 4th century cut out their butchness, literally. What is left in their hands? The bleeding remnants while the howling goes on outside all this. My next husband therefore needs to be some mask of this—the way one says FAUX BUTCH or something—just as I am myself, ORLANDO and BRUCE, the both of me, only a FAUX FEM at best. We owe VALERIE for this more than could be said here. This is dedicated to you, MS. SOLANAS! Hand on heart!

Did God make STRAIGHT MEN unaware of this for a reason, ignorant of the impersonated nature of their status as conquerors and possessors, like that chromosome JOHNNY COME LATELY on the EVOLUTIONARY scene making it that much more necessary for something new to INTRUDE? On this supposition THE NEW is the X itself, not the Y. I just read something about LACAN where he says that he's SUSPICIOUS of any MASCULINITY that takes itself seriously. "BEING AN INCOMPLETE FEMALE, THE MALE SPENDS HIS LIFE ATTEMPTING TO COMPLETE HIMSELF, TO BECOME FEMALE." VALERIE said that, which makes DARIO ARGENTO a DRAG QUEEN like all artists. The hormones have acted on what science will tell you is the naturally female state of the brain which takes crucial infusions of artificial hormone to alter it to its impersonated state: STRAIGHT-MALE. At the same time physiologists tweak and shrivel the famous ANTERIOR COMMISSURE which in gay men and women, they say, becomes a better-functioning CONNECTOR between the two halves of the brain. WHY IS THAT? And what is the connection with VIOLENCE in all this? SCIENCE, a little bluebird chirping inside ORLANDO, tells her that VIOLENCE is NEVER THE ANSWER. Can you make sense of this opposition now troubling poor ORLANDO, DEAR DAVID - - you with your big butch confident way of explaining things to ORLANDO that ORLANDO always loved, erotically anyway, while constantly kicking against the goads when it comes to a sense of the inappropriate behavior demonstrated by the very same butchness that attracted him SEXUALLY? You big butch queen. I'm still attracted. Be sure and write your:

ORLANDO

DEAR BRUCE,

LONDON AND VINCE - - those are the secrets. DON'T JUDGE YOUR-
SELF. LISTEN: Your name has FIVE letters. So does VINCE'S. ORLANDO
has seven, and substracting BRUCE's five, doesn't that leave TWO, the
number of the two of you - - VINCE and BRUCE? JUDY's message is so
clear. THE ROAD GETS TOUGHER LONELIER and ROUGHER, yes,
for HOW LONG? That's the question. Bruce, everybody loves you - - you
shouldn't get paranoid like this. You misconstrue messages by looking
only at a PART of the meaning, not the WHOLE. For instance in that
LONDON PALLADIUM CONCERT of JUDY's, besides the message of
the ROAD getting tougher isn't there another communication that you
might've mistakenly overlooked? Think about it! After the MAN THAT
GOT AWAY didn't JUDY add a message of HOPE for you in her OVER
THE RAINBOW - - a testament to a place where there will always be
PRETTY LITTLE BLUEBIRDS flying for you? BLUEBIRDS, LONDON,
VINCE - - isn't it to clarify the LARGER CONTENT of that message that
I'm intervening to write to you now? LISTEN UP BRUCE!! Could it have
been you alone I've loved, you queen of queens, and aka Orlando?

To realize what I mean all that's necessary is to go back and recall the
messages I've imbedded in my writing for you. For instance: in FLUSH,
my novel, named after ELIZABETH BARRETT BROWNING's spaniel,
consider what I wrote as a clue for you to read only much later and decipher
as the incentive to go DEEPER for comfort in your present situation. Why
do you think I wrote the following: ONLY A SCHOLAR WHO HAS
DESCENDED STEP BY STEP INTO A MAUSOLEUM AND THERE
FINDS HIMSELF IN A CRYPT, CRUSTED WITH FUNGUS, SLIMY
WITH MOULD, can't only she sniff out the meaning of a closed LONDON
bedroom as a mandala of DISCOVERY? VINCE, DECAY, LONDON. In
the dry dusty fungus-like smells of a closed LONDON bedroom leave it to
a pet spaniel named FLUSH to uncover the true meaning of VINCE's now
slightly MOLDY and MUSTY breath. HIV opportunistic infections? Or is
there another mode for the production of SPIRIT other than the DECAY
of the BODY itself, do you think?

FORGETFULNESS and REMEMBERING in LONDON. Since if eight's the number of letters in BLUEBIRD and seven in ORLANDO, what does the missing one stand for but a missing step? What's been forgotten in the attempt to get VINCE back? In the decaying sour breath of aliens probing and testing in surgically clean operating rooms deep in the space craft, don't abducted WITNESSES always see a paradox? Is evolving, and becoming HIGHER just another expression of the need to DEVOLVE, become LOWER, like a mushroom, a fungus, the sour breath in the mouth of your alien VINCE? Is the evolution we think is UPWARDS really just DOWNWARDS?! How to follow the path that leads us to the RECOLLECTION, the discovery of what's only apparently LOST? Like CHRISTINA ROSSETTI burying a secret code in the portent words of that famous sonnet by saying REMEMBER ME. Afterwards ROBERT ALDRICH would pick up on the clue and make CHRISTINA's "REMEMBER ME" the MOT DE L'ENIGMA as they say in FRENCH by turning it into an explanation of the mystery of the atom bomb in his 50s noir KISS ME DEADLY! Unraveling the plot of this mystery was it by chance that you BRUCE/ORLANDO, a generation later, seeing the film in repertory, would decide to make that phrase central to understanding the perils of nuclear destruction and ecological devastation, a desperate call to AWARENESS in your own essay for KEVIN KILLIAN's NO APOLOGIES? But why would the chain of transmission stop with you and not be destined to go on in this chain of un-remembering, like a virus replicating? Like the way BO HUSTON insists on recollection - - what SOCRATES called anamnesis - - by calling his own novel REMEMBER ME as well? I don't think any of this is in vain, do you Bruce? LONDON, home of CHRISTINA, then for a time of myself, VIRGINIA. And then JUDY comes in and sings her poor heart out on stage at the PALLADIUM for you a quarter century later - - is this just chance, BRUCE? Think on it. Could the clue to your understanding of your ex's - - VINCE's - - slow decline be related to my relocation back to LONDON? What do you think, ORLANDO? None of us know where we are going till we get there. Or is that redundant? It doesn't matter, LONDON, six, a middle between ORLANDO which has seven, and VINCE who is only five.

Superficial of me to say so? But if everything's connected, isn't it only natural for writing too to be superstitious, stepping as it must (mustn't it?) from visible to invisible? I did a bit of stepping myself that day when firmly but with difficulty (because weighed down by the stones in my pocket that were to keep me from floating, I thought) - - when as I say with difficulty yet firmly, I stepped into the OUSE RIVER. You could have for that matter as well called it the STYX given the way words of any kind are ultimately inapplicable when speaking of a BEYOND, aren't they? The letter I left for my husband LEONARD was to the point and succinct since as your own JACK SPICER liked to put it WORDS TURN AGAINST THEMSELVES. Perhaps it was the power of THE WORDS I used that brought me to this present fate when I began that note with the insanity hypothesis by telling LEONARD "Dearest, I feel certain I am going mad again." Everything is linked but I am very tired, since in this place it's with difficulty one raises oneself to write at all much less at length so I close here knowing your own alacrity and goodwill, DEAR ORLANDO, will read between the lines and benefit from the good intentions I can no more afford than I could in life formulate while at best remaining your

Virginia Woolf, born Stephen, aka Bruce.

These letters from *Carmen* exist only in manuscript, one long accordion-folded text from a dot-matrix printer, undated and completed sometime in the late 1980s. These excerpts appear here in print for the first time. Thanks to the Poetry Collection of the University Libraries, University at Buffalo, The State University of New York and their Bruce Boone Collection.

DAVID'S CHARM

FEET: I have little snapshots in my head of myself bent over, slavering. Why would I want to restrain myself? The feet ordinary, not dainty. Dealing with eros, a person has stopped dealing with facts, long since.

EYES: Eyes a lovely calm blue, changing in the light of a particular background, wherever we are—Noe St., Golden Gate Park near the autumn chrysanthemums, it doesn't matter. What gratified me was the slightest hint of animal terror I saw there. Oh, I tell you! My daddy's eyes held all of heaven's masculinity—cerulean, they were. A well-meaning Jove. A bit of a bumbler.

LEGS: Hot. Just hot. Sometimes we'd do "pushup" contests, take long runs in the park in the athletic glow of weekends, late afternoons, and I'd show my daddy I was, of the two of us, the better athlete. Daddy would show off his legs. Would I notice, winner of so many contests? I'd pretend not to—though he'd catch me out of the corner of his eye. Great, strong, "golden" thighs he had, born for tongue-worshipping, I used to think. Then later, when we got back, that's what they'd get, while I groaned. Light blond hair of leg outlined against late afternoon light in shadowed doorway while I made loud animal noises. But the calves good too, I thought—and the thought would lazily buzz like a fly—like Jonathan's are they?

COCK: With your cock in my mouth I'd invent strategies by the hour to debase myself, submit myself—in an agreement I made with myself, not you—to your higher power. While you resisted. The world outside changed, the seasons went by. Nothing changed. David, the creep, deliberately tormenting me, tantalizing, torturing with this one hope, desire to lead me on—"maybe I'll change, maybe I'll come in your mouth this one time, sweetie." Such was/is a cock's logic—a mind of its own as in the phrase, "he thinks with his cock"—which stirs desire in me still. Logic of love, unfolding like a peacock's train, a burst of light.

SOUL: Of course Bruce's daddy *had* one, didn't he? But sucking daddy, Bruce realized you can't have it both ways—and daddy became a bisexual stud, just so many pounds of meat on the hoof. I swear! I never thought of David's soul once—only my own, and I'd see it reflected in the admiration of David's eyes. My soul/David's body—our fair, gloomy agreement.

OTHER (except nose): I've forgotten them or maybe I don't want to talk about them anymore. To jerk off, I remember thighs, blue eyes, and a big fat dick in my mouth.

I guess daddy's gone to work now with his new white shirt on but of course Brucie realizes he'll not be gone for long cause he's gonna be back at the end of the day isn't he and uh huh such a nice surprise is it oh yes it is a nice surprise for Brucie flowers which he always liked so much and does while you are gone daddy I'm always a good boy you'll see I'm a good boy I've been making your favorite for you what daddy's boy knows daddy likes isn't it it's fried eel and drenched in tomato sauce doesn't that sound good and these cute little dim sums I got in Chinatown don't they look good they're made of haricot beans oh and for dessert daddy I know you'll love it a flan daddy a flan oh oh and now daddy is getting so happy he's patting my ass I think he's getting me ready for it I think daddy doesn't give a damn about the goddamn flan at all he's making me turn around while I stand at the stove with this stupid wife's kitchen apron on me frying up the eel while daddy the animal the brute the fuckin pig has got his hands all over around me patting my little ass good kneading and playing with it until my heart starts going faster, it's going faster and fluttering now my heart has leaped to my throat in terror I feel the terror of it oh daddy wants it from his boy uh huh daddy's gonna get it uh huh daddy's such a bisexual stud isn't he and his ex-girlfriend Margie is going to be so jealous when she finds out isn't she isn't, (faster and faster)

Then another time daddy gives *me* the daddy position—but it could only be for a little while, can it? (yes and no)

Sitting in the Guerrero St. kitchen, not the one on Noe St. I just described myself in—and there's this knock. Landlord Rich wants to come in, OK, OK, Rich—though I make sure to show Rich lots of teeth, so he'll get the point he's intruding. I think he has snooping in mind. Can he look at the paint job on the bathroom floor he did a couple days ago? Push push push with my pushy middle class politeness and I've got Rich to the bathroom and back again to the door of my apartment before he can do anything (ANYTHING) about it. Bruce glows with modest self-assertive pride. Not bad, huh? David looks up at me open-mouthed. Working class David. He can't buh-*lieve* how these middle class people know how to boss everybody else around by using so-called politeness, language, to their own ends. It's astonishing, David feels. I've spun around and caught these emotions registered on his face and—thud!—there's a pit in my stomach as I see David transparent with admiration for me, envy for the ability to *compel* people by using language a certain way—the skills he's attributing to me. My dick gets hard. I want to turn him over my knee, paddle him hard—real hard—till he cries. Fuck him then and there. David, if you were here with me now, I'd be trying to get up inside you—doing everything I could to get your pants off. Alas!

Postscript: Later that night I remember fucking David's face. He's giving me head with so much energy and willingness to please and submission written across his face I lean over to kiss his forehead like a puppy's. I'm so moved I hardly manage to hold back a tear from forming—a single tear. To feed David's face is to be a poet, I decide—and I know that sometime in the future (who knows when) I'll write of this. To his credit and mine. (what I'm now doing)

Here's something else. The story of how we met. David, the working class activist, straight man for ten long years, now coming out as bi—or maybe, maybe gay SOMETIME—tells me he's gonna be a therapist. David—I protest—then you'll be middle class! You won't be *working class* anymore, I tell him fretfully, scarcely knowing myself whether I mean what I'm saying. David crossly reminds me of how we met.

We met at the baths. What was I looking for? It was undefined, because it was taking place in an orgy room. I was perplexed and frustrated, since I usually go for some detail or details in a person that suggest that person's history, something about them besides just the basic equipment. The visual's as important for me as the sense of touch—so I was wandering in this darkened orgy room seeing only shadows, unsatisfied with the only exchange values I could see. Let something happen! I don't want to have sex with just ANYONE, you know—so how about a clue?

Then I see a silhouette across the room, a nose. It has some character to it, it's a good one, I decide. And the man *behind it*—I continued—what would *he* be like, I wonder? I decided there could well be an interesting story behind that nose; since, as I always believed, for those who know how to read them rightly, noses can be the very map of the soul, and this particular nose strongly intimated the INTELLIGENCE and PERSONALITY of its interesting-looking owner. Go for it, Bruce, I tell myself, go for it!

The other men in towels part easily before me as I push my way across the orgy room to the man's side. With his eyes he gives me unmistakable permission, acceding to the liberties I've begun to take with him. Then I'm down on my knees, giving him a great blow job. But when I look up I don't seem to see any particular emotions registering. Why isn't the guy reacting? What more does he want anyway? I continue—and slowly, slowly he seems to relax, get into it more, enjoy it. That's OK, he's into it now and showing it and I decide that all's well that ends well. Now the handsome stranger seems totally at ease and happy. He reaches down and lifts me slowly to my feet, then starts to return the pleasure-giving attentions I've just showed him. I become a rose blooming—a cherry tree in spring with white blossoms, a young apple free and supple brimming over with all the tingling sensations and pleasures you can imagine. I get hotter and hotter. I feel like I'm in a novel—aren't these the proverbial bells they talk about starting to go off and ring inside me now? Rockets they describe go off in the innermost parts of my sensitive inner ears, I'm THERE. WONDERFUL!—I think. This guy's got POSSIBILITIES—that, for sure.

Then we go find a place to be quiet, talk. Small world; it turns out we have a lot in common. So you know Fred Wasserman then? Well we're just roommates, David says, not lovers—but we live together. And then we talk about people from the old gay lib days, turns out David knows them all! We discuss theory next. David likes Guy Hocquenghem's—I prefer Mario Mieli but have an increasing partiality for David Fernbach. We talk about our pasts, his family of very "modest circumstances," mine not so. Futures— we'd both like to see money there, the question is, *how*? After a while David starts looking antsy. What's the matter? He says he'd like to see me again, but right now wants to go back to the orgy room and play some more. I think I probably reacted with some shortness. If we had as good a time as it seemed like, why doesn't he play with *me*! An odd person I decide, telling him—a transparent lie—it doesn't make any difference to me, since I gotta get home anyway, since I have to get to bed early, then get up early the next morning. He says he'll walk me to the door. At the last minute grabs an "introduction" card from the counter near the checkout window, writes briefly but furiously on the back of it, gives it to me with a kiss. I pocket it without looking at it, give him a friendly kiss, the attendant buzzes me through the closed door—and then I'm gone. The stars look great that night as I leave the bathhouse. They're all wispy and delicate, traceries, doilies for heavenly confections. If you have to decide one way or the other—I tell myself—never trust your emotions or you'll be sorry. You'll just get into worse trouble. Never trust them. Men are beasts.

Later: I'm looking at the card David gave me at the checkout window. It says, "21st St. Baths, 3244 21st St., San Francisco." It shows a drunken-looking street sign, cartooned, just above. One arm loops crazily one way and says 21st, the other says Bartlett—and the two arms look like they're embracing (staggering?). On the back I read David's tentative, vulnerable handwriting. "We discussed ambition, Hocquenghem and I gave you a great blow job. David Miller 387-8454 (M.F.C.C.)." The initials stand for David's projected therapist credential—by implication, a middle-class berth in life, no?

The Princess phone has put on its Hula-Hoop, shaking itself, a Hawaiian lei, started to dance like a cartoon cutout. R-r-r-i-n-g, r-r-r-i-n-g! all festive like the illustrated brochure the phone company sends, price list—somewhere between Trimline and Touch-tone. 9:30 in the morning, too early, isn't it?

Hlo? Groggy with sleep. A philodendron at the end of the room telegraphing infectious enthusiasm and waving its leafy green arms.

Hi dear, I just got to work and don't have time to talk. I'm calling to invite you to a party tonite at my friend Naphtali's.

Ng ng ng and inarticulate glugging noises.

So you wanna? We'll get a chance to unwind a little know what I mean?

The glottal stops now indicate Bruce might be on the verge of a choking attack, hysterical fit.

Sweetie? So think it over sweetie and I'll call you again at the end of day OK?

The hysteria's now definitely set in.

Sweetie? There'll be lots of food, I'll call you again at the end of the day OK?... Hello? Anyone there? Dear?

In the first I'm running up a heath, above me roll the ominous thunder-clouds. I've got to reach . . . it. "It" turns out to be Northanger Abbey, on account of a conversation I've had with Dodie about the vampire novel she's writing. As I reach the door, I wheel around to face my pursuer, a famous ex-San Franciscan who's into s/m. This person happens to be a lesbian and she's in her full leathers. I know she intends to go for my neck, but it's too late. The languor seizes me as she pins me against the huge medieval oak door of the Abbey and I give up. I can't fight this anymore. I've reached the end of my resources. She starts to rub up against me and I can feel her cruel metal-studded bracelets bruising my delicate flesh. Too late the realization dawns on me—this is what I'm made for, this is what I'm born for. I groan, ineffectually resisting the pleasure I've started to feel. I allow her to take her will.

Also: I'm at home at my family's house in Portland, Oregon. It's late in the afternoon, since it gets dark early here in the North country. So I turn on the lights in the bedroom I've had since I was a child. My mother comes in quietly and just stands there. For your punishment (but what was the fault?—I can't remember) I'm going to have to *ground* you—and a little tremor scurries down my spine. Brass gleams in the late afternoon twilight. I think, I *must* remember to get off my article for the *Poetics Journal.* Is there a deadline? I can't recall if there is.

In another I'm visiting my friend Martin at his pied-a-terre in the Silver Lake area, L.A. He's teaching a class in art criticism there and has rented this cottage temporarily. The warm evening floods us. Outside, banana trees are spotlit, L.A. style, wonderful yellow green against night. Where the traffic is down below, the streetlights make a frivolous diamond necklace. We're waiting for Martin's friend Tom to come by and take us to the bars. Why isn't he *here* yet? I demand. We're horsing around, then take off all our clothes so we won't be encumbered. It's obvious where all this is leading to, I think—I'm going to get to suck Martin's cock, why has it taken so long? But Martin suddenly changes the whole Scenario. He spreads my legs and tells me quite calmly he's going to fuck me. The proposal enrages me. What about AIDS! I tell him indignantly. Martin is very self-possessed. He remarks casually that I must be a very repressed person if I let a few vague fears stand in the way of a good fuck. I fall to the floor immediately and start a temper tantrum—Martin isn't taking me seriously as a person, I'm just a sex object for him. "I'm *not* your little boy and you *can't* tell me what to do!"—I protest disingenuously, hot salt tears in my eyes. The L.A. light goes cool, as in Raymond Chandler. And suddenly I think, but really—why not? My eyes narrow to slits. I'm a hot little bitch. I give Martin my ass, maliciously.

I want to add a note about sex as power. During the whole time I was with him, David was still crazy for women. He couldn't get enough of them. One part wanted to be gay of course. The rest was obsessed with what David called pussy. When we went out walking and saw women and he'd say stuff like "Nice tits huh?" I felt hopelessly outclassed, outmaneuvered. I realize I should have said something sarcastic like, Nice for *you* don't you mean, David? But I didn't, and maybe this was part of our dynamic. I was getting trade, straight dick. Should I stop loving them because they're shits?

David used to tell me how he beat off to the pussy mags or how he'd meet some nice woman at work and sneak off with her, they'd do it in her car or maybe in one of the empty conference rooms. Big deal. Then one time he told me about going to the Sutro, a local bi bathhouse, men and women both. David really likes bathhouses. When he turned the corner, there was this big guy, barrel-chested and macho, standing there, legs akimbo, arms folded across his chest. A couple of demented-looking women were at the crotch, sucking and licking and carrying on all over him. The trio was the center of interest of a larger circle of men around them, watching what was going on, beating off, and looking like hicks who'd never seen anything like this. The big man demanded of the women more and more insistently— this is what you want isn't it? Huh? Isn't this what all women want huh? According to David's story this had got the watching men so hot their tongues were lolling out and they were jerking themselves off like mad. "So what were you doing, David," I ask him. David looks at me like I got a screw loose. "I was jerking off too, what do you think?"

You just can't tell what, if any, of our sexual systems are going to survive. That's what I say. On the one hand, who wants terrible things happening to women? Not me; I identify with them too much, it'd hardly be in my interests to allow for stuff like rape battering etc. One thing I do know is I want hot sex, and that for me presupposes a power imbalance. Maybe the future will figure a way to put all this together. I dream of hot sex. I want it. My life depends on it to be happy. For the rest, don't ask me. I don't know.

Here's a snapshot. David and me are trading stories, we're talking about the history of socialism like we often did. He tells me about his political work, the relatives he found later in life who'd been stalwarts in the old CP. We're little boys in the 3rd grade again—trading baseball cards. I tell David about this wonderful/terrible quote I found from Max Eastman, when he'd gotten back from some conference in the Soviet Union (this is all in the 1930s). He'd discovered "scientific socialism in the process of verification." We both have to laugh. Such generous hopes betrayed by such stupid language. But the fact that David could laugh at this and is laughing with me, and is one of the few people I know who knows all the levels of hope and disillusionment and then hope again that this laughter means for me, kindles hopeless desire in me. It makes me want to conclude every story of David I ever tell with just one conclusion. Seeing me grow pale with desire, David decides to seize this opportunity to treat me like a thing, an object, takes me defenseless and sticks his big dick down my throat till I choke on it. That's the fantasy. Like I told you earlier, if I could reduce David to so many pounds of meat on the hoof I'd do it.

Onward, but to where. The news is, they come and they go. I haven't heard from David for at least a year.

Last time we talked, he said he had a girlfriend. A *girl*friend, David? He was at this dance and told her, I want to be completely honest with you—looking straight into her eyes and holding the glance to show sincerity—so I'm gonna have to tell you I'm a gay man. But if David was expecting to *epater les bourgeois*, did he ever get a surprise. The woman looks back at him equally straightforwardly and says brashly—well, I'm a dyke! And apparently that was the beginning of a very happy relationship. They're going steady now. They both really like getting it on; and what makes it all the more exciting is that, since one is a gay man and the other is a gay woman, obviously they don't have to feel boxed in. You are who you are, and they're not heterosexual. All the fucking in the world won't make you who you aren't. When David tells me this, he slightly averts his eyes. I like that actually. And really, I like David a lot. Just the way he is. With that slight gleam of animal terror in his big blue eyes. Don't change, David.

"David's Charm" was first published in *Storytellers: A Serial Fiction Anthology*, vols. 2, 3 and 4, edited by Benjamin Weissman (Los Angeles, Foundation for Arts Resources, 1986). The story was subsequently anthologized in *Men on Men: Best New Gay Fiction*, vol. 1, edited by George Stambolian (1986).

A NARRATIVE LIKE A PUNK PICTURE:
SHOCKING PINKS, LAVENDERS, MAGENTAS, SICKLY GREENS

Can storytelling satisfy without a bursting open, excess, slimy fluid to drip all over and taint what we tried so hard to keep separate?

Religion's a perverted but good start. Bataille likes to point to the *connection* between victim and sacrificers in old or nature cults. I wouldn't want anyone's heart to stop beating except that for the first time this might unite us. *Animal House*, pure crudity, combined with the serenities of Bresson's *Lancelot of the Lake:* the horses' hooves go by flashing and flashing as if something's being *torn open*. And it is. It begins with a pace or structuring, sexual and metaphysical excitement coming together. At heart it's the physical, a knife a person could get to love—Bataille and I agree. What could be more important than EXPRESSING?

What I mean: if Benjamin said take the auras OFF things, people have started to put them back ON—and violently. The modernist-defined world says there's just a gap, a big looming empty space between any A and any B. People things events are just units standing there, said our modernist ancestors. But radical NON-CONNECTION's now recognized as fraud; who could put up with this anguish of utter loneliness anymore? In another Bresson film, *L'Argent* (Money), there's a thief on the lam. In a (possibly comic) scene you hear footsteps of the thief running toward the subway entrance tunnel. Then the person comes into sight—a fast rush of visuals as he runs by the camera/onlooker. The footsteps are now heard clattering away, retreating into the subway tunnel proper, out of frame. They die away and Bresson's camera is trained on the interesting tiles. Is the film meditating/contemplating and inviting us to do the same? There's a revelation or directive in the sound (footsteps) across space and time. It links where I am with where I am not. This is something messy and viscous. If you go with the body, you go with perception: familiar borders stop looking clear or certain, don't they? A writing that's a body (and a body without a subject to control it is my death) goes up, out, beyond; where brilliant florid quasi-organic brutal patterns ("Millions of tiny fingers urging release! release!" said the Foot-Fixer ad on CBS Evening News at

7:00) push you out to the HOT/DARK—a black rose of narrative that's also an emotion of violence. To narrate: to explode. Feminists in the late 60s used to say—everything's connected, isn't it?—and it *is*, isn't it?

Modernists—partisans often of Empire—never believed this. Slap some lipstick on the modernists—would the stories they told improve? Subject and object for them had to exist with a *line of separation*. What Flaubert thought was—if I put MYSELF instead of my character Felicity into that nice soft white cotton flannel nightgown of hers, I'd BE her then, wouldn't I? If the thought alarmed, it didn't daunt Flaubert. And the idea occurred to make her, not him, go down on the Holy Ghost and call it a parakeet. Can the body be body and still spirituality? is a thought that didn't occur to them, the modernists.

So the leaky craft of historical progress continued on until it cracked up under the streaked and lurid skies we call today. Now the beautiful exteriorized waves of interiority of Southern California's suburbia stand for emotions trying to be freed in Eric Fischl's cover of Tom Raworth's new book. These feelings become problematic, have the blunt commercial intent of a Stephen Spielberg film. But I love their surge or rawness. And I appreciate the Olympic athletes, looking really great in their moment of triumph on TV. Rowdy Gaines, the glamorous heartthrob swimming champ who took gold medals he should have won earlier in Moscow but didn't—since we were boycotting the Russians then. When our national anthem struck up, the camera zoomed in to catch the emotions. I saw tears falling on the face of this athlete I love; he was a proud American and really into being this. 1936/Riefenstahl the metaphor I mean. Bruce, emotion's the human face of fascism—said Bob blandly the other day. If I'm in my body, I'm *linked* to you, aren't I? Don't answer, reader. The distance I feel is the mixed-emotion variety you get looking at the shockingly fetishized body of swimmer Rowdy Gaines, the hunk. Between image and body—a gap that's characteristic, postmodern: emotion experiencing itself in the mirror. And the image that's the meaning of image is the sudden perception of the lack of connection among people and things.

The art world proceeds on that recognition: image testifying to and forbidding its power to link up, relate through emotion. East Village painters go all out for the most direct emotions, horror, fear, terror—

but as pastiche. In Stephen Lack's expressionism Hitler kisses a little girl with blond braids in front of what's maybe a church? His "Your Parents Get the News You Are Dead"—great title—a National Enquirer weepie; for a frame he puts on sentimental tearing-fringe wallpaper instead of a regular one. Half of Rhonda Zwillinger's picture is teen lovers crossing soda straws, smirking, rubbing foreheads. The other's a backlit Statue of Liberty—postcard style. Are the truest emotions commercial? Recognize the commodity lie, then take part in it at a distance? The 23rd Olympiad— "Olympiad XXIII"—monumentality, spectacle, the humanness of other people's cultures lifted up, out, becoming commodities. In the spirit of the times it's hard to know which follows, which proceeds—High Art or Low? After a long time we have narration and the emotions again: so we have "life" not life. Start with the body. End kissing an image in this mirror (myself)?

Feminism enlarges the idea of image and decommodifies it partly. You get bigger than yourself. Narcissism isn't a bad word any more. Kathleen Fraser *(Something((even human voices))in the foreground, a lake):*

> A lake as big, the early wind at the bather's neck. Something pulling (or was it rising up) green from the bottom. You could lie flat and let go of the white creases. You could indulge your fear of drowning in the arms of shallow wet miles. You did not open your mouth, yet water poured into openings, making you part.

Focus on the *body*, perception—short-circuit ego structures, you hope. Is there an implication of death there? Beverly Dahlen thinks so in *The Egyptian Poems*, and her *A Reading* becomes at times a hymn to the drive and attractiveness of negativity: "As shoreward / as whatever gleams coming / a whatever there is / that might prove to be" her envoi. Does feminist writing also allow craziness? Can its promotion of transgressiveness toward the ordinary sense of subject-object division create schizzy-ness? For Dodie Bellamy's unnamed persona you could feel like you're from another planet: "The one in the black skirt loved him, but it wasn't a heavy passionate thing. More like fucking your Teddy Bear. Passion had never made her happy, anyway" (*Voices for a Valentine Birthday*). Fem-writing as a potential state of at least two minds Julia Kristeva described in *Powers of Horror*:

> The abject has only one quality of the object—that of being opposed to the *I*. If the object, however, through its opposition, settles me within the fragile texture of a desire for meaning, which, as a matter of fact, makes me ceaselessly and infinitely homologous to it, what is *abject*, on the contrary, the jettisoned object, is radically excluded and draws me toward the place where meaning collapses.

At what price decommodify? Remember Robert Mitchum in *Night of the Hunter*? Two little kids get shown a pair of opposing knuckles: one says l-o-v-e, the other h-a-t-e. Jonathan was just Jonathan before I put him in *My Walk with Bob*. Does it make me uneasy to know I've made my ex-lover into a commodity? If I didn't admit this also gratifies, I'd be dishonest— and on the *shock* of that realization I'd like to take my place in the writing of my time. What's the *positive* value of commodity?

So here I'd like to talk kink. With much gay writing now and some punk notoriously (Acker the big example), the sexual roots of aggression come into question. There's a scream of connection, the figure that emerges ghostly: life attributed to those who have gone beyond. So in Dennis Cooper's *Safe* there's a feeling-tone like a Schnabel painting, the ground is the fragments of some past, the stag, the Roman column, whatever—on them a figure that doesn't quite exist but would maybe like to. The person/ persona/thing the writer's trying to construct from images—

> Next to the bed is a Polaroid shot he shot of Skip. It's blurred because of the way Skip spun his head when Doug called to him. "Shit." He drops it into his dresser drawer, on ones of Todd, Dwight, Mark, Lon, Larry, and others, going way back. He's had a pretty full life, he decides, glancing over the pile, but not so full that the drawer can't be closed tight.

The Romans used to say "Ut pictura poesis," and I picture and would like to picture myself—only sucking, being sucked, moaning, being fucked, fucking, in the throes. In "Allegory" Robert Glück says: "Sexuality is often the community sublime for myself and other gay men" (*Ironwood* 23). And, Bob adds, "Cooper turns genre into pastiche with pastiche's assertiveness, so what was originally intended to engage now distances in order to accommodate new meaning." But when it comes to evaluating image in American culture, isn't something a commodity whether anyone likes it or not? You make your additions and subtractions from that point on.

So politics now is difficult, quite different from yesterday's, when it was taken for granted you could just be against this world, for the better coming one. If politics is between the lines now, ours may not be glorious, though it's still possible to be realistic. We're by the waters of Babylon making lists, I think:

> Nuclear catastrophes, destitution, famine, additives, melanomas, losing face, US involvement in El Salvador and Nicaragua, Puerto Rico, South Korea, Chile, Lebanon and Argentina, war in the Middle East, genocide of Guatemalan Indians and extermination of the native peoples of Brazil, Philippines, Australia, answering the telephone, resurgences of the Nazis, the KKK, auctioning off the US wilderness, toxic waste, snipers, wrinkles, cult murderers, my car, Jack's safety, queer bashers, South Africa, being unloved, considered stupid, considered second-rate, collapse of our cities, acid rain, the deforestation of the Amazon, etc. etc. (Robert Glück, *Jack the Modernist*)

So there's a modesty in these tears. But what will extricate? If I can't see, I feel. I express myself.

"A Narrative Like a Punk Picture: Shocking Pinks, Lavenders, Magentas, Sickly Greens" first appeared in *Poetics Journal: Non/Narrative*, no. 5 (May 1985).

HOLLYWOOD CELLULOID NUKE MADNESS

For gallows humor that comes close to stand-up comedy, a favorite of mine is Edward G. Robinson as Fred MacMurray's boss in *Double Indemnity*, telling MacMurray, the insurance rep, all the ways you can die accidentally. They're all down there in the tables, he tells him, in the actuarial statistics. Edward G. Robinson's at his best in scenes like this one, citing chapter and verse, ticking off on those plump fingers the categories of violence done to others. There's death by drowning, he notes, and death by falling from high places. There are deaths subdivided by location—by land, at sea, in the air. And death listed according to means—bathtub, auto accident, rope, shock. Each divides into still further subheadings, until at last you get this picture of a vast battlefield filled with severed limbs, crushed extremities, mangled bones. What a comic scene! But, concludes MacMurray's boss, suddenly puzzled and, in spite of himself, suspicious now, there are almost no statistics on death by falling from a moving train.

We enjoy MacMurray's complete deadpan reaction to his boss's confusion—since the last item mentioned happens to be the crime he and Barbara Stanwyck have just successfully carried out against her cranky oil-executive husband. Underneath, though, there's another aspect of the humor, and that's the list structure itself. How hysterically odd and funny it is that in the late capitalist society we live in, even death itself can be inventoried, be made just another item in our lives—even violent death. Death, like sex, by definition destroys the conceptual. So how can death go into any taxonomy? The monstrous, it turns out, is never far from the comic.

That's my gut-level reaction to the horror of nuclear disaster. Nuclear death is a G.E., chemicals are a Kelvinator, something else is a Kenmore or Amana. Want chemicals? Well, we can subdivide. There's Love Canal, or plastics in the wall, mold or asbestos in that old central heating system you used to have. And I give city telephone poles a wide berth, knowing that inside those insulators are PCBs. And at the collective level, there's Freon from spray cans—or wafting up from refrigerators? When the thin envelope goes, we get basted in our own juices, Thanksgiving turkeys in the oven of space. Only scale precludes this from our available imagination. What death is for me personally, is species extinction for group life? In such quandaries, humor arises. Without it, would our possibility for survival be as strong?

In emergencies, one of the most interesting forms of entertainment, for me, exists along the irony-to-sarcasm spectrum, based as it so often is on shared assumptions. Humor that's banal and vulgar? Sure! Like many an ugly duckling, it's going to be a swan. Its ability to 'vulgarly' expose long-standing contradictions may make you gasp and giggle at the same time. Humor like this is feisty. And the more it has to push back against, in terms of social repressions, the more obvious its raw aggression. Are faggots like me 'dishing' someone 'nice'? Yes, but only insincerely. Or how about black kids playing the dozens? Or class comedy in *The Sopranos*? The sheer rage bottled up in this humor shows through and is designated as 'side-splitting,' 'rib-cracking.' Something in you wants to break something—the mouth forms to a rictus of pleasure. 'Oh!' you think, looking at your neighbors for their reaction. Tears of rage that also mean joy? Is this one of those 'identities of opposites'? Possibilities like this might have motivated Brecht.

Commodity language may be the main instrument of the expression of our deepest feelings—our native tongue even? The oppositional quality of traditional avant-garde writing, experimental writing so called, on the other hand, makes it suddenly attractive. The training you have from working in an avant-garde tradition makes you very good at working with ideas. You can see concepts when they're only implicit, can draw them out for a progressive constituency and point them up, so they get addressed and people are urged to act.

And if it's not quite true to say that these two traditions—popular and mass art on one hand and avant-garde on the other—don't ever mix, it is true that most art gets limited to one, at the expense of the other. Most art seems schizophrenically attendant on only a portion of our lives. Two sets of strengths then, and how to unite them. In political writing—or a humane propaganda—don't you need to, absolutely have to, deal with ideas? Just as to make these ideas popular—and not cynically but appreciatively so— don't you want your ideas to be successful as entertainment too?

I think so. In 1955, Robert Aldrich made a sleaze vehicle called *Kiss Me Deadly*. In the Eisenhower years of the fifties, the 'nuclear theme' itself must have been a surprise. In a less obvious way, though, the bomb sequence at the end retrospectively interprets earlier materials, making them more surprising. Okay, great. There's an emotional critique of 'the bomb.' But in the end it's dumb, can't speak for itself, lacks the conceptual punch it would need to be used in any political sense. But what if—after the fact, naturally—we gave it the conceptual punch that's missing? What if, added to the film's lyrical evocation, there was a hardcore layer of explanation? This new *Kiss Me Deadly* would hardly be Robert Aldrich's—it'd be ours, in a larger, a more collective sense. And if it's propaganda, well, we'd hope it won't be authoritarian.

How does it start? First of all, there's Mike's girl trouble. Women! Always a problem for Mike! They pull guns on him, try to seduce him—and in their rottenness end up betraying him. In fact the Aldrich movie pushes your buttons so hard on this subject that you wonder if it doesn't have some buried critical, even proto-feminist intentions, however bungled. The opening shots are all violence. Christina, an escapee from a mental hospital, runs in front of Mike's sports car in the middle of the night, nearly getting herself killed. 'Stop! Stop!' Hmmmmm, she doesn't seem to have any clothes on under that trench coat she's wearing! Mike lets her into the sports car. The implicit promise of sex isn't delivered. Within a couple of short scenes we see her legs dangling lifeless at the edge of a hard desk. She's been tortured and murdered. Mike gets off with a beating, but when he wakes up you can tell he's thinking of revenge. Christina's last words to him are 'Remember me.' Life, as portrayed in this movie, is misogynist, violent. Sex is ambivalent, maybe lethal.

Soon artistic expression and ethnicity/race will seem problematic too. Meantime: lots of LA material, driving around in traffic, freeway shots, people manipulating cars with astounding aggressivity, like weapons. LA, city of modernity. You use—people and things—in this city. Like Mike and Velda do with each other, only Mike uses Velda more than she does him. Velda is Mike's lover, of course, but also a business partner/secretary of Mike's. Supposedly—according to the police lieutenant in this film—they play both sides against each other for added income in the divorce cases they handle in their private investigation business. When Mike gets back to his luxury apartment from wherever he's been, he turns on his answering machine and looks glumly out the window at the bleak traffic grid.

Something's wrong here, he's thinking—but what? Our Mike Hammer isn't a very conscious guy. His instincts just coerce—that's why he has the name he does. Won't a hardboiled guy like this at least be interested in great sex? Something always seems to keep Mike away from sex. Leering at a girl's better than fucking her, I guess. 'Look at the goodies,' he snickers in one scene when a good-looking blonde sashays down the sidewalk, but the remark's obviously meant more as a sneer than as a come-on. You wonder if he even likes Velda!

Velda and Mike are waiting in Mike's apartment, and apparently the modern art is getting to Velda. She feels uncomfortable and starts vamping Mike. She wraps her arms around his neck, fondles and inveigles, all to no avail. Mike gives her a tight-lipped little smile but won't budge. How come? His body language says he's made of steel. Would it be unmanly to reciprocate? we wonder. Both seem relieved when the doorbell rings. They stare at each other. Well, I guess we have to break this off, since that's the police lieutenant. And naturally that's exactly who it is.

Is it possible then that Mike really likes guys? Alas, probably not. The sign of it is Mike's manipulation of Nick, his Greek garage mechanic. Nick, on the other hand, really likes to get physical with Mike. Va-va-voom, says Nick. And Nick's octopus hands all over Mike indicates camaraderie. Mike's cheerful but calculating. His question: How can I use you? (Snicker, snicker.)

So he asks Nick to take risks for him that result in Nick getting killed. Too bad. On the other hand, since Nick's a small, dark foreigner, it's hard to really take him seriously, isn't it? He's dismissed. But, as in the black bar scene where there's a great blues song being sung, conversely, you see strengths in ethnicity—strengths that sail right over Nick's head. Nick's ability to love is shown as part of his Greekness. But that 'strength' is not for guys like Mike.

Ethnicity and women are a two-sided coin—but so is art, as we'll soon find out. Mike's need for a certain name, address, leads him to the (by now torn-down) old Bunker Hill area of LA, where a middle-aged Italian tenor is singing—is it Verdi? His arms are outstretched; he's accompanying himself on a record. And, in a touch that gets almost cute, there's spaghetti cooking on the stove. We get the point. Art and ethnicity go together, don't they?

Just as we've learned that art also goes with women. Or fags. The dead Christina was a poet, we find out, and the words she left Mike—'Remember me'—turn out to be the name of a Christina Rossetti sonnet. But back to Mike and the tenor. Mike needs information from the guy, so to show him he's serious he grabs the guy's record off his record player and smashes it in two across his big-muscled thigh. That's to show him he's not just fooling around. The man bursts into tears. Art is also weak, we learn. Which is a big problem. It's like the ladies. You can't help but need and want them, even though they're no good. No good for you, anyway.

Is modern art any different? Well, to Mike it curiously is. His apartment's full of it, and modern art gives Mike a sort of dubious pleasure. It's like the feeling he gets when looking out his window at the LA traffic, or when he's listening to his answering machine. When the camera pokes around—nosy, just as we are, for clues about this man's psyche—we see clunky fifties-type deco furniture, ugly pictures of Picasso-type women, faces distorted with anxiety or fear, and dangling mobiles, Calder style, dangling things everyone in this movie should be bumping into, they're so clumsy, obtrusive.

What's it all mean? we're asking ourselves by now. Don't worry, soon the answer is going to be clear as daylight—a thousand suns, as a matter of fact. But first our hero Mike has to get the address of the gangsters he's been looking for from a queer art dealer whose fear of Mike is played for laughs. He nervously swallows some sleeping pills so he won't have to be interrogated by Mike. Mike finds what he came for—then heads out to Malibu where the gangsters are holed up.

By now we have a pretty good idea what the jerks are up to. Earlier, Mike's police lieutenant friend has clued him in. The scene is very campy noir—two shadowy silhouettes talking to each other, like interviews with Mafia dons who don't want to be identified. 'I'm just going to say a few phrases, Mike'—here, a pause, to make the effect of horror really sink in—'and I think you'll understand.' It's so truly monstrous. 'Los Alamos . . . Trinity . . . The Manhattan Project.' Huh? Did he say what I thought he said? Yes he did. He said that. And as I watched this movie at the Castro Theater some twenty-eight years after it was made, the full horror did come back to me and remained. They're talking bombs.

And on account of this fact, the last moments of the film will seem curiously symbolic. It will light up 'tilt.' Something so big will be brought in that the film literally will not know how to handle it, and everything will get distorted, surreal. Sex and women will be revealed as a principle of evil, for instance. The 'object' the gang has in its possession is a box of uranium ore, or as it will also be called—Pandora's Box. 'All the evils of the world are in it,' explains the gangster chieftain.

It turns out he's a very cultured person, the criminal mastermind. He collects modern art too. That's of course in his spare time, since he's also an MD. But spare time is something this doctor has a lot of, since, when he's not out hustling uranium to sell to the commies, his medical practice is limited to discreetly pushing drug prescriptions to hoodlum friends. He's not a very savory person, you might say. But cultivated. Mike is the big goon. They're opposites, in the cover plot at least.

Or are they? The contents of that box contaminate our view of the mastermind's suave cultivation. And both are art collectors with a modernist temperament, both are thugs. The two become interchangeable instruments of the Enlightenment working together for the general deformation of society. A deformation that can be stopped—or completed—only by the explosion marking the end of the world . . . in terms of the movie, it blows up the problems that the director can't resolve.

I've seen the movie twice and the drama of the last scene remains completely riveting. You know something is really at stake. A woman Mike protected turns out to be the mastermind's lady friend, but she winds up double-crossing him too. She shoots the gangster boyfriend and, ignoring his dying words, opens the ill-starred treasure box to see what's inside. An unearthly light streams out and, with a gigantic shadow projected on the wall behind, it's clear she's in hell! Mike, in this interval, has freed Velda from the other room where she's been held hostage, and the two of them manage to stagger to the door. The gangster's moll, meantime, can't seem to let go of the lid she's raised. It sticks to her hand like phosphorus, she can't shake it, she starts to scream. The room begins to glow, heat waves roll up. Then there's a cut. Running down the beach, Mike and Velda look back at the place—they escaped from. Horrible! Ballooning out visibly at the sides, the beach house disseminates huge amounts of light, energy. There's a groan from the audience at this point. In the night sky we note clouds, heat waves slowly forming themselves from the house. In fact, it's a mushroom cloud, isn't it? It's a mushroom cloud we're seeing.

In my viewing, this ending is wonderful because of its ludicrous gratuity. Right at the end, has the film decided to just jettison all the realist movie conventions it's been following up to now? Atomic explosions don't come from the accidental opening of little uranium ore strongboxes, and probably they realized this even in 1955. This means the accent was put on the explosion itself, and the objectivity of a real mushroom cloud is something that causes you to want to account for it—but where? How? The explosion discredits the storyline, you could say, and recredits social reality—events in the world outside of this theatre. In place of Mike Hammer's sexy adventure stories, you get ban-the-bomb-ers, H-bomb development, Nevada testing sites, the Bikini Atoll.

Yet the movie clearly has something to say about causes. I haven't mentioned a lot of the violence in the plot—people getting blown up in cars, knifed and stabbed, pushed down stairs. An old man, a desk clerk, gets beaten up for not taking a bribe; another old man, the coroner, gets a drawer slammed on his fingers; women get thrown away like old minks. How far can you go in valuing cruelty, appreciating violence? Aggressive satisfactions are mixed up with social exploitation. And in the film it's a threat. Violence seems expressive of some huge but unnamed disaster about to overwhelm all of Western society. It ties things together that otherwise might not be related—a preoccupation with "art" and what's wrong with it, i.e., modern art, ethnic prejudices, implicit racism, the problematic nature of sex and relations of men and women, all related to the nuclear explosion at the end. The mushroom cloud as the meaning of a society that's turned against sexuality, against other cultures (racism), art, women and—finally—itself. Does such a culture even like life—for goodness's sake? Look at its view of sex. A woman opens a forbidden box. Since it's filled with uranium ore, this starts off the end of the world. You guess the moral.

Then this: who's the highest thinker in the film? Why, naturally, the criminal mastermind. He stands for science—white Euro science naturally—which arises from civilization to destroy civilization—and the world with it. Aldrich outlines a convincing aporia, which we'd inhabit if, like *Kiss Me Deadly*, we had nothing else to admire, love, lose.

Your subject can be anything. It doesn't have to be something from the sleazoid movie I've taken on. *Godzilla* would do. *The Matrix*. Who cares.

Anything goes. But with any 'deconstruction,' as we call it now (2004—as opposed to 1983, when I wrote this), find a subject that keeps people's attention. ENTERTAINS! (Sneak in the insights as you go.)

But what do I know? I'm only the writer!

"Hollywood Celluloid Nuke Madness" was first published with the title "Writing and an Anti-Nuclear Politics" in *Writing / Talks*, edited by Bob Perelman. Carbondale: Southern Illinois University Press, 1985, and subsequently revised and republished with the current title in *Biting the Error: Writers Explore Narrative* (Toronto: Coach House, 2004). The text that appears here is the latter, revised version of the essay.

MIRAGE—OR WHERE'S THE PARTY?

As usual this is me trying to think out loud about the future. What's *with* us writers writing in the USA today? . . . Now, if there's "Party Haha" and "Party Profession" as sides of literature, I get the feeling Bruce Andrews (whose writing, in deference to whose lovely first name I've always tried to pay attention to), to put it mildly, is far from fond of either of the two. In fact in an excerpt from a new book (it's in the latest *Ottotole*) he just about bursts a blood vessel slamming whatever occurs under that name. "Gestalt me out!," he begins intemperately and continues in a style which if unclear in offering whys and wherefores is all too clear when it comes to the *object* of this unprovoked display of pique. "Slang to the point of meat-eating, imperative ornament, dislike occurs. I refer to the Felony Augmentation Program; the tendency in art towards party." Now I like *that*! Cause all of the time I'd been assuming what the New York poet/professor's here condemning isn't shameful at all but in fact pretty close to being the *main thing*: the *point* of lit as a matter of fact. In the year 2287 will they be as bored with *our* writing as we are with the so-called giants of the past that's 300 years in the opposite direction? (Drydens or whoever.) Nothing lives beyond its era does it? But as busy grad students of that distant future exhume these books of ours that'll have been buried for centuries by then, won't they still have to wonder about and envy and maybe admire a little the aspect of us that came out when we got together and wanted to call ourselves *writers* . . . ??

By which I mean party. These observations aren't abstract, but they take place under the guise of a review of *Mirage*. Gossip, hanging out, calling up your friends on the phone to find out the dish on rivals, having fights and separations too, being allies or making innuendoes in your writing as a form of entertainment that you hope will make other writers in your group love, approve of, delight in you—I'm thinking of *Mirage* as party because I think it's quite possible that's the only way there is of being what's called "writers" now . . . in Late Capitalism.

Of course they say the *group* idea of writers (writers as a collectivity), some dare call it conspiracy, though I'm afraid that'll be in quotes, is what makes us modern or post or whatever. And I agree though you don't have to cite . . . uhhh, Schlegel and Young Hegelians or Breton with his Surrealism circus and Bataille going off into the woods with the Acéphale group for all of them to take down their pants (with Laure), or a New York School or Spicer Circle, Language Poets, New Narrative/Small Press Traffic Group, the Gay, the Black, the Women as groups of writers being together to show this as a fact! Kids who want to be writers but still are in school someplace (there's that fatal theme again: grad school!) concede the glamor of just being writers is the attractive thing, as if it's something "ontological," it doesn't matter really if you produce or not. . .

Though there's the other side as well: the entrance of rationality into this morass of sublime dark fun. "Party Profession": the foregrounding of light in what we do so that we, alas, also have a business and political side to us. Fun *vs.* work? Well: I'll concede the fact we didn't wholesale become the lawyers, doctors and CPA's our mostly middle class parents wanted us so badly to be doesn't mean that writing isn't a "party" in the other, more calculating sense of being an interest group too! "Party as Profession" this time around? Just look at Dodie and Kevin: they're smiling back at you from a recent *Mirage* cover so *competently*, I think the word is, name tags and all. "Let's tell it like it is, folks!" Dodie and Kevin and par-ty-ing—they're combining business with pleasure—they're in fact at a national fan club convention of a TV soap opera they're partial to—"Santa Barbara"—where they'll meet its "stars." And what might this say about a *Mirage* approach to arts, to literature? A theory of writing as fun plus interest?

The practice of this is a motto that I'm just making up at this very minute but want to attribute to Breton: Literature will be a party, I imagine him saying apodeictically, *or it will not be at all!* ** Now this is an interesting way of putting it because where the Dada people *were* thinking of lit as party but just a party, the Surrealists had already (busy, busy, busy, as Denis Hollier points out in his new *College of Sociology* signing canvases and checks) become a business, part of the art business. I'm using these two groups to show that I think our writing ancestors weren't schizophrenic enough and, with a somewhat European devotion to clear things, thought you have to choose one side of things against the other, that "naturally" one has to *exclude* the other. . .

But do they? What are you going to do in a society where everything's money? Exchange value? Just as it's nobler to frankly avow the *emptiness* of the signs that formally represent community, sublimity or the dark when it comes to the business of religion and, if it's important to you to join a church, be a TV adherent of the PLT Club, than have the unmitigated gall to decide you want to choose the side of *purity* by joining a "real" church like Anglicans (or . . . whatever), so I think the time has come to openly express the loss of the *dark* in the blinding, calculating *light* of writing today by reshaping what we do. If meaning has frankly departed from us isn't it better to acknowledge what we're doing not as writing but "writing"—in the sense of "sociology"? In the sense of having a *pretext* for getting together in secret clubs of gossip or whatever?

Our "God"'s gone anyway. This is just fact. There's no sense in telling people it ought to be otherwise . . . What we're doing with words (just like what so-called artists are doing with their hip avant-garde painting these days) is truthfully thought of as a *packaging* of art. The forms of the community, of the dark, are *business*. We're making a commodity out of Dark.

So community, from my point of view, would be like sex for gay men at a time of AIDS—you have to keep producing images of it, representations. You keep it alive this way until the reality that's supposed to be up ahead of us, still in the future, can manage to be more than—an idea? It's like sympathetic magic. You say the words and do the dance. You—click your heels together and repeat with eyes closed thinking on lovely inner truths—There's no place like Home, there's no place like. . .

And Dorothy's ruby slippers? Are they every real or are they—studio properties? (Gasp.) Say the "C word": is it "commodity" or "community"—and does one *equal* the other?

I don't know. Is *equal* too strong a word: should I say *equal for now*? What I *do* know though is about *Mirage* wanting (locally? or on the writing scene generally?) to try to be *really different* this way! In spite of a common interest in genres of sex, porn, horror, entertainment, etc. *Mirage*-published or *Mirage*-oriented writers, to any extent I can see (and I'd mean Killian and Bellamy, Bob Glück or me or whoever, a lot of different names coming to mind somewhat vaguely), don't have a quote unquote program across the boards. But I think it's fair to say though that we do make a business of turning business into pleasure. Dodie Bellamy's rewritings of *Dracula* in her Mina letters (as her talk at Bob Glück's recent Intersection residency shows) aren't Dracula, much less *Dracula*. And few will be tempted to confuse the—I hope wonderful—aestheticizations of porn, condensed, stylized and subverted as they are, in Cooper or Glück (or I guess you could say "me," though "less" of mine is out there) with say a *viewing booth*, as I think they're politely called, in the Tenderloin.

I will only be happy when it becomes *completely* popular to recognize writing as a giant PTL Club—because (*only?*) then will it be possible for anybody to start to think the next step, which obviously is all-important . . . (Oh Lord of Dark, if there's a once and future Lord to be, in my heart of hearts I have this inner intuition that it's *you* and not a Maitreya Buddha who we're gonna see arriving with your tacky thunderbolts and lightning . . . but by *then* will they be as "tacky" as they can't help but seem to us now?).

As a closing thought for this review I want to refer to the Dennis Cooper piece by Dodie Bellamy (aka *Mrs.* Kevin Killian . . . as I think she'd want me to say in a tip of the hat to the heroine's entrance and breathy first words into the mike at the end of *A Star Is Born*: "Hello everybody . . . This is Mrs. Norman Maine. . .") in one of the *Mirage*s of last year, where, first, she has a brilliant/funny/important critical discussion of that writer's work and then, contextualizing this text, adds this coda—"After his reading at New Langton Arts I walk with Cooper to his rented car. We formally discuss Writing for half a block when I say, 'I hear your next book is about shitting in people's mouths.' I know this isn't polite, but like in sex with Mark I want to make his professional surface messy. And it works. Dennis is momentarily disconcerted, keeps glancing at the people behind us, stammers, 'That's just part of it.'" Then she (as comment? query?) adds— "This is Life not art"—in her own voice, allowing the antecedent of that *this* to freefloat ("the events she's just recounted," or, "the recounting of the events that constitutes her essay on Dennis?"). Does the Community contextualize the Commodity in that way, with the ambiguity of a "C word"? A big C.

Will Community, if we keep praying for it (preying on it?) redescend on Commodity like a Holy Ghost on the abstract heads of Apostles at Pentecost? I can't see the future now, only—*Mirage* . . . illusion . . . commodities like yours truly and the only life he knows . . .

** Compare V.I. Lenin's famous saying "Literature must become party literature." I agree! Also with Leslie Gore when she tells us—"It's my party and I'll cry if I want to (you would cry too if it happened to you)." (!!)

"Mirage—Or Where's the Party" is a review of the San Francisco-based literary periodical, *Mirage*, edited by Kevin Killian and Dodie Bellamy. This essay first appeared in *Jimmy and Lucy's House of K* no. 8, edited by Benjamin Friedlander and Andrew Schelling, (January 1988).

FOR JACK SPICER—AND A TRUTH ELEMENT

Against the formalism in Jack Spicer, I think, is his meanness, his nastiness. That quality releases the texts from over-universalism. Or if the universalism is there it heads back afterwards to its particular home through spite. Spicer complains against the pretentiousness of others, including those who unfairly dismiss his poet colleagues—

> Tired wisdoms as the game-hunters develop
> Shooting Zeus, Alpha Centauri, wolf with the same toy gun.
> It is deadly hard to worship god, star and totem

(Zeus = Duncan and so on) though the defense easily turns inside out and becomes an attack, and he joins the enemies of his friends. Nothing here militates against the fact that Jack Spicer was greatly loved. In fact the opposite is probably true. Verbal dexterity is more and more considered a real advantage in society, and an unpleasant opposition to your friends' weaknesses may even increase their respect (if your luck manages to hold, that is).

I'd like to relate this often present irritability of tone in Spicer's writing to the opposition real/fake as a scaffolding around which, on which, much of the work is hung. That diction is obviously homologous to the Quest themes of the content—there's gay sex, Orpheus descending and so on that work this out. The real and fake only makes sense in terms of some always-seeming-to-be-impending disaster. You better be careful, is Spicer's advice—you'll miss the point if you don't. Which is fatal by definition. But this wisdom gets to be a very vexed question since foolishness, the opposite, just means you're too dumb to know you will be taken in (anyway)—

> All your heros are so polite
> They would make a cat scream

—as Gwenivere says of, to Lancelot.

These aren't abstract issues. They're intended to say something about social structures, a rotten society. When Spicer in a letter to Lew

Ellingham accuses Stan Persky of breaking faith about the name of a magazine, the sarcasm just spills over. Poetry isn't separate from how to act. Or rather it's pretty disgusting when it is. "Poetry is becoming like his father's used car business, or whatever it is, more every day"—says Spicer contemptuously. If you allow commercial values in your life, this probably means you weren't a poet in the first place. Anger about a rotten society doesn't have to be idealistic.

The dynamics of quarrelling seems to have the curious ability to get you on the right track. This means a relation to cruelty and negation. In dictated poetry (that brand of poetry Spicer called his own) no one—especially those senders or ghosts, as he called them, go-betweens between you and a larger scheme of things—believes in charity, to yourself or anyone. These muses are ghosts or, still more grimly—

> Determined funsters who have eaten half their skull away. These oldnesses are not human.

A quarrel is simply a useful railway ticket to these funsters for Spicer. You don't pick quarrels, but since they are occasions of a contact with ghosts, you don't avoid them. So, since Ferlinghetti's being for Spicer a bad poet and a business man is obviously an affront, he'll be revealed as only a nursery rhyme—or "nonsense syllable" as he's called in the "Ferlinghetti" poem in *Heads of the Town up to the Aether*. Morals aren't an issue here—unless it's the question of how a poet should live. The grudge gets nursed along until poetry results. Writing gets redefined.

Childish? Probably—but to call it that doesn't get you very far as an objection. The childish part comes from the fact that everyone knows that moral purity of this kind prepares a person (Spicer or anyone) for death—and in Spicer's case it did just that. "That is how we dead men write to each other," he said in *After Lorca*. But it's conceivable that being mature may make you unhappy—since that's the status quo. The disposition to be political may begin, and the seeds of it may be a childishness that wants to be *against*. So, Ferlinghetti owns a bookstore and Spicer—as an arbitrary act, as a preference almost—holds Ferlinghetti responsible. Speaking for poetry, he finds it ludicrous.

These potentially political values seem to come from a strong need for the real on Spicer's part—

> ... there was a beach, not a breach in the universe but an actual fucking beach

—marking, for all the ghost machinery, a love for what's here. In my mind I see something like an awkward but canny labor militant getting up in his union hall to bluntly set some record straight. The drive toward the American language's ordinariness will probably by itself, without anyone's help, show up the current idea of turning Jack Spicer into another French metaphysician. It's a *relation* to ordinariness though—and it's wise not to claim too much more than that. It's not distant from Jack Kerouac—two grown men using popular symbols, at the level of Catholicism or Oz, for quite sophisticated work.

The 60s showed us how out-of-sync the decade before was—but are we better now? A thought like this suggests a value of Spicer's writing. Example: imagine a middle class kid somewhere considering the idea of otherness (other than him naturally) in the degraded form of a studio mock-up. The spaceship music you hear is the bringing in of the Real, its signature. Now the hospital clutter is disassembled and put back in trucks, and even the intensive care unit's light are dim now. E.T. shyly opens one eye. E.T., you jerk, you weren't dead at all—were you! E.T., phone home, E.T., phone home—(he's muttering like a machine ready to go berserk). Where before they were wilted and peaked-looking, the flowers in the flower-pot have started to bloom again. Isn't this to say—don't worry, with the dead able to come to life again, won't everything be OK in the 80s after all? Capitalist society has embodied critiques of itself before. What's new here are religious overtones—the lost collectivity.

How awkward or plastic was the religious junk in Spicer's work in his own time—I mean Oz, Billy the Kid, the Grail, white rabbits and ghosts, the rest? Spicer's choice of this subject matter was pretty much on target, I think. I can't imagine it wasn't intended to seem tacky. Certainly, he must have known, if there was going to be a collective activity, a transpersonal kind, it would only take place in what was at hand. The specifically junk qualities in Spicer's writing relate very much to whatever religion it is that is at hand—is in this sense postmodern. The different myths are picked up and put down with an insouciance that might have met George Lucas's or Steven Spielberg's. They're only commodities among commodities! This might otherwise take Spicer toward *The Sound of Music* as it does Spielberg, except that the defining quality in Spicer's religion is aggressiveness—

> Fool—
> Killer lurks between the branches of every tree.

To say it again—Jack Spicer wasn't a very nice person. It would certainly be unfair to say that his characteristic emotion was contempt—an emotion that deals in repressing other emotions. But just as obviously any emotion was a danger for him—

> Emotion
> Being communicated
> Stops
> Even when the game isn't over—

so he needs to legislate. He makes fun of Verlaine and identifies with Rimbaud—

> Dare he
> Write poetry
> Who has not taste of acid on his tongue
> Who carrys his dreams on his back like a pack?

but sadly (no joy in this validation) since—

> The slaves of poetry are slaves in deed

as he tells him in the poem by the same name. Poetry is produced by the repression of (erotically-oriented) emotion. The poem should be the place where emotions cancel themselves—though you have to have them in the first place to get the poem going.

This is oversimplified though. The newness of Spicer's writing lies in its tendency to prefer schizophrenia to a received ascepticism (or Platonic writing), and the aggressiveness is stressed proportionately. It's not accounted for by the tradition of Black Mountain, for instance, or Creeley stripping away excess in the interests of (male) law. Spicer's sentences waste not, want not, give no quarter—but with the futile intention of thwarting the desire they produce. A response—solicited—is then made impossible. Is the current commodity nature of writing recognized here, its necessity? An impulse to go beyond this is factored in, in spite of everything (the aggression), gets back to the relation with an audience—

> I left in a huff with your hand
> Naked

—as he says. This poetry is against you (a non-mystical thought expressed mystically) because it's first of all for you. It's a recognition of the deformations of the world as it is now, a social inability to meet human needs (since they remain alienated).

Does a gay aspect of Spicer's eros fit in then? I think so. It's been part of our gay lives to extend libidinal drives, or try to anyway, to a beyond-the-personal. And—to be frank—that's the meaning of a back room. This has been part and parcel of our construction as gay men. And our narrating structure isn't so different from other communities in specifying this. In a core phase as a Sanctified (not Baptist or A.M.E.) Church, for instance, the black community has a narrative structure with similar aims—in "shouting," or being possessed by African gods given Christian names. This too gets a person beyond his/her/itself. The gay, like other pockets of community, at least partly, resists, reacts against the slow commodity death known as U.S. society.

And is feared sometimes. Like the prebourgeois or religious there's something frightening about it. Seeing the nonrational aspect of it—a crisscrossing of ego-lines, the shifter side of this community, its ability to short-circuit itself—the commodity world senses the presence of an

Underside to things—about to react and oppose it. Undoubtedly Spicer exploited these fears—and the thought of readers' alarm must have been a provocation difficult to pass up. (Remember from *Heads of the Town up to the Aether*, "He wanted an English professor—someone he could feel superior to, as a ghost"?). Childish? Yes, but then, is it less childish to forget about the darker, realer side of things?

> Have guts until the guts
> Come through the margins
> Clear and pure
> Like love is

—Spicer said in an "Admonition" to himself. He wanted—among other things, I think—his sexuality to be a rebuke, an opposition.

My admiration for the politics and courage of this attitude is unstinting. Opposition to commodities should be everybody's stance, though hopefully this won't be idealistic, but simply a practical matter. If you care enough about your own desire, you'll want to fight for it, won't you? But Spicer's desire to be against idealism is almost in itself a tendency toward it—

> This is a poem to prevent idealism—i.e. the study of images. It did not succeed.

Somewhere along the line Spicer loses bite. There's less enthusiasm in being dishy than there once was. Previous and focused energy that went into basically silly projects (seduction of straight love objects like Jim Alexander and Graham Macintosh) sometimes seems more genteel. The abstract pessimism of announcements like this in *Heads*—

> Now the things that are for Jim are coming to an end, I see nothing beyond it.

—only predicts trumpets, Wagnerian style. What follows is *The Textbook of Poetry*, romantic, severe, pedagogic—also, I think, aware at this point that we're more rapidly moving away from life—

And the human witness of this passion is rightly stunned by the incongruity of it. Lifting a human being into a metaphor.

The side of Spicer that begins to talk about the "Logos" (even when it's "low-ghost"), "God" and the "Word" is the side I have doubts about. I don't like my philosophy straight. Better to discuss such matters in terms of ball games or bitch fights (two fields where, thank goodness, Spicer excelled). Better in fact just not to see the intensely Christian feeling of the last book (*Book of Magazine Verse*) than to face some of the contradictions in Spicer. Or is it?

So is this where I should bring up the matter of Spicer's "isms"? They haven't been talked about very much publicly, but maybe they should be. For a person (Spicer, I mean) with so much common sense (usually) it's hard to understand how he could become anti-semitic, as he did at the beginning of Billy the Kid for instance—

> a poem with no hard corners, no houses to get lost in, no
> underwebbing of customary magic, no New York Jew salesmen
> of amethyst pajamas

—where nostalgia for frontier life went uncritically accepted. Had Spicer (temporarily) forgotten his own demand for criticism-poetry? "Stepping up to poetry/Demands/Hands," he said earlier. Or again when he said that

> People who don't like the smell of faggot vomit
> Will never understand why men don't like women

he was wronger in being sexist, homophobic even, than righter in reminding prejudiced straight readers of their nonstraight potential. These political faults can only be dismissed as nontextual to the extent that life and language/literature are separate. Which doesn't seem to be Spicer's approach anyway—separating them. Good taste wasn't this poet's strong point, thank goodness.

In a strange way I think these deficiencies can be accounted for by an *incomplete* transgressiveness—one that got stopped by conventions that theoretically at least it was Spicer's intention to thwart. He wanted his transgressiveness not to be tactical, but on principle. Hence, "In Robin's poetry," as he explains in a letter to Duncan, "Xt is the King and in mine the King is 'the King of the world,'" adding frankly, "evil."

And evil of course is also the *place* of evil—hell. (I think Spicer's a lot happier in his place of hell, the Cocteau-influenced *Homage to Creeley*, than in his abstracter Paradiso, *A Textbook of Poetry*). This is a place where a plurality of transgressions(s) permits boundary-crossing—

> Away we go with no moon at all
> Actually we are going to hell.
> We pin our puns to our backs and cross in a car
> The intersections where lovers are

—and it is also the place of language. The ontological qualities of language make it that—though naturally hell is a lot of other things too. It's where the Jews and homosexuals are—since by definition they've broken society's codes, "sinned against the light." And it's where sex is, sex that promises to be transgressive, that is. So all in all hell's the name of a certain negativity. Hell's an idea, but it's also *where* that idea takes place. (It has materiality.) A state and a place, a double-dealing—

> Being a [poet] a disyllable in a world of monosyllables

Puns are important—they reflect this. Another name is rhyme—"all," "hell." When you get there (rhyme, hell), you understand language's dissimulation (magic-like)—

> Or stop
> Morphemes in section

—of being-what-it-isn't. So for Spicer all of language—not just parts (like the pronoun "I"—becomes a "shifter" on this place. Hell understands (in hell you understand) that the inability to "shift" (to be flexible enough back and forth, the failure to understand that this is what *actually happens*) is historically the equivalent of a self-destruct order society gives itself—

> Troy was a baby when Greek sentence structure emerged. This
> was the real Trojan Horse.
> The order changes. The Trojans
> Having no idea of true or false syntax and having no recorded
> language
> Never knew what hit them.

Is there hope for the future then? A place where society and the world can be different? If there is, it might be like this description (Zen-like) of the snow in "Dillinger" (in *Heads of the Town*)—

> There is nothing left of it. Not even the water its crystals puddle
> into. These persons know reality for what they are

—and the relations of person and nonperson, society and the world, wave and matter, are—punningly—no longer occluded.

I don't think that Spicer's writing—in spite of its difficulty and playfulness and assumption that language=the world—is a formalism. After the pause of *A Textbook of Poetry*, the poems begin addressing real people again (much of *The Holy Grail*, the pivotal *Language*), though sometimes this takes place in cyphered form, as in the lines quoted at the beginning of this essay. Context is made more important again—friends in North Beach, gayness, poetry quarrels, baseball, jazz, and so on. Regular stuff from someone's life from the late 50s and early 60s, who lived that time and seemed to love it and still opposed it, to judge by his work. I'd like the etherealness and concreteness of Spicer to relate to each other a little better than they seem to be doing right now. More spite, for one thing.

"For Jack Spicer—and a Truth Element" first appeared in *Social Text*, no. 7 (Spring-Summer, 1983).

SPICER'S WRITING IN CONTEXT

For me Spicer's paranoia is an ability to project. That fact renews Freud's claim that religion and paranoia are flip sides of each other—it gives a value of objectivity to the paranoia we suffer: Words, worlds, appear in Spicer to have reciprocal relations. The problem and mystery are the same. "Nothing" generates this dynamic and yet it is there.

The power of belief is proposed as a negotiating factor. The risk that motivates the dynamic between words and worlds also weighs down and gives significance where there wasn't any before. As signifiers become more and more detached from their signifieds, the "nothing" turns into something. There is a public side. "Get those words out of your mouth and into your heart. If there isn't a God don't believe in Him." And: "God becoming human, became a subject of anthropologists, /history." In this quote God is the way He thinks He speaks when the public side shapes itself. The public side keeps changing shape. All its ability to go from something to nothing and back again can only be our own ability to two-time, which doesn't end. It regulates itself—

> [...] "Credo
> Quia absurdum," creates wars and pointless loves and was even
> in Tertullian's time a heresy. I see him like a tortoise creeping
> through a vast desert of unbelief.

The personal arises as a response to this. If my power puts on a face what does it look like? This is the other side of the cycle of reciprocities. Belief cancels out unbelief. The mystery is, it's still my face I see and the fact that it's still there, though a projection. Spicer thinks everything takes place to show how impossible the face is—or any connection. Nothingness sounds and it's there inexplicably, as beloved other—

> Nothingness is alive in the eyes of the beloved. He wears the
> clothes wherein he walks naked. He is fame.
> Sounded ahead by the trumpets of unreason. Barely accounted
> for by the senses. He is what he is because he is never where he is.

I cannot proclaim him for he is not mine. Eros, Amor, feely love, his body is more abstract than all the messages my body sends my brain of him.

To explain somehow that the beloved face I see in the void can't stop being void. They are reciprocal functions.

To put it another way, how explain a masochist community?

This community would inhabit the dividing line between where the beginning is (where we're conceived) and where an action takes place (where we're deceived). Spicer imagines this community as a benevolent projection that takes alienated form as otherness. In spite of all the aggression the community he describes is capable of, there's a real unwillingness to posit a final hostility of intentions that would cancel the otherness—the shape of the face. This is like Frankenstein. I am the bride of Christ. "If He wanted to," Spicer notes hopefully, "He could make a machine a Christ, enter it in its second person which is You." An ironized redemptive vision. If there are ghosts out there writing us, do they want us? need us? And what if there's a small part of me that believes in its/their good intentions merely from the fact that, for whatever unexplained reasons, they need us as much as vice versa. Such a community provides guide-lines for the ability we have to perceive in the first place—when we subscribe to it, we *undergo* narration. Is to make a community at all to be masochistic? Yes and no. To *be* made instead of to make.

This reminds me of the white sheets that Spicer used to dress out his fears in childhood "afraid to go to sleep because I would dream about ghosts—chasing me and singing in weird voices." Which he goes on to claim generates writing. "But I discovered that fear of the supernatural could be used in poetry and magic (if these things are different) and could give me a kind of contact with things outside of myself" (letter to Graham MacKintosh). Does narration—writing—take its cue from this projected hostility?

Anecdote: The long-standing friendship between my friend Bob and a neighbor, Mack, erupts, becomes a shambles. Bob recounts the homophobia of Mack's revenge, and my own friendship with Bob is increased, strengthened proportionately. Our common status as gay men gives us a mutual impersonal stake—doesn't it? If the community begins as shared differences, it *needs* fear. What if like Spicer you could conceive of a fear that founded *every* community? Fear naming the affections we have to the extent we have them in the first place?

If the face is the other, it's the face of the enemy, since it's human. But of the Enemy—since inhuman. For Spicer the capital cancels the humanness, thankfully. Mack's homophobia and Spicer's several "isms" (anti-Semitism for one) outline the fact of the otherness of the human project itself, an illusoriness that refuses to recognize itself as such. To write is to act as inhuman, Spicer thinks (Bataille described this as *perte* or loss, as *dépense* or expenditure). The ghosts of community, or community of ghosts. If only we could become ghosts, he thinks. . . .

Spicer takes Olson's "polis" and deepens it, gives it a future. Olson never considered the future of ruin—what Spicer calls "slums." Spicer realized that the key to this idea of city lies in its after-image. The future of any city, collectivity, the thought, being its ghosts.

So here's what I think of as a "prediction" in Spicer, the sentence at the heart of *A Textbook of Poetry*: "Every city that is formed collects its slums and the ghost of it." The follow-up (logical) on this is in Vancouver Lecture #1—"you will notice that the ghosts also inhabit the cities and the cities develop ghosts after they develop slums." The slums is the negativity is our future—that's clear for him.

A future—on condition of your being able to think of it as *no*, as *apparently*, an *as if*. "Poetry comes long after the city is collected," he adds and continues, "It recognizes them [the ghosts he means] as a metaphor. An unavoidable metaphor. Almost the opposite." It's as if you could *avoid* this emptiness.

Cooperating with what denies you making you a victim. And the meaning of masochism expands. Community lays down the Law which the other (Other) needs and wants to be constantly undoing. And this is nothing a bottom-y masochistic wouldn't be prepared to topple if she, he or it could. A community of ghost tops, toppling. To be named is already to be victimized. Needed.

In politics this certainly would be the opposite of Lenin's casebook refusal to go out at night to the Bolshoi, for fear it'd make him weak. But this politics excludes us—writers, artists, generally. Spicer's victimology allies him in a much closer way to the embrace of a fate that's against you, whoever you are. Your grave lies open before you. To write, fall into it— since falling and rising coincide. One of you going one way, while the other goes the other. Just like the doomed soldiers of the volunteer International Brigades, in Spicer's example, who fought for the left Spanish Republic. What are the uses to make of defeat?

> Then the thought of Merlin became more than imprisoned Merlin
> A jail-castle
> Was built on these grounds.
> Sacco and Vanzetti and Lion-Hearted Richard and Dillinger
> who somehow almost lost the Grail. Political prisoners.
> Political prisoners. Willing to rise from their graves.

Anarchism in writing pairs off with anarchism in politics. It's not true you win, but you write. Is this a loss? For whom?

And inevitably for Spicer this thought becomes eroticism. A vertigo of falling, a vertigo of rising in this dialectic. A stiffening of a President he uses for this purpose

> "I call it death-in-life and life-in-death." Shot
> In the back by an arrow, President Kennedy seemed to stiffen for
> a moment before he assumed his place in history. Eros
> Do that

punning on the arrows.

Invaders and their victims. In the s/m system of Hegel, Death is known as Absolute Master. Since I'm narrated by Invaders in a similar system of Spicer's proposing, how not to take my place there as masochist? On the individual, on a collective level—is to be narrated to be masochist?

I'm narrated by ghouls Spicer thinks in their grisly reality "seeking experience for specific instances." To combat an abstract level of existence, they need you—the body. "Drawing upon the pulp of the brain and the legs and the arms and the motion of the poet, making him see things that can be conveyed through their words."

Spoken as a recognition and acknowledgment of the illusion we, not they, are. This is a game for ghosts, he tells you frankly. "I mean that the reader of this novel is a ghost," not writer. To multiply themselves so they can continue to exist as the nothing they are, he says, "They try to give us circuits to see them, to hear them." To be narrated. What we most want can be traced perfectly here in what we most fear, most hate—to become somebody else. So aren't I as much a sadist in this game of writing? We vampirize the realities that we don't want to believe support us in the first place. To let us identify with these victimizing presences, Spicer makes us author of this text saying "You write poetry / For dead persons." He's who we are and vice versa. The future-to-be-believed-in isn't (believed in).

Everyone's broken. The circle of this dynamic's assured when the assurance of the community is broken. "Hold to the future," he urged patiently adding by way of explanation that "the future of your words matters [because] That future is continually in the past." Did ghosts show him this? Did his Muses or dead teach him that every community wants the assurance of its failure? Suspicion and failure and being against itself he thought was as important as the opposite of those for a community. This *goop* he called his. "An international criminal organization that talks to each other, makes passes at each other, sings to each other, clings to each other, is as absolutely alien to each other as a stone in Australia." Through words George, Fran, Lew, Jim or any other set of names becomes the objectness, that is, deadness of the text you have. A context. Spicer's or anybody's, any community's.

In contrast to Olson's city of Gloucester which is fullness, there's a divorce between us and our meaning, since as he said "A band of faggots (fasces) cannot be built into a log-cabin in which all Western Civilization can cower." We become small enough to disappear. Physical locales—Aquatic Park, whatever—are worshipped wisely as what he called "Distances / Impossible to be measured or walked over." The power of language to disrupt (surrealism) is always at odds with another heresy—Olson's sureness. Each mirrors the other.

(Thanks to Bob Glück for help making this.)

"Spicer's Writing in Context" first appeared in *Ironwood 28,* vol. 14 no. 2 (Fall 1986).

ROBIN BLASER'S NEW *SYNTAX* :
POINTING UP AHEAD, BEHIND, WHEREVER

The unsuspected problems life seems to have! If: writers are terrible wreckers of life and set on destroying or undercutting—then: writers this applies to have some explaining to do. My problem is to maintain writerly onesidedness (sadism) toward you and also keep up, intensify, the moving/elevated/democratic hopes and aspirations I have, just like Walt in olden days when he wanted to be your own true sweet brother, sister too, whispering softly in your ear as the green grass grows around. Should this wish to be sacred run into conflict with my also authentic desire to be frank and sincere with you? If it does, what then?

That's the projection I make of Robin Blaser (in company of Robert Duncan and Jack Spicer and the three of them making the Berkeley Renaissance as they called it) putting the legitimacy of writing into question. I'm thinking of the period of the late 40s thru early 60s. But isn't the parallel with the present—assuming rightly I hope that there are writers who want their writing to actually accomplish something, do something in this society—only too acutely evident? What's clear is you'll flop if you don't have the right language. And as inadequate as it hopelessly is, isn't that the one that people actually speak? This gets you to a problem: what happens if an ambition to inhabit a world of sacredness, queerness in all its senses, literary modernity too, (an ambition you might equally have yourself) were to run smack into the obstacle of a society, a community, that persist in negating each hope you come up with to express that community more satisfyingly? Can a language, anyone's, express what doesn't exist except maybe somewhere else?

In the 50s it's natural to suppose that the intention to express the inexpressible would involve pain. Everyone's walking around so numb but worse yet there're signs you yourself may be one of these very undead whose lives you are protesting. Does this resemble what happens when blood rushes into the arm I've scrunched too long? These prickly feelings—or pain—only mean I'm getting myself back again. What's expressed by the inexpressible isn't not there; it's there all along; only hidden in some way so people in general, that is my community (I'm one of them), don't know it. How to define that knowledge? How can I—the Berkeley Renaissance writers could have thought—say I'm part of you, the same as you, and still claim a Knowing that the zombie doesn't have? If I call you (myself) names, don't you (I myself) rightly resent this? Two sides. Affirming both is hard.

How to make connections? A Solomon's judgment! The experience of the Berkeley writers shows this. Spicer's wonderful snarl "The Big Lie of the Personal" meant that at least at some point in his life he didn't believe that the connection could be made. Blaser's more modest and hopeful and pragmatic. In the NO APOLOGIES 1 interview with Lew Ellingham he's at pains to make you realize his leading ideas (the OUTSIDE/INSIDE notion for instance) flowed from context, and real-life events (the soirees at Duncan's on Telegraph Avenue, tiffs over the ADAM'S WAY production) fixed ideas as well: a reciprocity. And Duncan? Duncan embraces a thought to deny it—affirm its opposite. His proposal (SOUP 1 talking with Aaron Shurin, Steve Abbott) that

> there's only one primal eros for all kinds of love throughout
> the universe and back of that is a terror we harmonize

comes hard on the heels of an opposing thesis, that only the gay content of his poetry explains it: the universal turns out to be gay. And how naked these contradictions become with Spicer! How to scan for instance the dour impersonal declaration he gives to Donald M. Allen's NEW AMERICAN POERTY that he "doesn't want his life written down," as he proclaims in a bio note there, with the evident fact his poetry systematically rhymes this sense of an impersonal, a Higher or Doctrinal content of it, with the personal, the many loves, hates, spites, friendships that make the writing he's left behind for us as autobiographical and intense as O'Hara's. Here's Spicer's comment to a friend he loved about letters he's sent him (*Sulfur* 10): "I measure their success by how well I can succeed in being deeply personal and deeply public at the same time. Like my poems." In IMAGE-NATIONS Blaser puns similarly, he uses allegory as a bridge. Then there's the loving way he uses his grandmother's personal name, Sophia— its Greek meaning, Wisdom, always being implied. There is a public and there is a private, isn't there? One side says this world: the other says the next. One side of things is for language. The other is against it, for an animal side. To link, to make communication between them.

The Underside's most vexing, an alienation. The hermeticism, obscurity and magical themes in Duncan's ADAM'S WAY, A PLAY UPON THEOSOPHICAL THEMES have been the great example of this. Blaser's 5th Image-Nation describes it, what happened when the participants seemed to take their parts as seriously as they did playfully when the drama was produced at the Tape Music Center. Spicer was across town apparently, stirring up trouble, judging a commercial presentation of any kind would have equaled sellout, wouldn't it? At Spicer's instigation George Stanley and Stan Persky picketed Duncan's production and Blaser describes the scene this way.

signs went up
the police came

'Fuck chi chi
I asked the author not to press charges
Fuck, I said, is a young word
I had stepped out of my part
in the play as an Atlantean lizard—
face swathed in a sequin bodice—
her perfumed sweat clinging
to the words I spoke through
the glittering cloth—trousers
of kitchen-foil scales

("Image-Nation 5")

In the theatricality of all parties to the dispute, in the mediating role Blaser presents himself in, in outsiders' sense of a fight with stakes not clear, purposefully obscured, is there an image of the Gnosticism Blaser, Duncan and Spicer each claimed as metaphor of importance? A map to negotiate perils maybe, and a terra incognita to be learned about.

How suffocatingly Light crowded you! In the catholic high school I attended in the 50s, I remember not breathing from it. The vertigo of the rational and all that's positive: the blinding excess toward the Light.

Is there a possibility then of groping toward Dark? The writing project of this Berkeley group wanted to speak to this, and isn't it today at least as pressing an issue (some say even—more urgent)? But if Duncan holds back, it must be he has his reasons: which we'll see in a moment! The boast of his—"I too loved the scene of dark magic"—also has a dollop of mistrust! What if I'm caught believing in illusions, rabbits out of the hat? Spicer makes the contrast at the opposite end. In an appendix of the Jack Spicer COLLECTED BOOKS he says the ruler of his poetry is "the king of this world—evil." It's hard to see how a person could be more absolute and equally difficult to understand how the position he takes could be more perverse too: if purely so. Where's Blaser? He's the junior member of the Berkeley Renaissance firm, so still minding his p's and q's: he hasn't yet come fully to be a writer in the early part of this time, so he's waiting. But thinking. How can writing, which is language, be against itself? Later in his 9th Image-Nation in IMAGE-NATIONS he'll say that

> there are shining masters
> when I tell you what they
> look like   some of it is
> nearly false

going to add "their blue hair": as example. It's the small bit of falseness that has to be factored in somehow. In Kafka the leopard comes into the temple, knocking over the sacred vessels so many times finally that's made part of the ceremony too. What can evil, negativity have to do with the community?

Start with Duncan since he's the most pro-community. Dissenters have their rights because Duncan's one himself. But it's also true you have to maintain a measure of respect—a real one—for the social whole. That's the message that can be found in a Duncan's famous gay essay, "The Homosexual in Society." He wants you to be aware he's writing as a gay and pro-gay at that: he's the first American writer we know of to do this. His protestations show the harm social oppression had done to us as gays. His second point is the overall rights of the larger group. The community as a whole can't be forgotten either. Smaller groups should make reference to this larger group, Duncan thinks. There's a particular "small-group" way of acting—he calls it cult behavior—that draws Duncan's special ire for this reason. Anyone, he notes in passing, can be guilty of it; he names some possibilities—gays, blacks and Jews too, whoever. But what about the small group of oppositional modernist writers? you might feel like asking Duncan. Can modernists be as guilty as anyone of going against the rights of this Community as a whole? Draw your own conclusions. Duncan probably had enough on his hands trying to bring up the subject of gays without opening another can of worms—the question of how independent of the community this other group he belonged to, the modernists, could afford to be. How far can you go in declaring yourself as someone who's oppositional or against? One indication: Duncan says he's against "minority associations and identifications" and when he adds they're

> an evil wherever they supersede allegiance to and share in the
>> creation of
> a human community good—the recognition of fellow-manhood

it's as if he's asking, well how far can you go along this Gnostic path of knowing evil? In "Tribal Memories" (BENDING THE BOW) Duncan writes

> For this is the company of the living
> and the poet's voice speaks from no
>> crevice in the ground between
>>> mid-earth and underworld
> breathing fumes of what is deadly to know,
>>> news larvae in tombs
>> and twists of time do feed upon,

> but from the hearth stone, the lamp light,
>> the heart of the matter where the

>>>> house is held

so that ultimately, if pressed to it, he'd have to say he chooses Light, wouldn't he? The fire, yes, that Light.

Spicer's direction toward the Dark, minatory. If writing infringes on the community, too bad for the community. The community's an ideal for him and lies up ahead in the future. For that reason writing, though a rebirth, is also "your funeral." Spicer believed in modernist poetry as what he called Dictation. Writing puts you in touch with the Other World so that a split is produced and now there are two yous. The first you that's associated with the material, physical, social side of reality disappears and another comes to appear on its debris. Spicer describes the process in his first dictated book AFTER LORCA.

> When someone intrudes into the poet's life (and any sudden personal contact, whether in the bed or in the heart, is an intrusion) he loses his balance for a moment, slips into being who he is, uses poetry as one would use money or sympathy. The person who writes the poetry emerges, tentatively, like a hermit crab from a conch shell. The poet, for that instant, ceases to be a dead man.

It's perverse and paradoxical. Only the dead live. Only the live are dead. The poet's existence resembles that of the vampire. It's at someone else's expense, namely that of the first you who's now a dead man. Spicer's complaint in THE HOLY GRAIL that poetry's "the cup the dead drink from" may be read as more properly as boast. Maybe the death you have in life is better, because less human, when the community's so degraded and superficial. Death as the destroying angel. So at the end of THE HEADS OF THE TOWN UP TO THE AETHER when there remain only

> trumpets proclaiming that they had been there and been alive.
> The silver voices of them

there's an incredible feeling of relief. You've entered the field of the purely Dark and Sacred and found it literally Nothing—a Nothingness. Was it worth it to hold for the Dark against the Community? Obviously there are arguments to be made on each side. But is the dilemma—the opposition—inevitable? What if you didn't have to choose between them?

That's Blaser's initial feeling, I think—the basic proposition of his writing. For Spicer, when you write you make something out of nothing. Language shapes the world out of what it isn't. Blaser's focus is on perception, and it makes him tend toward sensuality or the life of the senses. With Duncan human society has priority; Blaser's version of community is more private by contrast. For Blaser the body itself is community. Knowledge is made equal to perception is made equal to seeing.

Images in this poetic cult are really thresholds or borders. They're, as they say, liminary. In secular, everyday seeing, things remain just what they are and only that. In sacredness they are perceived as more. They are themselves and also what they are not. Writing lights up the borders of things. The line between outside and inside is not rigid any more

> there is a spilled glass of water, an ocean
> spreading on the table
>
> under the shine on the water, the pieces
>   ("Atlantis," THE MOTH POEM)

and the edges glow, a continuity across what formerly was thought of as separation. Even a volcano from yesterday could do this.

> The ash came from Mt. St. Helena
> They all fell
> as by the same wind
> Rooted in springs
> the stone-filled trunks
> stretch out
>   ("Translation," THE HOLY FOREST)

And the world's continuity extends across time.

> . . . an oak grows
> from the rock bark

Built on seeing, the senses open. The percipient body is the same as eternity. They supposed that.

The image is in motion, not static: a doubling. Your outlines must be very clear, must have edges—since if they don't, how would you find the pair of anything? The image is a doorway, a place where the thing or event and its cancelled and linked self pass each other going different directions.

> the white dog is blind
> intent upon its master's
> footsteps   walks into
> my black dog
>
> ("The Private I")

Or

> 'It's all right, mine's blind' he called.
>
> ("The Private I")

The image permits and negates the opposite behind it. In the early writing of Blaser sacredness is essentially the exchange of opposites. The visual's key—but not yet fully explained.

Blaser's middle period IMAGE-NATIONS expands this. The condition of doubleness is spelled out as linguistic and founding the possibility of human thought.

> The duplicity is especially the business of poetry because it is a
> primary aspect of thought and poetry is primary thought before
> it is vision, fiction or transcendence. [unverified]
>
> ("The Practice of Outside," Blaser's Afterword to
> THE COLLECTED BOOKS OF JACK SPICER).

He keys in on the ghostly afterimage of language.

> Through the arrangement of words (parataxis), there is a
> speech along side my speech, which allows a double-speech

[. . .] The operation of its duplicity is the poetic job [. . .] a co-existence

("Stadium of the Mirror")

Not that the movement's abstract. The two main aspects of it are that it goes back on or of itself and that it's linked with perception.

                                        the language
    reverses itself   it is that narration   (*gna
    gnosis   )   poetry is after   the author is
    after   the death of a poetry that is
    only a <u>cutting out</u>   a <u>rarefaction</u>

("Image-Nation 12")

So that narration is opposed to (the death of) poetry that's only abstract (the <u>cutting out</u>, the <u>rarefaction</u>). Blaser's SYNTAX and his still-to-appear RANDONNE, books of his most recent writing period, work this out as a poetic practice. In writing narration is a link between the world about us and telling of it.

    it's dawn and things move about quickly,
    a bird sound at the end of every sentence

("lake of souls," SYNTAX)

And this moves poetry toward religion.

    this indefinite spiritual condition   it is
    probably the secret of syntax itself

Words themselves move us toward religion.

So the lists in SYNTAX

    . . . Carnations, Indian pink, Marygold, Globe
    violet, Sensitive plant, Cockscomb, a flower like

Broom, Umbrella, Laurel

("The Truth is Laughter")

are seen as incentives. Seeing better puts you in touch with what's beyond all seeing: mystical. The narration is the narration of a series of images. Blaser returns his recent writing to the imagism of his earliest poetry. In CUPS there are the wonderful musical notation marks, physical notes fluttering on the page. In SYNTAX look for the scattered x-ings out or diagrams all over or the Radiant Finger poem with its literal pointing in every direction. In IMAGE-NATIONS there's the comment to the poem climbing up the margin: a scholiast commentator that reminds me of the mock or ghostly typeface at the bottom of certain editions of HEADS OF THE TOWN. Blaser sees corroboration of the self-evident in "using your eyes." Language is incorporated into the community in a physical way. "Language reverses itself" (the earlier quote from Image-Nation 12): it's a hieroglyph. When Blaser puts the *gnosis in parentheses in that quote you see with your own eyes: it's related to community. Perception founds and articulates that community.

Linking knowing and seeing tallies with human developmental account—Freud and Lacan for instance. We integrate ourselves outside us in an outside image, they say, because humans are born with a special nervous-system-weakness: we have to form our ego on that visual image out there. It's as if Blaser was thinking, how do I write out Rimbaud's I IS ANOTHER in a literal, visual way?

But—could serious poetry be made of "just images"? Blaser tries to come to terms with that problem in a poem called "Diary, April 11, 1981" in SYNTAX when he repeats an objection Charles Olson made.

    I'd trust you
  anywhere with image, but
  you've got no syntax

SYNTAX, uppercase, is an apologia to redefine syntax, lowercase. Olson's comment was first backhanded compliment, then a critique. The rebuttal is a book making nothing but images, insisting in its list structures, that the serial placement of images is syntax.

        the Wolf Fenrir is fettered by the chain
        Gleipnir made of six things: the noise
        of a cat's footstep; the beard of a woman;
        the roots of a rock; the sinews of a bear;
        the breath of a fish; the spittle of a bird

Process was of course the great idea preached at Black Mountain and Blaser
insists the movement for image to image is process. In Stadium of the
Mirror he says unless his poetry's read image by image

        there is no saving grace. They will be stopped by a
        diminished and interruptive present, a misreading of the
        one here that is flowing in every direction.

So the poem is a staging area for this movement. If poetry or writing is not
to be diminished, as he says, won't it have to be always beyond and outside
itself? It's worth noting that what results is also an erotic moment.

        the moth in the piano
        will play on
        frightened wings brush
        the wired interior
        of that machine

        I said 'master'

                                                        (MOTH POEM)

Naturally you don't have to be gay. But you have to be able to look up to
what's greater than you. Sex and religion encompass devotion.

    There's a sense of the postmodern at work. A writer's not required to be
original. For religious writing originality is almost by definition ineffective.
I go beyond my person to the extent I plug into qualities of group-life. Does
this recall Duncan's insistence that he's a derivative poet? Since Blaser's a
religious poet or writer of the scared, he doesn't have to MAKE IT NEW.
To air out the text common or obsolete language

the peregrine falcon, stately,
sits in the bare cherry tree

("Image-Nation 15")

isn't out of place, keeps out the modernist hysteria of the *new*.

Women's writing as it's recently come back to myth and religion (Kathleen Fraser, Beverly Dahlen, Judy Grahn raise these issues) has developed a similar *visual : knowing* connection. In the *Poetics Journal* special women's issue Leslie Scalapino wrote that it has

> The most abstruse hieroglyphs are the most simple memories, so seeing is in terms of surfaces. Certain sights or pictures through their lines are direct entrances to vision which occurs in over-mind consciousness. In *Thought and Vision*, H.D. says da Vinci for example "saw the faces of many of his youths and babies and young women definitely with his over-mind. The Madonna of the Rocks is not a picture. It is a window. We look through a window into the world of pure over-mind."

Perception putting you in touch with knowledge, Scalapino summarizes adding, "The over-mind is a lens, really two,"—and doesn't this doubleness recall what Blaser referred to as duplicity? A final question. Seen from a standpoint of eternity, are looking ahead, looking back, equally arbitrary impositions? I think of this segment of Blaser's talk with Ellingham mentioned earlier.

> Do you think language is behind you, or do you think of it as in front of you? Now, if you do think of it as behind you, this marvelously holds on to the entire tradition of the sacred, of the origin of language as actually being there. You see what I mean? Now, if you think of it, instead, as being in front of you, which I believe Spicer did, there was an incredible task, once again, to shape a world and it was, so to speak, adrift from what had been happening.

It's part of Blaser's wonder and charm as a writer that he supposes that both have to happen, at the same time.

"Robin Blaser's New *Syntax*: Pointing Up Ahead, Behind, Wherever" first appeared in *No Apologies: A Magazine of Gay Writing* no. 3 (Fall 1984). The Image-Nation poems quoted here appear in *Image-Nations 1-12 & The Stadium of the Mirror* (London: Ferry Press, 1974).

ROBERT DUNCAN AND THE GAY COMMUNITY:
A REFLECTION

I write about other people's phobias as images of something better. Right now I'm thinking of a passage in one of the Stan Brakhage articles in the old *Caterpillar,* where he says something like the following about gays—"I've proved they were wrong, he says, since I'm the person I've become. If they thought I'd never be a great film-maker just because I happened to get married, well, they should think again, the jerks!" But there's a secret admiration in Brakhage's contempt. What do conspiracies really tell you?

Brakhage, like many others in his generation, presupposed gays would somehow want to get together and make a *band,* a small or closed group, and that the result would assume common interests he might not share. Was it true about Duncan and the Berkeley Renaissance group? To me as a gay man the idea of gay writers getting together and forming a *band* of some kind is exciting, and I wonder if that idea might have consequences for the gay community today, engaged as we are in a period of reappraisal. I think of Duncan's own phobic vision of this ("The Conqueror's Song," *Caesar's Gate)*—

> Here women are nothing.
> The men lust at noon
> licking forms of men
> from the improvident clay

—as truer to that idea.

Among the major postwar writing groups, the Berkeley one is the only serious contender when you look for something to call a gay band. In spite of Duncan's temporary presence at Black Mountain isn't gay, nor is the New York School in spite of Frank O'Hara. The latter look gay while remaining mostly heterosexual, the greater sensitivity and gentleness of Ron Padgett, Kenneth Koch, Ted Berrigan and Peter Schjeldahl giving them, against their straightness and partly because of O'Hara, the alertness and graciousness of queens. The Beats of course are out of the running—Ginsberg is just the exception here. And the West Coast group of Robert Duncan, Jack Spicer and Robin Blaser—the Berkeley Renaissance? (I remember tall rangy old Professor X in graduate school looking over his shoulder to see if we were alone, then telling me: 1) they were *all* homosexual, you know! 2) I wonder why Jack finally stopped coming to see me?)

There's now a Duncan interview with plenty of gab on these subjects, part of a series the poet Lew Ellingham is making with the Duncan/ Spicer circle. What's most striking is the millenialist, vanguardist slant. Loyalty to something Beyond or Higher is tangible; exactly *what* is open to dispute. With Duncan this is related to a sense of having a calling, a métier (what he means by saying he's a "derivative poet"). That is, you belong to a caste, have a genealogy or lineage. For Duncan anyway, this takes you back through High Moderns like Pound or H.D. to figures of a more distant past with defining concerns for a/the public sphere. That sphere could be called polis or city or community maybe, would have been shaped by the likes of Dante or Brunetto Latini, the poetry of Provence or the minnesingers; is Utopian that way. Community and judgment. As in Jack Spicer's drawing the line—" I / Can- / not accord / sympathy / to / those / who / do / not / recognize / The human crisis." As in George Stanley's homoerotic community in the Pony Express Riders, "the men that fought and loved / they rode." Robin Blaser in his wonderful late 60s essay, "The Fire," makes clear that the basis of this community is in the Other World, in the "invisibility of everything that comes into me"—and loyalty becomes an issue. One's enemies talk against one. "He writes for a coterie, the poets talk only among themselves," Blaser hears them saying. And the group's sense of itself is key.

How should this loyalty be construed? Some say it's to a local history; others to the gloomy depths of the Occident itself. In the Ellingham interviews Duncan is quick to point to the connection of the Berkeley Renaissance with the learning of Northern Italy, and it's hard not to feel sometimes that the group considered themselves as clerks in their explicit relations to knowledge and history and particularly to the university (Jess associating the owl of learning with Duncan in paste-ups).

It's curious that this relation includes rejection. When Duncan talks about not having finished his degree at Berkeley there's a note of pride: isn't there an illustrious history of us autodidact poets? In Spicer's opinion, as it's recorded, the university damns you; it's an Enemy as constituted, takes the poetry out of you. And again the contrary movement—a respect among these men for the university as purveyor of lore—because after all there's still a doctrine of Correspondences:

> The Authors are in eternity.
> Our eyes reflect
> Prospects of the whole radiance
> between you and me

—says Duncan in "Variations on TWO DICTA OF WILLIAM BLAKE;" and books take up their relations with people, not institutions. How then?

There's a clue, I think, in the pivotal relations of the group with its professors and teachers, like Josephine Miles. Thomas Parkinson and Ernst Kantorowicz. In the Ellingham interviews there are definite signs of respect for those who transmit learning, for the idea that knowledge has to be passed *through* someone, that the correct name for this is authority. Duncan has a relation to Olson, who has a relation to Pound and so on. This aspect of learning is loyalty. In Germany you might have a *Doktorvater;* in France the person who made knowledge possible for you was your *maître.* For myself, I find it a rich fact that in his moving book of gay poems *(Slaves)* Stan Persky names Spicer as his master; and I put this in the same context as Duncan calling Sar Peladan Satie's master. All suggestive.

According to the Lew Ellingham interviews, the question "What do you know about the Albigensians?" is the very first thing Spicer says when he meets Duncan in 1945 or 46 in Berkeley. This is Duncan's account at any rate, and there's a whiff of sulfur in the air. Then Spicer brings up the topic of the Stefan George group or *Kreis,* and that's even more interesting. George's *Kreis* was actually a homosexual cult (!), so they say, dedicated to preserving the memory of the Master's dead teenage lover, Maximilian. All very campy stuff, but fascinating. Then Duncan goes one better. He says that this whole conversation, Spicer's and his initial encounter, takes place in Berkeley . . . at an anarchist study group! (They just happen to be there that evening.) Hearing that, I had the feeling that the antinomianism of the group was there, still there, integral to it. Why *shouldn't* these men have truck with anarchism, I thought. The memories of a Wobbly and syndicalist past still linger in the Bay Area—with its Tom Mooney case and Wobbly hall. A general strike closed down San Francisco in 1934. And it was never the Communists or Trotskyists who were sympathetic to gays in this period, but the anarchists, only them. "Let me await thee, Prince of the Morning" writes Duncan in "Apprehensions" (*Roots and Branches*), of a Prince some have called Satan. Duncan calls him only "the Lord of Love."

Gossip and more gossip—but can it suggest a conceptual direction? In the anecdotal material I've laid out I'd see four or five strands converging, structuring the Berkeley Renaissance group, making it new to literary history. I'd suppose these points: the Berkeley group stood opposed to institutional authority on grounds of bohemianism or anarchism; but authority was probably important to them on some one-to-one basis as an erotic glue to hold things together; learning's so important to them it's probably the core of what they want to do, all the misappropriations of the university notwithstanding; the key to their gay-identified-ness is in some relation to a long distant past; and all these factors would be meaningless if not seen as an ensemble or nexus working together. This makes the Berkeley poets new on our horizon and gives to the young Duncan, finding his voice in the decade of the mid 40s to mid 50s, an emplacement, a context to define him, even when *after* that he discovers himself as an opposition within—not outside.

Pure chance, randomness, sometimes teaches in this small talk. We know for instance from Duncan's letters to Spicer in the *Collected Books of Jack Spicer* that Kantorowicz was highly esteemed by them as a scholar and thinker and that his work and that of his teacher Gundolf were especially important to Duncan in the writing of his own book *Medieval Scenes*. But there's something else coming through Duncan's letters on the subject. After all, isn't a professor in the end . . . a professor? It's not as if Kantorowicz was a poet, is it, so why is Duncan making a fuss about him? So I think about the problem of Duncan's excessive excitement and my own (by some sympathetic magic?) gets equally stirred. Then one day I receive an unexpected letter from Lew Ellingham, hard at work on his Interviews project. He tells me he's corroborated (courtesy of a professor in the German Department at UC-Berkeley, Gerd Hillen) some information on Kantorowicz that might interest me. In his earlier days at the University of Heidelberg this Kantorowicz who is Duncan/Spicer/Blaser's teacher was himself a member of the inner circle of the *George-Kreis*! He's part of it throughout his life, even while teaching at Berkeley. And at the time of the poet's death (1933—the year of Hitler's accession to power, so that George's non-residence in Germany seems to reflect favorably on him) Kantorowicz even makes a special trip to Switzerland to keep vigil over the poet, according to the Swiss custom, until burial. This was exciting news for me. Didn't it confirm my own sense of Duncan's emotional excessiveness in those letters? I begin to believe in the power of the Homintern conspiracy. I call up the wonderful scene from Murnau's *Nosferatu*—Dracula's beautiful black coffin on a sinister-looking merchant vessel making its way downstream on the Danube to the world-port of Amsterdam. And from there, won't the pieces of that same Dracula be propagated to the *entire world*? I shiver with delighted anticipation. Could I give my sense of the Berkeley group's aura of romance and mystification a solid basis in Duncan's texts?

It's obvious, from a conspiracy point of view, that these texts aren't writing at all, but ritual. In a recent issue of *Salmagundi* on Homosexuality, Herbert Blau says modernism, feminism and gay-ness have now begun to join forces in a desire to push an already tottering Western Civ over the edge. He notes with alarm that basic values are being questioned; the West as we (?!) know it is at stake. The advantage of this viewpoint is to underscore the meaning of Duncan's pun write/rite, a conjunction that makes a lot of sense for and of Duncan, I think. Stein, for one, set some kind of precedent, a woman as notorious for being modern as for being queer. Duncan sees in Stein, as in other strong women modernists (H.D., maybe Laura Riding), a real *precedent* (Duncan's sense of being "derivative"); he adds to them, reinforces, in a common cause. The addition has something to do with words actually *causing* things, the

> . . . I too loved the scene of dark magic, the sorcerer's sending up
> clouds of empire and martyrdom

of "What Do I Know of the Old Lore?" for instance, testifying to Duncan's Orphic shamanism. Magic assumes an ability to speak for something larger. If you're part of a community, these verbal patterns will help defeat enemies, you trust.

So you get in Duncan's definitely odd book *Writing Writing: A Composition Book* a sense of private languages as rituals. Say in Gertrude Stein's *Tender Buttons* or in "Miss Furr and Miss Skeene" wasn't there a fooling around and gay joking toward you/women/readers? I think this looniness carries over to Duncan but with a hysterical edge that's intended. Duncan takes a Sitwell-style, playful Auden-style, or English nursery story-style in "I Am Not Afraid" and deals with danger at a distance by casting a spell:

> I am not afraid of writing a great poem.
> I am not afraid of writing a perfect lyric.
> […]
> I am not afraid of sounding like Stein.
> I am not afraid of being inspired.
> I am not afraid of your growing tired.
> […]
> I am not afraid of not knowing Greek.
> I am not afraid of allowing no one to speak.
> I am not afraid of ever being seen.
> I am not afraid of being a queen.

The poem insists, how can you understand this unless you know Duncan the person? Example: Duncan's fear that he speaks too loud or isn't always mannerly in listening to a conversational partner—"allowing no one to speak," he says. Or the whistling-in-the-dark assertive, non-assertive declaration—"I am not afraid of being a queen." Such wistful private language—why not say it straight out? There were dangers, constraints, that other pieces in the book reflect, like this—"Another ido. Cross eyes. Aimiable cross eyes."—referring to Duncan's non-alignment of eyes, from an early accident. What needs to be explained is how he can call the condition "aimiable," since that implies *accepted*—or even acceptable. As in "Crosses of Harmony and Disharmony"—

"Gladly, the cross-eyed bear"—the cross
rising from the eye a strain of visible song
    that Ursa Major dances,
    star notes, configurations

—where in the weight that "cross" and "strain" bear, as issuing in poetry ("song"), I wonder if it's possible to see a reference to *gay*. If there *is* an acceptance of the equation gay=flaw=poetry, I think of Spicer as catalyst and comrade in formulating it. Probably any approach to either of these writers remains incomplete if it doesn't take the other into consideration.

Duncan says in the Lew Ellingham interviews that, in contrast with himself, Spicer arrives on the scene already having a voice. If this is true there are two questions: 1) How do you say what Duncan's voice is, the integrity of it, when he *does* get it? and 2) what was he *before?*

The question of voice has "reverberations." Art isn't separate from life—and the issue is one of confidence or belief, how you can come to be your choice of yourself. A sexual dimension is inseparable:

> And the other feeling I had with Jess was when I said yes, and I
> have a strong—that while I made promises with myself for other
> people, for other reincarnations, that I would not ever, I mean
> I would never want to leave him. If you really want to be with a
> person just this once, just these years, then that's the character of
> those years. And I do then, in reincarnation terms, I find *that* is
> real to me. This is something I have to know, is teaching me, is
> bringing me to know something that only love, that love brings
> me to know. And that I have faith in. Yes.

This disclosure—in *Soup* no. 1 to Steve Abbott and Aaron Shurin—though about love is also about art. The rewards of maturity or commitment aren't naive; they imply a realization that in choosing one thing, you are by definition not choosing another. A sense of limits; and that these choices still *remain,* even as you decide against them. So Duncan's recognition of this—

at the same time I have many, many rueful reflections upon domestication as repression, as loss of—denial of—

is for me echoing a basic stance. To choose Jess is an act of responsibility to oneself, but in no way rules out an awareness of the plurality of selves one is and remains. To the extent it remains, perdures, a sovereign choice is by definition arbitrary, not "given."

It's interesting that the pre-Jess years largely co-incide with the Spicer years. Though there's no indication Duncan and Spicer were ever lovers, the relation is intense and important enough, I'm convinced, to stand as a counterweight to the time of—and poetry of—the years of commitment with Jess. *Contrary* to Spicer's, Duncan's work changes. I'd go further. What most characterizes Duncan's work is a constant striving to redefine ego boundaries, to be, you might say, what it *isn't*. Duncan makes an incantation to show this: "As I was then I am, a circling man." And in the process to *evade:* "We have left, of course, witchcraft, sleight / and shifting of shapes." Wanting to be (in) the flux of things, Duncan's most himself when he changes.

This is true in Duncan's pioneering 1944 essay, "The Homosexual in Society" (Dwight McDonald's *Politics*) beginning—

I propose to discuss a group whose only salvation is in the struggle
of all humanity for freedom and individual integrity

—which, surprisingly, develops an argument for gay behavior over against and at the price of a gay identity. Yes, he's for gays, but not in the way the gay community is now. So too, characteristically, in the work of Duncan's maturity, where eroticism is more often of tone or atmosphere—

Father expected, Father conceald
Father who has hidden His law in my heart,
Father who has given me keys to joy

(from the H.D. Birthday Sequence)—of individuation with archetypes that are eternal (Indian deities peering out of modern machines, cityscapes as mythic, in Jess's paste-ups for *Caesar's Gate*) rather than expressive of any group identity or sense of identification with the gay collectivity that Stonewall and Gay Lib brought about. And indeed, in "The Homosexual in Society," Duncan had said it explicitly:

> But my view was that minority associations and identifications were an evil wherever they supersede allegiance to and share in the creation of a human community good—the recognition of fellow-manhood.

In terms of gay-ness anyway, being part of a small group is part of the problem, not a solution. It's a concrete and eternal sexuality that interests Duncan—not an identity. Spicer contrasts here. You get identity taken so far there's little actual sexuality left, or rather *sensuality*—since with Spicer sexuality is a way of opposing the status quo. A politics.

In *The Opening of the Field* (1960, but reflecting earlier work) Duncan makes an arrangement of elements that ratifies this dilemma: behavior on one side, identity on the other. There's an idea of male sexuality and an idea of community. Both are accented positively but they remain separate and autonomous. No longer tied down to the idea of a specific community which would historically be its (real) expression, Duncan's concept of male-on-male sexuality glows, mystical and idealistic:

> I thought a Being more than vast, His body leading
>   into Paradise,   his eyes
>   quickening a fire in me,   a trembling
>
> hieroglyph: At the root of the neck
>
> *the clavicle,* for the neck is the stem of the great artery
>   upward into his head that is beautiful
>
>   At the rise of the pectoral muscles
>
> *the nipples,* for the breasts are like sleeping fountains

of feeling in man, waiting above the beat of his heart,
shielding the rise and fall of his breath, to be
awakend

[...]

For my Other is not a woman but a man

the King upon whose bosom let me lie.

It doesn't matter if this Hero/Lover/King is Jess or not, since what's at issue is transpersonal. The language, theosophical in tone as much as it is Biblical (Song of Songs), shows it. What's important for man-with-man sexuality is man-ness, so that the philosophical language enhances the expansion in this, how the Other becomes the *self.* Loving another man=loving yourself. Elevated idiosyncrasies, like the Being capitalized at the beginning of the poem ("The Torso/Passages 18"), stress the wonder and marvel, since the loving involved is a figure for what reality does, is. This flowery language is a kind of doctrinal dance—there's an aspect of teaching to the sensuality.

Sex as learning or teaching, you might say. And in another avatar the King/Lover or Canticle of Canticles figures will become the one Duncan names the Master of Rime—

The Master of Rime told me, You must learn to lose heart. I have
darkend this way and you youself have darkend. Are you so blind
you cant see what you cant see?

—whose sarcasm seems directed at those who refuse to yield, give up, a "self," a "pride," whatever. You can't stay the same; there's always a something *more* in the "not-you." "Learn to lose your heart. Let the beat of your heart go" is this Master's humorous—but loving—advice. What's at stake for the Master of Rime is a radical understanding of process. For Duncan this knowledge-journey becomes magic, an incantation:

O brother of the confined! O my twin lord of the net rime has
tied in the tongues of fire.

—and under this Christian sign of a Spirit-Descent (Pentecost) poetry and
sexuality are seen, heard, as becoming world.

These are high flights. How do we know that the purveyor of this
wisdom won't take a spill from time to time? Didn't Olson, Duncan's
self-acknowledged Master, once famously warn *against wisdom as such*? In
"Reflections" (*Bending the Bow*), by juxtaposing it with another paragraph
celebrating the Dance, Duncan reinterprets this caution—

Charles Olson, how strangely I have alterd and used and
would keep the wisdom, the man, the self I choose

—hoping it exonerates. Maybe it does. But if not, the question is certainly,
what's excluded by wisdom? And that would be a question to be asked by
gays, a very material question about the function and nature of any kind of
sex, I would think.

Let me put it another way. To their lasting credit, Duncan's Fire Master,
Lion, Master of Rime and King are far more sensual (musical) than Spicer's
Billy the Kid for instance, who is after all devoted to death. Yet the question
remains—what if the forces of sexuality can't be tamed without there being
a terrible penalty? What if it turned out that the domestication of sexuality
involves compromise? In Duncan there's an assumption you can put sex
into music, that the two are—even with loss factored in—reconcilable.
The price extracted for making the opposite assumption—that they're not
reconcilable, that there's a radical cleavage between things sexual and things
human—was Spicer's, and may well have accounted for his increasing
alcoholism and premature death at 40. One can't turn one's back on society
and live. The perils being obvious—Dionysius. Duncan's hero is Apollo, the
culture hero and patron of poetry, and his sensual and musical rendering of
sex largely *excludes* violence, rupture. One can legitimately wonder why;
what redounds to your credit if you give up the *rawness* of sex?

The benefits of that choice were preponderant. The wisdom archetypes that
characterize Duncan's verse amount to a strategy of sensuous abstraction—

that allowed him to present gay sexuality from a positive, loving, celebrational viewpoint. But there were drawbacks. Duncan's breakthrough took place at the cost of a break with the then-existing gay community.

The writing from before that break would include *Medieval Scenes* and *Domestic Scenes* but would be represented by two other books: *The Venice Poem* and *Caesar's Gate: Poems 1949-1950*. The subject matter of these, in one way or another, is the gay subculture. It's a writing that is full of conflicts, doubt, self-laceration. But this period of Duncan's writing shouldn't be overlooked by gay people, and as far as I'm concerned it's unique in dealing with certain issues—such as the butch/femme polarity, usually written off as politically incorrect through much of the 1970s and only now up for reconsideration. Insofar as it comes firmly down on the side of breaking down barriers between gay and non-gay, Duncan's poetry here raises the issue of assimilation vs. separatism. Is it possible, one wonders, without rolling back advances for gays in the form of rights, social cohesiveness and a greater, earned sense of self-esteem—to push out the boundaries of our identification so they can apply less narrowly, more generally? Duncan's particular, effective brand of combining gay emphasis with universalist humanism deserves real consideration. There's a deep sense of acceptance, love of the world itself in the

everything I see / glows or shines

of the "Epilogos" from *Bending the Bow*, and it moves out into the specifically gay dynamics of otherness in "I see in your eyes your sight of me." "Man himself moand in me," writes Duncan, and in the pun on the first term the human/male dichotomy groans too.

Butch/femme. What's interesting here is how early Duncan was to give a positive valuation to the femme part of that opposition, to insist on it as a matter of fact. To judge from Duncan's accounts, he accepted an identification at the femme end of the spectrum—surely even more difficult then than it is now. I don't want to press the point, but you can see genuine anguish in the pages devoted to this subject in the *Caesar's Gate* introduction, with the horrendous quote from Anais Nin's *Diaries* (Duncan had met her and they had been friendly for a time in the early 40s in New York)—

His face became that of the coquette, receiving flowers with a flutter of the eyelashes, oblique glances like the upturned corner of a coverlet . . . the stage bird's sharp turn of the head, the little dance of alertness, the petulance of the mouth pursed for small kisses that do not shatter the being, the flutter and perk of femininity, all adornment and change, a mockery of her invitations, a burlesque of her gestures. . . etc., etc.

—as he records it in the form of Nin's indictment of him. (An unfair expression of dislike for those who seem too much like oneself maybe.) The soul-searching that follows in the introductory pages of Duncan's gay book will go far, I think, to explain to the puzzled why Duncan—more than Ginsberg, Burroughs or Norse, even Spicer perhaps—might have had such a hard time of it coming out. It's noticeable in patriarchal society that femme gays are treated more harshly than their butch brothers. And Duncan, choosing the femme end of the spectrum, got some of the worst of this bigotry. In a *Gay Sunshine* anthology of interviews, the Boston poet John Wieners gives a different, probably fairer portrait of Duncan. Without a particular ax to grind. Wieners' description strikes me as arguably more human, both amused and amusing:

He had all the effeminacies of a bar habitué but it was truly more than that—a rush of language that sprang out of his mouth. His conversation was far from *sotto voce* as well; it was very effeminate and loaded with authority. We had stopped at Sharaf's to eat, and ostentatious is hardly the word.

Duncan took note of the strong femme side early on. In the *Soup* interview he describes his early sense of himself as a "flirt" and as "casting a spell." Duncan here corroborates the sense of danger often witnessed to by poets on the vatic, or "receptive" side of poetry: blind Homer, acquiescence in the inevitability of a price to be exacted for the gift. But it's a mixed message you get from Duncan. "Casting a spell" describes a vocation as well as a temperament, it's a way into poetry—yet it's also a punishment. Why? In an anecdote he relates, Duncan vacillates between acceptance of this traditional, prejudiced point of view and its condemnation. A man, a drifter who's recently come to town and noticed the young Duncan, decides—with an arrogance that's familiar to women as a traditional justification of rape—that if the youthful Duncan was smiling at him, that meant he had to put out—or take the consequences. Did the drifter suppose that a murder attempt was only just desserts for a prick-teaser? A person has only to think for a moment, what would have transpired for the young man, Duncan, if he had chosen a more encouraging butch role for himself. I see Nin here as an ideologue for a course of action the drifter happens to put into practice—with bloody consequences, near loss of life.

The trauma of sexuality is on Duncan's mind from the very earliest poems. Is there a strong impulse to want to express gay sexuality, to talk forthrightly about it? Duncan begins by not being clearly able to say—

> Among my friends love is a painful question.
> We seek out among the passing faces
> a sphinx-face who will ask its riddle.
> Among my friends love is an answer to a question
> that has not been askt.
> Then ask it.

—so that these earliest poems are still practicing up. "Then ask it"!, say the Berkeley Poems, from which the segment I quoted stands out. There's an enormous confusion, floating above them like death, in lines like—

> Lost, lost such peace, and Persephone lost

—and

> We remember in symbols such violence

—that it seems a classically Freudian situation of substituting one thing for another in the effort not to have to say what's really on your mind; it's that depressing. And so too we get the disease imagery in this early Duncan—to express blockage of the "real" topic, but getting closer now. Yet the lyricism

Duncan says he got from Auden in this beautiful and moving section from "Passage Over Water"—

> We have gone out in boats upon the sea at night,
> lost, and the vast waters close traps of fear about us.
> The boats are driven apart, and we are alone at last
> under the incalculable sky, listless, diseased with stars.

—or the velvet fist in lines like—

> our love like a knife between us

—remain testimonials to the policy of endlessly delaying what's really in question. It's the legitimacy of dissimulation that's at issue here even though—

> My music not Apollo's but that of Mercury the Thief the Dissembler, Lord of the Musical Comedy turn. But name me there, and I shall be offended Apollo.

We're talking about the 40s and 50s. Recently, in *Mother Jones,* Allan Bérubé has shown that there was actually a great deal of flexibility about gender roles in American society in World War II. With the postwar years came a terrifying crackdown and return to "normalcy." You had to take it for granted that, if you wanted to be an accepted artist, you had *in some way* to agree with your fellow Americans when they called you "sick," "crazy" or "evil." So the poetic ideology of a gay "cult of evil" in men like Kenneth Anger will come into existence as the product of a larger social system, and will be antagonist by definition. While certainly made up of guilt feelings in part, under its trope of "evil" it takes sexuality far more seriously than U.S. society was generally able to do. The darker image of the sexuality of faggots stands out against the predominant bleached "white" image of sex; and it *attracts* on that score.

How then could Garcia Lorca's poetry, essays—which we know the young Duncan read at this time—not have come for him like a bolt from the blue. The Spanish poet's Duende essay, for instance, with its accent on demon power, or the Walt Whitman Ode! In Duncan's intro to *Caesar's Gate* you get a good idea how suggestive these pieces must have been for Duncan, addressing his coming out as a literary problem. Would Lorca be any help—Lorca, slain by the Spanish Civil Guard, it's said, out of revenge for his anti-fascist "Song of the Civil Guard" and on account of his gay sexuality? One of the most lyrical sections of *Caesar's Gate* insists—

> García Lorca tasted
> death at this drinking-fountain;
> saw a dead bird
> [...]
> García Lorca drank
> life from this drinking-fountain;
> witnessd the witless poor
> [...]
> García Lorca stole
> poetry from this drinking-fountain
> sang and twangd

—and then later in the *Soup* interview Duncan scans that "drinking-fountain" image as what it obviously is, gay sex. Already there are three terms or themes interrelating: 1) gay sex as bringing death, 2) as somehow bringing life underneath that, and 3) poetry making these apparently incompatible ideas compatible. In the Spanish poet's "Ode to Walt Whitman," for instance, one would have found perhaps as extreme a hostility to the actual realities of gay life, what we now call the ghetto, as Duncan himself had expressed in his "Homosexual in Society" essay, in a wish not to allow sexuality to come to the point of contravening laws society takes for granted. Didn't Duncan's notion of sexuality take for granted some concept, in its inner logic, of death as a term? How far can you push sexuality? In another of the *Caesar's Gate* lyrics Duncan puts it this way—

Torches, we light our own way,
nor, in passing, notice our burnd bodies

—with all the accents of high tragedy, the black and white of, say, a Motherwell's *Spanish Elegy.*

And the third term, the one that reconciles the first two by going beyond, is poetry. Here's Duncan talking about what the work of the Spanish poet meant to him and Spicer—

> It seemed to us, to Jack Spicer as to me, our conversations of 1946 and 1947 as young poets seeking the language and lore of our homosexual longings as the matter of a poetry, that Lorca was one of us, that he spoke here from his own unanswered and—as he saw it—*unanswerable* need.

What did the "one of us" imply? A chain going back to Rilke maybe? As far back as Orpheus in confraternity? Orpheus has already made his appearance in Spicer's early poems, and Orphism is already there in Duncan's early *Heavenly City, Earthly City*—not without a knowledge of the Renaissance tradition of Orpheus' second life, the life of a poet who is gay, I think. That need, here very explicitly sexual, is in Duncan's formulation, unanswerable. Underlined as this is by Duncan, it makes a strong statement:

> I watch with pain my hairy self
> croucht in his abject sexual kingdom
> writhe in that brief ecstatic span
> as if he took the sun within himself
> and became a creature of the sun

—as Duncan has it in *Heavenly City, Earthly City.*

There's strong indication that we have a mixed message here. Duncan seems to approve of Lorca's idea of gay love or sex as being "impossible." That's surely the meaning of unanswerable. Here on earth at least you can't find satisfaction. So doesn't that mean you should start thinking of the *above*?—however defined, as the gods, the dead, the invisible world? That seems to be how Duncan finds himself in agreement with Lorca. But on another basis, the *effeminacy* discussed earlier, Duncan is equally explicit in taking issue with him, realizing how necessary it is to go farther than Lorca here:

> But draw the line, Lorca, as you do, and I stand with them to whom otherwise I do not belong, though my heart longs for you. . . . Already there is about me the irremediable stench of H.M.S. Bearskin I will not disown and you will not love.

The H.M.S. Bearskin he refers to is the queen-caricature Duncan develops in a short subset of poems half-way through *Caesar's Gate.* For the time being the agreement with Lorca is more important. Duende is a bargain struck with the Invisible World. By giving up lovers you get poetry.

What this comes to is renunciation. In writing his serial poem *Medieval Scenes* (1950), Duncan had started to develop this idea, only in a different context. The series proceeds like a set of meditative abstractions from the poetry-doctrine of the Albigensian love poets and minnesingers. Later Duncan commented:

> The poem is above all things an attempt to picture, to imagine— how gods, demons, lovers and companions are interrelated in history. . . . The ritual is the ritual in which any EXPRESSION of love at all is specifically excluded

—and, I think tellingly, the "companion" series called *Domestic Scenes* is dedicated to Jack Spicer, "For Jack Spicer, Until his Return." The Spicer friendship is crucial and I'll come back to it. Meantime I want to note the nadir at which Duncan's feelings of despondency over the possibility of gay love were shortly to arrive, a brief period when rejection of sexuality and love seem unqualified, as in the long *Venice Poem*—

> Buggary stirs enmity, unguarded hatred.
> Cocksucking breeds self-humiliation

—which, if not characteristic, is still there and can't be ignored. But then there's the answering refrain, a simple statement of acceptance—

> Yet here seeks the heart solace.
> Nature barely provides for it.
> Men fuck men by audacity.
> Yet here the heart bounds
>   as if only here,
>   here it might rest.

I'd like to relate some of the troubled aspects of Duncan's poetry of this period, even the distortions of self-regard that appear from time to time, to a femme aspect of his poetic project. That dynamic is important. One takes it as an argument in simple justice and fairness that the more macho aspects of other contending gay writers of the day should no longer be seen as normative. The argument for the high-writerly greatness of writers like Ginsberg and Burroughs can get along quite well on its own, I think, without approval of their apparent "butchness" being thrown in for good measure. My proposal for considering femme-ness more fairly is only a suggestion for clearing the air so a discussion of literature proper can emerge. What's more interesting to me is the possibility that there might well be something worth considering in the ancient idea—here linked with "femme"—that the *capacity to do poetry* has something intrinsic to do with receptivity as a stance or attitude toward the world. This would make Duncan's notion of "renunciation" more comprehensible. Ideals of renunciation in life translate into "Dictation" in poetry: what the Berkeley Renaissance called Dictated Poetry.

Robert Glück once pointed out a way Duncan and Spicer differ along these lines. With Duncan, he said, notice how the love object is characteristically a man. With Spicer it's a boy. I agree—I think it's a definite direction. I think for instance of the resplendent but rather terrifying Apollo figure of *Heavenly City, Earthly City* who "pierces" the muses till they "break," "crack." With Spicer the identification seems on the other side of the fence: "The poet is a counterpunching radio," that is, a prize fighter, even if he goes down. I imagine these respective temperaments to have been on occasion points of issue for them; it's not difficult for instance to think of a side of Spicer *bristling* at this or that indication of a "femme"-ness perceived in Duncan, nor of Duncan reacting *defensively* if this was so. One has to assume that theirs was a relation of competition as well as friendship. Nor is Duncan slow to admit this. In an unpublished essay ("The Underside") he interprets the

Words-

      worth
Nods
He heap good
Gray poet
English department in his skull

of Spicer's poem, "Dover Beach," as having him, Duncan, as its direct target.

But I think, myself, there's another way that femme-ness comes into play in the Duncan-Spicer relation, one that suggests more tender, and amative, underlying feelings.

Looking at the tokens of these years, it's hard not to suspect coded or wistful valentines. The "in all these years (I have) realized no gracious way to love you" [not verified] in one of Duncan's letters or the "bed-conclusions" and "what was lost in my not-touching you" you can find in the same letter. From Spicer, there's a childishly drawn sketch of Duncan sexually excited—now in Duncan's archives. Do you stir up love to thwart it then? That would be medieval.

I don't think though that Duncan "bought into" that ideology to the extent that Spicer did, even when you take into account the fact that as older and more experienced, it was Duncan who initiated much of the actual content or terms of this poetic ideology. My sense is Duncan brought to Spicer most of the ideas like Dictated Poetry and the Invisible World—metaphors for carrying through poetic inspiration. Spicer carried them through—with inexorable logic—so they were not metaphors any longer. In his own interview with Lew Ellingham, Robin Blaser hazards the opinion that probably Duncan didn't believe in the

Invisible World. Spicer did, and it was literal for him with results I've talked about in another article (*Social Text,* Spring 1983)—opposition as Utopian. This of course didn't particularly make Spicer a happier person; everything says the opposite. In any case the fact remains that the two poets for something like a decade had much in common—in theory as in practice. Once Duncan's, the idea of "serial poetry" becomes both of theirs. And though Duncan seems later to have junked the key concept that unhappiness in sex goes with success in poetry, for a time this opinion was common to both. The methodology of magic, techniques of randomness for making poetry were common. And then there's the religious stuff—God (Calvinist, theosophical or other); the sleazy ghost machinery from Yeats; Oz and children's stories and Romantic ballads as correspondences-with-something-greater. I have this sense of Spicer picking up the ball that Duncan tosses him and running with it—to extremes with which Duncan will take issue. The strategy question is this: can sheer oppositionality, so important once as a technique for breaking up the massive uniformity of the 50s *(still)* be effective in a no-longer-conformist, *pluralist* 80s? The corollary for gays: how to go beyond *separatism* without negating its advances?

Duncan's work is a good place to ask questions like this because it's not "gay-community" minded and for that reason remains more open in its sexuality. It's the opposite of Spicer's concept of the gay clan that way. Spicer doesn't want Billy (the Kid) but effectively *is* him and his outlaw band. This foresees the whole development of gay community in the 70s with its legitimate emphasis on sexuality as such. But to what extent are ideals of sexuality and community actually compatible? The question needn't be hostile but does lay out the essential ambiguity of both notions. What if—an "anarchist" thought, surely—what you got was sexual sectarians? Or—Duncan quoting Spicer—a community of "unloved lovers."

In its movement away from ideological questions and toward a perception of the physical as rhythms of being, Duncan's accent on "simple" or uncomplicated sensuality implicitly raises these questions—

> Earthly city in which I walk, the light, your sun,
> is the golden heart of that deep body,

the darkend city that gleams in the tide
of that inward sea. Dumbly, I hear its voices

—forcing all notions of community (polis) to be as inclusive as possible,
and general. The upshot is a sexuality that's understood as part of nature,
not against it. A kind of "body mysticism" in other words—

Organized, as perfect as an army there
your body lies. It gleams upon the sweet
unorganized, the field of dark.

—where the hope is "dark" to keep it from being naive. This is a program of
inclusiveness that hopes to be exhaustive.

I like the sense of conflicts not resolved in Duncan. It shows common
sense, like Whitman. "Poems then are immediate presentations of the
intention of the whole," writes Duncan (intro, *The Years as Catches),* "the
great poem of all poems, a unity, and in any two of its elements or parts
appearing as a duality or a mating, each part in every other having, if we
could see it, its condition—its opposite or contender and its satisfaction or
twin. Yet in the composite of all members we see no duality but the variety
of the one." As I say, like Whitman.

"Robert Duncan and Gay Community: A Reflection" first appeared in *Ironwood*
no. 22: "Robert Duncan, A Special Issue," vol, 11, no. 2 (1983).

REVIEW OF ROBERT DUNCAN'S
GROUND WORK: BEFORE THE WAR

If the mood of the country now (the recent elections and alarming manifestations) is to let things slide, put off urgent ecological, social and political changes everyone knows are desperately needed, Robert Duncan in *Ground Work: Before the War* is as much a radical as ever, maybe more. Cassandra style (better: like Blake) Duncan demands we start giving a lot of serious attention to signs of Negativity we can see all around us: isn't the penalty for not doing this some great apocalyptic event? Duncan's *Ground Work* (part two of it's to be called *Ground Work: In the Dark* but isn't due out till 1989) is an exciting, swirling view of all Duncan's latest on society, nature, politics, us—in relation to the growing Dark. This in itself wouldn't make it a must-to-buy, as the *Voice* would say. But there's also an extremely personal, poignant, autobiographical note in this collection, and I think the best thing about *Ground Work* is the way the two collide—

> the wave of a life darker than my
> > life before me sped,   and I
> larger than I was,   grown dark as
> > the shoreless depth

—he says, catching his breath, giving the main thing obliquely, *between*.

The Dark and Death's as complex, ambiguous as it can be for Duncan. As far as style goes, the poet's awareness of ecological, social and other disasters at the heart of the collection doesn't make it a particularly public or open book. Duncan's for himself completely the singer, the lyricist—and the new stress on personal just enhances this. Ginsberg's by contrast polemical: if once in a while he picks up an instrument to accompany himself, well, that doesn't change things. You're what you are *through* the changes when you're a really good writer. Facing limitations of age and death, Duncan's very moving first-person quality becomes the life of the new collection, gives real in-depth urgency. Duncan here is self-defined as a champion of Light, as he always has been. So the big question of

BRUCE BOONE • 331

the book, as I see this, is how any person—you, I, whoever—can start to reconcile this stance of attraction to the same Dark that's on another level so threatening. Put in the context of the late '60s (much of the book being written then)—can a person be against the war in Viet Nam, the horrible eco-menace of capitalism, its globally destructive way of life etc.—and still be *for* all the Dark urges that sometimes seem to lie *behind* them? An important question. And it's evident Duncan wants very much to answer. Yes, though he's also still working on the question. And anyway—are we being given the choice?

So there's a certain shiftiness, elusiveness here. Take the long poem called "Santa Crux Propositions." The hyper-rationalism, destructions of capitalism, the poem seems to be saying, inevitably are going to bring about some cosmic retaliation, a righting of the balance by the universe. And then

> *SHE* appears,   Kālī dancing,   whirling her necklace of skulls
> trampling the despoiling armies and the exploiters of natural
> resources

and so on. As a reader, you take this pretty much at face value. But then—and there's where the surprise comes in—Duncan announces these lines (at least the passage) aren't his, but are taken from something by Denise Levertov, a friend with whom he's then fighting, separating from in fact. So the *meaning* changes. Was the eco-discussion a red herring? No, but the ground's shifted. Text's become meta-text; speaking voice, the one spoken. And this is a very *epistemological* shift, isn't it? Is a shift of this kind in writing part of the Dark too?

Does Duncan's reflexivity—textual "self-awareness"—put him in the same general grouping as current "text" writers like Ashbery or the Language Poets? Duncan's writing *uses* textuality, but as a means. Textual writing *stays on the page*: with Duncan the writing tends outward, elsewhere, to a beyond. Duncan's writing is Romantic and emotional. In spite of using the language of Western myths (though not as much as in the past—this collection uses simple and direct language as a strategy, I think) this links Duncan with popular writing. Sometimes only horror writing in our time (Bram Stoker, Stephen King, etc.) has been able to achieve the expressive, *mystical* feeling about the Dark that Duncan has. In lushly beautiful lines like these for instance—

> the sea
> comes in on rolling surfs
> of an insistent meaning,   pounds
> the sands relentlessly,   demanding
> a hearing.   I overhear
> tides of myself all night in it.

—you get Duncan's writing practice. Meaning breaks down. Out of that comes a connection. From the Dark—

> Fugitive evangel of morning
> I don't know in what sense you are *"mine"*.
> Yet I was waiting.   Were you
> barely fitting the shadow of an old desire
> the mind would not let go,   or
> do you come as the river of fire in the poem comes
> surpassing what the mind would *know*

—a possibility of a face companion.

This review of *Ground Work: Before the War* by Robert Duncan was published in *Poetry Project Newsletter*, Issue no. 111 (Jan-Feb. 1985).

BEAT POETRY'S POPULISM

It looks like the concept of populist writing has gotten a new lease on life among progressive/left writers these days. How carefully, as a cultural approach to the eighties, is the idea being worked out? The recent publication of two books from New Directions—*Endless Life: Selected Poems* by Lawrence Ferlinghetti and *Herald of the Autochthonic Spirit* by Gregory Corso—gives us a chance to look at this issue in a critical spirit.

To begin with, and on the organizational level, it's clear that left and progressive writers are going back to the populisms of other times for inspiration. There's been a spate of writers' congresses and conferences in the past few years—from San Francisco's Left/Write to New York's (*Nation*-sponsored) Writers' Congress to more pocket-sized events like the underpublicized Art Works for People at the San Francisco Women's Building, the anti-World War III gatherings, and so on. In addition, serious efforts to set up writers' unions are also under way, though there are some problems—jurisdictional conflicts, for instance, between already existing local writers' groups and the proposed national union.

Journalists and freelancers have been more receptive to these organizing efforts than poets and fiction writers, who historically have been first to speak out their fears and suspicions of organization. But the precedent should be taken seriously. In the past (the paradigm CP of the thirties, for instance) left cultural policies were characteristically bureaucratic and manipulative regarding writers, and this heritage is still a force to reckon with. Looking for a collective way to be a committed writer you may for instance join a "brigade," start viewing your writing as "cultural work" rather than elitist-identified "art," and so on. In spite of successes, perceived sectarianism has limited the effectiveness of even the best political writers' groups of the late seventies and early eighties (Union of Left Writers, Mainstream Exiles, Women Writers Union, the Roque Dalton Brigade, to name some important groups in the San Francisco Bay Area). This revival of older forms is properly the strategy of an intermediate period, an era of marking time, a post-modernism.

Fringe aspects of commercial culture, similarly, sometimes show a progressive side. Take the renewed interest now felt in the Beatnik period.

Jack Kerouac's writing is being read enthusiastically by younger people. There are the strong beatnik allusions in dress style and in New Wave music culture (the Voice Farm's "Beatniks / They are absolute!"). If the beatniks were a cutting edge of cultural/political rebellion in their time, so the argument goes, doesn't their beat rejection of formalism, dead tradition, make our reliving of that period an attractive possibility? By a similar principle there can even be a masscult critique of masscult, as monster movies of the fifties are reshown in a spirit of camp, sponsoring new analytic attention to the problems of commodity alienation. To borrow a slogan, it's "the presence of the past" in our period.

For the left, that past has a sometimes suspicious kinship with a discredited Stalinism. As in other areas of politics proper, on the left, basic cultural politics also seem to be up for reevaluation these days. Should we junk the Gramscian and democratic-socialist trends of the seventies, girding ourselves for battle with a more bureaucratic program? When, on the other hand, would a populist stance begin to erode our writing? In the conflict of questions of this order the tentative revival of beatnik writing styles seems attractive. Beatnik writing expresses broad political opposition (or at least *can* do that, as the writing of Ginsberg and others seems to show), but on the other hand isn't usually seen as tainted with the deficiencies (manipulativeness, etc.) of Popular Front culture from the thirties. In the sphere of leftist writing, in short, Beatnikism is also a "postmodern" tendency.

The problem with such a proposed politics, however, is that you have to have an actual, real constituency for your writing. The beatniks never had a social base. This becomes quite clear when you contrast them with the community praxis (cultural production, reception) of, say, Latino/Latina, black, lesbian and gay or women's writing. Inasmuch as these "new social movements" emerged as radical leaders of the seventies, socialists wondered if the cultural forms of these new movements shouldn't be accepted, vanguard style, as the norms for the entire leftist community. This seemed like a reasonable idea, and throughout the seventies many socialists tried to "impose" the cultural codes of the new social movements on those who didn't come from these movements, implicitly and sometimes explicitly codifying language, dress, even entertainment idioms. If straights, middle-class people, whites and males had their own cultures—which at the time seemed doubtful—that didn't necessarily mean they had a right to express them. After all, they weren't oppressed groups.

To nobody's great surprise, I suppose, this supposition proved untenable. And in the backlash that developed in the late seventies through the beginning eighties, a number of straights, whites and others began insisting, rightly, that left and progressive culture should be inclusive, not selective, in the way it addresses existing communities, and that cultural codes should no longer be looked at as commodities transferable at will from one group to another. This seems like definite progress. Once disengaged from its always possible racist, sexist and homophobic potentials (easier said than done), the backlash critique offers real insight. It might be seen as part of an overall left awareness of the need for a post-modern cultural politics—using elements from several pasts to create a more usable mixed culture of the present. More radical change will have to wait on the back burner for quite a while.

At this crossroads, Ferlinghetti and Corso may look as much like warnings (what shouldn't be done) as like harbingers of a glorious culture to come. Be that as it may. The new populism of the left is still taking its baby steps.

I think the most positive thing you can say of Lawrence Ferlinghetti's *Selected Poems* is that it's an "accessible" reworking of French surrealism in an American context. For Ferlinghetti that context includes native literary traditions (Whitman, but mostly Carl Sandburg) as well as American "populist" institutions (Fourth of July bombast). All this in a We-the-People voice, as in this proclamation to brother (sic) poets, to

> All you house-broken Ezra Pounds,
> All you far-out freaked-out cut-up poets,
> All you pre-stressed Concrete poets,
> All you cunnilingual poets

to overcome divisiveness in a spirit of bonhomie and "utter the word en masse"(a steal from Whitman) and, though the revolution doesn't seem to have arrived, prepare for it by "putting up the barricades," becoming "subversive" and "subjective." A poetic invocation of Revolution that's fatuous, labored, cranky, and sexist—is this the deep social change that socialists long for?

Ferlinghetti's interest in revolution, sincere though it is, pales in comparison with the really interesting subject—Ferlinghetti himself. When it comes to true admiration, F. only has eyes for Number One. Here he is speaking of the charms of that subject in a poem called "I Have Not Lain with Beauty All My Life. . ." It's a cautionary note that begins with a warning on beauty's dangers and ends like this—

> Yet I have slept with beauty
> > in my own weird way
> and I have made a hungry scene or two
> > with beauty in my bed
> and so spilled out another poem or two
> and so spilled out another poem or two
> > upon the Bosch-like world (40)

Such verse is the arrogant, swaggering side of populism, frankly contemptuous and superficial. In what regard does this verse promote actual social change? It's a sensibility, a kind of bourgeois bohemian freedom to do what you please, that the poet really seems to have in mind-and its limits are pretty obvious.

You encounter them for instance in a poem titled "An Elegy to Dispel Gloom" (1978). After so many protestations of a belief in rebellion on the poet's part, you may be surprised to find in this poem nothing but—counsels to calm, admonitions to forgiveness and mature resignation. So why this sudden about-face on Ferlinghetti's part? Why the unexpected discovery of virtues of Christian mildness? It turns out the poem's about the death of Harvey Milk, gay San Francisco supervisor—who was murdered by the ex-cop Dan White. What's Ferlinghetti *learned* in these past thirty years when he counsels *resignation* at an anti-gay murder? Not, by the way, that his basic attitudes toward nonwhite people are much better (though they are well-intentioned). The difficulty is Ferlinghetti's urge to stereotype. So . . . Happy-go-lucky baseball players, Chinese dragons, etc.. A populism like Ferlinghetti's would probably be dismissed as "vulgar" by current neopopulist theorists—yet to my mind it's a clear warning sign of dangers to be squarely faced as we evaluate proposals for a new politics.

So why don't I feel this way about Gregory Corso's *Herald of the Autochthonic Spirit*? I definitely like this book. Corso's got such talent. It's hard to be pessimistic about him, though his book's pessimistic to the limit—all kvetching and complaining. Maybe a person's life-experience does influence their writing ability in significant ways after all. Ferlinghetti the businessman, owner of City Lights and the publisher of City Lights books, vs. Corso the impoverished Failure? In any event, it's difficult to be tough on populism's dangers when you've got a populist poet with talent to deal with—like Corso. Maybe Corso is beatnik populism with a "human face."

As a by-now seasoned, veteran beatnik, Corso's latest tack is to be coyly modest (for him) and a bit of a curmudgeon. So things are more subtle in this man than in Ferlinghetti. Think of the multiple slynesses that lie in a quote tike this

> The pope doesn't really love me
> nor I he

says the rueful Gregory. And typically, he'll improvise, slowly but surely, layer on layer till we reach a pratfall—

> It's always a bad day for someone
> Pain, Death
> The Big Lie of Life
> The apothecarian earth blooms the poppy
> at best

—that yields laughter that's surprising by factoring in human misery.

This doesn't, of course, make Corso populist-political in any conventional way. You could spend a lot of time regretting, I think, the fact that Corso doesn't speak on public issues like Allen Ginsberg does. Corso is usually more complex than Ginsberg and when he does speak to distinctly public issues, as in this poem called "Bombed Train Station, 80 Killed,"

> And in the world the world at large
> there is talk soft talk of bombs
> Carter talks like a monk whispering psalms
> of bombing Russian bombs
> of bombing the Russians in charge
> even Brezhnev and the cars in his garage

—it's in rhythmic strains that are far more witty and skewered than Ginsberg's usually are. Look how skillfully in the last couplet Corso undercuts possibilities of rant with his deft suggestion of a parallel consumerism, a parallel hierarchism in each of the two societies. There's more genuine democratic values in Corso, I think.

This is a poet who can be oppositional to the society he lives in and, with bleak humor and doubt, include spaces for talking about the Big Questions of life. Corso is a modest person really—

> I feel there is an inherent ignorance in me
> deep in my being
> to the very core

—and his poetry turns out to be a domestic coinage—

> O what a heavy fall
> I'll have if I fall
> in all my light
> down ill-carpeted night

—of everyday household concerns. There's quite a bit of "the personal is political" here, ahead of its time. Cautious, canny, Corso's domesticity ends up a collective, popular mode, not an individual one. It speaks of surviving trials and tribulations. In Corso, working-class experience parodies and takes on an Everyman/Everyperson stance, with all the sharings in between.

Who wouldn't wish this poetry the best of luck!

It's asking for a lot to have a neopopulist literature that's radical, popular and anti-authoritarian at the same time. But aren't the elements for this mix already in place, waiting to be combined? One wonders, though, if there will be a sense of play and respect for democratic values in this as well as a necessary commitment to deep social change.

"Beat Poetry's Populism" first appeared in *Socialist Review*, no. 73 (Jan./Feb., 1984).

THE QUEEN BEATS

Glamour and sleaze: masochist doors that open on another world. Could it be the world of spirit? Is masochism in postmodern times ousting modernist sadism? Tho terms like this do have a sexual meaning, maybe the rehabilitation of the likes of WIENERS and SPICER and the increasing boredom with the likes of ALLEN GINSBERG or WILLIAM BURROUGHS suggests the spiritual meaning I want to get at here. Is the return of the queen beat writers an indication of a change of fashion?

Think about it. Just look into yourself, deep down. For whatever reasons—environmental catastrophe, political decay, infrastructure collapse, it scarcely matters—don't you really want to identify with some kind of FAILURE more and more often these days, and in the process turn your back on stupid images of SUCCESS? Yo, bitch or prick: If at first you don't fail, try try again! That's the message of the QUEEN BEATS I'm interested in. JOHN and JACK, not WILLIAM and ALLEN. These days, people want all the masochism they can get. They aren't satisfied with small amounts. Isn't masochism the only spiritual door you can find with a growth potential that can promise a future? MASOCHISM EQUALS SPIRITUALITY.

What brings on this sea-change of expectations then? I'm trying to explain it even to myself. Do me a favor, think of Wieners' pathetically masochistic whimpering ("DANA DANA MY HUSBAND WHERE ARE YOU? NOW!?!?," or something of the sort, to paraphrase my feelings about a lot of Wieners' writing). Now compare this admirable loser's mentality with the unpretty SADISM of someone like ALLEN GINSBERG or WILLIAM BURROUGHS and who comes out ahead? If you have to choose? Is it possible to be spiritual in this or our era without being a loser? As I said, think about it. Don't the attractions of WIN exclude the rewards of LOSS in any and all ways in the work of an overinflated pig like MR CITY LIGHTS? In modernity, winners win. But hey isn't this at postmodernity, if not beyond? There's been a big flipflop hasn't there, I mean doesn't winner equal loser now and loser equal winner? And retrospectively then doesn't spiritual relevance belong to the loser whining Wienerses of this world and not that winner big-time-celebrity hounds like

Ginsberg and Ferlinghetti—if you think about this seriously? The world has changed hasn't it? Isn't dissolution looking more and more attractive these days? (You might be thinking of these thoughts as sort of Bataillian—but Bataille was no loser in reality only in writing. Can I call him just an armchair LOSER then?)

Watch the skies, as the tag-line of that 50s ufology film had it: hey isn't there a NEW STAR now a-borning from some far-flung nebula? Of all the plates in Blake's long-poems isn't the finest one that of LUCIFER seen from behind—seeing HIS behind like the Lord God showed Moses according to the bible when Moishe went up the mountain to see what he could see of his maker? These are two instances of butt—of man-cave or man-pussy, whatever term you like—and aren't these sort of hints—hints about the LUCIFERIAN, that is to say LOSER, mentality promoting a new spirituality? I guess!!

But where should we look to discover this regnant new star—where in the era of what's been used up, physically, mentally, and in every other way? Occluded by its dark like any exoplanet unless discerned by space-telescopes tracking such dark planets only by the registration perceived in the planetary SUN's slight and momentary oscillation as it, this dark planet, transits otherwise unperceivable. This is what I'm telling you. Reformist queen beat writers excluded (Ginsberg, Burroughs et al.) what's there to see, what's remaining on the horizon of our expectations and desires other than the ones, the writers, the other selves of us—who LOSE! Like John Wieners, Jack Spicer, babe? As the Harmony of Difference and Unity (zen/chan chant often chanted still today in zendos despite its great antiquity going way back to Tang!) puts it so excitedly (to me) when talking about a dark LIGHT, a sheer luminescence that happens, just happens mind you, to be . . . occluded dark. That's what's going on here. With queen beat losers who looked to spirituality in the dark of losing, as we do now—we can at last trace our lineage, can't we? Isn't DOWN the new UP and vice versa UP the new DOWN to you—and me? There's a big hole on the horizon if you take the trouble to look up at the nighttime sky some time and if you can get thru the smog to see at all—then, duh! Isn't that a big hole to nothing up there that's our future—I mean mine, of course, but yours too especially since I'll probably be dead by the time you read this and the future will have lost its meaning (LOST!) to me—and isn't it yours alone to deal with? Future: is it JUST climate change and science deniers and religious evangelical nuts and invaders from outer space—JUST that? I don't think so!

How about an example. Despite the perception of SPICER's misogyny—partly justified no doubt but surely also a bum rap generated from his rant against Denise Levertov—and given WIENERS' contrasting feminine identifications, is it conceivable to think that these dark stars who are so present to other masochist-spiritual fag writers seem to reach all the way to the likes of DODIE BELLAMY today? Just asking. My mom used to tell me where there's smoke there's fire. But hell, how do I know—was mom wrong? In the hippie days Levertov showed up at a beat reading wearing white gloves and a lady-like outfit amid the hundreds of hang-loose hippies marveling at her on the stage until, imagine our surprise, with the appearance of a guy bopping up and down the aisle toward Denise in a clown suit calling himself the People's Prick, there emerged a scream from Denise that seemed to confirm her lady-likeness. Was it this that Spicer was really aiming at I wonder? That was then, this is now: you decide.

The sex-spiritual homo-radicals of the WIENERS-type are true losers. What did Wieners get in his lifetime? Recognition? Hardly (except among a small cognoscenti MAYBE). Money? Ha! Celebrity? Double up on those haw-haws because outside that cognoscenti, who?

There was one time when Wieners at least seemed at FIRST to be a celebrity. It was in 1990 at the Victoria Theater in San Francisco and after Wieners read his poems, Kevin Killian interviewed him on stage. "John who do you think of as the most important influence on yr writing?," he asked,—and John, totally serious, says "the Virgin Mary" and everyone burst into a hilarity of laughter reducing John completely to this stupid piece of shit, as if he were a demented moron. I kid you not. I was there. After that, nothing but losing. On to more poverty, aloneness in old age, loss of everything, death without achieving recognition at all. Talk about SPIRITUALITY!!! (And I could double up on this if there was space enough for twice as many exclamation points—but you know, time's winged chariot and all . . .)

Degenerate breakdowns in other words are the key to this dark spirituality still coming more fully to be present. It will take new forms, y'all. So get ready. There's a death star headed our (your) way. Are you ready for it—in your writing at least—in the new forms you'll build to accommodate this? You'll have to junk present (past) influences: not just the Beats but New Narrative, Language Poetry and whatever it is you want to call what's going on now. Think: breakdown. Then you'll have it. New texts yet to be determined wherein spirituality depends solely on LOSING—huh? I won't be here to help! You'll have to discover all this yo-sefs. I mean obviously—not enough to be a degenerate loser. More's required. What about all those still-to-be-discovered loser-FORMS of what you write? Yo!

To redefine a terrain in other words: not Beats, but a (non-)future. If I were to do your thinking for you for a second I'd say there'll be a lot of looking into non-dualist categories like the GLOSSOLALIA of SPICER and WIENERS when considered not as aberrant but as constituent, like the A E EI O OU (the seven Greek vowels, the seven planets) that occurred in a sketchy fashion to SPICER and BLASER for instance (look 'em up yo'sef). Oooohs and aaahs are not necessarily onomatopoetic but incantatory in a frankly LOVECRAFTIAN spirit if you ask me—and if you are still reading this you HAVE asked me, right? I guess! This implies from quantum physics the notion of periodicity paralleling more ancient Vedic concepts of spreading waves of darkness-light for instance. If once perceived around the head as a nimbus can they not also be spread out—a non-local, as they say in quantum, electro-magnetic probability wave that redefines luminescent darkness as the essential (non-)being of infinite potentialities existing everywhere and nowhere at this time and all times, until, that is, locked down so to speak by the gaze of a viewer/reader thereby causing, by this gaze I mean, the utter and total collapse of the wave into the registration of a particle on the photographic paper meant to track its collapse from everything and nothing into a banality called THIS PARTICULAR EXISTING NOW only in this specific space and time. Get it? Will your new poetries be up to this? It is not sheer nothing— but the ability to, as probability waves do, ECHO, BE PERIODIC. Like someone tossing a pebble into the pond and seeing the waves expanding out: that's what I mean. Do you too? Will you if you don't yet? Can you still? Figure it out.

Spreading waves in verse—neurons misfire in loser-crazy WIENERS's head and voila you've got your above-mentioned GLOSSOLALIA don't you? I got it anyway. You too? To let in the Holy Spirit as is well known you've got to cause some kind of radical breakdown. Take Kaufmann in North Beach during the Beat era, for another example. He didn't give a shit—just threw all his finished poems on the carpet and there, truly, wouldn't BE any KAUFMAN left for us if it hadn't been for his wife who decided to save them for posterity by picking up after KAUFMAN's clear determination to LOSE them. Get it? Another glossolalia adventure—that misfired though. She should have left them alone, shouldn't she have? But it wasn't exactly her fault, I imagine, but the fault of the totalitarian sexism/misogyny of the period that relegated a very intelligent creative woman to the role of care-taking for a flaky man: remember Valerie Solanas in the late 60s saying that there isn't an intelligent capable woman who wouldn't think twice about sticking a shiv into the first man that came her way?

GLOSSOLALIA is nothing more than the seven vowels. Vowels are defined in linguistics as openings (consonants are not), which is why Gnostics think to equate them with the seven holes in the sphere above that go by the name PLANETS but are really the piercings of the shells surrounding this earth that when pierced allow the brilliant LIGHT of . . . what? . . . godhead, eternity, probability waves to shine thru, each shell built up around this earth by giving the correct password to the archon guarding that hole, or gate as we might also call it, and they rhyme from smaller (initial, in eternity, as in Plotinus's explanation) to constantly expanding bigger sounds. Woooooo! Wooooooooooooooooooo! Wooooo ooooooooooooooooooooooooooooooooo! Like that. You get it now, don't you? KAUFMAN didn't put this into words but after having his brains fried a few times I think he must have sensed the openings thru which his vowel-like oscillation circles spread.

The result of all this (go re-read if you haven't got it all the way yet) is obviously GLAMOUR. I personally went on the death-trail of a real loser in life, Valerie Solanas, after she died and nobody in the newspapers seemed to know anything about how, except that this all took place somewhere in San

Francisco didn't it? I said to myself: Bruce, let's go down to the HEALTH DEPT cause that's where the death records are. What do you think? I go. Get her certificate with last known address on it. And wouldn't you know it's in the deepest depths of the Tenderloin—the pit of all pits—in a hotel that's the very bottom of any abyss within an abyss you can think of. I proceed to the front desk where the manager is uninterested in my queries about Valerie. But just from good luck and the power of shining negativity there happens, mind you, to be these three whores sitting on the broken naugahyde sofa. They're cute and I chat them up. It's like talking with a few nice gay boys. "Oh so she was FAMOUS?" they ask . . . "Uh huh," I go. "Well, would you ever know? Out hooking every night like that?" And I go, "Really?" (I mean the girl did truly hate men!) Yaaas. She had to find some way to pay for her meth habit didn't she? You bet, I get it, yes, Bruce thinks to hisself. Then he asks the rent-girls about how she looked. Rent-girls: "Oh fabulous, you know speed really helps you cut down on the weight and all and . . . ," (pause, as if a little reluctant to reveal the heart of the mystery) ". . . she looked so damn good in that SILVER LAME dress that she always wore for hooking!" "Tell me!" And they do.

The story emerges of a dark dark end, of poverty, meth-addiction, giving up all her honorable ideals of giving the shiv to all men, only to be driven to the very opposite, of serving them instead. In my mind Valerie shines in GLAMOUR, pure shining luminescent dark nihilism. She lost everything, to become for us a shining nighttime star that shows the way for all our future writing? No? Think of it. Silver lame!!! Talk about the midnight sun, y'all. She was it, like you could be too.

Or the painter JEROME. He's probably been forgotten about now but he was the best thing in painting to come down the pike in decades— and living here in San Francisco, where for some reason he used to cruise me at the HOLE IN THE WALL, probably the sleaziest bar that ever existed, where you could see homos in the bathroom, just a long urinal and that's all, and at the end of that there'd always be some homo waiting for some dude to point his junk at the dude's mouth and spritz out a golden shower. I'm telling you, SLEAZE ALLEY. That's where JEROME hung. Sometimes in ripped fishnets. Sometimes just skuzzy all over. He was my hero. A homo hero of negative shining dark spirituality. I loved him with all my heart and isn't it thru HIS lenses as well as WIENERS' that we ought to be looking at the comet of the future (and yo bitch, it ain't HALE BOPP!). Comet means hair in Greek, a long tail of it as it streams on by shedding its light in the dark—that is what we, you, have to look forward too isn't it? Fess up now. It IS isn't it? Yes is the correct answer I think. Yes yes yes.

Back to the B.V.M. (Blessed Virgin Mary—to you) and JOHN being interviewed on stage at the Victoria Theater in the Mission. She gave John messages. He transmitted them into vowels and sang their ever expanding circles to us, after originating in the outermost shell and spreading as they would, and could, and should, violently penetrating new holes in the shells of stars surrounding us—or giving the AEEIOOU inflections to the archon gatekeepers as they plunged across a sky, in truth never more brilliant for a plunge into their non-being. The rebarbative audience-cynicism of that laughter then—has it not undergone a sea-change into a respect for the GLAMOUR of SPIRITUAL LOSERS like JOHN? I mean what planet are you on if you do not yourself now experience the expansive influences of the B.V.M? Perversion is the gate. The finger that now writes, does it not— also is raised in silent homage to what is above whispering, to explain to you, HA SHEM! Glamour from the name. Glamour from the B.V.M. It is SO spiritual. It is plunging, like a comet! And that's why deluded ones like the HEAVEN'S GATE persons of that time took kool-aid and a quarter to reach it if they could—as corpses.

So now we come to ultimates. The ultimates of spiritual-negative-future writing. Tangentially in WIENERS, almost in BOB KAUFMAN. In new writerly forms must it not be? Of silence. Nothingness. The future writer can only be a failed writer, a non-celebrity, a failure even in the sense of being a writer only by not-writing. Spirituality of this new era, and you will soon be in it. A FOXY ROXY of derision will be your only thread to hang on if you wish to be true to the coming non-existence that will shortly hold sway among us in forms still unknown—except as adumbrated above. Writing will have to become an immensely chemically powerful and intoxicating self-destruction (think 99% pure crystal meth) such as will hasten the onset of a glamourous spirituality with the shiv to be applied to oneself. Silent SCREAMING, a new set of vocables to use as its basis.

There are hallucinatory conclusions. Tho any less real? A mandate has gone out from the Shah of Shahs: requiring the modeling of poetry on the model and meth-scale of trailer-trash. If you can't cook 99% pure negativity then try again and just quit. Quit writing. That's your only real goal for a foreseeable future, isn't it? As crude and effective as a yawn—this dark. As unreflected as the corner drug dealer of spirits—there are no more words such as you used to know but only yowls now. And the yowls are all vowels—that is, passages.

I am exhausted. I myself can write no more—ever. This is the last. Failure. Spiritual grandeur. My nothingness. None of these can be separated from you. The coal mine's canary. Is me. Grace abounding to all that pitch their tent in nothingness.

Cut off now from the PENIS. Since Valerie. Cut off from our female masculinities and our male ones, powerless. And yet—how can this be? In the discarded and degraded member lying in the dreck, can the HOLE not be seen where we escape to otherness, the only eye of god at the end of this penis we'll see thru in the future? Boy howdy!—as Jamie used to say. Future writers, peep thru THIS hole because it is the only true spiritual eye left—it is the eye of a true cunt—she who retains only an eyehole to see thru while the instrumentality of it lies in the dust, *vorbeigegangen*. This is the true disintegration of the world you await, as should you not? The fulfillment of BOB KAUFMAN's plural electroshocks into true neuronal transformation by way of LOSS. He lost his balls, he lost his prick—to become a cunt, not a true one but the best imitation possible— thru the shiv employed so effectively by Valerie. Reduced to a vowel, an opening—to all other non-worlds that exist or don't, faithful to the coming non-existence of the world. That hole in the dead penis is God's eye closing—and soon we won't be seeing at all. The only luminescence is electroshock.

This can be taken up and qualified of course. But do you want to? Those QUEEN BEATS showed the way, in all the emasculation you can be capable of if you truly wish it. And, writers of the future—DO you, do you in fact, do you REALLY wish it? This is up to you of course. Cunts of both sexes such as we are. The glory of being losers shining inward but not outward like that of real men.

Here I would just add another premonitory note, a celestial hints it and holds in the skies. Look up when you read these words from the poet who spoke them to embrace his eradication: he has become a cunt not just in memory like any "negro" or fag of the 50s but a blazoning unrequited gift in mantic oracular intuitions *avant la lettre*: say the words with me, please!

> She dwells with Beauty—Beauty that must die;
>   And Joy, whose hand is ever at his lips
> Bidding adieu; and aching Pleasure nigh,
>   Turning to poison while the bee-mouth sips:
> Ay, in the very temple of Delight
>   Veil'd Melancholy has her sovran shrine,
>   Though seen of none save him whose strenuous tongue
> Can burst Joy's grape against his palate fine;
>   His soul shalt taste the sadness of her might,
>   And be among her cloudy trophies hung.

The banner to be raised, the far-foreseen future embraced in this. What more? The time even for str8 men to become cadet cunts alongside the superwomen of the future who write in nothingness their vowel openings and luminescence of coming night. As Keats. Themselves now cocksuckers as the QUEEN BEATS themselves. What more? New political writing of the nothingness that makes sacred—in loss—in losers. That writing of vowels, future apertures of future nothing. A cocksucker-becoming-cunt now. Hellmouth, said Beverly Dahlen instead of cunt. A hole, whole oncoming nothingness. Dejection. Kink. The glory of spirit arriving in the lowliest. A world of light.

$E=mc^2$, what does that mean? That only a smallest particle of matter or body explodes by exponential magnitude that bursts into spirit light you can become. M for matter, in being destroyed. E the explosion's spiritual brilliance no longer imprisoned and in the splendor of a million suns transforming the dark of a previously material universe into the infinitely light future of only spiritual energy—unfulfilled drifting pure and non-local probability waves again as we all once is, again being—that holograph of pure empty mind existent in light alone.

You may be thinking, Where is JAY DEFEO in all this falling-apart-ness?

The decadence of the body exposed to its unrecognized life begins to shine thru. There is a rose. That is, there is a cunt. The cunt (as per Ms. Solanas) begins to fall apart from both the weight it carries and the weight ascribed to it by pussy-envious men. There remains the non-recognition of men of this fact. Instead men, men with balls, not men-cunts, project from a pussy-envy that leaves them yearning for womanhood to take counter-measures: the traditional male iron-clad but rusting armaments of macho, the definition of a strength they in fact lack, the attempt by posturing competency to deny the greater calmer more rational multi-tasking competence of a proud and coolly competent woman, or cunt, a real cunt they attempt to appropriate for themselves.

Thus a painting of a rose, "The Rose," the most heavily impastoed painting ever made, with a thickness defying the laws of gravity, must impress the viewer with the inevitability of its crumbling. It is a crumbling cunt. It deconstructs the illusion of timelessness by its all too apparent declension thru time—its degradation. A prick on the other hand, that is, a man with balls, attempts in reification to stop the flow of time in the constructed armor of what he considers his impermeable and non-changing exterior—supposing nonetheless all the while that this false consciousness constructed thru his pussy-envy is a womanly attribute, one that he can freely appropriate—and does—while falsely so thinking. Falsely because by definition in its passage thru time all matter disintegrates. Does he not realize this? He kids himself. He games himself into thinking that decay—as in the inevitable decay of the painting called "The Rose"—can be resisted. As the passage of matter thru time failed to imply permanence rather than the impermanence he attributes both to art and to himself. He cannot stand the odor of decay.

Thus too he cannot stand what Jack Spicer called the smell of faggot vomit, the puke of ball-less men on the floor of the lavatory which rather than being some magical suspension of the laws of nature—is rather a most vivid illustration of those very laws understood with the realism of the senses rather than with some abstract but illusory conception of the passage of time: whose most vivid realization is in the realm of the senses, in

the repugnance generated by the smell, sight, and touch—of decay.
The Queen Beats join hands over "The Rose."

May this work of mine turn all FALSE MEN, or pricks, into the cunts that inside themselves they most truly attempt to appropriate without being willing to imitate. RABBI JOSEPH BEN SHALOM OF BARCELONA: at each moment a thing's status is altered and for a fleeting moment the mystical abyss of nothingness is crossed and becomes visible. This however will never be done without the acceptance of a masochism that lasers thru the myriad deceptions contrived and constructed by the world of men as we currently know it. And them!

"Queen Beats" was first presented at the Queer Beats Conference, which took place at the San Francisco Art Institute on Nov 17, 1997, presented by the Harvey Milk Institute in conjunction with the Poetry Center at San Francisco State University. "Queen Beats" was revised for this volume, where it appears in print for the first time.

H.D.'S WRITING:
HERSELF A GHOST

I wonder: what did H.D. think at night? Debatable answers require debatable questions, don't they? The value of predictions is their openness, isn't it—she thinks. So every disappearance's appearance then—she ponders in her bedroom. What appears—is based on *nothing at all* then? Hmmmmm. Otherworldly H.D. considers she's opposed by unnamed enemies for not putting her shoulder to the wheel—for not making of her writings, which they call scribblings, something useful. These cast-offs are claimed with a vengeance. Pearls are made from such irritating stimulants and in *Trilogy*—of these writings—she says we

> take them with us
> beyond death; Mercury, Hermes, Thoth
> invented the script, letters, palette

born as we are—beyond. Does faith, for instance, overcome illusions by disputing them?

Do you believe you're dead when you're dead? Far from it! she'd answer—returning from Egyptian Karnak to London, presenting in exclamatory haste her great discovery to her friend Pearson—London *is* Karnak—you know? Meaning partly the Blitz is going on outside her window. When a roof falls down on you in London, this *reveals* something (think of Virginia Woolf resolving on, successfully attempting suicide because of an intuition that comes to her: this is WWI all over again!). And when ruins come to light in the sand—that's when you *know* something. And this becomes a fable of permissiveness of death, loss, and what Bataille would call *perte:*

> there, as here, ruin opens
> the tomb, the temple; enter,
> there as here, there are no doors

Negative vampires emerge from the tomb in front of H.D.'s mystical wish that meaning exist where none is or *can be...*

So is this an experience of a *beyond* shining like the cold hard light that glances off the text-body of Bataille then? Hardly. Living and dancing on tombs in their giddiness and sheer *frilliness*, H.D.'s vampires unlike Bataille's have the appearance of *omens*. Necromancers, for then the present talks only of a *future* that

> connects us
> with the drowned cities of pre-history

Experience means the present for the French author. For her, a glistening *goal*!

The brightness of it proportionately excludes any clarity—the intensity and imprecision going together. Kaspar's alternatives and the end of *Trilogy* as arbitrary and luminous to him as to us reading H.D.'s account of this X decades later. He sees a blank, fits what he wishes there—reads what he wants never being able to get really clear on the idea he's experiencing, whether what he feels is

> a sort of spiritual optical-illusion
> or whether he looks down the deep deep-well
> of the so-far unknown
> depth

of things, whatever is. The future's tea leaves are left for us at the bottom of the cup. Has H.D. then given us permission to see in her lines whatever's there *for us*? Wasted surface of nuclear-holocaust planet, empty holes that used to be ozone layers once upon a time, green slime that they say in yesteryear might have been strong Amazon liana jungle vines from them, those who lived in that time then . . . ?

And *Helen in Egypt* is what I call her most *I Ching*-type book of them all, because going furthest in its ability to provide wherewithal for those looking in to make their own forecasts. The ghost lines initiating this *oeuvre* only let out their spiritual quality or ghostliness in parentheses as a taunt in the guise of an uncalled-for confidence we're surely not taken in by when they sweetly urge—

Do not despair, the hosts
surging beneath the Walls
(no more than I) are ghosts

as if that hollow *emptiness* the parentheses encloses and entombs might
be given the right conditions and *for us?*—rise again? And now since
Helen's ghost-writer is herself a ghost, as she foresaw, will this emptiness be
contagious? Will those who read these words of mine when I'm dead one
day empty *them* of meaning I intend for them—in a fairness proportional
to me—as I've done with *her?*

(For Kevin and Dodie, ghost-aspirer like me)

"H.D.'s Writing: Herself A Ghost" first appeared in *Sagetrieb,* vol. 6 no. 2 (Fall 1987).

BEVERLY DAHLEN

It's been some decades since I first met Bev Dahlen. There we were on the sidewalk ignoring the rain and drenched to the bone as a storm broke around us. I can't recall any of the topics, only the amazing vital energy we had in conversation together. Finally we noticed and realized: we need to be out of the rain. Should we try Bob Glück who lived nearby? We should and we did. These were post-hippie days so people still did things unannounced. We received shelter and dry clothing from Bob, who also cooked for us, as if a matter of course. And he listened, as two of his friends had just made their first significant encounter. That's how things began for me. Personally.

Bev was nearing the end of her boho period and drenched by the rain. Did she seem a bit impoverished, or bag-lady-ish? So be it. Her grouchiness became her, it kept her grounded. It contained both the wit and brilliance that makes them so common-sense. And full of compassion.

Were these misapprehensions? Yes and no. Intellectualism is one side. The sky-side you might say. Or transcendence. The other was the impoverishment that grounds it. Through this world I used Bev to help me enter the other, while remaining a citizen of this one. That was certainly one of Blake's aspirations, and Flannery O'Connor's, too. Bev is in good company. To demand that the ecstatic sky-glories of one world remain simply the flip side of the impoverishment of our own world. One grows out of the other—as the other grows out of this. Osiris grows in the dark as Bev shows in her Egyptian poems, just as in decline that light produces dark, with wrath making up the good measure that a sense of justice always calls for.

Here I'll fast forward a bit. At a reading a couple of years ago, I applied to her *Eighteen Sonnets* the word "dyspeptic." She giggled at that. Because of the strangeness of this Dr. Johnson kind of word, or because it somehow hit the target?

The dreary homecoming. Going home from her job teaching newcomers, Bev inevitably took the Mission Street bus. What a bleak postindustrial landscape can be revealed there! What calls out for a whole inventory of smaller darknesses: dyspeptic ramblings and mutterings.

The protagonist and narrator of these sonnets, by the light of slightly vatic intuitions, calls things as she sees them. Protest against this world is inevitable, necessary. To reach the other world you must rant, and rant against the spiritual archons responsible for such urban desolation. There are "hell-streets" with clear resonance that traverse both Bev's sonnets and her writing in general.

This is really the opposite of Gregory Corso ending one of his poems with the following: "Life—the Big Lie!" If you can't laugh like that, what can you do? It always sends me personally into howls of laughter. The problem with vaticism then is the issue of how not to get trapped in a non-relation of this world and the other. Yes, this world is truly a place of desolation. But to the vatic soul, like Bev's, this opens on another that, while other, coincides with it. It is not separate.

I mentioned the connection with O'Connor. Between the vatic urbanism of Bev and the rural impoverishment of Flannery O'Connor, there is something familiar. The red raw hills of the beginning of stories and the violence of endings landscaped with the jagged line of pines in many of O'Connor's stories are the moral equivalent of Bev's more urban landscape. The transcendence of the other world is this world's immanence. Only starting by using scraps of paper, words from the Mission Street gutter, vatic comes to mean the way the dirty and the ecstatic coincide.

Hence, the *Egyptian Poems*. The primary statement of the Other World in Bev's writing—Dendor and Luxor, the Book of the Dead—and this made physically beautiful by a choice of papers, scraps of gold leaf, fine typesetting. Instead of Mission Street looking up at it, it is looking down at Mission Street. Neither denying either. Neither being separate from the other, yet also not identical.

Bev uses Gnosticism as a set of usages both of content, or teaching, and of form, or technique. Helen only seems to remain at Troy while in actuality her real body remains in Egypt. You might compare, though Bev doesn't, the two Jesuses of the Gnostic tradition. A fake Jesus, a Jesus appearance, is nailed to the cross and this nothingness dies an agonizing death. While the true Jesus hovering above like a bird of prey, laughs at the masses' credulity. But can the true Jesus and the false one be entirely separated? This is the question I'd put in Bev's mouth, if she'd let me.

To hold together two divergent realities in the same place and time, with neither superseding either. Flaubert will have none of this—it is either/or or neither/nor, but not both/and. When the deluded old woman while dying sees her parrot as the Holy Spirit, for Flaubert the bird must be either just a bird, and if the Holy Spirit, then just the Holy Spirit. Bev undertakes a battle in her poetry against this kind of dualism.

All this is a footnote to *A Reading*, Bev's great work. I wanted to mention some of the sometimes forgotten qualities of the poems that make up these books: snippets of conversations, words of a bag lady, complaints against a dehumanizing desolation around her. But the ability to see beyond the present and the here and now into something more human that awaits us is vatic. And that is the Bev I first saw working her way through ancient Egypt with its hierarchical sense.

Bev writes in hierarches: like the real Helen snatched away in H.D. to another place while only a phantom remains to be called by her name. This is the ability to see thru the impoverished reality you confront daily to a mystical, greater one. Something of this sense of a replacement of the present postindustrial dreariness is transcended, glows with the reality that real being always has, and has had in poetry at least since Blake.

It's not that I want to say that *A Reading* is somehow like the *Sonnets*. Or that they can be said to be like the *Egyptian Poems*, in luxury. That goes too far. The technique can vary. I'll give one example here. The way the *Egyptian Poems* coincide with the ascent visions of Nag Hammadi Gnosticism. There is a great deal of prominence given to the technical tool of question and answer. Bev will pose a question, for instance, followed by "Explain this," or "Explain it." A Gnostic candidate reaches the Keeper of Gates (Bev retains the word "keeper" as she does "watcher") and before progressing further must answer questions. "Who are you?" "I am a child of starry heaven," reads one of these ancient questions that ultimately is found on one of the gold plates of Pythagorean mysticism. There are other examples, but I don't have time. Clearly, Bev has read her Robert Duncan!

Yet it is something that can only be whispered, or grumbled, and that is where the vatic poet and the bag lady become the same. She sees what the rest of us don't, while remaining only too aware of the degradation around us all the same. The gold leaf on the *The Egyptian Poems* seemed to say it all, a luxury product with fine paper and fine typesetting. The Trojan War has whisked the real Helen away just as the violence and poverty of this world whisk away the other: and yet—there must be connections mustn't there? Who is to say them?

Or the way little wisps and bits and snatches of muttered conversations make their way through *A Reading* like a sample book of the dead: sayings from this world seen by the seer, luxury palaces and temples you must wander into to see. And Bev does.

We all become bag ladies by doing this. The woman who comes out with the bedeckings of a Pharaoh, whip in hand, cobra at the top of the head is not the woman we see: that one is different. She is in fact the muttering, impoverished lady about to exit or enter a bus going up Mission Street. Bev's poetry stretches between the two, and brings them together. It's a text made of the weft and woof connecting the two world systems we live in.

Is this how Bev wants you to read her *A Reading*? It may not be her choice to decide this. The poet starts with the heavens or the earth. And it is they, the two aspects of our existence, and they alone that can decide how a book is read, or how in another time and another place it will be read differently.

In reading *A Reading* you may find yourself flip-flopping from one of these two sides to the other. There are too many other things to be said about *A Reading*. Just take this as a footnote, one that may or may not help illuminate for you the phrases and conversations, the apparent lacks of connection, the strong but invisible thread of thought in Bev Dahlen's writing that takes us from the deep abyss up to the sacred transcendent Egypt, and maybe back again. The impoverished and the profane become illuminated Blakean glories of a heaven seen by the seer alone, the prophetess in her cave at Cumae, whose books prophecied Rome's futures.

(Do you remember Bev's great Hellmouth essay? It must have shocked some feminists when it appeared. Out of this darkness—by now a familiar dynamic—comes light, but less familiar—from that light, the dark again. In the essay, Bev goes about her business with a frankness that seemed to many at the time as obscene.)

The personal: the image of a woman carrying her cane and moving slowly along the sidewalk. How many times have she and I met to chat, to sit on a bench, to spend an afternoon at an art show, or, instead of writing to each other now, telephoning or emailing. This is my personal context, the context I use to create my own Bev Dahlen.

A context is not a text, though each will condition the other. Will this writing of mine be yours too, the one you create?

Bev has been a friend and a teacher both. Her great contribution—a zen contribution—has been to help bridge that western dualism, an effort like that of Georges Bataille after WWII. Bev has made that dualism a little less lop-sided than it might have been, I think. I write in praise today of my teacher and my friend and in praise of writing that influenced so many.

I offer this in celebration of a woman I have known for an eternity: as a woman and as a poet. I can't separate the two. And don't want to. This instead will be just my memories of a woman and poet who have meant a great deal for me. As I hope they have for you too. I hope my friend's words will long continue, often change, and always provide the lighting I need to continue to read her.

"Beverley Dahlen" was first presented as a talk at A Beverly Dahlen Reading & Tribute December 8, 2008, sponsored by Small Press Traffic, held at Timkin Hall, at California College of the Arts in San Francisco.

STEVE

First a white boy growing up. Then a white man, all grown up. That was Steve. And now in death he's white ashes. Such a white person, he was. So ghostly, he was. Us white people: ghosts, who have forgotten our bodies, tied a string around our fingers trying trying trying to remember. Steve was more this way than anyone—anyone who I can think of.

Strangely I mostly remember him nagging. Isn't that strange? I liked him a lot. People rarely admit that they like it when people nag them—it means they think a lot of you somehow just the same—doesn't it? Over my shoulder now, I sense Steve there, telling me: Bruce you have to be sure to give me credit, all the credit I deserve, Bruce. He wanted that and that's what I'll do in this story—for him.

Did I say ghostly, he was ghostly? You know how it is when a person dies: tick tock, time keeps going by though there's something bothering you—nagging even can I say?—but what, exactly—what? It eats at you: ghosts all want something and you don't know what it is. But how can I tell now—considering where he is, or isn't—exactly what it is he wants. I'm going to use this essay to try to figure out what.

I can feel his presence, and there's a picture of him above this computer—he's somewhere in France in front of what looks to be a cathedral, wearing his Levi's jacket, underneath it a pink pink shirt: political in death as he was in life. I will tell you now a little bit about what I know about his life.

First what I know about his Nebraska boyhood: He had a dog named Spot. This would remain a source of the infinite pleasures of mean-spirited laughter among us. Imagine. The name of a pet that sounds like it comes from a third grade reader. We would double over with laughter at this. The other side of this—Steve's innocence—somehow escaped us. Did it escape the other friends? Where he is, he doesn't care if I remember he was born in Nebraska. Strike that. Or that growing up he had a dog named Spot, a fact we laughed at. What was more risible to us big-city sophisticates than someone naming their childhood dog Spot?

In other words wasn't there something about Steve that would make you want to be careful with him, so you wouldn't bruise him, hurt him? He was so very vulnerable. You could say, for instance, that all the doorways to his soul were always open, and you could so easily just walk in—into the little prairie house of his soul, and I guess Steve's friends must have felt to Steve like those horrible murderers in Kansas, that author Truman Capote used to write about, the serial killers. Except for Steve this wasn't about the murder of the body but of the soul. You could have trapped that thing in Steve as easily as you or I would bird-lime a twig! Soul murder, a terrible thing! And it was up to you to restrain your hand so you didn't commit that awful deed against Steve. Didn't you stay your own hand from such a thing? You had to nurture Steve because what was the alternative, torturing him?

He was so easy to make fun of, for instance. It was—and isn't this unusual in the life of a writer?—as if Steve hadn't any natural defenses of any sort. Life kept hurting him, over and over, and he kept accepting that hurt. Was he a masochist then? Oh probably not. I just think of it as genetic, you know, a DNA type thing: The pores of his cells would open wide naturally, welcome whatever foreign or alien thing decided it wanted to pass across the threshold of him! This is my prayer now for him: oh naughty world, at least now can you not keep yourself at bay from this little lamb of yours, now that he's gone anyway? Or can the long hand of the world even reach where Steve now is? Who knows.

He was a teacher. Not formally, though he did have a bit of formal training to be sure. He would discover the most recherché things, rare books just translated from France, and show you their marvels: he introduced people to higher stages of learning through the strange books he was always reading—and passing on. About this he was almost careless, or as I said vulnerable. He made use of outdated slang, for instance his hippie-period talk, almost as if without noticing that this was what he was doing. He was always talking, long after you stopped listening.

He used to ask me to write about him when he was dead and I always agreed, and at last here I am complying—Steve would be proud of me! He wanted me to credit him with introducing me to the study of Georges Bataille, a French philosopher, someone whose books I later translated. In his hippie-esque way he would urge, "Bruce, I turned you on to Bataille!"— after I had just begun reading the French writer. He wanted credit just for reading this author: how much more would he want credit if I've now gone on to translate the man? Oh Steve! Oh humanity! Oh Bruce!

"Bruce, I turned you on . . . " Which of us even then would have resorted to that hippie phrase as a locution without appropriate quote-marks around it, as a usual way to put things? As I told you, we—we others—we were sophisticates. And Steve? Like I said, a lamb, a baby lamb. A white baby lamb. As with the others, so with me, he saw a need I could surely fill and he wanted me to realize my possibilities in life. He thought in translating this philosopher I would do myself proud. (Whether I did or didn't isn't my decision—it's up to you now). "Bataille is an important writer, Bruce!" Steve was very solicitous of you, he wanted you very much to succeed. He pushed and prodded you into doing just that.

He was both maternal and childish. He took good motherly care of his friends when they were there, as friends, though toward the end didn't they diminish in number as Steve more and more counted as friends only young boys? You could say that, I think. Being a teenager, being immature, Steve loved the immature, he loved those in their teens. He was, as I say, both maternal and childish. The maternal part would invite you to dinner if it thought you were depressed—just to cheer you up. The childish in him competed with his own daughter, and for the same sexual partners! Childish indeed. She would bring home her boy-friends, and he would interest them in talking books with him. He'd pick out an exciting new book, then start talking. And talking. Until ending in bed with his new listener. And as if sex were but a side thing and it was books that was the issue. Was this a pretense? No, it was just Steve, a strange undersea creature of new species only recently discovered—a glowing phosphorescent spiny thing with feathery tentacles whose sole purpose was pulling you in to his soul to stave off the awful loneliness of life that he experienced as its principle feature. He sought sex partners as he sought intellectuals: they made him feel less lonely. Helping people made him feel less lonely too. Besides introducing me to the glories of Bataille, Steve wrote an article in the local newspaper that made me curious about a local zen teacher, and later it made me take up zen meditation and gave me the spiritual practice I had been longing for for so long. Steve was maternal as I say.

I've mentioned only a couple of Steve's childishnesses. I now mention another. He gave his daughter the education he himself had always wanted: he put her through the local French School, a tony downtown establishment that catered to the elite. And so, through her, his daughter, he accomplished a goal he otherwise had failed at—he too began to speak French.

He avoided open conflict, preferring the feline—and sometimes feral—ways of women. He had sex, not just with boys, but with women too because after all he liked them too didn't he? He loved them as he had loved his wife. As he had loved her as a hippie bisexual in love with everything once, everything at least that didn't remind you of Nebraska. Everything came from his home. He was escaping the palor of whiteness of his childhood, of the bleached out existence of the empty city streets of the nearly empty state of Nebraska. He let this boyhood go—while holding onto it with a string so it floated above him somehow, no longer harming him, but like the tight little balloon that could, drifting far above to heaven.

His days floated by as from the bay window of his Haight-Ashbury flat. He watched them langorously. He watched the whole world from his window. As he watched life go by, he wrote about it from his sequestered couch, never forgetting his primary duty: to nourish. Even when he dragged in teen boys from off the street, he wouldn't just use them but had to make sure to feed, bathe, even play with them. And that was the origin, ultimately, of Steve's seroconversion to HIV eventually, and too, of his final struggle, his death. For, in the image of child with child, Steve and the young man would shoot up together, bringing in with methamphetamine of course the specter of AIDS too. And finally, this became not just the specter for Steve, but the reality itself. Was it even what he wanted? The world hadn't recognized him and his writing as he had hoped. Why not just take leave?

This doesn't mean he didn't feel guilty about the meth though. He told me of a terrible meth run ending with his, Steve's, visibly seeing a giant pale-veined and greenish insectoid thing slowing flapping six translucent green wings at him from across the room behind an armchair, with a skull-grin. Meant for Steve. It was, as Steve said, that he recognized even then the sign of his coming death.

There was something very strange in what happened next. A kind of postmodernist experience of virtual reality, a kind of experience of the priority of sign over signified.

As it happened, Kush, a filmmaker friend of Steve's, had made a tape of a talk of Steve's, or a long monologue, I should say, a talk done another time, one we just happened one day to be watching on Steve's couch together. One Steve was beside me, another is the talking head on a TV monitor now, together looking at the tape of a rambling and quite incoherent talk. What would be the relationship when the present Steve was dead but visually anyway left only in this movie. Which would be Steve?

Then Steve told me something else, a bit ghostly. He said, Bruce when you watch this after my death, think of me, think of me watching my own image on the screen before I died—all right? That seemed to give Steve immortality, sort of, I guess.

He wrote a number of books. A few of them were good—SKINNY TRIP TO A FAR PLACE after Bashō and LIVES OF THE POETS, a small book of selected quotes from the births and the deaths of poets. He also wrote several quick potboilers. And he wrote criticism, though not very well, and a column in the local gay-community newspaper. This was his literary output.

Dying he got a priest sent to him from his parents all the way back in Nebraska. Despite that Steve already told them about being a Buddhist. So our zen temple took him in and he was one of the first Maitri patients. I'd go see him every so often. So would Phil Whalen, though not so often.

One evening I received a call—from hospice. Come soon if you want to see your friend, they said. I quickly walked the two blocks to the hospice next to the temple to see Steve before the end.

When I was about to get up from my chair and leave for the night, the nurse checked his vitals. Steve's breathing had slowed considerably. The nurse looked up, our direction—"a breath every 45 seconds," she said. Even I knew that wasn't good and decided to stay. There was a delay of only a couple more minutes. Then, as softly and gently as you would want for yourself, Steve just stopped breathing. No one moved. We looked out the open window expectantly. Did we expect to see him ride out and into the free air and up to heaven like E.T.?

Maybe.

We sat there, stunned. He was dead now, wasn't he? So . . . what now? Steve's daughter appeared in the doorway, asking to be alone with Steve. Which was fine. Then came something I hadn't expected: would I myself, as Steve's friend, like to spend a few moments with him alone, myself? My first thought was, why would I want to be with a dead person, a corpse? I wasn't sentimental. But I thought maybe I should be polite and stay with Steve a few moments as they were suggesting. Then we were alone, Steve's body and myself. All alone.

Reader, do you wonder why I emphasize the "alone" part? I'll tell you. In fact, to my shame, it wasn't Steve that drew my attention in that room alone with him—but the two beautiful Jerome miniatures that Steve owned and that as it happened right now were still where he placed them, in a small nook on the other side of the room. Who, I asked myself, who would notice if these were gone, and who after all would be emotionally fit enough to construct the time-table needed to know who took them? I considered this proposition. In some ways attractive—since certainly that daughter of his would never appreciate fine art like I would! And, I added, wouldn't Steve have wanted me, as the artistic one, to be the recipient of his two lovely little Jerome pieces?

All this ran through my head in a moment—but then I came to my senses. Bruce, are you really considering stealing from the dead? I blushed. What a shameful thought! And I rejected it—for good. My temptation had lasted but a second or two. Shameless, blameless. I made my goodbyes to Steve and left.

To conclude: he got burned up, or cremated, when he died. He wanted his ashes to be strewn in the river Seine in France. And so they did.

I guess the only other thing is this: In my helium balloon metaphor, Steve is still rising, he's on his way to Andromeda or something. To my way of thinking this pale white man's destiny is with the stars. Steve belongs to the cosmos now.

He was my friend.

"Steve" was first published in *Satellite Telephone* no. 2, edited by Robert Dewhurst (Winter 2010).

INTRODUCING *HE SLEEPS WITH THE ANGELS (PINK SPERM)*

He Speaks with the Angels (Pink Sperm) is a road novel set along I-5. Emptiness is its heart and core. Everything can be substituted for everything, and everybody in it becomes a shifter. When there is an "I" it could be Courtney or Kurt, Bean or Bruce. You'll have to figure it out! The past is spliced up and becomes the future, every part of space or time can be any other part, so your hat or arm or liver might turn up temporarily on or in me. I've conveniently chosen the road trip genre because as the landscape passes and becomes different, everything is exchangeable. And as soon as things can be exchanged they seem to acquire a commodity value that's total, or maybe totalitarian. You get the drift.

What follows are several excerpts from this long work. To me, these pages—like the whole from which I've drawn them—are dead, although their space-and-sperm imagery keeps haunting me, as does Kurt Cobain, wherever he is, and just as Jamie, my lost mate of two decades, does too. Does Kurt = Jamie? Oh, I don't know, maybe. There are invisible ties that we all have with each other. But you know this already, don't you?

FROM *HE SLEEPS WITH THE ANGELS (PINK SPERM)*

Eat me, write me, pour me down the drain. I can't hear you here. So NOT Björk! Sad dad, dead dad. Can a fetal position curled like a kidney be a BEAN? The question decrypts the wrong message. Spattering our garage door. The grease on the floor. The flesh piece they take away by stretcher. Can you guess the message of this? I was poured down the drain. The vortex drowned me upward and I'm with the angels. In stars.

That was then. This is now. A controversy about Courtney on a magazine cover—a spectacle. Distorted NSA communications from the Space Needle all the way from here to Portland along I-5. On the cover of VANITY FAIR, I'm an angel with wings, Amy Semple McPherson style but in pink—for Love. Our love. Turned into a band. Named HOLE. Things never stop do they? They just change and change. I distorted an original, there is always white noise. Isn't everything always interrupted? You were misinterpreted but interrupted. That will never change. I hope this Venus I'm fighting for is worth it. Over a dead body.

Heart with the zombies tonight—it's cold out. Up here in space, in the deep deep freeze, I miss me. The wrong message saved and missed me. Now I am the message, right or wrong.

A stink bug. Pieces of me left over. They stink bad and that's a message too. Which in the silence I don't hear. In the rain on Lake Washington, what is the confusion? Am I fetal—or fatal? She's got herself curled up like kidney, Bean, dad dead and the shotgun of Love, his angel. They're confused. I shot myself out of love.

So def un-cool. So def un-def. Space pulls on words like salt-water taffee— s-t-r-e-t-c-h-i-n-g us out and back. First you're here now you're not. Love, I'll miss you. Me, I'm here all alone—I miss you. But I am always the wrong message and what's wrong with that? Ick you stink bad, where are they taking the pieces left over of you? I see clearly from space and they cloud your eyes. I'm only crying because there's always rain in Lake Washington.

Oh dear I'm dead, quite fetal. Fatal. A curled up kidney bean on the garage floor, my shotgun by my side cuz a man has to have one. No! Def not-kool. When you're in heaven looking down it all disappears.

Was I born like this, vortexing down? To sink is to stink. Like a bug. Screaming waves of funk are me. Find me, they said, and I did. Ascending to Jupiter's moon. I was like tears in rain. I emoted a moon of my own and owned it like a mormon-god gone right. The languages were interrupted but recoded. I understand that this is all I ever will be. One of me (sank and stunk and bodiless) ascended, laser-beam pointing. Find him, they said, and I did. Now in a sea of space on Ganymede looking down. Like tears in rain. Like tears in rain. My words never meant it. My music did—I emoted and for that was promoted to a moon of my own. Like a Mormon owning her own planet. Someplace in Andromeda, a galaxy next door, a hard worker, a genius and dope fiend, said the Space Needle transmission in a language to come. I don't understand you, the syntax of rain, graphemes of tears. Am I the language you don't understand? I didn't understand myself even.

A big yawn, I guess. Or gulp? Does time continue and never stop up here? In the mothership cyborgs dream in their pod-sleep. Kool! As a kid I made songs out of Douglas fir needles as they fell. Why signless now—here? Wordlessness keeps me under the pretense of these sexless emissions. Vibrations in a sleepy-time silence. Lonely. When you die, die completely, a great man said once. (And I did). Do slipping continental shelves in five centuries care? Yawn. Dawn yawn.

The heart beats faster. Space so much colder now, clearer from here. Huh! Was Teen Angst just a fad looking back? I guess. My washed head needs its hoodie back home to keep away this celestial chill. In VANITY FAIR, angel wings mean love. That means me. He once said I'd shrivel without him. I didn't. You did. What is a Hole without something to fill it? Pronouns have confused and deformed love. That is the voice I heard in my head driving I-5 to Olympia once. Her voice. The car lifted up into the air like kids' bikes in ET—to where it's so cold. A shivering of space, suppressing attraction, revulsion. Pink Philip K. Dick light, jetsam of straying pronouns, adverbs innocent of relationship, the only apparent coherence of page after page driving me crazy. Who am I now? Am I Courtney or am I Kurt, who cares—in the deep deep cold doesn't my lack of movement imply you're like me? In the dark cold can one idiot see another? Another what? It's the same, always the same.

A zombies' message is dead—on arrival. Does communication change YOU or is it the other way around? Hello towhead—is that mop of hair me or you. Shifters created the stretcher carrying him in me, or her in me on that stretcher. Out the garage down the driveway to the coroner's truck, glowing starlight greeting me. The whole Milky Way strung out in beauty like a bag of white heroin—pushing me on, pushing me further. Mom and dad like two teeny spots under the bridge near the river where I had to sleep, kicked out of home. An orphan angel. A teen angel and rushing years attacking like oncoming headlights on high. To get high as the spirit rushes out from the worthless bag of skin, his body, thought Courtney of herself. Do the charges stick? Every teen angel from Frankie to the Big Bopper to Buddy Holly in a straight line heading to destroy me—for the spirit's sake. Doesn't every artist have to punish then kill this bag of flesh—just to make music?

He's a stink-bug, say the powers. Step on him. Hard. Like a run-over bug on a country road. Penny Royal for the inter-uterine baby. That's another message but I don't have time for it right now. Check the transducers under the floorboards of your little Seattle cottage and you'll see. As long as you don't look they won't be there. And that's another message. From the inter-uterine world of Penny Royal. Downed baby drowned baby dead.

The heart zombies keep coming. Why? A quarter-size baby from the cum on my jeans. Only the voice is reborn. Then it gets boring and I want your prick, dad.

The laser communications cackle like falling icicles of freezing rain. It's cold here in the New Mexico desert. Trinity. White Sands. Decrypt this.

You are better off not knowing how light packs a punch. Until no one is left standing. Better to get it wrong, misread the text. My music told you— better not understand me. And you didn't. You're better off…

… glistening you don't always have to follow the laser's directions do you? A black hole holds it. Never letting it go. Don't follow the laser beams. Oh dear, dad, I'm dead. Or you are. It's always a new message. Always a wrong one. You stink bad. Bugs on you. Rolled up, a bean on the garage floor like her instead me like a kidney bean. Quite fetal. After a while everyone will stink and be dead. Why? Def not-cool. I'll jump into some vortex before her, Courtney, or Bean—then just fall fall fall. Even before I was born wasn't I falling even then? I was special. Singled out. I must have slipped on the grease on the floor of dad's garage first. The second time it worked. That's what the laser-beam tells me. Unless you believe in some stupid Princess Leia and dumb C-3PO droids. But space is something different, I've learned. My heart beats faster. Without a space suit now for the first time, don't I see clearly now? Everything is pure and clean, that's how it is. Spots, blemishes, they're pretend. You're playing a game of pretend. I am.

Daddy's a drooling doll-dork, I told him. My little beady eyes, a doll's body drolling like a dork. One d-word away. Go figure. You know. I was just under a bridge in ABERDEEN lately. If the magic marker works you can erase it—whatever you want. Then someone threw rain in my face. Dude, I said to him in my vibes—do you know what hell means?

Up here in the Northwest, as windshield wipers wipe the shit out of your eyes, you open them again and see the most beautiful fuckin' trees you even thought little ewoks were destined to die in. In so much beauty—why should an ewok die? Doesn't matter. Turns out the eye was made of glass anyway. The gelatinous thing busted when I stepped on it splattering all the way to Clark County and back to Multnomah. She should know—she danced there. Portland's a place for fools in the rain. Drip drop drip drip. Is she what I mean? She wiggles her ass back and forth for the customers then just sits down to cry like the rest of the customers. Everybody cries in the Northwest don't they? HEY—I was talking to YOU! OK OK you don't have to bust a blood vessel about it. If you want to put cigarettes out in your palm that doesn't make you a rock star. A rock star is just a doll to play with. But aren't you too, sister?

My mind's eye's a doll's, shooting up. Programmed to do this believe it or not. In the Mothership of Hale-Bopp? Hell-Bopp. What's going down the drain as I speak—all the fuckin' tears nobody cares about? Hey dad, where were YOU when all this got started? In the garage with all your tools, the buzz saws stole aboard the ship. A buzz saw or sees a problem behind the eye camouflaged as the transducer it isn't. Sadness is just joy. That was now, this is then.

It was pretty glamorous back then pushing a broom or rather NOT pushing one so that's why I got fired. He's no janitor, he's a bum. Dad and mom and me, little bums living in a bum-house or a doll-house. Hi mom hi dad I wave from in front of the tv cameras whose cable plugs into my back. It had to be sawed open and sutured closed or I wouldn't get enough heroin to make it. I can't tell you how exciting it is when it zooms up your brains, I mean veins, I guess really I don't care enough to bother to set foot on a trap door. Little man in a glass suit looking like Darth Vader—only a white guy. We decided our doll-house, painting a droll-house black. I mean pay them back—for what they done for us. I forgot, but what? What if all of the things you forgot made a necklace of eyes on a string you use for a necklace, would that be kook or what? When it breaks do the eyes go swimming. But not too fast. You don't want the sperms to catch up to them is it? Swim little sperms, swim to mommy. Do you think that's really glamorous? Really?

You're a wandering swamp. Please throw so much water at you up here it just mooooooshes everything. Down the rubber hose it comes, even more. Does she think she can be my penis anytime her little cunt THINKS she can? Well FUCK her. Have a child dear, she says. Did I paint my house white? White's closer to having no body at all. That was a dream one night. I thought I was about a hundred years ago you know when they wear all those long pajama things to bed. Outside, every cunt thought it had the right to be watered. We were sloshing in it. When it threw up down the vortex it went. The eyes of the body are black, the arms I paint with blue, these fingers that use guitars are just a swamp. Come as you are. As if. Like which one, dude? All we know is we're in trouble and it's not going to stop. Do you think a knife to your throat will stop it that way. What do the clouds say? What do their puffed up mothers the starship from another galaxy have to say to your dribbling attempt to communicate with a girl with your penis? I know. I'm just a prick.

I would take it up the ass you know, just because I'm fuckin sensitive. That doesn't make me a fucking AXL ROSE fag does it, honey? There was nothing for me to say. Except that's glass too. It's all glass. Except for HIS dad, a deadbeat for some ARYAN NATION conspiracy. We were sloshing when I said that. I guess it didn't come across the way I meant it. I said I'll make you a bet. And he said whaaaaaa? I said DUDE LISTEN to me, all you got to do—for HER sake, your girlfriend's I mean—is cut off your dick and put it in my mouth. I mean how long have you been wanting to make me a fag, DUDE?

I could see that got me. It spun him around like the storms up here, the way they broadcast secret messages for anyone who has a transducer beyond their head. Is that you. Gimme a fuckin prick, penis-head, I told AXL— and after that he just sort of backed away and said dude you are a real loser. They don't make guys like you. And I said SHIT YES MAN!

For her dad, me. BEAN I mean. The one who's so NOT Björk probably won't be born until. . . . See what I mean? The vortex of this drain where I live. Even that's alive. I told them under a bridge in ABERDEEN—do you think that's true? This piece of shit—this garment—my body. The eyes of body are small and glass like a doll. My MIND'S eyes see by some reprogramming or other. I guess you weren't aware of that. Get used to it. I was sloshing around down in this black black vortex. That's what my MIND sees. It's not nice here. Like someone throwing rain in my face, it all goes by so fast. The MIND never left—no problem there.

FOR BEAN: I HATE MYSELF AND WANT TO DIE. When you're, oh I don't know, maybe 20 or 21 and get to all this shit written about me, you'll see, oh that was his original name for his IN UTERO record. Put your arm out the window, I have to keep both on the steering wheel. Is it raining out there? Does it smell like forests smell? That was in the contract. Very Northwest—rain. Douglas firs, etc.. ADOBE on my computer can give me that as easily as the masochism that's passionate enough to LOVE. Look at them signs, honey, as we drive by 'em: NO WHITE TRASH ALLOWED. Don't they know I'm the one that HATES white trash? All rednecks are my dad.

How long since I been talking or typing? When you're no longer able to tell genders you can't tell which communication medium I'm using. Or the pronouns. You. You're using. That's my friggin OUTFIT, don't use it, use your OWN OUTFIT. MEAT DOLLS eating their own freaking excrement. What? Oh it's talking again, you know, like something thru the electricity plug. It's the SPACE NEEDLE. Ha ha, get it? I said OUTFIT back there now I'm doing NEEDLES again? FUCK I'm too stupid, they WILL CATCH UP with me. Like this man in a trench coat and RAYBAN wraparounds and like DUH it's raining outside. Got it? HE comes up and says uhhh got a match buddy? The French Unit stutters. They're on.

It's on the table. It's not on the couch. That's a mistake in their worlds, not ours. You can't say table when you mean couch in this world. I'm so tired of curling up like a spirulina and then getting all dry, dry as a bone, and just umm like blowing away. First there's a giant Douglas fir, then they cut it down. They kill monkeys, lambs, cows, elephants—anything that moves— it's all some BUFFALO BILL movie. So down it comes, oh it doesn't matter, the tree, the Douglas fir or you cut the lamb to pieces because why shouldn't you? You CAN. And what happens? It stinks for a while. This is if you leave it alone outdoors where it should be. Then other things eat it like—right now, honey—the larva of something that smells real bad too is gobbling this corpse they used to call me. So anyway you wait a little longer, decades some places, centuries other places and after a while if you put it under this bell jar it just gradually turns to sawdust. That's all. All there is.

Look at the hourglass over there. You turn it upside down and you watch all that lovely lovely sawdust go thru the hole a grain or three or four at a time. Down the hatch. It's all going someplace. Down a drain where I am. No not me. But that me-thing-body that you CALL Kurt. I don't. An arm is not a leg. A girl is not a boy. But they WILL be, from your perspective. This has already happened. RAYBANS. They keep you from seeing what is really happening. Throw them away, honey. Your daddy just says throw 'em away, baby.

They're so stupid. Remember some of those conversations, or else I will. Obliterate like a pig? I couldn't make BEAN fat enough. Like COURTNEY IS? So like Björk, who hasn't come along yet. But a mistake will. It will wind up coil up spiral up in this vortex in the sky. Dark clouds cluttering. They seem inky like on this paper. BEAN: wake up stupid-head, I'm not Björk. Don't wanna be either. Everything that gets put down on paper is an exception. MEAT DOLLS eating their exceptions.

Ok Daddy, up! That's right. Off the floor, you minx, in teeny bits. If you're you then smell your stink. I wanted very much then. This is me, BEAN, now thirty years later writing some memoirs of something—to make it not THEN but NOW. Go away, time. Go back or forward. Program me to do this and I promise you I'll be as depraved as you'd like—now get out of here. You stink the way daddy does. EVERYBODY KEEPS SHOUTING IN MY EARS BUT REST ASSURED DEAR PAPA THAT THESE ARE MY VERY OWN THOUGHTS. Did someone else say that? It's original. Who's the author now? It's FRANCES BEAN, isn't it? I'm the future. First you dream then you die. A littered battlefield, space-junk and you don't think empty, it's just empty . . . empty . . . empty.

This excerpt from *He Sleeps with the Angels (Pink Sperm)* first appeared in New Yipes Reader, no. 8 (April 2006), produced by David Larsen, for the occasion of Bruce's reading at 21 Grand Gallery in Oakland.

THE SENSE OF UTOPIA:
BRUCE BOONE IN CONVERSATION
WITH ERIC SNEATHEN

ERIC SNEATHEN: Much of the research for this Open Space series was conducted following repeat listenings to Forrest Baker's *Capri Tapes*, which are the result of his desire—more than a decade into the AIDS epidemic—to collect people's memories of the bar, The Capri, before even more of his friends from those years died. I'm hoping you can say a bit more about Forrest and how you got to know him, what he was like.

BRUCE BOONE: It must have been at a bar, and it must have been at The Capri. That's the only thing it could have been. I remember going home with him to his place in the Outer Mission in the middle of winter. That's how I met him. There was no heat, and he was living with Michael Ford and a few others. I knew it would be one of those hippie things, where you just have sex and then become friends. We were like sisters. Forrest was a rush of energy, explosive, big, loud, delicate, crude. You know, as I've gotten older, as I've thought more about friendship, I think there are limits to every relation. You meet someone and it's a bed of roses. Things explode and then there's a pause, you set up conditions around that relationship and you have to figure out whether this is worth it or not. If it is, you can move on, and it's really solid. That's how it was with Forrest. He had an impeccable political consciousness and was incredibly good-willed. But he was big, awkward, loud, and pushy. Big in stature and big in confidence. He was president of his high school and valedictorian, too. He was fearless. I'll add this: another shock for me was seeing Forrest's great energy, his vitality dwindle over years. Years. One day he rang me up to say, "Okay baby, this is it," because he knew he was dying. Michael had moved to Portland by this point, so he wasn't there to help. So Forrest and I got into the taxi together and went to UC Medical Center, which is where you went for AIDS treatment, what there was of it at that time. He had no money. He knew he wouldn't be able to stay at the hospital, but he wouldn't let me come inside. His partner at the time wouldn't let me visit him later, either. He said, "Okay, you won't see me again. This is goodbye. Kiss, kiss." And it was another few weeks—he was sent to a nursing home—but he correctly foresaw his end. At the curb with the taxi, that was it.

For a person of such gargantuan stature, he was cut off so early in life. It was terrible. What would he have been if he could have lived longer? So many talents, so much to offer.

ES: Listening to the tapes, it's hard not to fall for Forrest. He's so charming and gregarious. Big laughs, deep romance, he was so sweet and so passionate. Did he ever live with you and Michael and the rest at your commune on Divisadero?

BB: Michael, his ex, and someone else—we were all in a commune together, though there was always someone floating in and out. The commune, it scandalized me because . . . in a way I think that principles are a middle class thing. You can't afford principles unless you are at least middle class. And I grew up with lots of principles. They were things that were all for the betterment of humankind, how to behave, what's proper, all that. I'm *still* trying to throw them out. The commune was on Divisadero near Washington, and it was an old Victorian, which at the time were cheap because they were thought to be shit. I was really scandalized because there were no principles, either in terms of the treatment of others or in terms of politics. Like there'd be a march against the Vietnam War and I would think it's important, of course, and want to go. But these guys would laugh at me. And when we disbanded, they stole everything in sight from that place: doorknobs, finials, everything. I had never met people who really *stole* before. This, also, went along with my own restraint when it came to drugs. It seems like a parody, and it's a scene in my play *Fucked Up*, you know. We shared the space, and we pooled some resources, bought some food in bulk: beans, lots of red wine, dope, the necessities. But it just shocked me to the roots of my bourgeois principles that there was a back porch where everyone would leave the garbage bags, until they nearly reached the high ceiling by the time we left.

ES: Is there anyone else from the days of The Capri, or the '70s more broadly, that you'd like to say more about?

BB: My choice would be Don Lee, as he illustrates both a different set of friends than so far have popped up as Capri groups and because he illustrated the supposition that we all shared at the Capri scene. I think most of us were really misfits. Like hippies in general, gay hippies to me seemed often to have not just social-group-outcast status in general, but in some personal way to feel psychologically, well, "damaged." Jim Mitchell might be the exception. And for me, I think The Capri and gay hippiedom were harbors from my agoraphobia and terminal shyness. I expected I would never fit into any society but would have a respite of a decade or so of hippie play and then perish early as we all were destined to do. Most of us lived from day to day not thinking of the future—not because of some "Be Here Now" perspective, but rather, I think, because many of us were assuming that there wouldn't be a future for us, that we'd die early. It felt a bit like the movie *Cabaret* or the Isherwood Berlin stories: wasn't there a bit of the essence or perfume of Weimar in the air? The gay hippie deaths seem, in retrospect, a run-up or preview to the AIDS deaths of the '80s and '90s. Bodies falling constantly. Rumors that the mafia had finally caught up with Arlene Arbuckle—the owner of The Capri—and that they had finally done her in. The two Karl Johnsons dying violently. There was the melanoma that killed Paul Egger. Johnny Pippetone, the scene's connection to the best drugs, in Chicago continuing on in his criminal career, was found in forty-eight pieces. Suicide attempts transpiring all too often: so many friends and former lovers, perched on that edge.

ES: And Don Lee?

BB: From someplace in Indiana originally, he had been abandoned by his father, came home one day in high school to find his mother's body dangling from a chandelier, a suicide. He arrived in San Francisco more or less after graduating high school, an extremely bright young man but very much precarious even at that tender age.

Donnie and I met one morning—he was drunk—in the kitchen of the Bachelors' Quarters hotel, a block from the Capri on upper Grant Ave. I recall our engaging in a furiously intellectual conversation about the meaning of the Second Letter of Paul to the Corinthians, which we considered a major text. We ended up in his closet-size bedroom drunk, trying to engage in sex—then vomiting all over each other. Though one bout with him was enough for me, he saw himself as a charmer and continued to flirt outrageously. We'd see each other near-daily. Each of our fiercely intellectual natures engaging, challenging the other's, and he'd make a practice of returning us to his hotel room for a few moments, the reason for this soon becoming apparent. He'd need to change clothes. He'd pull down his underwear-less jeans and turn his back provocatively to me and say, "You know I could get any man I wanted with this ass of mine, don't you?" I had already had some time in grad school by that point. And though Don barely had finished high school, through his own learning he had or was in the process of gaining real and serious knowledge. Don pushed me to Sartrean critiques and the language of the Existentialists. We would walk and have coffee and talk constantly. Then he would snicker as we passed a building wall and sneer, "Bruce, isn't this the very meaning of Sartrean 'facticity'?" One special morning we got up early to go to a place overlooking the Bay and take some LSD. We popped our Purple Owsleys, sat fraternally next to each other, watching the sun come up as the acid came on. Donnie turned to me with a look of joy: "Bruce, isn't this just like the first pages of *Being and Nothingness*!?" He was filled with delight. So was I. That moment was way, way closer than sex. We were seeing the universe as it really was.

ES: When was the last time you saw him?

BB: Well, by now Don was a full-on heroin addict, a speed freak, an alcoholic, and connoisseur of a full spectrum of uppers and downers. He had with varying degrees of seriousness tried to take his life many times. I was his last friend. And I had become something like an adult guardian for him, I believe. I wanted to be the one friend who wouldn't desert him. One day I told him I was going to have to leave town for a few days, no more than three or four. I had to drive a friend back to Chicago after he had attempted to end his life, but that he shouldn't worry, I would be back. Donnie went into a tailspin of despair. He accused me of wanting to abandon him. I thought of this as just another scene, full of drama, but not really amounting to anything. I was wrong. Getting back from Chicago the very first thing I did was to go over to his hotel to check up on him. I approached the front desk for permission to go to Don's room. The wizened and somewhat cynical old clerk didn't bother looking up from the paperwork he was engaged in. He croaked, "He's deceased." I stood there, shocked, and for a moment couldn't move. It seemed like the end of an era. Looking back now I suppose I'm recounting this in an effort of disclosure or honesty. To emphasize that in addition (like Weimar again?) to the great joys we had as gay hippies living like mayflies, it wasn't as if the experience didn't have its dark side. And wouldn't I be remiss in failing to note that darkness as a part of this exciting communal time, of trying out new ways of well, not necessarily living, but just being? Don meant a lot to me. Later on, returning to Berkeley, and after writing my dissertation, on the title page I wanted to remember him. After the dissertation title, I put: "to Don Lee" as a dedication or in memorial.

ES: That's a beautiful gesture, Bruce, and thank you for telling me more about Donnie. It seems so fitting that he would be attached to your dissertation, which is a study of Frank O'Hara's poetry—how it evinces, through Frank's lexicon, his robust participation in the gay world that was coming together in New York City in the 1960s. I'm struck, as you're recounting this story, by how you, Bob, Jim, and all these others are doing the same in your work a decade later. Donnie wasn't a writer, but he's part of the milieu, like Forrest. And it seems that New Narrative, because it was genuinely a part of the local community and founded at the back of a small, independent bookstore, was able to keep these others close to its history. How did you come by O'Hara in the first place?

BB: In the early '70s, a friend took me to City Lights, and my friend, Brett, said, "Here, I want to show you a book I like." And it was *Lunch Poems*, prominently displayed in their basement. And unlike Spicer, who I really didn't understand, I was mesmerized on the spot. I just knew that I had to find everything he had written, and I had to keep up with him, and he was gonna be my main man. Though he was dead by then.

ES: It seems there's an interesting parallel between the poor reception of the Cockettes in New York City in 1972, and you all getting turned on to the New York School throughout the 1970s.

BB: But the Cockettes were so lousy! Unlike the Angels of Light, whose shows were paradise on Earth thanks to Hibiscus, there was no form. Everybody was high and drunk and couldn't remember their lines. I know that's the minority report, but—

ES: I'm trying to bring out this possible sense of overlap, I guess. That here are these two countercultures, each radical in its own ways, with its own techniques. Though, yes, the Cockettes flopped in New York, while the relationship between the New York School and the unaffiliated gay hippies writing in San Francisco was virtual, and fostered by way of letters, books, and short run-ins here and there. There's a certain thrill of representation at this time, something in the language you're attracted to— the embeddedness in gay community that you talk about with O'Hara, for example. Is that too simple?

BB: No, that's pretty much on the mark. I would say the counter to that is John Wieners, who I met at that time. Did I tell you about his reading in San Francisco? It was in some church basement downtown.

ES: Which meeting was this?

BB: Maybe thirty people showed up. And John was there in a transparent raincoat—and nothing else! *That* was John.

ES: [Laughter] What?!

BB: Well, you know, there was a precedent. Robert Duncan revealed himself to the world by taking off all his clothes at one point. Taking self-revelation so literally.

I recognized something that was really great in John Wieners, but I felt scared of him. Perhaps it was my bourgeois upbringing, or whatever, but I thought he was such a loser, and I felt a little scared. A little scared. Then afterwards, I had liked his poetry so much that I approached him and we began talking and talking, until we were the only people in the basement. He said, "Oh, why don't you come up for some tea in the apartment I'm borrowing from a friend..."

ES: And?

BB: And I was still a good Catholic boy. I thought, *Oh, he's such a great poet, I'm so lucky*—and then he wanted to give me a blowjob. I was shocked!

ES: Bruce, how could you be shocked?

BB: I was *shocked* because I was still a good Catholic boy.

ES: So you gracefully declined?

BB: It's one of the things that still makes me feel ashamed. Like, what the hell? He was a great guy and a great poet. Why didn't I just unzip myself and say, "Here it is, all yours babe."

ES: I have always known you as a permanent fixture of this city, but can you remind me what brought you to San Francisco?

BB: I came to the Bay Area when I begin attending Saint Mary's College in Moraga, which is where I attended school as an undergraduate. I double-majored in Philosophy and English. And in fact, that choice, which seems so fortuitous or arbitrary, so insignificant, now comes back and seems to explain my enduring interest in all this Bataille, Hegel, Marx. Perhaps it explains all of the philosophical tangents in my work.

ES: Say more about that. I can't imagine you think philosophy is a *tangent*.

BB: Honey, I was trying to be modest. [Laughter]

ES: And when do you graduate from Saint Mary's?

BB: 1962. Then I go into the novitiate for a year and a half up in the hills above Napa. There was one monk, Brother Timothy, who was a wine master in charge of about four hundred people making wine. I was a postulant and took temporary vows. But when it came time to submit my name to the Council so I could take my permanent vows, mine was rejected. I was the only one not to be passed, though they said, "Well, the Holy Spirit is telling you, Bruce, that you are not ready now, but you certainly have permission to stay another year and try again if you want."

ES: Did they give you a reason why they didn't pass you?

BB: No, the Holy Spirit doesn't give reasons, doofus. [Laughter] It's the Holy fucking Spirit!

ES: I don't know. I thought maybe it was because they thought you might be gay, like, you know, they could smell you out. There's something up with this guy—

BB: Oh, most of the novices were sleeping together. It was just that I was the only one who wasn't doing anything about it. The reason I didn't get passed, I think it was more political. I asked too many questions. I challenged them because they would all turn on each other during confession of faults, but I refused. I thought, this is mean, and meanness is not Jesus's way. So I'm not going to do this. I mean, I was almost faultless, such a perfectionist. But I wasn't going to get up there and point a finger at my brothers. And they saw this as rebellion, when I planted my foot to say, "I will not do this. This is wrong." They didn't care if I messed around with the others, sexually. But they would not abide a loose cannon, so I left instead of completing another year.

ES: And so you moved back to the Bay Area?

BB: I moved to Berkeley and completed a semester in their English department as a graduate student. I couldn't stand it. And that began my long history of graduate school. I just got so . . . I felt like puking. Everything about graduate school was wrong. But I knew I had to get a graduate degree if I was going to get a berth in life as a teacher. So I figured, because I still had all these Jesus-ideals, why not go to Germany and become a Catholic lay theologian, under the tutelage of Karl Rahner. He was the guy who laid the foundations for Vatican II. I did that for a year, visiting the most exquisite Baroque churches instead of eating. I would go in and pray. *Jesus, tell me, I just want to go and have sex with these beautiful German boys, and I know it's against your law… but is it? Because I know that that's stupid, and I don't think you're a stupid person. Enlighten me.* It took about a year. But the Holy Spirit enlightened me and said, "Well, you're right. It is all stupid. All these things. The only things you can know for sure, you know from experience. Jesus was just a good guy. Forget miracles. Forget the Church. Go be a hippie. Fuck your brains out. Take lots of acid. And be happy, dear." So I did.

ES: [Laughter] Suddenly the Holy Spirit is so verbose. You came back?

BB: I flew back to the Haight-Ashbury, and I staggered everything from them on, in terms of money. I knew I'd need an income, so I went back to get my Ph.D. because I couldn't think of anything else. I'd put in a semester and then quit to be a hippie for a semester when I couldn't stand it. Back and forth like that through the rest of graduate school. I got my degree in 1976.

ES: Okay, so that helps me figure out where you're at when you meet Jim at the Rendezvous. And you do teach at Saint Mary's at some point.

BB: A year and a half, part-time. This is just paying the bills, but I was halfway between a celebrity and a scandal. I had long hair down to my shoulders, wore dark glasses, took drugs, and I hung out with the kids, because I was really more their age. I think I was a very good teacher, though. Or at least many students said so. I taught World Classics.

At one point Saint Mary's sent me to a drug conference in Los Angeles. At that time, drugs were in the air, of course, and they wanted to send someone who was friendly with the kids. Who do they pick? Doctor Boone, of course. I think I only went to maybe one of the sessions. What I learned of drugs was just whatever we took while we were down there. It was only later that it struck me that they never asked me for anything in return. You might naturally expect that they would want you to prepare a report of some kind, but I didn't. I didn't even think of it. I have felt guilty about it for all this time. Still do, kind of. I should have known. That still gnaws on me.

E S: When I think about New Narrative, I'm always so glad, so encouraged to think of you all—real people in real time, inventing this thing together. And there's this question of time. Do we talk about New Narrative in the present, or is New Narrative something that has been, that we continue to mourn its passing?

B B: The latter.

E S: [Laughter] Well, you get to say that, authoritatively—

B B: I just think, for practical reasons, you could never have had a conference on the scale that you and Daniel [Benjamin] made it, without a certain quantity of people involved. But I think that the idea of New Narrative is way overrated. It was basically a small handful of people, and after that it gets so diluted. How do you even talk about a group of people so small? It's not like the New York School or Black Mountain College or Surrealism. For me, it doesn't get beyond that small handful of people. There are many people who took up some of the techniques, some of the principles, and that kind of widens the circle. But it was basically that handful of people in a little pond. An iteration that could recur, and probably does, all over the world without much notice. We happened to be in San Francisco and a spotlight was cast on us here. It wasn't cast on others for various reasons. There might be thousands of communities like ours emerging, ones you'll never hear of.

E S: I want to agree with that. But if we think of New Narrative strictly in the past tense, arising from specific conditions that will never return, we have to acknowledge that New Narrative continues, has continued, into the future. Not just because people have read the books and the histories, been inspired, and taken what they want to into their own work. New Narrative has a present tense.

BB: Where do you see that? Which aspects of it are in the present tense? How is it not dead?

ES: In the strictest sense. Bob's *About Ed* has yet to be published. Camille is still writing. Kevin and Dodie are still writing. You have a book forthcoming. All of these books, which I'm looking forward to, from what I've glimpsed, are all bigger than what's come before. And they are not all relics, fossils, petrified pieces exhumed from the glory days. New Narrative continues to be forthcoming, and I'm excited for people to see these things, though it may not be for years in some cases. The work for this Open Space series began after we had wrapped up the New Narrative conference, when Matt and I drove over to your house to return the artwork you had lent us for the gallery show. That night you gifted me a copy of *Veins of Earth*, which has several early poems by you, Jim, Stephen Mark, and Michael Ratcliffe, alongside artwork by Norman Jensen, mostly printed on vellum, so it's occasionally possible to read snippets of poems through drawings of swirling, winged phalluses. Thank you for the book, but also for pointing me toward this treasure trove of stories, reveries, lost poems, and visionary work. Though Daniel and I put in a year of research and organizing for the conference, I had only the slightest clue of all that there was awaiting me. What do you think—why go back to the '70s? What is there that's worthy of reconsideration?

BB: Utopia. It's one of the things I'm grateful to Fred [Frederic Jameson] for, because he fronted the idea of utopia in his criticism. There's Rob's [Rob Halpern's] essay that so thoroughly and carefully connects what we were writing with what Fred was doing, to what we were doing as hippies or whatever. The reason this whole period is so important is for the sense of utopia. Every so often conditions conspire such that people, rightly or wrongly, and so far it's only turned out wrongly because it's always reversed by the powers that be—people get the idea of living a fully human life, as if for the first time. To say yes, in such exaltation, we *will* do all this. That's the reason—I think, that's the reason to remember at all.

This conversation was originally commissioned by SFMOMA's Open Space Blog, where it appeared in July 2018, as part of the series Life Blasted Open, organized by Eric Sneathen and Gordon Faylor.

A STELE FOR JAMIE

After he died, I found a voicemail message from him, left over from a few days earlier in the morning. It went something like this. "Hi darlin' I'm not used to not seeing you this early in the morning" (time-stamped message, 10:30am from the day it was sent). After a few practical matters, his voice breaks. "You'll never know how much I love you. No. You will. You will." Then some more stuff from a couple of days before he dies then this. "When you die I'll come and find you, even if I have to SMELL you out!" This was said a few times and it made sense, made me think of his rural/ranch background, the fact that his dad was an official trapper for the state of New Mexico. It was just this total reality thing and pierced like nothing else he could have said.

After that, I listened several times a day. I remember thinking (you know how I'm hardly gifted in practical affairs, a total wash-out like with spatial-mechanical stuff other people do without the slightest trouble) that this message is the only physical part of him still left, and I want to keep it forever not letting it slip away. That worked. For about three weeks. I would enter some other reality state where listening to the voicemail would bring back my dead man. Then that impractical part of me took hold. I just blissed-out on hearing the real physical sound of Jamie's voice saying he loved me. The impractical part of me forgets there's always a limit for voicemails. Then they're erased. I get up one day about three weeks later and click! There's nothing but the white noise of nothing or outer space there. What happened. My brow furrows. I remember there's a time limit for these messages. I realize now I've lost forever the physical record of the voice of the only one in life I've ever really loved. The last remnant of what anchored me. I'm desolate.

What was there? Now there was nothing, if I didn't and don't consider the quote unquote ashes as real physical parts of him. Isn't his voice more him than leftovers of his body, his ashes? And now with the voice gone he's really gone. That I know. He's disappeared and been scattered with those so-called ashes out into the cosmos he came from, the emptiness. Or are parts or it/him in the process of getting whirled or spun out somewhere past the Solar System in separated different parts now, though starting to reconfigure and being themselves reshaped by other shapes, each thing taking a part of him, another part and in the process all his former parts being transformed, changed, changing into something else?

Hitting the despair button, Bruce? Yeah, I think so. Despair first crawls into my body thru the mouth. It makes its way down my throat then gets all over the thorax and now it's slowly starting little pathetic protests like, uh! uh! uh! And now upping the ante as my dog-growling comes on howling at full throttle, omg!

Desolation. Suffocating lungs in panic mode wanting to turn back the clock and reverse time and get Jamie back thru blackmailing the universe by yelling and screaming at the top of my lungs. Tho something unexpected's happening. There's some counterintuitive thing I start to notice. The mental pain, and physically the body's muscles and inner organs and tissues are affected cramping up painfully or contracted then expanding the pain out again, not just locally but globally, all over me! The dismantling of the Jamie-Bruce love machine part by part, this binary that is us, strangely seems to be constructing or reconstructing some other thing, a pneumatic thing, a binary love-thing that now, as a pain-outcome, seems to be somehow even possibly a love that's even a little stronger maybe? How weird. It's still a stupid evil universe but . . . I'm paying attention.

I was sitting on the edge of the bed, perched with dangling legs while the pain comes on even stronger now hitting real hard right in the solar plexus! Pulled-up knees oooooooh. Bent over chest. Ohhhhhhh. Howling. . . . And this goes on all night long.

Next morning, a protest note from the neighbors, against Sadie (our Yorkie's) rudeness. She had joined my cries. They didn't have the honesty to complain about me so they bitched about Sadie's howls. Fine. She howled and next door they couldn't sleep. Why the blame on Sadie instead of me except for cowardice of not wanting direct confrontation. I was unsympathetic.

As I had listened to Jamie's voice message there was something really calm about it. I didn't know why. Was it that thing about "you'll never know how much I loved you"? Well yeah. But more, maybe. It was the drawl, the cowboy drawl in the physical sound of it—the physical was even more important than words I guess. Not entirely tho. It was also the way he always so casually used the word "darlin'" to me. That got me in the gut directly. That was the howling pivot. If he hadn't said "darlin'" like that maybe it wouldn't have quite so much turned me completely upside down crazy. But it did. His native cowboy drawl. It was a knife in my heart.

Can Jamie's pronunciation alone, even heard just on a machine, spin me into more love? And of course the sound of the other shoe, that dropped g. When my mind and ear go back to that sound I see that it's a tipping point, the thing that smacks me hardest in the gut with the love-pain that's to bring me something very weird and wonderful and alien and maybe—even higher than it was when on this earthly plane with Jamie and me. No pain no gain as is said. If it doesn't hurt is it real? How can your lover make you love him without causing pain as well. It's almost formulaic. If he doesn't hurt you he's not making love to you. And you'll be stuck on this world of boring normals instead of, like, thru maximizing the love-interaction-thing, getting your binary to a higher and this time truly alien plane? Darlin': as I mouth it now while writing it here. I want you to shape your lips to say it with me. Say it. Darlin'! And a greater and stranger love is now present for you. Grab it if you can.

Now, no one can separate Jamie from the country and ranching culture that made him, can they? That was all in that "darlin'" and it was soaked in the blood of him growing up dirt poor in this very hard culture under a few desert mountains outside town before there's nothin' but greasewood as far as you can see. It merged with me, confused me. Ranching was magical and though mostly positive there's also this dark side. It's prejudiced and cruel. Against that background was a foreground of him that wasn't that. But still. The looming mountains, the hot desert you can't get away from. His family wants to be against this nature but really they're actually part of it though they don't know. What a bundle of contradictions.

Love and pain. Things reverse themselves. As we reversed pronouns listening on the boombox to a Buck Owens tune he loved. Didn't the music itself make the shifters do their thing?

> *There goes her memory kicking in*
> *It's that same old hurt again*
> *It makes me crazy now and then*
> *It's her memory comin' in.*
> *"It makes me crazy now and then*
> *It's her memory kickin' in.*

Listening to this I'm still transported. Buck Owens was a country fave of Jamie's, mine too. Who would have thought I'd ever be a country fan? Along with so many other country classics Jamie knew this by heart oh boy did he. He loved them. Me too for that matter, maybe for his sake then but maybe for mine later. We had this thing. In country songs we re-gendered pronouns. Making her a him. And honestly? I still do that. "It's HIS memory kickin in" is how I sing. According to the grapevine, Buck meant a someone, a real boyfriend of his, even if Buck wasn't "out." And Jamie might have meant me. And of course I mean him, Jamie, now.

Jamie just did stuff. He didn't look at everything from all angles, then pick stuff apart. And I'd look at Jamie listening to every word coming from the boombox with me. Then in my mind I'd go, puzzled, now what exactly is it that is going on in that cowboy mind of his? How would I know anyway? Jamie wasn't one to analyze. Or, for that matter, harbor. He took things as they came. I was the opposite and Jamie, he would always wonder, like, Bruce why do you torment yourself like that? You always an-al-ize. He would take the word apart partly in frustration, partly wanting me to do better and just live in the moment. Not to "take things apart" and analyze. He took pleasure in whatever was there. Could be country-western music. Could be anything. I always wanted to "take things apart" and analyze. I couldn't help it. My destiny wasn't his destiny.

We held Buck Owens in great reverence and Hank Williams Senior too. They were special among all, together with Loretta of course. Buck's "straight" songs would have bothered us more if we didn't know all the while he had this good ole boy of his stashed away, somewhere. That's country.

Even now listening to some Buck song and dancing, I really feel him, I feel Jamie. Eyes moisten and a big flood starts up and I hurl myself onto the bed crying my heart out IT HURTS doing this of course and it's a violent weeping, bending over, yowling and yelling hurt, like there' no tomorrow. Should I stop this? I couldn't. That was a path to forcing the presence of my baby from his absence. It was the only thing I knew. So there was a time I did it over and over and over and each time it cut deeper, hurt more. You have to grieve. If you love someone it will come out. One way or another.

Pain is the best place—for grief. He's standing there in front of me. I reach out and touch that beautiful body and soul of him. It's the suffering and sobbing that makes this magic work because if you don't start in on pain, how is he going to be present. It's all absent without the pain. He's really here with me, can such a thing be? Who knows. Is it "step one?" A dialectic? Step two—having the sense to grasp the experience. Time flows on and the more it flows the deeper it gets and then despite everything you have this awareness that you can get him back into you again. "Despite." I mean despite everything. And who's to say otherwise.

Beyond reanimation. And beyond death. And even beyond beyond. You say impossible. But little by little it starts. Your cell structures porous to each other. Is it conscious? I am you, Jamie, you are me Bruce. Letting you into each other—a new grid-structure. Sorry, I can't describe it. Or can I?

Make us be merged okay? Seen from one angle separate but from another merging. Grief making these thoughts. Inside my head fusing and confusing them with other things, thoughts? What kind then? Is it a double helix, so one image images the other and which is the false and what one do you want to call true then? Two separate people impossibly together. Did Stoicism say that. Or did St. Paul make his multi-focal body of Christ out of just us, Jamie and Bruce? Or is both neither. I'm confused.

Cells of him merging mine, I mean merging in mine, of mine don't I. Something is new. Remember telling you about the voicemail message and the period just after he died? Was it like that then? A two-entity thing above us like a dirigible now floats higher. Out the window. Into the skies. To eternity. I better forget everything, words concepts images whatever, completely—it's an us-entity now. And it's beyond the beyond and beyond realms of perception or sensation or thought or consciousness or anything. There's no hereafter here just nothing and that's okay. What's wrong with nothing. No hereafter. Okay. A big nothing. That's okay too. And these merging entities are so far out of reach can they even be described in writing to make sense? Okay you can allude to something. But to find us you'll have to see the blank spaces between the words here. That's it. This is goodbye, isn't it Jamie? Is it? Bye Jamie. Bye Bruce. Bye bye Darlin'.

Two in one. The big velcro experience. Is there a window into that? Laminated and regular as normal as everyday-life. Velcro is my road now. Beyond the beyond—velcro how I love you.

An upshot? Well it doesn't take half the number of valiums it used to to put me to sleep now. And this is either a good thing or a bad thing but I don't wake up at night and still reach over the bed-space for his body because it's not there now. That too. Is that a plus is it a minus or what? Touching him is touching me. How to you go and SAME yourself. Dunno. Got pronoun problems. You, me. Is he a nothing, Bruce, has he become a nothingness, Bruce? You bet. What makes you think I haven't. Damn. Well at least I don't take the pills to sleep now. Why?

Combine must be on my mind right? I'm single but a unity, it's him, the same, it's me, it's different, none and both. Everything mixes everything with everything. Tho Jack Spicer said "alone as a stone in Australia." Do I think that applies?

Tho in Munich, Germany I had a very crude Australian room-mate. With him I was alone as a stone. With Jamie the opposite wasn't imaginary anymore. I wasn't alone any more for nearly two decades with him. That's what you have to say to write my life. The two parts of the velcro are still laminated. That's what you say. And that should do it.

Oh his funeral. I got together with David, my monk friend and he helped me pay tribute to Jamie and Jamie's would-be type Buddhism. Some nice colored sheets draped over a couple of boxes, and that was the altar. Some Buddhist images. We cooked up a zen-non-zen funeral for him. Invited people. Xerox copies of the Heart Sutra were on the folding chairs. Incense, candles, the whole thing. In the middle of our ceremony David directly addressed him as JAMES HOLLEY after pausing his prayer to look straight at Jamie's ashes there on the altar. Time stood still. It reminded me of some French I learned once. If you're dining and there's a long pause you can say, voila un revenant. Something must be haunting us, a ghost! When David called out it felt like that. An unexplained cold spot in the middle of the warm room.

It ended. Everybody chanted the Heart Sutra with David leading them as priest. "All form is emptiness, all emptiness is form." Jamie now gone, utterly gone, gone completely, gone beyond. But don't you doubt it—still laminated with velcro. Hah. It's like the act of writing. Now you see it, now you don't.

What to do? A year later I still have the (so-called) ashes. In the trade they say cremains, what an ugly name that is. There's a spot I wanted parts of him to be in, Sutro Forest above UC Medical Center. A couple of friends and I trek up. Ivy covering the forest floor. Downed trees. The smell of the eucalyptus, its tangy citrus-y odor. Looking for a spot we pass the rich-man university chancellor's house that really annoys me—it's so corrupt and proud of itself. Nearby too I can hear screams from the UC animal experimentation labs where they torture monkeys that howl thru the whole forest.

Then ivy, fallen trees, eucalyptus. We're walking up the path and I'm looking for a stump with a hollow. Here it is! Ivy falling all over it and nearly covering it. There's a prayer, we put his ashes into the stump hollow, out of respect then bowing. Did I cry or let a tear fall? Boy howdy. For a while. Then time to go. I remember the only fork in the path so I can come back sometime. Will I remember?

What about the rest of his "remains"? I have this Ming-type vase in my computer room along the wall beside the door. Wouldn't that be good? Now it's got just a bit of bone in it, his. Because what you get back from cremation isn't ashe, bone pieces mix in too. In a plastic bag. A Ming vase is more elegant.

Go back. We rip off a few branches on Mount Sutro to cover up the ashes we put in the stump. No one's going to miss them tho this must be against state law. And it's against the law to scatter "human remains" in the city. I'm a criminal. Should I feel bad? The first good rain will probably take the ashes and wash them away downhill. Being criminal is also being alien. I prefer that. I've always been alien. You know that don't you?

Maybe someday if I'm lucky friends will haul ashes of me up that same hill to the tree stump and impart what's left of me to the Jamie parts that are left. That would be nice.

"A Stele for Jamie" is excerpted from bruceboone.wordpress.com, a blog journal that dates from August 2010 through August 2011.

BRUCE BOONE's published work includes—*Karate Flower* (1973), *My Walk With Bob* (1979 & reissued in 2006), *Century of Clouds* (1980 & reissued in 2009), *La Fontaine*, co-written with Robert Glück (1981), *The Truth About Ted* (1984), *Wallpaper* (2019), and a variety of essays in small press journals. In addition, Boone has translated the work of Georges Bataille, including *Guilty* (1988) and *On Nietzsche* (1994), several works by Pascal Quignard including, *On Wooden Tablets: Apronenia Avitia* (1984) and *Albucius* (1992), and Jean Francois Lyotard's *Pacific Wall* (1989). He lives in San Francisco.

ROB HALPERN lives between San Francisco and Ypsilanti, Michigan, where he teaches at Eastern Michigan University and Huron Valley Women's Prison. His most recent book of poetry, prose, essays, letters, and manifestos is *Weak Link* (2019). Other books include *Common Place* (2015), and *Music for Porn* (2012). Together with Robin Tremblay-McGaw, he co-edited *From Our Hearts to Yours: New Narrative as Contemporary Practice* (2017), which was listed among *Entropy's* "Best Non-Fiction" books of 2017.

NIGHTBOAT BOOKS

Nightboat Books, a nonprofit organization, seeks to develop audiences for writers whose work resists convention and transcends boundaries. We publish books rich with poignancy, intelligence, and risk. Please visit nightboat.org to learn about our titles and how you can support our future publications.

The following individuals have supported the publication of this book. We thank them for their generosity and commitment to the mission of Nightboat Books:

Kazim Ali
Anonymous
Jean C. Ballantyne
Photios Giovanis
Amanda Greenberger
Elizabeth Motika
Benjamin Taylor
Peter Waldor
Jerrie Whitfield & Richard Motika

This book was made possible by a grant from the Topanga Fund, which is dedicated to promoting the arts and literature of California. In addition, this book has been made possible, in part, by grants from the New York City Department of Cultural Affairs in partnership with the City Council and the New York State Council on the Arts Literature Program.

State of the Arts
NYSCA

NYC Cultural Affairs